*Y*ou're About to Become a
*P*rivileged
*W*oman.

INTRODUCING
PAGES & *PRIVILEGES*™.

It's our way of thanking you for buying
our books at your favorite retail store.

— *G*ET ALL THIS *F*REE —
WITH JUST ONE PROOF OF PURCHASE:

◆ **Hotel Discounts up to 60% at home and abroad**

◆ **Travel Service - Guaranteed lowest published
airfares plus 5% cash back on tickets**

◆ **$25 Travel Voucher**

◆ **Sensuous Petite Parfum**

◆ **Insider Tips Letter with previews of
upcoming books**

◆ **Mystery Gift (if you enroll before 6/15/95)**

*Y*ou'll get a FREE personal card, too.
It's your passport to all these benefits— and to
even more great gifts & benefits to come!

There's no club to join. No purchase commitment. No obligation.

As a *Privileged Woman*,
you'll be entitled to all
these *Free Benefits*.
And *Free Gifts*, too.

To thank you for buying our books, we've designed an exclusive FREE program called *PAGES & PRIVILEGES*™. You can enroll with just one Proof of Purchase, and get the kind of luxuries that, until now, you could only read about.

*B*IG HOTEL DISCOUNTS

A privileged woman stays in the finest hotels. And so can you—at up to 60% off! Imagine standing in a hotel check-in line and watching as the guest in front of you pays $150 for the same room that's only costing you $60. Your *Pages & Privileges* discounts are good at Sheraton, Marriott, Best Western, Hyatt and thousands of other fine hotels all over the U.S., Canada and Europe.

*F*REE DISCOUNT TRAVEL SERVICE

A privileged woman is always jetting to romantic places. When <u>you</u> fly, just make one phone call for the lowest published airfare at time of booking—<u>or double the difference back</u>! PLUS—

you'll get a $25 voucher to use the first time you book a flight AND <u>5% cash back on every ticket you buy thereafter through the travel service</u>!

FREE GIFTS!

A privileged woman is always getting wonderful gifts.
Luxuriate in rich fragrances that will stir your senses (and his). This gift-boxed assortment of fine perfumes includes three popular scents, each in a beautiful designer bottle. <u>Truly Lace</u>...This luxurious fragrance unveils your sensuous side. <u>L'Effleur</u>...discover the romance of the Victorian era with this soft floral. <u>Muguet des bois</u>...a single note floral of singular beauty. This $50 value is yours—FREE when you enroll in *Pages & Privileges*! And it's just the beginning of the gifts and benefits that will be coming your way!

$50 VALUE

FREE INSIDER TIPS LETTER

A privileged woman is always informed. And you'll be, too, with our free letter full of fascinating information and sneak previews of upcoming books.

MORE GREAT GIFTS & BENEFITS TO COME

A privileged woman always has a lot to look forward to.
And so will you. You get all these wonderful FREE gifts and benefits now with only one purchase...and there are no additional purchases required. However, each additional retail purchase of Harlequin and Silhouette books brings you a step closer to even more great FREE benefits like half-price movie tickets...and even more FREE gifts like these beautiful fragrance gift baskets:

L'Effleur...This basketful of romance lets you discover L'Effleur from head to toe, heart to home.

Truly Lace...A basket spun with the sensuous luxuries of Truly Lace, including Dusting Powder in a reusable satin and lace covered box.

ENROLL NOW!
Complete the Enrollment Form on the back of this card and become a Privileged Woman today!

Enroll Today in *PAGES & PRIVILEGES*™, the program that gives you Great Gifts and Benefits with just one purchase!

Enrollment Form

☐ *Yes!* I WANT TO BE A *P*RIVILEGED *W*OMAN.

Enclosed is one *PAGES & PRIVILEGES*™ Proof of Purchase from any Harlequin or Silhouette book currently for sale in stores (Proofs of Purchase are found on the back pages of books) and the store cash register receipt. Please enroll me in *PAGES & PRIVILEGES*™. Send my Welcome Kit and FREE Gifts -- and activate my FREE benefits -- immediately.

NAME (please print)
_____

ADDRESS _____ APT. NO _____

CITY _____ STATE _____ ZIP/POSTAL CODE _____

▶ DETACH HERE AND MAIL TODAY! ▶

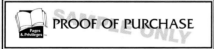

PROOF OF PURCHASE
SAMPLE ONLY

NO CLUB!
NO COMMITMENT!
Just one purchase brings you great **Free Gifts** *and* **Benefits!**
(See inside for details.)

Please allow 6-8 weeks for delivery. Quantities are limited. We reserve the right to substitute items. Enroll before October 31, 1995 and receive one full year of benefits.

Name of store where this book was purchased_____

Date of purchase_____

Type of store:

    ☐ Bookstore   ☐ Supermarket   ☐ Drugstore

    ☐ Dept. or discount store (e.g. K-Mart or Walmart)

    ☐ Other (specify)_____

Which Harlequin or Silhouette series do you usually read?

_____

Complete and mail with one Proof of Purchase and store receipt to:

  U.S.: *PAGES & PRIVILEGES*™, P.O. Box 1960, Danbury, CT 06813-1960

  Canada: *PAGES & PRIVILEGES*™, 49-6A The Donway West, P.O. 813, North York, ON M3C 2E8   PRINTED IN U.S.A

"I was good enough to sneak around with, but not good enough to bring home to your father," Justin taunted.

"You don't understand. You never understood," Megan cried. "I couldn't tell anyone."

"That's you, Megan. You've always kept your dirty little secrets. Does anyone know you promised to marry me?"

"Let me g-go!" She pulled frantically at the door. "I didn't mean it. I'm sorry."

"Sorry you agreed to marry me, or sorry you threw it back in my face? Are you sorry you couldn't marry the town bastard?"

Jerking open the door, she gave him one last glance. He saw the tears on her cheeks and the hurt in her eyes. His anger died, snuffed out by a wave of shame.

"I'm sorry you're back. That's what you wanted to hear, isn't it? You wanted me to be sorry. I am. I truly am." She slammed the door shut behind her....

Dear Reader,

Though author Susan Mallery has written numerous contemporary romances and historicals under the name Susan Macias, *Justin's Bride* is her first book for Harlequin Historicals. This delightful Western from an author whom *Romantic Times* describes as "a terrific writer," is sure to touch the heart of every reader. It's the story of an outcast who finally returns home to set the past to rights and claim the fiancée who jilted him years before.

Also this month is Ruth Langan's *Highland Heaven,* another tale in her dynamic Scottish series, which has included *The Highlander* and *Highland Barbarian.* You won't want to miss it.

Our other titles include *Redwood Empire,* a reissue of the Western saga written by talented authors Ann and Evan Maxwell writing as A. E. Maxwell, the powerful story of a woman torn between a ruthless businessman and his renegade son; and *The Saxon* by Margaret Moore, the sequel to her award-winning medieval, *The Viking.*

We hope you will keep an eye out for all four titles, wherever Harlequin Historicals are sold.

Sincerely,

Tracy Farrell
Senior Editor

Please address questions and book requests to:
Harlequin Reader Service
U.S.: 3010 Walden Ave., P.O. Box 1325, Buffalo, NY 14269
Canadian: P.O. Box 609, Fort Erie, Ont. L2A 5X3

SUSAN MALLERY

JUSTIN'S BRIDE

Harlequin Books

TORONTO • NEW YORK • LONDON
AMSTERDAM • PARIS • SYDNEY • HAMBURG
STOCKHOLM • ATHENS • TOKYO • MILAN
MADRID • WARSAW • BUDAPEST • AUCKLAND

ISBN 0-373-28870-0

JUSTIN'S BRIDE

Copyright © 1995 by Susan W. Macias.

This edition published by arrangement with Harlequin Enterprises B.V.

® and TM are trademarks of the publisher. Trademarks indicated with ® are registered in the United States Patent and Trademark Office, the Canadian Trade Marks Office and in other countries.

Printed in U.S.A.

Books by Susan Mallery

Silhouette Special Edition

Tender Loving Care #717
More Than Friends #802
A Dad for Billie #834
Cowboy Daddy #898
+*The Best Bride* #933
+*Marriage on Demand* #939

+Hometown Heartbreakers

Silhouette Intimate Moments

Tempting Faith #554

SUSAN MALLERY

Susan Mallery has long had a love affair with the West. A recent move has brought her to the Lone Star state, where she lives with her hero-material husband and their two attractive, but not very bright, cats. When she's not hard at work researching cowboys— (and Oilers)—she can be found exploring the wilds of Texas. Susan loves to hear from readers. You may write her directly at P.O. Box 1828, Sugar Land, TX 77487.

To Maureen—
a friend, fellow sufferer in this insane business
and soul mate. If it hadn't been for you,
I would have convinced myself not to give this
historical thing a second try.
Thanks for the support and the nagging.

Here's to bigger and better things,
to success beyond our wildest imaginings,
to the laughter we've shared
and that is yet to come.

Chapter One

Landing, Kansas—1878

Justin Kincaid was back.

Between the rustling petticoats of the ladies looking at the current issue of *Godey's* and the rattling of nails being weighed on their scale in the back corner, Megan Bartlett heard talk in her general store. The nearby farmers, in town to buy their spring supplies, mentioned the news to one another. The old-timers said it couldn't be the same boy. He wouldn't dare show his face back in Landing after what had happened to him. The newer settlers wanted to know what exactly this Justin Kincaid was supposed to have done. Vague talk about boyhood pranks and no one's ever having seen his father made them shrug. The town needed a sheriff, they said. If this Kincaid fellow could protect them and keep peace, they didn't much care about his past.

The women, clustering by the bolts of fabric and the new shipment of fashion books, whispered that he'd been as handsome as sin.

"And sin makes its own kind of trouble," Widow Dobson said, shaking her head as she walked away from the group of women toward the front of the store and her small table and dresser that served as the United States Post Office. She maneuvered her considerable bulk around the furniture and plopped down in her chair.

Megan looked up from the inventory papers in front of her. The first big shipment from the East had arrived.

Spring was always a busy time. Settlers and farmers came into town more often. They needed seed and new tools, clothes and whatever supplies they'd run out of during the cold Kansas winter.

"Who's making trouble?" Megan asked, even though she knew the answer. Like everyone else, she wanted to talk about Justin. Had he really come back? Did he remember her? She shook her head. She was being silly. Of course he remembered. How could he have forgotten the way they'd parted seven years ago? Megan drew in a deep breath. Who could have known he would come back?

Mrs. Dobson stopped counting her small inventory of stamps and raised her head. She tugged at the bodice of her jet black gown. Ten years after Farmer Dobson's passing, she still wore mourning. From her perky feather hat set at an angle, clear down to her shoes, she wore black. Privately, Megan thought it was because the buxom widow, with her fading red hair, knew she looked especially striking in that color.

"Those women." The widow jerked her head toward the small group clustered at the far counter. "They're jawing on about Justin Kincaid. Saying he's handsome. Well, the boy was always more handsome than a body had a right to be, but he was always trouble, too. That kind never wants for female attention."

Megan set down the papers she'd been examining and smoothed her suddenly damp hands over her full skirt. "Maybe he's changed."

Widow Dobson turned in her chair. Her bright green eyes narrowed as she looked across the dresser, pinning Megan with her stare. "You weren't one of those harebrained misses who was sweet on that Kincaid boy, were you?"

Megan raised her chin and met the other woman's gaze. Her light laugh sounded confident, even to her own ears. "Did you ever once see me with him? Can you imagine him coming courting at my house?"

The older woman leaned back in her chair and smiled. "Of course not, Megan. You always were the right kind of girl. Respectable." She turned to her stamps. "Not that I would have blamed you for noticing him. Hard not to. And he wasn't all bad. I'm willing to admit that. Still, he's going to be trouble. You mark my words.''

Megan gathered her papers together and escaped to the back of the store. Behind the calico curtain was a short hallway. To the left was the large room holding her inventory. To the right, a tiny cubbyhole that served as her office. She closed the door behind her and leaned against the desk.

Like the rest of the store, this small space was clean and tidy, with everything in its proper place. Even as she struggled to still her pounding heart, Megan placed the inventory papers in the right pile on her desk, and slipped around her chair to the little table in the corner. After pouring some water from the pitcher into the basin, she rolled up her cuffs and washed her face.

It didn't help. The oval mirror above the basin showed her that the flush she'd felt on her cheeks was still visible. Her eyes glowed, although whether from panic or excitement, she couldn't say. Her mouth quivered. She touched her finger to her lips but couldn't still the trembling.

Justin Kincaid had come back.

Maybe it wasn't him, she thought as she refastened her cuffs. It could well be another Justin Kincaid. Both names were common enough. She'd met a family of Kincaids two springs ago when a wagon train had camped close to Landing. She'd asked a couple of the women settlers, but they'd never heard of Justin.

She smoothed her hair, then made her way back into her store. Andrew, her assistant, was wrapping up a purchase of bleached muslin for one of the young women in town. No doubt she would be making a pretty dress for the Fourth of July dance. The celebration was months away, but people started preparing well in advance. Thinking about that dance didn't ease her mind nor make her forget Justin. In fact, it made her think of other dances when she'd been held by proper young men but had watched Justin out of the corner of her eye. He'd danced with almost everyone but her. He'd made those girls laugh with his easy humor and flirtatious winks.

Once, at one of the dances, on a magical night filled with stars, he'd found her out walking through a grove of trees. No one had been around, although they could still hear the music of the fiddler. Without saying a word, Justin had taken her into his arms. He'd pulled her closer than the other boys did. Close enough that she'd felt the heat of his body, his warm breath on her face. Close enough that her heart had pounded harder in her chest. They'd danced for what felt like a lifetime, circling, staring into each other's eyes. His fingers had burned into her back. For a moment, while they'd waited between songs, his head had dipped low and he'd brushed his mouth against her cheek. Then he'd looked at her and—

"Oh, Megan," she heard someone say. "I need to order a few yards of silk."

Megan blinked several times and found herself standing in her general store. The woman in front of her went on about her daughter's upcoming wedding and the need for the young woman to have something pretty to wear her first night married.

Megan flushed. She'd never had a wedding night. Had never had a wedding. At twenty-four, she was an old maid. And a businesswoman, she reminded herself as she hurried forward to help the customer. So what if Justin had come back? She didn't care. She didn't have time to care. But as she continued to work that afternoon, she could hear the faint sounds of the fiddle from that long-ago night and her cheek tingled with the soft echo of Justin's kiss.

By three-thirty, Megan couldn't stand it anymore. If one more person came into the store and asked if it was true that Justin Kincaid had come back, she was going to scream. Everyone wanted to talk about the possibility, but no one was willing to find out the truth.

Widow Dobson talked on and on about what a mistake it was going to be, and how someone born to trouble usually died from trouble. Even if it wasn't his fault.

"You mark my words," the older woman said for at least the fortieth time that day. "It's easy to hope a boy like that will turn out right. But a body never knows for sure. I can just see—''

Not willing to listen to the widow for one more minute, Megan marched to the rear of the store and slipped behind the curtain. In her tiny office, she picked up her hat and set it on her head. She paused in front of the oval mirror long enough to make sure the hat was straight and that no stray hairs had escaped from her morning coiffure, then she picked up her cloak and drew it over her shoulders. After closing the fasteners at her throat, she reached for her gloves and reticule, and headed back into the store.

''Andrew, watch things for me, please,'' she called as she sailed down the center aisle.

''Where are you going?'' the widow asked.

Megan paused by the door and pulled on her gloves. ''To find out the truth.''

The older woman gasped. ''You mean—''

''I'm going to the sheriff's office.''

''But you can't. My dear girl, if it *is* him, well, he's one of *those* kind of men. What will people think?''

The question made her hesitate. Megan knew the power of what other people thought. She lived her life by what other people would or would not think of her actions. Between her late father's rules and having a minister for a brother-in-law, she always had to think about other people's opinions.

But she also had to know. She would go mad if she didn't find out the truth. If it wasn't the Justin Kincaid she knew, then she would simply introduce herself and come back. And if it was him...well, she would figure that out when she saw him.

''It's the middle of the day,'' she said, and opened the door. ''The sheriff's office *is* a place of business. It's not as if I'm going to a man's hotel room, Mrs. Dobson. Why would anyone say anything?''

Before she lost the little courage she had, she stepped out into the afternoon and turned right.

Her ankle-high buttoned shoes clicked on the wooden planking in front of her store. The boardwalk continued to the stage office, then came to an abrupt end ten feet from the butcher shop. From there it was a wide river of mud until the planking started again in front of the sheriff's office.

Spring was almost here, she thought as she took a firm grip on her skirts and pulled them up several inches. She eyed the moist muck, planning out her path to avoid the worst of the puddles and a still-steaming pile of manure left by the stagecoach horses. With a quick prayer for the state of her shoes, she stepped daintily across to the planking several feet away.

A couple of farmers nodded as she passed them. A lady she knew said hello. Megan smiled and kept on moving, hoping no one would ask where she was off to.

When she reached the safety of the wooden sidewalk, she stamped her feet to get rid of the loose mud, then dropped her skirts to the ground. Her heart thundered loudly. She raised her chin slightly, trying to ignore the fear that fueled the pounding in her chest and made her palms damp against the kid leather of her gloves.

She approached the one-story wooden building. Two windows flanked the door. They hadn't been washed in weeks, so she couldn't just peek inside and find out if the man in question was the Justin Kincaid she had known. Besides, she scolded herself, it wasn't seemly for her to go around spying on others. She would simply open the door and step inside, as any good citizen could. She would see for herself, then leave.

"Afternoon, Megan."

She spun toward the voice. Mrs. Greeley, the butcher's wife, strolled by her.

"Good afternoon." Megan almost choked on the words. She'd forgotten that guilt made her throat dry. "Fine weather we're having."

The older woman hiked up her skirts to almost her knees and waded through the mud. "If you don't mind a little mess," she called over her shoulder.

Megan stared at the front door. Indecision gripped her. Oh, just get it over with, she told herself firmly. She had to do it now before someone else she knew came along. What was the worst that could happen?

She gripped the door handle and turned it. The door swung open silently, and she stepped inside. Until that moment, Megan hadn't realized she'd never been inside the sheriff's office before. She'd had no reason to come here. She'd never sworn out a warrant against another or been accused of a crime. Her father had conducted his business with the sheriff in the small office in the back of the general store.

Standing by the door, she slowly studied the room. The walls hadn't been papered. Posters of wanted men hung on the bare wood. Dappled sunshine highlighted the floor scarred by boot heels, spurs and tobacco burns. Three desks, two smaller ones on each side and a larger one in the center of the room, took up most of the space. There were two doors leading into the back. Both of them were closed. Except for the furniture and herself, the room was empty.

She stepped inside and breathed a sigh of relief. There was no one to witness her potential humiliation at the hands of Justin Kincaid. Of course, there wasn't any Justin Kincaid, either.

She moved closer to the large desk. A box sat on top. The cover had been pushed aside and she could see pencils and papers, along with a pair of handcuffs. She saw the edge of a pocketknife at the bottom of the box. Initials had been carved into the side, but she couldn't read them. She didn't have to. Justin had always put his initials on his pocketknife. No doubt the JK carved on this knife would match the one she kept in the bottom drawer of her jewelry box.

It *was* him. He'd come back.

"This is a surprise."

She jumped when she heard the man's voice, and her head jerked up. He stood by the back door, beyond the afternoon light filtering through the windows behind her. She had trouble making out his individual features. Even so, she knew the man. She recognized the broadness of his shoulders, the tilt of his head and the easy grace of his stride.

As he walked toward her, he moved in and out of the shadows. For a second, his face was clear to her, then hidden, then clear again. She hadn't realized she was backing up until the desk was between them. It should have made her

feel safer, but it didn't. She took one more step to the side
and the sun illuminated him fully. She wished she'd left him
in shade.

His hair was as dark as she remembered, and as long as
ever. The dark brown layered lengths reached to the bottom of his white shirt collar. Equally dark eyes flickered over
her face and body with all the impersonal appraisal of a
horse buyer inspecting a brood mare. But she was too intent on her own study to take much offense. The lines by his
eyes had deepened. Was it from the weather or had he had
reason to laugh and smile these last seven years? The hol-
lows of his cheeks made his mouth look fuller than she remembered. His square chin and angular jaw were still thrust
forward in stubborn defiance. She'd told him that once.
He'd asked what other kind of defiance was there.

She'd laughed then, and he'd joined in. Their laughter
had led to kisses, and then he'd touched her waist. His hand
had slipped higher and—

"So. You've come to welcome me back," he said, taking
the straight-backed chair in his hands. He turned it neatly
and straddled the seat, folding his arms along the top of the
back. "I'm honored. Is it me, or do you welcome all new-
comers to town?"

She stared, not quite able to believe that he'd actually
taken a seat without offering her one. She shook her head.
Why was she shocked? He was behaving exactly like the
Justin she remembered.

"Come now, Megan, are you here simply to stare at me?
Has it been that long since the carnival came through town?
I don't remember your being this quiet."

She gave him her best glare. "Welcome back, Justin. No,
thank you for the kind offer of a chair, but I prefer to
stand."

He raised his dark eyebrows. "Oh, a temper. I don't remember that, either. Did you want me to get you a seat?
You'll have to forgive me. Being the town bastard, I tend to
forget my manners."

She flinched as if he'd struck her. Before she could gather
herself together enough to think about leaving, he rose to his

feet and grabbed a chair from behind the desk on his right. He carried it over and placed it next to her.

"Please." He motioned to the chair, giving her a mocking half bow.

They stood close, now. Close enough for her to see the pure color of his eyes. No flecks of gold or green marred the deep brown irises. She'd never been able to see what he was thinking, and today was no exception. She was close enough to count the individual whiskers on his cheeks. Close enough to study the scar on his chin. Her fingers curled tightly against her palms as she remembered what it was like to touch that chin. The contrast of textures. The rasp of the stubble, the hard line of the scar, then the damp heat of his lower lip.

His scent surrounded her. The fragrance of his body, a unique blend of man and temptation, filled her lungs and made her knees tremble. It had been so long, she thought as she swayed toward him. So very long. His eyes locked on hers. She felt her fear fade as a fiery weakness invaded her. Her breath caught in her throat and she exhaled his name.

"Sit down, Megan," he growled, holding the chair in one hand and pushing her shoulder with the other. "Sit down and tell me what the hell you're doing in my office."

His anger completed the job his nearness had already begun. Her knees gave way and she sank onto the seat.

"I'm sorry," she said. Embarrassment flooded her, making her duck her head in shame. How could she have reacted to him that way? She stared at her hands, twisting them together on her lap.

She didn't hear him move, but when she finally gathered the courage to look up, he was back behind his desk, straddling his chair. Nothing in his expression gave away his feelings, but his anger lingered in the room. She could smell it when she breathed.

"This was a mistake," she said. "I should never have come here."

"Why did you?" he asked and folded his arms on the back of the chair.

He wore a black vest over a white shirt. Convention required that all the buttons be fastened, even on the warmest of days. There was still a bite of winter in the air, but Justin wore his shirt open at his throat. She could see the hollow there, his tanned skin and the hint of the dark hairs on his chest. Once, when they'd sat on the edge of the creek on a summer night, once, when she'd sipped from his flask and felt the heat in her belly and the languor in her limbs, she'd kissed that spot. She'd tasted his skin and felt his heat. Once, he'd moaned in her arms.

Foolish memories best forgotten, she told herself. He was angry at her. She couldn't blame him, of course. He had every right to be angry, more than angry. He should hate her.

"I came to find out if you were really back." Megan reached up and unfastened her cloak. It slid off her shoulders and onto the chair back. "And you are."

His gaze narrowed. "Don't play your games with me, Megan. You could have asked any number of people if I was back," he said. "Why are you here? What do you want from me?"

"Oh, I couldn't have asked about you. People would have wanted to know why. I couldn't have them think—"

She bit back the rest of her sentence, but it was too late. For the second time, he rose from his seat. He didn't bother concealing his anger. It flared out from him, tightening the line of his jaw and pulling his mouth into a straight line. His arms hung loosely at his sides, but his hands were balled into fists. She shrank back as he approached.

"*What* couldn't you have them think?" he asked. He came to a stop in front of the desk.

"I—I didn't mean to say that, exactly."

"What *did* you mean? Exactly."

She couldn't look at him. She couldn't bear to see the censure in his eyes. He did hate her. She saw it as clearly as she saw the man before her.

She buried her face in her hands. "I'm sorry," she whispered. "So sorry for all the things I said."

"But not for what you did."

He spoke so softly that at first she thought she'd imagined the words. She looked up. He sat on the corner of the desk in front of her.

"You're sorry you called me the town bastard, but you're not sorry you didn't come with me."

He said the words flatly, as if they had no meaning. She searched his eyes, hoping for a clue to his feelings. Nothing. The brown depths offered nothing except tiny twin reflections of herself.

"I'm sorry I hurt you," she said, hoping her apology would be enough.

"Oh, no, Megan. It's not that simple." He moved quickly, stepping in front of her and crouching down. He stared at her face. "It's the words you used that bother you. Not the deed."

"Stop it," she commanded, but her voice was weak, and she had no power to make him stop. She couldn't even escape. She would have to push him away. To do that would require her touching him, and as surely as she knew her name, she knew if she touched him, all would be lost. "What do you want from me?"

"The truth, Megan. For once in your sorry life, tell me the truth. I'll accept that instead of your apology."

Now *her* temper flared, quarreling with the confusion inside of her. She didn't know this angry stranger. He wasn't the Justin Kincaid she remembered from her childhood, or the young man who had made her fall in love with him seven summers ago. He was hard and frightening, mocking and cold. She wanted to run away and forget she'd ever been here. She wanted to forget the heat of his stare and the scent of his body and the way his hands reached for hers, holding them tight.

"The truth," he growled. "Say it."

His fingers squeezed hers. His hands had always been hard from his long hours working in the livery stable. Time hadn't changed that. He pressed until her fingers dug into her own palms. The sharp pain shocked her into action. She jerked free of his touch and sprang to her feet. Stalking across the room, she drew in deep cleansing breaths.

"Yes," she said loudly, turning to face him. "Yes, I'm sorry I said those things, but I'm not sorry I stayed here. I'm not sorry I didn't go with you."

He stood and smiled at her. There was no humor or kindness in the curve of his lips or the flash of his white teeth. She felt chilled and folded her arms over her chest.

"Are you satisfied?" she asked.

His smiled faded. He returned to his seat. "No," he said without looking at her. "But you told me the truth. At last. Does your husband know about your habit of avoiding the unpleasant?"

"Husband?" Oh, Lord, he thought she was married. Megan was glad her gloves hid her bare left hand from him. Married. When he found out she wasn't, was he going to assume she'd waited for him? Oh, he couldn't. She hadn't, of course. There were plenty of reasons she hadn't married, and none of them had anything to do with Justin Kincaid.

"I don't avoid the unpleasant," she said, staying well away from him. "What about your wife? Does she know you accost strange women in your office?"

This time his smile was genuine. She'd forgotten about the dimple in his left cheek, and the way his eyes crinkled when he was amused. Against her will, her own lips turned up at the corners. Justin had always had the ability to charm her, no matter how hard she tried to hold on to her anger, or her sensibilities.

"You were hardly accosted, Megan."

"You know what I mean." Cautiously, she approached the chair he'd given her. She sank onto the edge of the seat, prepared to spring up at the least provocation.

"No, she doesn't know I accost women in my office."

His words shouldn't have surprised her, but she felt as punctured as a pincushion. Who would have thought he had married? She recalled her worries of that morning. How she'd wondered what she would do when she came face-to-face with him. She'd been torn between hoping he would remember what had gone on between them, and fearing that he would want to continue the relationship. Now there was no question of that. Married.

"Who is she?" she asked, hoping he wouldn't notice that her smile had faded.

He folded his arms over the chair back. "Who?"

"Your wife."

He gave her a lazy wink. "What wife?"

She sighed. "Justin, even you cannot treat your wife with such disrespect. Who is the woman you married?"

She could see his humor fade, and with it the man that she remembered. The cold, angry stranger returned. "You mean, even the town bastard should know how to treat a lady? What makes you think I married a lady?"

"Your time away has taught you a quickness I cannot match." She picked up her cloak and drew it over her shoulders. "I apologize for any insult I may have spoken. It was, I assure you, unintentional. I wish you and your good wife well."

"There is no wife, Megan. A widow woman tempted me once, but I managed to escape."

Her anger was gone, battered by his overwhelming presence. She wasn't afraid, what with half a room and his desk between them. Her knees still trembled from his handsomeness, but she would be able to overcome that weakness. Which left only confusion. Why did he toy with her? Was this his punishment for her actions seven years ago?

No. If he sought punishment, that would mean he still cared for her. It couldn't be true. Even if it was, nothing had changed. He was still Justin Kincaid and she was—

The door flew open. "Megan Bartlett, what on earth are you doing here with that . . . that man?"

Her sister, Colleen, swept into the room with all the fiery determination of an angel entering the devil's domain. Megan wanted to crawl under the desk but there wasn't time. Or room, she thought practically, knowing she would never be able to slip past Justin, even if Colleen hadn't seen her.

"Ah, Miss Bartlett," Justin said, approaching her and smiling. "How good to see you again."

"It's Mrs. Estes, sir. What do you think you're doing here with my sister?"

"Why we were just . . . talking."

Megan groaned and sank lower into her chair. There had been enough of a pause between the words *just* and *talking* to give Colleen reason for concern. When combined with Justin's suggestive smile and the wink he shot her, she knew her fate was sealed. Colleen would lecture her for the next three weeks. Megan had always regretted being the sister-in-law to the town minister, but never more than right now.

Just when Megan was telling herself it couldn't get any worse, Justin reached for Colleen's gloved hand and brought it to his mouth. Before the woman could snatch her hand back, he kissed it. Colleen squealed.

"Unhand me, sir. Do you know who I am? Megan, tell this . . . this creature who I am."

Megan looked up at him. Behind the mocking facade, behind the quick smile and easy charm lurked anger. She saw it in the stiffness of his body and the lines around his mouth. Like a wolf sunning himself on a warm day, Justin would revert back to the wild at any moment. No one would be given any warning, least of all her.

Justin Kincaid was back in town. The tingling in her fingertips told her nothing was ever going to be the same again.

Chapter Two

Justin glanced from Megan to her sister and back. There was a time when the Bartlett girls had looked so much alike strangers had trouble telling them apart. Time had changed that. Colleen had grown matronly. Her once-pretty smiling face seemed pinched, her expression sour, as if the fragrance of life was more than she cared to smell.

As for Megan, she'd grown more beautiful. Justin should hate her for it. Instead, he hated himself for giving a damn. Why couldn't she have become old and ugly in the seven years he'd been gone? Or at the very least, why couldn't she have married and moved away?

He looked at her and caught her staring at him. With his left eye, he gave her a wink.

She flushed and bit her lower lip.

He knew Megan was wondering if he'd caught her sister's salutation. He saw it in the panicked expression in her eyes. She was hoping he hadn't noticed Colleen had called her Megan *Bartlett*, instead of by another man's name. He'd noticed. She hadn't married while he'd been gone. He moved his gaze down to her full bosom, then back to her heart-shaped face. It wasn't her looks that had kept the suitors away. He remembered the taste of her mouth and the passion she hadn't been able to control. That wouldn't have contributed to her unmarried state, either. Seven years ago she hadn't known exactly what went on between a man and a woman but she'd been eager to experience as much as convention allowed an unmarried couple. She'd even been willing to experience a little more, he remembered, then cursed the heat that flowed to his loins. So why hadn't she married?

"I say, do you know who I am?" Colleen demanded a second time.

Justin had grown bored with the game. He walked back to his desk, turned the chair around and sat in it. He moved the box to one side and picked up a sheet of paper.

"I remember everything about you, Colleen, including the Sunday you went running out of church so fast that you didn't see the pile of horse manure right below the steps. You slipped and got green muck all over your dress. You cried because you smelled, and no one would sit next to you."

Colleen flushed an unbecoming shade of red. From the corner of his eye, he saw Megan's shocked look. Justin sighed. Maybe he had gone too far with the story, but he didn't care. Colleen had been younger than most of the other children Justin had gone to school with, but her tender years hadn't gentled her spirit. He recalled how, during recess, she'd stood with the older children and taunted him. At five, when her soft voice had still lisped like a baby's, she'd sung the singsongy school yard refrain of "Justin is a bastard." Megan had been one of the few who hadn't joined in. She'd turned away from the taunting children.

The mocking song had continued until he was strong enough to beat up any boy too dumb to shut his mouth and until he'd become good-looking enough to distract the girls. But he'd never forgotten.

Colleen tugged at her cloak and approached his desk. Rage radiated from her. He wasn't impressed, although Megan seemed bothered by her.

"My husband is an influential man in this town," Colleen said.

"Why doesn't that surprise me?" Justin leaned back in his chair and smiled.

"You'll never be sheriff here, Justin Kincaid. I'll see to that." She pointed at the box on his desk. "Don't bother unpacking. You'll be gone before sundown." She turned to glare at Megan. "I'm glad Papa's dead and not here to see you shame the family this way."

With that, Colleen spun on her heel and marched out of the room. Justin stared after her. When he'd first seen Landing on his return to town, he'd realized there had been a lot of changes in the time he'd been gone. New buildings had sprung up along Main Street. Most of the people he'd seen were strangers to him. But he counted on some things to be the same. He'd expected trouble and had assumed old man Bartlett would still be around to give him hell. He'd spent his whole life trying to hate that man, but found he couldn't even dislike him. The man was Megan's father. Justin knew that if he had a daughter like her, he wouldn't have wanted a boy like him around her, either. He'd always understood Mr. Bartlett's feelings, even though he'd never let on.

"I'm sorry about your father," he said. "I didn't know he was gone."

Megan looked surprised. "Thank you," she said cautiously, as if she wondered if he was going to say something else. "He passed on about five years ago."

"Who runs the store? Colleen and her husband?"

Megan laughed. The sound hit him square in the chest, like an unexpected blow. Her laughter always made him think of summer. He didn't know why, but even now he pictured the two of them on the banks of that stream east of town. Her blond hair streaming around her shoulders, her hazel eyes gazing up at him in adoration. He shook his head to banish the memory. He had no time or interest in the past and if he remembered anything, he would do better to recall their last hour together before he left town. That would be enough to cure any man of dreams.

"Colleen married a minister." She leaned forward in her seat and lowered her voice conspiratorially. "Mr. Estes. I think he was here before you left. He's a few inches taller than you, but he has no hair." She giggled. "He did have hair then, I think. Or parts of it."

Justin smiled in return. "A minister? Figures. I'm surprised you didn't marry one, yourself. Megan Bartlett."

She swallowed. The blush climbed rapidly from the collar of her dark blue dress up her pale throat to her cheeks. Unlike the flush of rage that had made Colleen look harder, this pink hue made Megan more beautiful. He studied her mouth. It was uneven, with the bottom lip fuller than the top. He'd teased by telling her that it made her look as if she was always pouting. When she'd become self-conscious, he'd whispered all the things her pout made him think about doing with her.

Stop! he commanded himself. He couldn't keep doing this. He couldn't keep going into the past and finding the good memories. He had to hold on to his anger until he could come to grips with seeing Megan again.

"I never said I was married," she said, smoothing her hands over her full skirt. "You assumed."

"So neither of us married."

"I didn't wait for you," she said hastily, as she raised her chin higher. "Don't think I did."

Her words brought another revelation. After all this time, Megan still had the power to hurt him. Of course she hadn't waited. She'd made it very clear what she thought of him and his marriage proposal. He gripped his hands so tightly, he thought he would split the skin over his knuckles. He forced himself to relax. Eventually, he wouldn't care anymore. Time away from Landing had taught him that.

"I never thought you waited for me," he said mildly and rested one ankle on the opposite knee. "Until you mentioned it."

"Justin." Megan shook her head. "You haven't changed at all."

"Oh, but I have, sweet Megan. I'm a different man. Much more dangerous."

"I suppose you're right. There are parts of you that seem the same, but other things are different." She studied him. He liked the way her gaze lingered on his face, focusing on his mouth. It was almost like being touched by her. The steady glance, the sudden panic as she realized she was staring. The careful looking away, only to have her eyes flicker back again and again.

"What has changed?" he asked, liking the way he flustered her. She might not have waited for him, but she hadn't forgotten what they'd been to each other.

"You used to be nicer."

He'd expected many comparisons but not that one. He threw back his head and laughed. "Nicer? I was never nice."

"You were to me."

His humor fled and with it his desire to continue this conversation. "Are you surprised? After what happened?"

"You're still angry with me."

He wanted to deny it, but what was the point? They both knew the truth. "Yes. I am still angry. It's been seven years, and I figure I should have forgotten it by now, but I haven't. If nothing else, Megan, you were supposed to be my friend."

"I was." But her actions then belied her words. She dropped her gaze to her lap, where her fingers twisted together nervously.

"Then why didn't you believe me?" he asked.

"I wasn't sure. Everyone said you did it."

"I said I didn't."

She looked up at him. Sadness widened her eyes, darkening the hazel color to gray. "I know. Later, when I knew you were innocent, I didn't know where you were. I wanted to write and tell you I was sorry."

He stood, walked over to where she was sitting and held out his hand. She stared at his outstretched palm for several seconds, then placed her gloved fingers on his and let him help her rise.

She was tall for a woman, but the top of her head only came to his chin. She smelled of some forbidden flower. With her blond hair pulled away from her face, there was nothing to hide the pure beauty of her skin, the large almond-shaped eyes, or her trembling mouth. How many nights had he lain awake picturing this face, trying to forget...desperate to remember? How many times had he begged God to let him hear the words she'd just spoken? The statement of his innocence.

"It's too late," he said. "It doesn't matter now."

She blinked. "Oh, Justin, it has to matter. As you said, whatever happened, we were friends."

"Not anymore." He wouldn't forgive her, couldn't trust her. "You don't want to be friends with me, Megan. I'm still the town bastard."

"I'm sorry I said that. You frightened me that day. I didn't know what to do."

"You could have said you'd changed your mind."

"I was afraid you would persuade me." She bit her lower lip. "You always had the power to persuade me."

Did he still? The thought tempted him. No, it didn't matter. None of this mattered. He'd come back to Landing to make his peace with the town. To prove to them, and himself, that he was more than a troublemaker. When his year was up, he would move on and find a place to put down roots. Until then, he would stay as far away from Megan Bartlett as possible. She had always been his greatest weakness. Chances are, that hadn't changed.

"Go home, Megan," he said. "Go back to your respectable life. I'm not here to make trouble."

"You've made it already, and you know it. Did you think that you could just come back here and be sheriff? Did you think people wouldn't notice...or remember?"

"I'm counting on them remembering."

Her delicate eyebrows drew together. He loved her frowns. They made him want to kiss away the lines in her forehead and hold her close until her worries faded. He drew back a step, putting more distance between them. He'd been right to want to avoid her. She was more trouble than he had ever been.

"Then why are you here?" she asked.

"You wouldn't understand."

"I would." She stepped closer, close enough for her to touch his arm. Even through her gloves, the brief contact seared though his shirt to his bare skin. Instantly, his body reacted to the heat as his blood flowed quicker. "Explain it to me."

The fire of need ignited his anger. He jerked his arm loose and walked over to the desk. After picking up a single sheet of paper, he waved it at her. "This is all you have to know, Miss Bartlett. The town council of Landing has signed a contract with me. Unless I commit a criminal offense, I *will* be your sheriff for the next year. I don't need your friendship, or anything else from you."

"Fine." She reached for her cloak and drew it over her shoulders. The heavy fabric swirled around her, brushing against his legs, taunting him like a too-brief caress. "Keep your secrets and your friendship. I'll be sure to tell everyone you're back in town and that you've only changed for the worse."

"Why don't you tell them the rest?" he asked, knowing he was pushing, trying to hurt her the way he'd been hurt. "Why don't you tell them the real reason you're so afraid?"

She picked up her reticule. "I don't know what you're talking about."

She started toward the door, but he moved quicker and slammed his hand against the wood, preventing her from leaving. "Tell them your dirty little secret. No one knows, do they? No one knows about our times by the stream."

"Stop it."

She reached for the door handle and pulled, but the door didn't budge. He leaned against it and folded his arms over his chest.

"Tell them about how you liked my kisses, Megan. How you liked me touching you."

"Justin, no."

She raised her head to him. Tears glistened in her eyes. But the visual proof of her pain didn't ease his anger. If anything, it made him want to her hurt her more.

"I was good enough to sneak around with, but not good enough to bring home to your father."

"You don't understand. You never understood." She raised her hands in front of her, palms up. "There are things you don't know. I couldn't tell you. I couldn't tell anyone."

"That's you, Megan. You've always kept your dirty little secrets. Does anyone know you promised to marry me?"

She choked on a sob. "Let me g-go." She pulled frantically at the door handle. "I didn't mean it. I'm sorry."

"Sorry you agreed to marry me, or sorry you threw it back in my face? Are you sorry you couldn't marry the town bastard?"

He stepped back and she jerked the door open. She gave him one last glance. He saw the tears on her cheeks and the hurt in her eyes. Suddenly, his anger died, snuffed out by a wave of shame.

"I'm sorry you're back," she said and escaped onto the boardwalk. "That's what you wanted to hear, isn't it? You wanted me to be sorry. I am. I truly am." With that, she slammed the door shut behind her.

He thought about going after her, then shook his head. It was too late. He made a fist and hit the wall beside the door. The sharp pain wasn't enough to distract him. Megan was right. He wasn't nice anymore. He sure as hell hadn't been nice to her.

"I'm sorry," he said, staring out the window at her retreating back. She walked quickly, not greeting the people on the street. He saw her hand rise toward her face and wondered if she was wiping away the tears.

"Come back to Landing and set the past right," he muttered. "You just made a hell of a start."

He owed her an apology. Whatever had gone on between them seven years ago had nothing to do with the fact that he was the new sheriff. He had no right to treat one of his citizens so rudely. Williams would be damned disappointed.

Of course, it was Williams's fault he was here in the first place. "Meddling old goat," he said affectionately. His friend and former employer had been the one to come up with the idea that Justin needed to make peace with the past. He'd been the one to find the notice soliciting applications for a sheriff in Landing. Then he'd bullied Justin into applying. And here he was.

He turned away from the window and stared at his small office. Maybe this had been a mistake. It would have been better to take another job. After all, small-town sheriffs weren't that easy to come by. Especially in Kansas. He could have gone further west, or maybe south to Texas. But no. He had to come back to Landing and prove them all wrong. It was a great plan with only one flaw.

What if they hadn't been wrong? What if *he* was the one who was wrong? Maybe he wasn't better than a born trou-

blemaker. He picked up the signed contract and stared at it.
He had a whole year to find out the truth.

An hour later, he grabbed his coat and hat from a hook
on the wall and left. Suddenly, the office had seemed too
confining. He crossed the street, jogging to avoid an on-
coming wagon pulled by six horses.

It was late afternoon. The sun was already sinking behind the buildings, leaving half the street in shade. A stiff
breeze tugged at his open jacket and hat. If it rained, there
could be snow, but the skies were clear in all directions.

He stopped and stared at the livery stable. Someone had
told him it had burned down three years ago. The new
building was larger. He'd worked there from the time he was
thirteen, until he'd left Landing at twenty. He liked being a
deputy and he was fairly sure he was going to enjoy being
sheriff, but he missed working with horses. Maybe when he
left here, he would find a bit of land and raise them. He
shrugged, then kept walking. Any plans for the future were
a waste of time. He still had to get through his year here.

Next to the livery stable stood a small brick building. The
bottom floor belonged to the town doctor, the top to a lawyer. As he walked by, the front door opened and an older
woman stepped out, wrestling with an oversize basket. Her
mud-caked shoes slipped on the stone steps. She spun to re-
gain her balance and cried out.

Justin ran up the steps, and grabbed the basket with one
hand and the woman with the other. He held on to her arm
until she was steady. She clutched at him, her small black
straw-and-feather hat shaking in the late-afternoon breeze.

"Thank you, sir. I just about tumbled down those stairs.
At my age, that would be enough to send me to meet my
maker." She straightened and looked up at him. Small green
eyes focused on his face. She let out her breath with an audible whoosh. "Well, well. If it isn't Justin Kincaid."

Justin stared down at Widow Dobson and groaned silently. Of all the people to run into. He gave her a forced
smile. "Afternoon, ma'am. If you're steady on your feet,
I'd best be—"

"You just stand there and let me look you over, young man." Her tone said she wasn't willing to be argued with. "I'd heard it was you, but I couldn't believe you'd come back to town."

Mrs. Dobson had never had any trouble speaking her mind. Looks as if that hadn't changed. She'd also been the only person in town who had cared when his mother had taken sick. She'd brought soup and home remedies to their small, dark room, and sat up with his mother until she died. Justin wanted to hand her back her basket and walk away. He couldn't. The widow had never wanted to hear a word of thanks, nor had she accepted the money he'd tried to give her. Listening to her berate him was a small price to pay for such a large debt.

She looked exactly as he remembered. Small and plump, with a generous bosom, and dressed entirely in black. The thick wool cape that fell from her shoulders gaped slightly, exposing a dark dress underneath. He didn't recall her caring about Mr. Dobson as much in life as she seemed to in death.

"I'm back here, ma'am," he said politely. "For the next year. I'm the new sheriff."

"I'd heard that." She pointed at him. "Take off your hat. Let me get a look at your face." He let go of her and did as she requested. She shook her head. "The women always said you're handsome as sin. You know what I say?"

"No, ma'am."

"Sin makes its own kind of trouble. Are you here to cause trouble?"

"I'm here to keep trouble from happening. I enforce the law, Mrs. Dobson."

"I hope you're right. It's my recollection that trouble seems to find you whether you want it to or not." She gave a little cackle. "Tongues are wagging over you. Guess you've set everyone on their ear. Now, help me down these stairs and be quick about it." She softened her words with a smile.

He'd always thought of the old lady as one of the judgmental old guard. But after she'd tended his dying mother, he'd realized her gruff words hid a tender heart.

He held out his hand. She placed hers on top and he backed down the stairs, making sure she stayed balanced.

When they reached the planked boardwalk, she shook her head again. The black feather on her hat danced with the movement. "There's folks who aren't going to be happy to see you back here."

"I kind of figured that. I aim to win them over to my side of things."

"Is that why you came back?"

He handed her back her basket. "You be careful, ma'am. I wouldn't want you to take a tumble. I might not be there next time."

As she grabbed the basket, it shifted suddenly. A soft sound drifted out.

"Now, you girls hush," Mrs. Dobson said. "We'll be home soon. I've got some cream for you." She looked up at him. "Kittens. Doc Ramsey told me their mother is a good mouser."

She drew back the red-and-white-checkered cloth that covered the basket. He bent down. Three kittens were curled up together, feet and tails overlapping. Two were black-and-white with bits of marmalade color on their faces, the third was a small calico with big green eyes.

"I only wanted the two, but old Doc Ramsey snuck the third one inside with the others." She glanced down and patted the kittens. "Silly thing is too small to be much good. But he said if I didn't take it, he'd drown it." She pulled the cover over the basket. "I've never had cats before. My dog always took care of the mice, but he didn't make it through the winter. And with my fence in need of mending, another dog seemed like too much trouble." She shifted her burden to her other hand. "So now I've got three cats. We'll see if we like one another."

"I'm sure you'll do fine."

She glanced around as if suddenly realizing how long they'd been talking. "Mercy, I've got to get on home. It wouldn't do for me to be seen talking to a handsome young man. What would people say?" She gave him a quick smile, then turned away. "Thank you for helping me."

"You're welcome." He watched her walk by the public water pump. Her basket bounced wildly as if the kittens had decided to start playing. They sure were cute, especially the little calico one.

He got the thought about the same time his feet started moving. It was a silly idea. Then he grinned. Why not?

"Mrs. Dobson," he called as he hurried after her.

She stopped, turned and looked at him.

"If you don't want the little cat, could I have her?"

She couldn't have looked more shocked if he'd tried to steal a kiss. "You want a kitten? They're not going to let you keep it in your room at the hotel."

He didn't bother asking how she knew where he was staying. The widow had always known everything about everybody. The only secret he'd ever kept in this town was the one about him and Megan. No one had known they'd been spending time together. No one had known that he'd asked her to marry him and she'd said yes. No one knew what she'd said to him that last day when he'd asked her to come away with him.

He pushed away those memories, knowing he would have to face them sometime but not wanting it to be today. "It's a gift for someone."

"A girl you're bringing in from wherever you used to live?"

"There's no girl coming, and no, I didn't go and get married, either."

Mrs. Dobson didn't even have the grace to flush. She tilted her head. "You trust this person to take care of the cat?"

"Yes."

"All right." She reached in the basket and pulled out the little calico. "Here. She's probably hungry, so don't dawdle."

He hadn't been accused of dawdling since he'd been about eight, but there was no point in correcting her. He thanked her, tipped his hat and hurried toward the Bartlett General Store.

The kitten curled against his chest, then shivered. The wind was picking up in force and the temperature had dropped. He pulled open his coat and set the kitten into an inner pocket. After making sure the animal was comfortable, he carefully held the edges of his coat together tight enough to keep out the chill, but not so tight that she couldn't breathe. He could feel the tiny vibration of her purring.

When he crossed the street in front of the general store, he stepped carefully so as not to jar the kitten, then shook his head in disgust. The little creature had probably received plenty of jostling in Mrs. Dobson's basket. Still, he moved with care.

He was so intent on his passenger, he didn't realize he was close to the store until he stopped in front of it. The big windows, ordered special from the East, gleamed. The painted name looked freshly touched up. Lace curtains hung over the glass in the door, and between the glass and lace was a sign saying Closed.

He swore under his breath. He should have remembered that the town kept winter hours until well after the spring thaw. Blizzards could crop up without warning, trapping the unwary for the night. Everything closed up early so that the shopkeepers had time to get home in the light. He shouldn't have taken so long with Mrs. Dobson. No, he shouldn't have taunted Megan in the beginning. Then he wouldn't have to waste his time apologizing.

He was about to turn back toward his office, when he heard a door close. He looked around the side of the building and saw Megan walking briskly away from the back of the store. She was heading home. Justin started after her. If her sister had gone and married the town minister and Megan's father had passed away, Megan most likely still lived in the Bartlett place on the edge of town. With her long dress and ladylike shoes, she would have to keep to the path. If he hurried, he could cut through the grove of trees behind the land office and beat her there.

"Hold on," he told the kitten and circled around the front of the general store. He nearly bumped into a large man wearing a bloodied apron under his coat. "Evening, Mr. Greeley."

"Evening. Justin Kincaid? Is that you?"

Justin didn't bother to stop and chat. He tipped his hat and hurried along the boardwalk. Once past the land office, he headed directly into the trees. Without green leaves to hide the path, the way was easy to spot. He cupped one hand under the kitten and jogged through the grove.

When he came out the other side, he could see the Bartlett house sitting at the top of a small rise. It stood three stories tall, looking like a graceful old lady. Bare oak trees reached past the peaked roof. The setting sun reflected off the front windows. A wide porch circled the house, but all the outdoor furniture had been pushed to one side and covered with oilcloth. Bare patches of dirt showed where the garden would be, come spring.

He moved closer, fighting the memories. How many times had he stood just inside the grove of trees and stared at this house? He'd often willed Megan to come out and join him. Many afternoons, she had. One night, she'd crept out the back door and met him by the creek. They'd laughed and talked almost until dawn. Until he'd sent her inside because he'd wanted her so badly. Even as a young man, he'd known that Megan Bartlett wasn't the kind of girl a man had his way with. She was the kind of girl a man married. That was why he'd proposed.

The familiar ache in his chest made him push the memories aside. He didn't want to remember any of it. He wanted to apologize and be on his way.

He walked over to the front steps and sat down. Megan would be along any moment. The path she'd taken was longer, but only by about five minutes. He checked on the kitten. She'd fallen asleep in his pocket. He stroked the soft fur on her head. She stirred, blinked sleepily at him and yawned. Her tiny teeth made him smile. She sniffed his finger, then closed her eyes. Her soft purr faded as she went back to sleep.

The sound of footsteps on gravel made him look up. He could see Megan approaching. She carried a wrapped parcel under one arm. The other swung freely at her side. She looked up at the house and came to a complete stop.

"What are you doing here?" she asked.

"I came to apologize."

"Why don't I believe you?"

"I don't know. It's the truth."

She started walking again, this time moving quickly toward him, then up the stairs. "Nothing is ever simple with you, Justin. Do you know the kind of gossip there would be if someone spotted you here?" She opened the front door and ducked inside. "Hurry. Get in here before someone sees you. You might not care about the talk, but I do."

He rose slowly and stepped onto the porch. For the first time in his life, he was going in through the front door. He should have been pleased, but he wasn't. He'd been a fool to come back. Nothing had changed. Megan Bartlett still cared about her reputation more than anything in the world. And he was still just that bastard Justin Kincaid.

Chapter Three

Megan held the door open impatiently as Justin slowly stepped inside. If she didn't know better, she would swear he was taking as long as possible. Probably to punish her, she thought, shaking her head. She'd seen the anger in his eyes when just moments ago she'd accused him of not thinking of her reputation.

As soon as he was in the foyer, she slammed the door shut and adjusted the curtains on the side window. Her father had built the house on the far edge of town, opposite where all the new buildings had sprung up. He'd bought the surrounding land and enough of the woods to ensure privacy. Megan didn't get many visitors, but it would only take one to see Justin sitting on her front porch. Within hours, the entire town would know he'd been there and her reputation would be ruined. Not that he cared.

She glared up at him. His brown eyes met hers and flashed with equal fire. The tension between them crackled. She wanted to stomp her foot with irritation.

"Aren't you going to invite me to take a seat in the parlor?" he asked, his lazy drawl a direct contrast to the stiff set of his body and the angry, thin line of his mouth.

"No," she said curtly, even as the reminder of good manners made her feel guilty. It was wrong to keep a guest standing in the foyer. But Justin wasn't a guest. Thank goodness her father wasn't alive to see this moment. Why he would have—

She swallowed hard as she met his stare. The tension she'd been aware of moments before charged the air. Like a summer electrical storm, when bolts of lightning ripped across the sky and loud claps of thunder echoed so forcefully the house shook. But during those storms there was no rain for relief, no soft patter of individual drops to provide counterpoint to the violence and beauty. And so it was in this room. There was the combination of anger and the past with nothing gentle to ease the intensity between them.

The skin on her arms puckered and a shiver raced down her spine. She lowered her gaze from Justin's dark brown eyes to his mouth, then to his broad shoulders and chest. His thick coat only made him look more powerful. And masculine.

He was a man, a man who had always been able to make her forget what was right and proper. He'd always been able to make her forget herself and all her good intentions. The ticking of the clock in the parlor suddenly sounded very loud. The steady sound seemed to echo in the house, reminding her she was completely alone with him. There were no witnesses, and no one to come to her rescue.

''What do you want?'' she asked, her voice low and quavering.

He shook his head, as if coming out of a dream, then moved away from her. There was very little light penetrating the curtained windows and soon they would be in darkness. Justin walked to the lamp she kept by the front door. Without asking her permission, he lit it. When the wick caught, he adjusted the flame until it burned brightly. Casually, as if he had the entire evening, and more time besides, he unbuttoned his coat.

Megan clutched at the fasteners at her throat. He hadn't done anything untoward, but she suddenly felt vulnerable, as if he'd started to undress. It's just a coat, she told herself. Most people took them off indoors. But most people hadn't kissed her on summer nights while sitting on the bank of the stream. Most people hadn't touched her waist and then moved higher to delicately caress her—

Don't think about it, she commanded herself. What she'd done with Justin had been a madness born of youth and the night, and that bit of whiskey she'd sipped from his flask. It had been a dream. In the light of day, she'd felt ashamed.

Liar, a voice inside of her whispered. *You felt wonderful.* She ignored the voice.

"I told you, I came to apologize." He paced to the bottom of the staircase that circled gracefully toward the second floor, then turned and glared at her. "God knows why I bothered. I should have remembered nothing is more important to Miss Megan Bartlett than what the rest of the world thinks."

It was a familiar argument, one they'd had countless times. "Not everyone enjoys flouting convention."

"Maybe, for once, you could figure out yourself what matters instead of letting other people tell you," he said.

She clenched her teeth together and unfastened her cloak. After setting it on a hook on the hall tree, she stepped in front of the mirror and pulled the pin from her hat. She could see the flush of anger on her cheeks. It reminded her that she could deal with Justin better if she stopped letting him think that his comments had any power over her.

"I form my opinions after reflecting on the Lord's, the laws of the day and dictates of society," she said calmly and set her hat down. She turned to him. "Despite your urgings, I don't believe I should place my opinions above theirs."

"That's always been your problem. You need backbone, Megan."

Her temper began to burn at the edges of her self-control. She firmly gripped the singed edges. "In your absence, I seem to have survived the loss of my father and kept the store running successfully. Rather large accomplishments for someone with no backbone, wouldn't you say?"

He stepped toward her. "But everything you do, every thought, every action is dictated by what other people think. What are you so afraid of?"

"Harming my reputation," she snapped. "Something you wouldn't care about, being a man. But I'm a single woman in a small town. If I expect to keep my place, I must concern myself with others' thoughts. If you don't share my concerns, you should at least understand them. After all, your mother had a bad reputation and look what happened to her."

The second she spoke the words, Megan wanted to call them back. She clamped her hand over her mouth, but it was too late.

Justin froze in place, halfway between her and the stairs. The flame from the lamp danced with some slight draft, casting shadows on his face. His mouth straightened into a grim line and the muscle in his right cheek twitched. Something dark and ugly stole into his eyes.

She stepped away. Not out of fear, but out of shame. "I'm s-sorry," she stammered. "I didn't mean to say that. It was wrong of me. Completely wrong. I know you loved your mother and that she was a good woman. You made me angry." She twisted her fingers together in front of her waist and shrugged slightly. "That's a stupid excuse, isn't it? It's not your fault and I shouldn't try to say that it is. It's mine. I'm sorry."

He blinked and it was as if he'd never heard her slight. His face relaxed into its original mocking expression. "Don't apologize on my account. I've heard worse in my time. Your comments weren't original, or even harshly spoken. I don't care enough about you to be wounded by your opinions."

He'd changed so much in the time he'd been gone. The young man who had taught her about kissing and passion had been replaced by a dark stranger. Just as well, she told herself. The old Justin would have tempted her too much. This man was unknown to her. If she kept it that way, she wouldn't be at risk.

"Wounded or not, I do apologize." With a sigh, she moved past him into the parlor. The last rays of afternoon light slipped through the drapes and outlined the large pieces of furniture in the room. She moved to a corner table and lit a lamp. She placed the smoldering match in a small metal tray, then turned to him.

As she'd suspected, he had followed her into the room. He rocked back and forth on his heels as he looked around at the furnishings. She followed his gaze, wondering how the parlor would appear to a stranger.

Overly furnished, she thought, glancing from the three settees, to the scattered tables and covered chairs. Her father had had a fondness for expensive things. There were lacquered boxes and silver candy dishes. A beautiful ivory fan bought in New Orleans from a ship that had been nearly around the world. Cream-colored wallpaper and heavy, dark blue drapes provided a backdrop for the ostentatious display.

"Who would have thought I would be so blessed as to finally see the inside of the famed Bartlett mansion?" he said. He raised his eyebrows. "You must be very proud living here."

"I'm not. You know that, Justin." She glanced at one of the settees and thought about sitting down, but she was afraid he would sit next to her. With her heart already pounding in her chest and her palms damp, she didn't think she could deal with the consequences of him being so close. "This house means nothing to me. It is still my father's home, not mine."

"Yes, of course. You could be happy in a small sod hut somewhere out west. Fighting snakes and scorpions, watching your children die from the elements."

"You twist my meaning."

He thrust his hands into his trouser pockets. The smile pulling at his mouth was anything but pleasant. "Are you saying you would be content in a single room above a saloon? Like my mother? You could hear the noise from below, you know. The yells of the drunken men, the squeals of the saloon girls. And the smells. Tobacco, sweat and—"

"Stop!" She moved toward him until she was directly in front of him. "Please, stop. I've said I was sorry for what I said about your mother. It was thoughtless and cruel. I have no excuse except for the truth." She dipped her head slightly and stared at the center of his broad chest.

"Which is?"

He had been in town less than a day and already her life had been turned upside down. "When I'm frightened, I tend to speak without thinking. It's a failing. I beg your indulgence."

"Beg" had been a poor choice of words. She saw that instantly when she risked meeting his gaze. The fire had returned, but it wasn't fueled by anger.

He had the most beautiful eyes, she thought, staring into their deep brown depths. Thick lashes framed the pure color. The dark slash of his eyebrows added to his handsomeness, making him look sardonic one minute, gently teasing the next. Justin's moods changed like the surface of the stream, quickly and without warning.

She blinked several times and looked away. Yes, the anger was gone, but that which replaced it was much more dangerous.

"What are you afraid of?" he asked softly.

"Your return."

She turned away and walked over to the fireplace. Logs and kindling were kept stacked in readiness for guests. She crouched down and lit the fire. When the smaller pieces had caught, she rose to her feet and motioned to one of the settees. "Please, have a seat."

He shook his head. "I'm not going to be here that long. Why are you afraid of me?"

"I'm not afraid of you," she said, then smiled. He was the least of it, really. *She* was the problem. Being around him, thinking of him, made her act differently, as if the respectable woman she worked hard to be was just a false covering, like a storefront. As if the world saw her as a gracious two-story mercantile, but inside she was just a squat saloon.

She smiled at the analogy. He seemed to addle her brain as well as her senses.

"So, you're going to be here for a year," she said.

His gaze moved over her face, then dipped lower. She told herself to be insulted, but the frank appraisal left her feeling warm and tingling. Justin had often looked at her like that in the past. The appreciation in his eyes had made her proud to be female and that which he desired. It had frightened her a little, for her inexperience had left her with more questions than explanations. But in his arms that hadn't mattered.

He'd tempted her with his soft kisses. Despite his time away and the changes in both their lives, he still tempted her. Pray God he chose to ignore her.

"Yes. As I told you earlier this afternoon, I have a one-year contract with the good citizens of this town." The mocking tone had returned.

"Why did you come back? To punish them?"

He shook his head. "To make peace with the past, although that doesn't seem to be working."

"What are your plans while you're here?"

He raised his eyebrows again. "I'm the sheriff. I'll enforce the laws, try to keep people out of trouble and generally make my presence known."

She bent down and picked up a lacquered box from the table. The smooth surface felt cool against her heated fingers. "There are those who will oppose you."

"Your sister, you mean?"

"Not just her. I know Colleen has become a—"

"Prig?"

Megan smiled. "That's quite unkind of you." She set the box back on the table, then straightened. Her smile broadened. "But yes, she has. And her husband is worse. I've heard the whispers, what people are saying about you. Eventually, everyone comes into the store. The new settlers don't mind that you're sheriff. As long as they are free to get on with their lives, they'll have no complaints. But the old-timers, the ones who were here when . . ." Her hand fluttered toward him. She didn't want to speak of that time, or that day. She didn't want to recall the ugly words she'd spoken to him, or the pain in his eyes. She didn't want to know how much she'd hurt him. And herself. In the deepest, darkest part of her heart, she knew she'd made the right decision. She couldn't have gone with him. But she'd been wrong in the delivery of the message. She'd been so afraid he would convince her to come with him that she'd lashed out in fear, speaking harsh words that could never be recalled.

"They won't forgive you," she said.

"They don't have to. I appreciate your concern, but it's misplaced. The contract's binding. Unless I commit a crime, they can't get rid of me. For the next year, they're going to have to get used to having me around."

"When the year is up, what happens then?"

He looked past her toward the fire. "Then I leave this place behind and never come back."

"So it's just for a year?"

His eyes met hers. She saw the amusement. She was so grateful he would eventually be leaving, she didn't care that it was at her expense.

"Yes, Megan. One year. Then you'll be through with me for good."

She could bear anything for a year, she told herself. "I think it best that we try to stay out of each other's way during that time," she said.

Instead of answering, he smiled. She knew that smile. It made her knees weak and her fingers tremble. It made her remember his kisses, and more. It made her wish Justin Kincaid had been respectable, the son of a farmer or a business owner. It made her wonder what would have happened if she'd gone with him.

"Why is it a problem if we see each other?" he asked, the glint in his eye reminding her he was dangerous.

She couldn't answer that question. He might suspect the truth, but he wouldn't *know* for sure. "Why are you here?"

"I told you, I'm the sheriff."

"No, why are you in my house? Why did you come to see me tonight?"

"I want my question answered first. Why is it a problem if we see each other?"

She didn't think he'd moved, but somehow they were standing closer together. The snapping of the burning wood in the fireplace filled the silence. The scent of the smoke mingled with the fragrance of the night and the man. She could feel his heat. She had to tilt her head back to look at his face. Her hands clasped and unclasped.

He reached out toward her. She thought about stepping back, but she couldn't seem to get her feet to move. He was going to touch her, and she was going to let him. She needed to know if he could still affect her, she told herself firmly. It was a scientific experiment.

His thumb whispered against her jaw, then swept across her chin. Sensation shot through her like the unexpected warmth of sunlight after a storm. The room grew hot, her muscles clenched tight.

"Why aren't you married?" he asked.

"No one ever asked."

The lie was so automatic, she shocked herself. Why had she said that? She'd been engaged for months. It would be better for Justin to know the truth, but she couldn't say anything now. She was confused. Nothing made sense, and Justin was moving closer.

"I find it hard to believe you never tempted a man," he said. "Are they all blind?"

She should have been pleased at the implied compliment, but she was too caught up in that single word. *Tempted.* Had he known that was what she was thinking? Did he know he tempted her?

"I'm not interested in temptation," she murmured, wondering why her voice was so soft. She tried to swallow, but her throat was dry. Against her will, she found herself staring into his eyes, watching the fire reflected there. The light seemed to dance about, then darken. The night closed in around them. She could feel the heat from the fireplace behind her and the heat of the man. It was like a dream where she couldn't move, couldn't call out. Could only bravely accept her fate.

But instead of the frightening demons of her dreams, she only had to face Justin. Not so difficult a task.

"I'm interested," he said, reaching his hand up to cup her face. His lean fingers held her gently. She felt the rough calluses against her skin.

"In what?" she asked.

"Temptation."

His face drew closer. The flames in his eyes grew brighter. She vaguely thought it couldn't just be the reflection of the fire behind her, it had to be something else, something . . .

When his lips touched hers, all conscious thought fled. Her eyelids must have closed for she could see nothing, hear nothing. There was only the moment and the flood of memories filling her with the bittersweet taste of the past.

His mouth was firm, yet yielding. The powerful passion she recalled was now carefully controlled. He brushed across her mouth, back and forth as if familiarizing himself with her. She raised herself on tiptoe to mold her shape to his. The correct and proper side of herself screamed it was foolish and wrong to be doing this. She didn't care.

Justin wrapped his arms around her shoulders and drew her closer. From chest to knees they touched. Through the layers of her skirt and petticoats, she couldn't feel much but the general shape of him, but he was all she remembered him to be. The rightness of it brought a burning to her eyes.

She wanted to hold him, as well, but couldn't bring herself to acquiesce that much. She held her arms at her sides, her hands curled into tight fists.

His fingers slipped under her chignon and kneaded the back of her neck. He moved down her spine, touching, pulling her even closer. His mouth angled against hers, his lips pressing harder now, taunting her with passion.

It wasn't supposed to feel so good. Other men had kissed her. Not many, but one or two. Why did he have to be the one who made her feel this way? She swallowed her cry of protest against this cruel trick of fate.

His hands encircled her waist. Her breathing came faster now. He dipped his head lower, moving his mouth to her jaw, then down her neck to the collar of her dress. She arched against him, ignoring the way her movement caused her corset to dig into her. The pain didn't matter, and neither did the fact she couldn't draw in a deep enough breath. When he returned his lips to hers and his tongue swept across her sensitized skin, she released her last hold on sanity. Her mouth parted and her arms came up toward him.

As he dipped inside, she prepared herself for the onslaught of madness. He would make her forget herself, forget everything, and she didn't care at all.

Her hands splayed across his chest, feeling the strength of him concealed only by his white shirt and long underwear. He was hard to her soft, angles and planes where she was curves and swells. She reached under his coat to hug him tighter, all the while savoring his kiss. She moved her hands over his ribs and bumped something in his pocket.

The lump moved, then meowed softly and stretched. Justin broke their kiss.

"What's that?" she asked as soon as she could get her mouth working again.

He reached inside his coat pocket and pulled out a tiny calico kitten. "Her mother was a good mouser. I thought you might like her." He grimaced. "I'm sorry about what happened in my office today. That's what I came by to tell you. We've had our problems in the past, but that doesn't change my responsibilities to you or the town. I was rude to you and I apologize. I brought her for you."

He held out the kitten. She took her and cupped the small creature in her hands. Bright green eyes blinked sleepily. The kitten nuzzled Megan's chest and exhaled a deep breath. The kitten's purring became muffled as she buried her face under the tip of her tail.

"She's so sweet." Megan glanced up at him. The dampness of his mouth and his knowing look reminded her what had just happened between them. They were still standing close together. Too close. She stepped back. It didn't help much. She had a bad feeling she could walk clear to the other side of Kansas and it wouldn't be far enough. Justin's apology made her want to forgive him everything. His hot kisses and thoughtful gift made her feel more than was safe. She should ask him to leave right now. Before any more damage was done.

"Would you like to stay for supper?" she blurted out.

He shook his head and started buttoning up his coat. "That wouldn't be a good idea. You're right. We aren't supposed to be friends. It would be better for everyone if we tried to stay out of each other's way. I know Landing isn't that big, but if we work at it, I think we can avoid too much contact."

She wanted to ask why he'd had a sudden shift in attitude. She bit her lower lip. Was it the kiss? Had he been disappointed? Had she shocked him by responding? Did he think she wasn't a lady?

She walked with him to the front door. She held the kitten close, savoring the animal's warmth and the faint rumble of her purr.

"Thank you for her," she said.

"You're welcome." Dark eyes met and held hers. She couldn't read his expression. Justin was such an odd combination of known and unknown. A stranger, and yet—she squeezed her still-tingling lips together—someone she would never forget.

"I apologize for what I said about your mother."

He shrugged. "Goodbye, Megan." He reached for the hat he'd left on the hall tree when he'd first come inside, then stepped onto the porch.

Instinctively, she swept her gaze across the bare garden. In the last lingering illumination of twilight, she didn't see anyone standing around. Thank goodness. Heaven only knew what would happen if her sister or someone from town saw him leaving her house.

"You aren't going to say anything to anyone, are you?" she asked.

He looked at her over his shoulder. Confusion pulled his dark eyebrows together, then his expression cleared and she could read his contempt. "No. I won't say a word. Your precious reputation is safe with me."

He stalked away. Megan stared after him. She thought about trying to explain, but he would never understand. He didn't know the danger of being ostracized. He didn't know what fate she would suffer. So many times she'd started to tell him the ugly secret from her past, but she hadn't. She'd been too ashamed.

So instead of calling him back, she closed the door and locked it, then headed for the kitchen.

"I have some cream," she murmured. "Would you like that?"

The kitten stirred in her arms. The small warmth wasn't enough to banish the ghosts from the past and the chill from her heart, but it was so much better than facing them all alone.

Justin pulled up his collar against the cold night air. As he made his way back to town, he cursed himself for still being a fool. Damn Megan and damn himself for caring. Her precious reputation had always been more important than anything else. Why was he surprised that hadn't changed?

He shook his head in disgust. He hoped her reputation kept her company in bed at night, otherwise she was going to have a long and lonely life. Not that he cared. He was only sorry that he'd wasted his time with her. Going to see her had been a mistake. Kissing her a bigger one.

Suddenly, he laughed out loud. His breath created a small cloud. He slapped his arms over his chest and walked faster. Kissing her hadn't been a mistake, it had been mighty pleasurable. He'd wondered if anything had changed between them. Now he knew it hadn't. The passion, the fire, had still flared, and she'd tasted as sweet as he remembered.

Just thinking about her yielding body pressing against his was enough to make his groin harden. Unfortunately, even the cold didn't ease the swelling. He hoped thoughts of their kisses were bothering her as much as they bothered him. He grinned. It had been worth it, that's for sure.

Justin walked around the back of the Bartlett General Store, then across the muddy street toward the sheriff's office. He had to lock up for the night before he could head back to his hotel room. As he passed the saloon, he heard the familiar sound of music and yells of excitement. No doubt there were a couple of poker games going on inside. He should probably make an appearance, but his duties didn't officially start until the morning.

He paused across the street from the building and stared at it. This saloon was newer and larger than the smaller Golden Landing down the street. He made himself walk toward that one, wondering what it would cost him to go inside.

The old building hadn't changed. The worn sign still needed painting. Three panes of glass had been covered over by boards, so little light filtered onto the boardwalk. Upstairs the windows were dark. The women hadn't started their "hostess" duties yet. It was early and most of the customers hadn't found their way to the saloon yet. Tinny piano music covered the sound of conversations and clinking glasses. Justin knew that in an hour or two the raucous noises would drown out the sound of the piano, and by ten o'clock, the man playing the instrument would give up. He knew the sights and sounds and smells of that saloon. The Golden Landing had been the first wooden building constructed in town. His mother had worked there for as long as he could remember.

Without trying to he could recall the sound of her weary footsteps on the stairs as she'd climbed up to their room. Year after year she'd worked washing glasses, serving customers, cleaning up after everyone had gone home. Time and time again she'd been offered money to warm a man's bed. With a growing boy to provide for, she must have been tempted to take the easy way out. But she hadn't. She'd kept their tiny room spotless, him in food and shoes. Every year he'd watched her grow weaker. He'd quit school to work, but the extra money hadn't helped improve her cough, or changed the gray tinge to her skin.

He swallowed hard, fighting the memories. His mother had been a decent hardworking woman. But no one in Landing had cared. She'd worked in a saloon and hadn't married his father. That was all anyone had needed to know.

He turned away from the building and the past. As he had several times already that day, he wondered if he'd made a mistake by coming back. The idea of returning to Landing and making his peace with the town had sounded so easy. Now he wanted to forget he'd ever heard of the place. And Megan Bartlett.

Without trying, he could feel her body pressed against his and taste the sweetness of her mouth. Damn. He'd never been able to resist her. He wouldn't have come back if he'd known she was here. Why hadn't she married and moved away? Now he was going to have to deal with the fact that he'd once offered his heart to her, exposed his most secret self and she'd thrown all of it back in his face. She'd reminded him he was just that bastard Justin Kincaid and that he'd been a fool to think she might have cared about him.

The anger might be old, but it still lived inside of him. He wished it would burn hot enough to allow him to make her pay for what she'd said and done, but that wasn't possible. He could never hurt Megan. Which is why he had to stay out of her way.

As he crossed the dark, empty street, he noticed light shining out of the sheriff's office. He hadn't lit any lanterns before he'd left, so he must have visitors.

As he approached the building, he saw two men standing in front of his desk. One of them turned toward the window. The muscles in Justin's stomach clenched tight. He recognized the light brown hair and mustache. It had taken Wyatt the better part of five months for it to grow in that thick. He'd been so proud of his mustache that Justin wasn't surprised to see he still wore it, after all these years. He didn't know the younger man standing next to Wyatt, but he knew who they were. The gleaming silver badges on their chests told him. His deputies.

He walked softly toward the door, then paused before entering. Wyatt had been one of the boys who had taken pleasure in beating Justin up. When Justin had grown big enough to hurt back, Wyatt had given up his game. Justin wondered if his old enemy knew who the new sheriff was.

He opened the door and stepped inside. The two men turned toward him. The stranger gave him a half smile, but Wyatt stared as if he'd seen a ghost.

"Evening, gentlemen," Justin said. He walked closer to the men. "I'm Justin Kincaid, the new sheriff of Landing."

The smaller, dark-haired man held out his hand. "Daniel Thomas, Sheriff. It's a pleasure to meet you." They shook hands. Justin studied the younger man, taking in the firm set of his jaw and the straightforward appraisal of his eyes.

"Thomas," he said. "How long have you been in town?"

"About three weeks, sir. I worked as a deputy up North for a while. I'm sure excited about this job."

"Good." Justin turned his attention to the other man. "Evening, Wyatt."

"Justin." Wyatt's blue eyes met his. Justin read the confusion there, the shock and anger. Then all the emotions were banished, and the other man smiled. "Welcome home."

Justin walked over to his desk and picked up a piece of paper. "I've got a contract that says I'll be here for a year.

I won't accept less than complete loyalty and obedience. You can either work with me, or move on. Which is it to be?"

Wyatt shifted his weight and brought his right hand up to rest on his waist, right above the butt of his pistol. Justin didn't blink. He wasn't armed, but that wasn't something he cared about right now. Wyatt wasn't going to draw, the man was just testing him. He didn't mind the testing, what he cared about was Wyatt's decision. He would rather be a man short than work with someone he couldn't trust.

Thomas glanced from him to Wyatt, obviously confused. Wyatt stared at Justin. "I heard the name but didn't believe it. If someone had told me we were going to meet in a sheriff's office, I would have guessed you'd be on the other side of the bars."

Justin smiled. Wyatt was right. After all the trouble he'd caused in town and the reason he'd been run off, it made sense to assume that. "I almost was," he said. "But I've learned from my mistakes. I've been a deputy over five years. I've studied law, even been offered a turn at being a judge. My qualifications were enough for this town. I don't give a damn about whether or not they're good enough for you. I just want to know where you stand. I won't watch my back. Either you're with me, or you find yourself another job."

Wyatt relaxed and dropped his hand to his side. "Take a good look at this man, Thomas. He broke my nose when we were both twelve. Did it again when I was fifteen. All right, Justin. I've learned my lesson, too. I'll work with you."

Justin's gaze narrowed. That was too easy. He didn't trust Wyatt.

Wyatt shrugged. "I know what you're thinking. It's not only your besting me in a fight. We all know you didn't beat up that woman. If you'd stuck around long enough, you would have found out for yourself that you were cleared of the accusation."

Justin settled on a corner of his desk. "No one else was willing to wait around to find out I was innocent," he said. "They were all anxious to attend a hanging. Leaving seemed best."

Wyatt nodded. He walked two steps closer, then held out his hand. "My sister admitted to me that she was sweet on you. Told me she'd cornered you after a barn dance. Said she kissed you, and, ah, made it clear she wouldn't say no. She told me you sent her back to her mama and warned her if she was foolish enough to make that offer to another man, she would find herself in more trouble than she could handle. I'm obliged to you for that."

Justin took the man's hand and they shook slowly, measuring each other. He still didn't trust Wyatt, but he was willing to give him a chance.

Thomas still stared at the two of them, bewildered. "Sir, I don't understand."

"You will." Justin slapped him on the shoulder. "I used to live here. I was a hell-raiser and troublemaker. My mother worked in a saloon, but she wasn't a whore. I never knew my father and my parents didn't marry. That makes me a bastard. Some would be happy to tell you that's not the only thing, either. I work hard and I expect the same from my men. I hold on to my temper." Except around Megan, he thought suddenly and had to fight back a grin. "I don't allow drinking on duty, or gambling ever. Aside from that, what you do with your own time is your business. Any questions?"

Wyatt shook his head. Thomas gaped at him, apparently overwhelmed by the information and instructions.

"Thomas? You have a problem with any of that?"

"No, sir."

"Good." Justin took his seat, then lowered the box containing his belongings to the floor. "Anything been going on in town that I should know about, Wyatt?"

Wyatt walked over to his desk and picked up a couple of papers. "I was writing up a report for you. Everything has been quiet around here." He handed Justin the sheets. "Except for the murder last month."

"Murder?"

Wyatt shrugged. "Some saloon girl was found beaten to death on the edge of town."

Justin stared at the other man. The coldness in his stomach quickly spread to the rest of his body. He was careful to keep his face expressionless as he studied the details of the case. There weren't many. According to the report, Roberts, the previous sheriff, had investigated for a couple of days and had concluded that one of the many drifters who had been in town at that time had been responsible for the crime.

The hairs on the back of Justin's neck stood up. Something wasn't right. "What kind of sheriff was Roberts?" he asked without looking up.

"Decent. He kept the town clean."

Not clean enough, Justin thought, fighting the ghosts that threatened to suffocate him. For a second, he entertained the notion that Roberts had ended the investigation because he'd been bought off. No way to prove that. But he didn't like any of it—not the murder, the brief nature of the investigation or the fact that the victim was a saloon girl.

"According to this, he didn't interview anyone but the saloon owner. There's no proof she was murdered by a drifter."

"If it wasn't a drifter, then it had to have been someone in town," Wyatt said. "That doesn't make sense. Who would want to kill her?"

Justin had no answer for that. He glanced over the paper once more, then focused on her name.

Laurie Smith. The cold knot in his stomach tightened. She was the same woman who had been beaten up seven years before. She was the reason he'd been run out of town. He'd been accused of the crime. He hadn't done it and as soon as she'd regained consciousness, she'd cleared his name. But it had been too late. He'd already left Landing, swearing he would never come back.

Well, he was back now. And a saloon girl had been murdered. In keeping with this town's attitude about someone they thought was less respectable than themselves, no one gave a damn. But he did. It was possible the two crimes had been committed by the same person. And he damn well wanted to find out who.

"I want to reopen the investigation."

He glanced up at Wyatt. The deputy shrugged. "You're the boss."

Justin set down the paper. He had something to prove to the town and himself. He would solve this. He had no choice. The case hit far too close to home.

Chapter Four

It was late afternoon when Justin left the livery stable and stood alone on the boardwalk. The blue Kansas sky stretched on forever. It was warmer than it had been the day before. He buttoned up his lined coat and adjusted his hat.

Two women carrying overloaded baskets walked along the boardwalk. He stepped back out of their way and touched his hat brim. The younger of the two smiled and nodded until her companion leaned forward and whispered something in her ear. Then both of them glanced at him and hurried away.

He'd had that kind of trouble all the day. Most of the old-timers remembered him and weren't pleased to have him as their sheriff. And, as Megan had told him, the newer settlers didn't much care about him or his past, as long as he kept the peace. Neither group had any information about the dead saloon girl. They'd answered his questions patiently, but he'd seen the questions in their eyes. Why did he care about the likes of her?

One or two people had tried to be helpful, but most couldn't bother. He hated that some lives were valued more than others. As long as he was in charge of justice in this town, that wasn't going to happen. Unfortunately, he was too late for Laurie Smith.

"Will there be anything else, Sheriff?"

Justin turned back toward the stable. "No. If you think of anything, I'd be obliged if you'd come tell me about it. Or one of the deputies."

"I'll sure do that."

Rumors about his presence in town and what he was asking everyone about had spread so quickly that by the time Justin got to the livery stable, Zeke had simply come out shaking his head. Said he'd never met the girl, hadn't known she was dead. Zeke man was so frail that Justin doubted the old man could have raised his hand against a good-size dog, let alone a woman. But as far as he was concerned, everyone else was suspect.

"Afternoon, Zeke."

"Afternoon, Sheriff."

He shoved his hands into his coat pockets and surveyed the town. He'd sent Wyatt to speak with the other saloon girls, and Thomas to find out what he could from nearby farmers. Justin had asked questions at every business in town. Except one.

He started down the boardwalk, then jogged across the street between two wagons. He wished he knew if he'd been putting off talking to her, or saving her for last. Better for both of them if he hadn't had to think about it at all. Best if she hadn't still been in Landing, or if he hadn't have given a damn about seeing her.

It was too late to change what had already happened between them, he reminded himself. Too late to take back the kisses that had kept him up half the night. If only she'd gotten old, fat or bald. Even a husband would have been enough to keep him at bay. Now there was nothing between him and Megan Bartlett except his good intentions. They would provide as much protection as cotton sheet in a blizzard.

His boots clunked on the boardwalk outside the general store. He wished he didn't have to go inside. He didn't want to look at her and know that she was still bent on protecting her reputation more than anything in the world. He didn't want to know that just seeing her was enough to make him act like a fool. Megan had been nothing but trouble for him. From the moment he'd first laid eyes on her, he knew he had to have her or die. In the end, she'd almost destroyed him.

But right now, he didn't have a choice. There was a dead girl buried by the church and no one to bring her killer to justice but him. That was more important than any woman, or any feelings either he or Megan might have.

He opened the door and stepped inside the store. As the door slammed shut behind him, he heard the faint tinkling of a bell. Despite the big windows in front and spaced on the sides, it was dimmer inside than out and it took a moment for his eyes to adjust.

Before he could see all the merchandise in her store, he could smell it. Leathers and perfumes, burning wood, tobacco, coffee, salt brine from the barrels along the wall, and underlying it all, exotic spices. He inhaled deeply, remembering how, as a child, he'd loved visiting the general store. Old man Bartlett had chased him out quick enough, fearing the young Kincaid boy was as likely to steal as a cow is to eat hay. So his trips had been furtive, planned out in detail as he tried to enter hidden by the full skirt of some respected matron. He took great pride in the fact that he had never stolen anything, despite his reputation. All these years later, when he had every right to be in the store, he couldn't quite shake the urge to look over his shoulder.

Although the bounty of the store was similar to what he remembered it had in the past, Megan had changed the organization. Instead of a hodgepodge of goods piled around, she had rows of neatly stacked items for sale. Bolts of fabric were at the front of the store, along with tables of pattern books and magazines. Behind them were the household goods. Dishes, steel knives, pans, pails, brooms. There was even an adult-size coffin tucked under a table. Display cases down the center of the store held jewelry and pistols. On the left of the room was the food. Barrels and bags, jars, tins, boxes. A dozen or so customers filled the aisles.

"Good afternoon, Justin. Have you come to see me?"

He turned toward the voice and was surprised to see Widow Dobson sitting behind a desk by the front window. Her black dress, different from the one she'd worn yesterday, but no less severe, clung to her generous form. The buttons over her mammoth bosom seemed to test the strength of the fabric.

"Not specifically," he said. "But I do have a few questions." He motioned to the store. "If you're done with your shopping."

She cackled gleefully. "I'm not shopping, I'm working." She spread out several letters in front of her. "Should I be looking for mail for you?"

Of course. She ran the small Landing post office. He shook his head. "No. I'm not expecting any letters."

Her bright green eyes danced. "We can always hope. From a young lady, perhaps?"

Just what he needed. A matchmaking, meddling old woman spreading gossip about his correspondence. A sharp retort sprang to his lips, but he held it back. He reminded himself again that Mrs. Dobson had been kind to his mother. He owed her for that.

"How is my kitten?" she asked, leaning forward and resting her bosom on the table. It smothered some of the letters and pushed others aside. He wondered if Mr. Dobson had ever felt inadequate at the sight of such largesse.

Kitten? He stiffened. The one he'd given to Megan last night. "She's fine."

"It's puzzling," she said. "Megan came in this morning with a kitten. Just like the one I gave you. I didn't know you and Megan were acquainted."

The hairs on the back of his neck rose as he scented danger. The older woman could make trouble for Megan. He didn't trust her with the truth, so all that was left was a bluff. Slowly, he reached up and removed his hat. He slapped it against his thigh, then met the woman's gaze. "I'm sure I don't know anything about that."

Her green eyes narrowed as she studied him. He waited to see if she would call him on the lie. Instead, Mrs. Dobson leaned back and straightened the pile of letters. "I see. You said you had some questions for me. What are they?"

"I'm investigating a murder that occurred here last month. One of the saloon girls was beaten and left on the edge of town. Do you know anything about that?"

Mrs. Dobson stood and glared at him. "Because I know you didn't mean to insult me with that question, I will pretend I never heard it. I'll ask you to go on about your business."

"I'm not implying that you had anything to do with her death, ma'am. I'm just trying to find out information."

The woman continued to stare at a point just left of his shoulder.

"Did you ever speak to her?"

Her gaze didn't waver.

"All right, Mrs. Dobson. Good afternoon."

He walked toward a young man behind the counter. Widow Dobson's reaction had been the same as most women's in town. They wouldn't discuss the girl's murder with him. It was frustrating and he didn't know what to do about it.

A young man in his late teens looked up when Justin approached. The stitched name on his apron said Andrew.

"May I help you, sir?"

Justin needed a minute to let his temper cool off before he spoke to Megan. Starting a fight with her the moment he saw her wouldn't help his investigation.

He glanced at the counter in front of him and pointed. "A penny's worth of candy." He pulled the coin out of his vest pocket.

Andrew measured out the hard sweets, then dropped them into a piece of brown paper and twisted the ends together. "Anything else?"

Justin took the offered package. "I'm the new sheriff in town. About a month ago, a woman was killed and I'm looking into her murder. Her name was Laurie Smith. She worked in one of the saloons. Did you know her?"

Andrew's still-pimply face blushed bright red. He ducked his head toward his chest. "N-no," he muttered, his voice cracking on the single syllable. He cleared his throat. "I don't go to saloons much. My ma doesn't approve."

"You never paid for her company?"

Andrew looked up, his gaze stricken, then looked away. From the deepening of the flush on his cheeks, it looked as if the boy had never had the pleasure of bedding a woman. Justin shook his head. He felt old. Very old.

"Your time will come, son," he said.

Andrew's answer was unintelligible.

Justin glanced around the crowded store. Several women were having a lively discussion over a fashion book. A couple of farmers had spread out packages of seeds. He glanced back at the clerk. "Where's Miss Bartlett?"

"In the back."

Justin started in that direction.

"Sir, you can't go there. It's private."

He shot Andrew his coldest look. "Official business, young man."

That froze the boy in place. Justin weaved through the shoppers and ducked behind a curtain.

Megan bent over her task, trying to tally the number of bolts of calico she was ordering. They would arrive in plenty of time for the fall Harvest Dance. With spring and summer crops bringing in extra coin, lots of people liked to buy an extra garment or two. She wanted to be prepared.

But as she moved her pencil down the neat row of figures, the tiny calico kitten batted it away.

"You're not helping," Megan said, trying to sound stern.

The kitten looked up at her. Her pretty face was as multicolored as the rest of her, as if God had changed his mind about her several times, but hadn't bothered to erase what he'd already started. Her belly, paws and half of her face were white. There were blotches of orange, black and an intriguing sprinkling of tabby on the rest of her body. Her tail was ringed all the way up to the solid black tip.

"You should be as ugly as a groundhog," she said, picking up the kitten and holding her close. The little cat nestled against her chest and purred contentedly. Megan leaned back in her chair and stroked the little animal's soft coat.

"I see you're working hard."

The male voice shocked her. She straightened immediately, causing the kitten to meow in protest. Megan looked up and saw Justin leaning against the doorway of her office. The room was small enough without him taking up all the space. She scooted the chair back to put more distance between them, but the file drawers behind her didn't give her anywhere to go.

He was too tall, too broad, altogether too masculine. Her father had been gone long enough for her to have removed all traces of him from the office. This was her domain now; she was in charge. But just seeing Justin standing there made her feel helpless and fluttery. With his hat pushed back on his head, she could see his eyes, but she didn't want to look there. She didn't want to see his expression and perhaps know what he was thinking.

His scent came to her—the cool freshness of the sunny afternoon, the faint smell of her store and something else, something wholly male and wholly Justin. She recognized the fragrance. It had clung to her clothing last night for a brief time, reminding her of his kisses.

She set the kitten on the desk, then stood and smoothed her skirt. "Good afternoon, Justin," she said, hoping her voice sounded calmer than the thundering of her heart. "This is a surprise."

"I came to make a purchase." He held up the small paper package, then nodded at the kitten. "And to check up on her. She seems quite happy. Have you given her a name?"

"Alice."

He raised one dark eyebrow.

She tilted up her chin slightly. "She's my cat. I can name her what I like."

"Alice?"

"I've never liked those silly names like Boots or Snowball. I wanted to give her a real name. Something she could be proud of."

He took a step closer. In the tiny office, that action left less than two feet between them. She tried to slow her breathing.

"She's just a cat," he said.

"I know, but . . ." Her words died in her throat when he reached toward her. Her body began to hum in anticipation. Her palms got sweaty and her blood heated. He was going to touch her, right here in her office where anyone could come in and—

He stretched his arm past her and picked up the kitten. "Good afternoon, Alice," he said softly and stroked the animal under the chin. The kitten looked up at him, then started to purr. Her rumble seemed far too loud for a cat her size.

Megan abruptly sat in her chair. She understood exactly how Alice felt. If Justin had touched her, she would have purred as loudly. She'd told herself she could survive anything for a year. This was the second day of his stay and already she was in trouble. She had a bad feeling it was going to be a very long twelve months.

"I want to talk about the murder," he said. His voice was still low and pleasant, but when she looked at his face she saw the tightness in his expression. "About a month ago a saloon girl was killed. What do you know about that?"

"Nothing. Why would I?"

He set the kitten on the desk. "Because someone who lived here for many years was brutally murdered. She didn't die in her sleep or have an accident. Someone found her and beat her to death."

Megan folded her arms in front of her and clutched at her waist. Justin's anger was a tangible force in the room. It filled the small space and used up all the air until she felt as if she couldn't breathe.

"I'd heard—"

"Nothing. I know. Damn." He took off his hat and ran his fingers through his dark hair. Brown eyes bored into hers. "What is wrong with all you people? Why doesn't anyone care about her? Why didn't you want to know what happened?"

"I didn't know her. Of course, I'm sorry she met with such an unfortunate fate, but there is no reason for me to know a saloon girl."

"That makes her death all right with you."

"No." She grabbed the arms of her chair and glared at him. "Not at all. I wouldn't want anyone to die like that."

"Weren't you concerned for yourself? Your safety?"

She drew her eyebrows together. "Why should I be? Someone who wanted her dead wouldn't be interested in a respectable woman."

Justin bent over her and placed his hands on the arms of her chair, trapping her fingers under his. His coat fell open, blocking her view of the rest of the room. His face was inches from hers. "How do you know?"

She wanted to get away, but squirming would be undignified. She refused to let him know how he was upsetting her. "The sheriff said her killer was just a drifter. There were several in town around that time. He said it was an argument over...services." She could feel the heat on her cheeks.

"And no one cared."

"You have no right to ask me these questions or to make me say these things."

"Explain that to Laurie."

"Who?"

"The dead girl. She had a name, you know." His dark, angry eyes refused to release her. She tried to look away, but she couldn't. "She was just your age, Megan. Not much taller than you. Not nearly as pretty, though. But because she worked in a saloon and took money for what you offered me for free, it's all right that she's dead?"

"No!" She jerked her hands free and pushed at his chest. "I never offered you anything." She banished the memory of their times by the stream. Nothing had happened.

But she'd wanted it to.

Justin straightened. Only then did she realize the door was open and that anyone could have overheard their conversation. She sent up a quick prayer, then rose and moved around him to close it.

"Keep your voice down," she said quietly.

"Ah, yes. Your precious reputation." He mocked her, then took her chair without asking. He stretched his long legs out in front of him, trapping her by the door.

She glanced at the desk. Alice had curled up on the order forms and had gone to sleep. The sight of the sweet kitten reminded her that Justin had brought her the cat as an apology for the harsh words he'd said yesterday. Here they were, arguing again.

She tugged at the waist of her dress, then looked at him. "You didn't really expect me to know her, Justin. I'm sorry she's dead. I'm sorry I don't know anything, but you can't blame me for her life or her death."

He placed his hat on his lap. "I suppose not." He thought for a minute. "Did anyone demand a more thorough investigation?"

"Not that I remember. Sheriff Roberts told everyone it was one of the drifters who had killed her."

"That's it?"

She nodded. "Justin, I'm sorry. He was the sheriff. Why wouldn't he tell the truth?"

He leaned forward in the chair, resting his elbows on his knees. He dangled his hat from his hands. "I'm not saying he lied on purpose. I just wonder why he didn't bother looking into the case further."

"You think there was another killer?"

"I don't know."

He looked desolate. Megan had to hold herself back to keep from going to him. She wanted to touch him and tell him that everything was going to be all right. Except she didn't know that to be true. And even if she did, Justin wouldn't want comfort from her.

"Her name was Laurie," he said.

"You told me."

"Laurie Smith."

Megan grabbed on to the door handle for support. She stared at his bent head, then watched as he looked up at her. She tried to school her features, but couldn't. Heaven knew what he saw on her face. His dark eyes gave nothing away.

"So you remember."

"Yes," she whispered. "She was the one—" She swallowed the bile rising in her throat.

"The woman I was accused of beating seven years ago. Interesting, don't you think?"

"She cleared your name."

"So I heard."

"But you don't know how."

"What do you mean?"

Megan was sorry she'd said anything. She didn't want to have this conversation with Justin. There was no way for her to talk about it without him guessing how much she'd been hurt. No one had known the truth, she reminded herself. That was the only thought that had kept her alive during those awful days. When she'd heard the story, she'd known she'd made the right decision about staying in Landing. What would have happened if she'd left with him and then found out? She would have been destroyed.

"Megan, tell me what you're talking about." He rose from the chair and approached her. With the closed door behind her, there was nowhere to go. He tossed his hat on the chair and gently held her upper arms. "Tell me."

"I..." She looked up into his face, then away. "When she said it wasn't you, the sheriff wanted to know how she was sure. He told her it had been dark. She said—" Her voice caught. She swallowed again, then closed her eyes. It was easier to speak of it without looking at him. "She said she would have known you anywhere. That you'd been with her several times, some of them in the dark." She blinked back the tears, but could do nothing about the pain. "You spent those summer evenings kissing me and tempting me on the bank of the stream, but you spent your nights with her. You went from me to a w-whore."

His fingers gripped her tighter. "Sonofabitch."

She flinched at the harsh word.

He released her then, and turned away. "So even if you knew anything about her death you, wouldn't tell me," he said.

"That's not true. If you think that, you don't know me at all."

"You're right, I don't know you." He picked up his hat. "It's been seven years, Megan. Despite the past we shared, we're strangers."

Then why does my heart beat faster around you? She didn't ask. He would have no answer, at least none that she wanted to hear.

"I'd better go," he said, turning toward her.

She feared what she would see in his eyes, but for once his lack of expression was a blessing. "I really don't know anything," she said.

He nodded and moved past her toward the door. She wanted to say something, anything to make it right between them. There were no words left. He was right; they were strangers.

He opened the door.

"Justin?"

He paused.

She raised her hand toward him, wanting to touch him, then let her arm drop to her side. "I don't know if this helps or not, but there was another saloon girl killed about four years ago. She was beaten to death, as well."

"What happened?"

"I don't know." She held her palm out. "I was caring for my father while he was ill, so don't yell at me for not being concerned about her death. I don't know any of the details, but they sound the same as those surrounding Laurie Smith's death. Maybe it will help."

"Thanks for telling me. No one else bothered to." He grimaced. "I don't suppose you would consider asking around about Laurie? Maybe people would tell you something they won't tell me?"

She wouldn't have been more shocked if he'd asked her to take off her dress and parade around in her petticoats. "I can't. What would people—"

"Think," he finished grimly. "Stupid of me to ask."

"That's not fair. No one I know would be familiar with a saloon girl."

He stepped into the hallway. "Tell me, Megan, does it get cold and lonely being perfect?"

He didn't wait for an answer, he simply walked away. She stared after him, biting her lower lip and fighting the tears. He wasn't being reasonable. He wanted too much. And he was right. Her world was much colder and emptier than he could ever imagine.

Justin stormed along the boardwalk, then stomped through the mud on his way back to his office. Damn Megan for her heartlessness. He pulled his mouth into a straight line and barely had the good manners to nod as one of the new settlers in the area greeted him.

She couldn't risk her precious reputation to ask a few questions about a dead girl. Laurie Smith had never hurt anyone; she'd been the one hurt.

His steps slowed as he remembered the look on Megan's face as she'd tonelessly spoken the words that had proven his innocence. That Laurie knew Justin's form in the dark because he'd bedded her. More than once.

He drew in a deep breath and let it out slowly. He'd been so young, then. So infatuated with Megan, so determined to do the right thing. But night after night of kissing her and nothing more had left him as randy as a stallion teased by a mare in heat. He'd taken his release with Laurie because she was young and smelled sweet and because if he closed his eyes, he could pretend her curves were Megan's. He would have cut out his heart rather than let Megan know what he'd done.

He shook his head but that didn't banish her look of hurt and shattered pride. She was too innocent to understand the needs of a man, especially a foolish young man. She wouldn't know that time and experience would temper those needs and that spending his coin on Laurie didn't mean he had loved Megan less. Things would be different now. He could handle the temptation without giving in. He had developed self-control. Not that it mattered. There was nothing between him and Megan and there never would be. When his year was up, he was leaving and never looking back.

He stalked around the pile of manure by the sheriff's office, then jerked open the door. He was so intent on forgetting Megan and trying to concentrate on her news of another murder four years ago that at first he didn't notice Thomas cowering in front of a tall, large-boned woman.

"Sheriff," Thomas said as Justin stepped into the office. "I'm real glad you're back. This lady here—" he motioned to the poorly dressed older woman "—needs to speak with you."

The woman turned her cold stare on him. There was something meanspirited about her and Justin understood why his deputy was squirming.

"Are you the last person I got to explain this to, or should I just hold my tongue a spell? I ain't fond of chewin' my food twice."

"I'm the sheriff here," he said and motioned for her to take a seat. He took off his hat and coat and hung them on the hooks by the door, then offered her his most charming smile.

The woman glared at him and sat. Her gray-streaked hair was pulled back into a bun. The afternoon sunlight caught the strands, highlighting the oily film. Her coat and dress were old and dirty, her face none too clean. Only practice kept him from recoiling when her odor drifted to him.

"How can I help you?" he asked.

Her gaze narrowed. "I've been to that church there. The pea-eyed lady done told me she don't care for the likes of my trouble. Not that I blame her. I don't care for it none, neither."

Justin perched on the edge of his desk and looked at Thomas. The deputy shrugged. "I'm not sure, sir. We had just started our discussion when you walked in."

"I'm gettin' to it," the woman said impatiently. "Girl, get over here."

Justin saw something move away from the corner. He looked closer. With all the commotion, he hadn't noticed the child standing so quietly. At the woman's command, the girl stepped forward slowly, but kept her gaze firmly fixed on her shoes.

If anything, her clothing was worse than the woman's. Her dress and coat were too short. Patches of lining showed through on the sleeves and what he saw wasn't too thick. Her legs were thin, bare and scratched around the knees. Her littlest toe on her left foot poked through her shoe. The soles were probably missing altogether.

Anger welled up inside of him. He understood families being poor. God knows he and his mother had had their share of tough times. "Are you saying the lady at the church wasn't willing to provide you with food and clothing for your daughter?" How like Colleen, he thought grimly. She would save all her Christian charity for the well-placed citizens of towns, the ones who needed it the least.

"She ain't mine," the woman said. When the girl was close enough, she grabbed the child's arm and pulled her in front of the chair. "Say how-do."

"Hello," the small child whispered. Her voice was shaking. She couldn't be more than five or six and was obviously terrified.

"I'm afraid I don't understand," Justin said.

The woman scowled. "It's real simple. That whore, Laurie Smith, paid me to take care of her bastard girl here." The woman poked at the girl. "She's dead, and the money's run out. I don't run no orphanage. I got babes of my own to feed and there ain't no extra."

Justin curled his fingers into his palm, just in case his temper got the better of him.

"Madam, I would thank you not to speak like that in front of the child."

The woman stood up and shrugged. "Say all the fancy talk you want. Like I said, the church lady didn't want nothin' to do with the girl. I ain't gonna keep her. As I sees it, she's your problem." The woman moved to the door, opened it and walked away.

Chapter Five

Justin stared at the little girl and wondered what he was supposed to do now. She continued to study her worn shoes. Thomas came back into the office after having followed the woman.

"She disappeared," he said, between breaths. "She must have had a wagon somewhere. I'm sure it won't take me long to find out where she lives and who she is. I could—"

Justin cut him off with a shake of his head. He crouched in front of the little girl. Long matted black hair hung past her shoulders and shadowed her face. She was as dirty and smelly as the woman had been.

"What's your name?" he asked.

"B-Bonnie."

"Was that lady your mother?"

"No. My mama's dead."

"I'm sorry, Bonnie. Was that lady taking care of you?"

The girl nodded. "Mama couldn't be with me, so she left me with Mrs. Jarvis. Mrs. Jarvis told me whores go to hell, and that I'm going to hell, too, to be with my mama." She swallowed. "Is this hell?"

Despite her slumped shoulders and trembling voice, Justin smiled slightly. "Sometimes I think so, honey, but no. This is Landing. Mrs. Jarvis brought you to town."

Her small, dirty fingers twisted together. He could see several cuts and scrapes that were red and inflamed. He reached his hand toward her. She flinched.

"I just want to look at your pretty face."

He touched her chin with his forefinger and tilted it upward. When her tear-filled blue eyes met his, he felt as if he'd been kicked by a horse. She had Laurie's eyes, and her mouth was the same shape. At least he thought it was. It was hard to tell because her lips were swollen and there was the faint shading of a bruise on the side of her face. Someone had slapped her hard.

"Are you gonna take me to hell?"

"No. No one's going to hell." Except possibly Mrs. Jarvis if she ever showed her face in town again. Justin stood and glanced at Thomas. "From what the woman said, she took the girl to Colleen and was turned away."

Thomas looked surprised. "I haven't heard of a minister's wife ever doing that."

"You probably haven't had the pleasure of meeting Colleen Estes yet. You'll be less surprised by this when you do." Justin glanced out the window. It was already getting dark. "Bonnie needs a place to spend the night."

Thomas looked panicked and started backing up toward the door. "I'm staying at the boardinghouse, Sheriff. There's eighteen of us to a room. That isn't a place for a little girl."

"I know." Justin tried to think of someone in town who could help. Megan flashed through his mind, but he dismissed her. Someone that respectable wouldn't want to be tainted by the daughter of a dance-hall girl.

Beside him, Bonnie shivered. As soon as he'd let go of her chin, she'd gone back to staring at her shoes. He touched her shoulder, and was shocked to feel her bones. "Have you eaten today?" he asked.

She shook her head.

He bit back a curse. There was no one he trusted, no one he could turn to. Looks like the responsibility was his, at least for tonight. "Come on, Bonnie. I'll take you back to my hotel and get you something to eat." He started toward the door. "Thomas, you wait for Wyatt and find out what he learned. If it's important, come tell me at the hotel, otherwise it can wait until morning. While you're here, see if you can find any information on another murder. It hap-

pened about four years ago. Another saloon girl. The two
cases may be related.''

Thomas raised his eyebrows. "How?"

"I don't know," Justin admitted. "It's just a feeling."
When he reached the door, he realized Bonnie hadn't
moved. The little girl stood where he'd left her. She was still
staring at her shoes. "Come on, honey. I'm going to take
you home with me. You'll have something to eat, and maybe
a hot bath."

Slowly, she raised her head toward him. Big blue eyes
shone with terror. "It's going to be all right," he promised.

She didn't budge. He thought about picking her up, but
that would probably scare her more. Besides, she was filthy.
He settled for holding out his hand.

"Is there really food?" she asked.

He nodded.

She took several shuffling steps toward him, then shyly
reached for his hand. Her fingers were chilled. He bent over
and touched her coat. It was threadbare. How could Laurie
have left her daughter with that woman? He cursed silently, figuring he would never get an answer now.

He led Bonnie out of the office and toward the hotel. The
three-story building was the largest one in town. It had been
built in the last year and contained every modern convenience. When he entered, tugging Bonnie along with him,
the desk clerk looked up, then turned bright red, as if he
were about to have apoplexy.

"Mr. Kincaid, that child! She's filthy."

"I know, Newt." Justin stopped at the front desk and
reached into his vest pocket for several coins. "There's a
room adjoining mine. Is it vacant?"

Newt adjusted his glasses, leaned over the counter and
stared down at the child. "Yes, sir, but I don't think—"

"Good. Send up a maid with hot water for a bath, and
deliver two dinners from the dining room."

"But sir!"

"The key?"

Newt turned around and pulled it out of the box. "Mr.
Kincaid, I think I need to discuss this with the manager. You
can't bring a lady in here alone."

Justin rolled his eyes and took the key. "She's five years old."

Bonnie tugged on his arm. "Mister, I'm six."

"She's six. Tell them to hurry the water."

Justin tossed the coins on the desk and started up the stairs. Newt was still spluttering behind him. When they entered his room, he let go of Bonnie's hand and unlocked the door between the two rooms.

"You'll be in here," he said, motioning to the adjoining bedroom.

He glanced around. It wasn't quite as spacious as his room. The bed was smaller, the windows not as wide. But it would do. The hotel was clean, the rugs were taken out and beaten regularly, the sheets changed weekly. He walked around the room and pointed out the pitcher and basin, opened the armoire, showed her the lantern.

She stood in the doorway between the two rooms and stared at him. Big eyes got bigger. Both her arms hung at her sides with her hands balled into fists. For a heart-stopping second he thought she was going to cry.

"What's wrong, Bonnie?"

She shook her head and didn't speak. Before he could ask again, there was a knock on her door. He opened it. Two teenage boys carried in a tub, followed by three more with buckets of hot water. When the tub was filled, a maid came in, bringing towels and soap.

"Will there be anything else?" she asked.

He glanced at her, then the water. "I think there might be. Would you mind bathing a rather small little girl?"

"Sir?"

The maid wasn't much more than a child herself, he realized, studying her upturned nose and brown eyes. With her neat cap and apron, she looked older, but she couldn't be older than sixteen.

"What's your name?" he asked.

"Alice."

He grinned.

"It's not a funny name, sir."

"I know. It's just..." He paused. He didn't really want to explain that Megan had just named a calico kitten Alice.

"Alice, there's a little girl in my room. She needs a bath. I think it would be easier for her if you helped her rather than if I did."

"Yes, sir." Alice smiled. "I've got seven younger brothers and sisters. I know plenty about bathing a young'un."

"Wonderful." He turned. "Bonnie, Alice here is going to—"

But Bonnie wasn't standing in the doorway. He frowned and walked into his room. She wasn't there, either. Everything was as he'd left it. He glanced toward the door. Had she run off? No, he would have heard her leaving. Then where was she?

He walked around the bed. Part of the carpet had been turned up, as if someone had tripped over the edge. He bent down and touched it, then got on his hands and knees and looked under the four-poster bed. Bonnie lay on her belly up by the headboard. He could see her face. She had her eyes tightly shut.

"Are you hiding?" he asked.

She opened her eyes and looked at him. "Yes."

"Why?"

"I'm scared."

She looked so small huddled there. With her tattered clothes and dirty face. She also smelled like a sheep.

"Are you afraid of taking a bath? There's a nice lady, whose name is Alice. She's going to help you. They sent up some soap. I think it smells nice."

"Will it hurt?"

"No. It's warm water. You'll feel toasty when you're done. Then we'll have something to eat. Would you like that?"

Instead of answering, Bonnie shimmied out from under the bed. Alice stood in the doorway between the two rooms and smiled encouragingly.

"Hello," she said. "Can I help you bathe?" She held out her hand, then wrinkled her nose. "What do you want me to do with her clothes, sir?"

Justin opened his mouth, then closed it. "Wash them?"

"Does she have others? These won't be dry by morning."

"No, Mrs. Jarvis didn't leave anything." He thought for a moment. "Here." He opened the armoire and pulled out one of his shirts. "Put her in this after her bath. Take her clothes outside, brush them and let them air. In the morning, I'll find her something else."

When he was alone in his room, he sank onto the window seat and sighed. He'd been back in Landing exactly two days. In that time he'd fought with Megan twice, kissed her, found out about a murder, insulted half the women in town by asking them about a dead saloon girl, learned about a second murder and found himself responsible for a small child.

A knock sounded on the door. A cheerful male voice called out that it was a delivery from the dining room. As he rose to let the man in, he hoped they'd remembered to bring whiskey because he sure as hell needed a drink.

The little girl who was escorted to the table set up by the foot of his bed wasn't the same child who had disappeared thirty minutes before. Instead of a dirt-encrusted waif, this girl was all pink and white, sweet-smelling with beautiful, shiny black hair that fell halfway down her back. His white shirt dwarfed her, dragging on the floor. Alice had rolled up the sleeves.

"Here you go, sir. One clean girl. We had fun, Bonnie, didn't we?"

Bonnie nodded. Justin wondered if she ever smiled.

Alice held the child's dirty clothes in her arms. "I'll see what I can do about these and leave them outside her door in the morning."

"Thank you." Justin accompanied the maid to the door, then tipped her generously. When she'd left, he turned back to Bonnie, who stood beside the laden table staring as if she'd never in her life seen that much food.

"Why don't we start with some soup and bread," he said, pulling out a chair for her. If she hadn't been eating regularly, she wouldn't be able to hold that much. He didn't want to make her sick on her first decent meal in God knows how long. She glanced from him to the table setting and back. Confusion darkened her blue eyes, and fear, or maybe hunger, made her tremble.

"Don't be afraid."

He picked up a biscuit and handed it to her. She stared at it, then snatched it from him and shoved it in her mouth. While she was busy chewing, pushing and swallowing all at the same time, he lifted her and set her on the chair. Her head barely cleared the table.

Justin frowned. That wasn't going to work. He grabbed the pillows from his bed, picked her up with one arm and shoved the pillows under her behind.

"How's that?" he asked.

She swallowed the last of her biscuit. "Nice."

He grinned. "Try the soup." He lifted the cover of the tureen and ladled some broth into the bowl in front of her. The aroma of chicken and spices must have enticed her because she licked her lips. He tucked the napkin into the collar of the shirt she wore, then handed her a spoon.

"It might be hot," he said. "Blow on it first."

She stared at him as if he'd told her to ride a pig to market, then obligingly bent forward and blew on the soup. After a couple of minutes of listening to her huff and puff, he told her the soup should be fine now.

Before he'd even chewed more than two bites of his steak, she'd finished the bowl and set the spoon neatly on the table.

"You still hungry?"

"Uh-huh."

He handed her another biscuit. This time she ate it slowly, a bite at a time. Her big, blue eyes studied him. He wondered what she was thinking. He cut another piece of his steak and chewed slowly. After swallowing, he took a sip of the whiskey that had come with his meal, then leaned back in his chair.

"You mind staying here tonight?" he asked.

She shook her head.

"I've never had a little girl around before, so you tell me if you need anything. And if you want to know something, you just go ahead and ask me. You're safe here. Mrs. Jarvis isn't coming back."

She set the half-eaten biscuit on the tablecloth and wiped her hands on her shirtfront. He could still see the faint outline of the bruise on her face. It made him want to find that wretched woman and show her what it felt like to be bullied by someone bigger and stronger.

"What's your name?" the child asked.

"Justin."

"Is that for me?" Bonnie asked, pointing to a glass of milk.

"Sure is."

She took a long drink. "Am I going to stay here with you?"

Justin didn't know how to answer that. "I'm going to see if there's a nice family who would like a pretty little girl like you. Until then, yes, you'll stay here with me."

Bonnie carefully set the glass on the table. "Mrs. Jarvis says no one wants me. I'm a burden." She tossed her black hair over her shoulders. "A burden is a bad thing, ain't it?"

He didn't know how to answer that. She was only six years old, yet she sounded older, as if she'd experienced a lot of life in her years. "I don't think you're a burden."

"Mrs. Jarvis took me to see that lady at the church." She shivered. "She had a mean smile. I thought smiles were happy, but hers wasn't. She said no one would take me in 'cause my mama was a p-postute." She frowned and wrinkled her nose as she stumbled over the unfamiliar word. "Mrs. Jarvis said whores have bastards same as other people. Mrs. Jarvis always said Mama was a whore. I'm afraid to ask her what that is. Do you know?"

Justin stared at the pretty child across the table. He studied her big eyes, the bruise on her face, the now-clean scratches on her hands. He'd seen enough of life to know evil people flourished everywhere. He shouldn't be surprised by the cruelty. But every now and then something caught him unaware.

He fought the anger, knowing it would frighten Bonnie. Mrs. Jarvis was a poor uneducated dirt farmer who had probably grown up in poverty and would die that way. Colleen Estes had no such excuse. She was the wife of a minister. She was supposed to be an example for the community.

He gripped his glass so tightly he thought it might shatter. He'd come back to Landing with the best of intentions. He was beginning to wonder if he was destined to relive the past without a chance to change the outcome.

"The lady at the church was wrong to say those words, Bonnie," he said slowly. "I knew your mama. She was very sweet and pretty. I haven't seen it yet, but I think you have her smile."

The solemn little girl brightened a little. "I thought Mama was pretty, too. When she came to see me, she would let me brush her hair. When she had to leave, she would cry. She said they were good tears. Her 'I love you' tears, she said. Why does crying mean you love someone?"

"I don't know."

She took the last bite of the biscuit.

"Do you want some more soup?" he asked.

"No." She rubbed her tummy. "I'm full."

He noticed the dark shadows under her eyes. If her bedding had been as disgusting as her clothing, she probably hadn't been sleeping very much. It was still cold at night and he suspected Mrs. Jarvis didn't provide much in the way of blankets for her young charge. But first he had to find out what the little girl knew.

"Bonnie, do you have any family?"

She shook her head. "Mama's dead. Mrs. Jarvis said she's never coming back." Bonnie blinked several times, then picked at the tablecloth. "I miss her."

"I know, honey. There's no one else?"

"I asked Mama about my father once. It made her cry sad tears." Bonnie took a drink of milk. "She said we didn't need him."

Justin swirled his glass of whiskey. The bastard had probably run out on Laurie when he'd learned she was pregnant. Figured. The same thing had happened to his mother. He watched Bonnie, hoping the town would treat her better than it had treated him. Not for a single day had he been allowed to forget who he was and what his mother did for a living.

She yawned widely.

"All right, little girl. Let's get you to bed."

He helped her down from the chair and escorted her into her bedroom. When she climbed up onto the mattress, her shirttails flapped around her skinny legs exposing the back of her thighs and three ugly bruises. Justin balled his hands into fists. The marks could have been caused accidentally, but he didn't think so. The child had been beaten.

Bonnie settled on her back and stared up at him. He pulled the covers to her chin.

"You warm enough?" he asked.

"Uh-huh."

"I'm going to be right next door. You holler if you need anything."

"Am I going back with Mrs. Jarvis tomorrow?"

She reached her hand up and brushed her hair out of her face. Without stopping to consider the action, Justin caught her small fingers in his. He squeezed gently. "You're never going back to her, Bonnie. I promise."

Big blue eyes held his as she seemed to weigh his words. There wasn't a lot of trust in her expression, little hope for a better fate than the one she'd endured. He knew how that felt. It would take time for her to learn to trust again.

"Good night." He released her hand and stood. After turning down the lantern in her room, he retreated to his side of the door and shut it partway. He sat himself at the table once more and stared at his half-eaten dinner, but his appetite had deserted him.

He would keep his word to the child. He wouldn't send her back to Mrs. Jarvis. But what was he going to do with her? He knew firsthand exactly how Landing treated the less fortunate who lived here.

He leaned back in his chair and sipped his whiskey. He wasn't that half-grown boy who'd been taunted at school, he reminded himself. He was the sheriff now. He would do everything in his power to make sure Bonnie didn't suffer the same fate he had. She deserved better and he was going to make sure she got it.

"Well, you can imagine how shocked I was." Colleen pulled off her gloves and set them on the counter.

It was early yet. Not many customers were in the store. Megan stared at her sister and tried to remember the last time she'd seen Colleen up and dressed at this time of day. Her dark brown cloak, matching hat and gloves were of the latest style. Megan had ordered them and knew exactly how much they cost. If not for the inheritance left them by their father, Colleen would be hard-pressed to buy her expensive clothes. Megan wondered how her brother-in-law felt about his wife spending so much money on what he would no doubt consider frivolities. Not that he would tell Colleen to stop. Not many people were willing to stand up to her sister's temper and vicious tongue.

"Why were you surprised?" Megan asked. "It *is* a church. People have brought you orphans before."

"I know. It's a burden." Colleen grimaced. "This one was worse than all of them combined. She was filthy and smelled." She waved her hand in front of her face. "I don't know why people allow themselves to sink to such a state."

Megan stared down at the box of buttons. For almost a month now, she'd been promising herself she would sort them by size and price. She drew in a deep breath and prayed for patience. Once Colleen told her story, she would be gone. Casually, Megan glanced at the clock and wondered how long it would take.

"Children don't usually have a choice about keeping themselves clean," Megan said curtly. "You can't blame the little girl if her mother didn't bathe her."

Colleen leaned over the counter. Her thick cloak completely covered the box of buttons and scattered the piles Megan had already sorted. "But the woman wasn't her mother."

Colleen glanced at the two other people in the store. Both were men. One was old Zeke from the livery stable. He couldn't hear too well. The other was Cameron Forbes, a handsome widower with a large farm just south of town. Cameron was at the far end, looking at some gardening tools Megan kept along the back wall. Even so, Colleen lowered her voice to a whisper.

"Yesterday, our new sheriff—" she said the last word with a sniff of contempt "—was going all around town asking about that dead prostitute."

"I know." She was still smarting from his accusations. It didn't matter that she'd tried to explain. Justin hadn't cared. Megan wondered why he was always so quick to judge her.

"It was her child."

"Who was?"

Colleen glared at her. "Will you please pay attention. I'm trying to tell you. A horrible woman, her name was Mrs. Travis, or Jarvis, something like that. Anyway, she came to the church with the dirty, disgusting girl and told me she'd been paid to take care of her. The prostitute died, there's no more money and she wanted to thrust the child off on me." Colleen touched her pale white hand to her chest. "I was shocked. Gene was gone, of course. That man picks the most inconvenient times to visit sick people. I had to deal with this woman myself."

Megan pulled the box out from under Colleen's cape and started sorting the buttons again. "What happened?"

"I told her the truth. That I wasn't interested in the bastard child of some whore." Colleen smiled. "I told her a few other things, too, and sent her packing."

Megan stared at her sister. At times she found it hard to believe they'd had the same parents, grown up in the same house and lived similar lives. "You turned away the child?"

"Not *just* a child. I told you. A bastard. And her mother is—"

"Yes, I know what you said. You seem to enjoy saying those bad words, Colleen. Do you find it exciting?"

Her sister drew herself up to her full height, only an inch above her own, Megan told herself, refusing to be intimidated. "Don't you speak to me in that tone."

"I'll speak to you any way I like. You're not my mother."

Colleen's small hazel eyes narrowed. "I am married to the minister. You'd best keep that in mind."

The threat wasn't a new one. Megan knew she should be used to it by now, but every time her sister made it, she got a tight feeling in the bottom of her stomach. "You turned her away. But she's just a little girl. Where is she going to go?''

''Why should I care about that? My heavens, Gene forces me to do charity work, as it is. That's enough for anyone. You can't expect me to take in a bastard.''

Megan scooped up the loose buttons and dumped them back in the box. She reached for the lid, then fitted it in place. ''She's just a little girl,'' she repeated. ''It's not her fault who her parents are. Why are you so cruel?'' She started toward the back of the store.

Colleen came after her. ''I have a duty to this town and to the church. As the minister's wife, I must set an example.''

''Exactly.'' Megan came to a stop and spun toward her sister. ''An example of charity and caring.''

''If you could have seen her. It was disgusting. And her father. He could have been anyone.''

''I don't care if her father was the devil himself. How could you turn her away?''

''Don't you lecture me, Megan,'' Colleen said, her voice shrill. ''I know my place in this town. We have a position to uphold. A family name. It's bad enough that you're a spinster and running this business on your own. Don't forget that my acceptance means the town's acceptance. The lines are very clear, so you make sure which side you stay on. I do more than my share. I know my duty.''

Megan stared at her, noting the rapid rise and fall of her sister's chest as she got carried away by indignation. The knot in her belly didn't seem so tight all of a sudden. Instead of worry or fear, she tasted sadness. She thought about their mother and her fate. Something that Colleen never wanted to discuss.

''Are you always so sure you're right?'' Megan asked quietly.

Colleen opened her mouth, then shut it. ''Of course.''

''I'm not.''

''Sure that I'm right, or sure about yourself?''

''Both.'' Before she could continue, she felt a light touch on her arm. She turned and saw Cameron Forbes staring down at her. He wore a thick, lined winter jacket and his hat pushed back so she could see his face.

"Are you all right, Miss Bartlett?" he asked.

His voice was so low it should have sent shivers racing down her spine. With his dark-haired good looks and tall, well-muscled frame, he was any maiden's dream. When his perfect smile was combined with the faint sadness in his eyes, he should have been as irresistible to her as a brightly colored ribbon was to her new kitten. He'd been in Landing almost five years. They'd spoken after church services, had even danced together twice last year at the Fourth of July celebration. He should have made her heart race. But he didn't.

"I'm fine, Mr. Forbes."

"Why wouldn't she be?" Colleen asked. "I *am* her sister."

Cameron ignored the interruption. Cool gray eyes met her own. "You're sure?"

"Yes."

Colleen sniffed. "Well, I never heard such nonsense."

"I'll be right here in the store if you need me." He touched his hat brim. "Ladies."

Cameron returned to his study of the gardening equipment.

"Who does that man think he is?" Colleen asked, turning her head so that her voice was sure to carry to the handsome farmer.

"A good customer," Megan said, watching Cameron pick up one hoe, then disregard it in favor of another. "With his experimental crops and new ideas, he's always ordering special from back East. And he's a friend."

Colleen raised her eyebrows. "You watch who you're friends with, Megan. You're a single woman and Landing is a very small town."

She looked at her sister, wondering when they'd stopped being friends. "I know."

Colleen began tugging on her gloves. Her mouth got that pinched look, as if she'd tasted something sour. "Despite your low and very misplaced opinion about me, I do have that bastard child's best interests at heart. There are places for a girl like her."

"What does that mean?"

"An orphanage. The church will pay for her train ticket."

It was probably better for the child, Megan thought. If the little girl stayed here, Colleen would make her life miserable. She watched as her sister adjusted her brown hat, and checked the angle of the dyed feather. At one time, they had been so much alike. When had all that changed? When had Colleen become meanspirited? Was it after her marriage to Gene or before?

Megan tried to remember. It suddenly seemed important to know. There was a time when she'd confided everything to her sister. Once they'd almost looked like twins. Although younger by almost two years, Colleen now looked much older. Her hair had darkened to a mousy brown and there were lines around her eyes. Discontent pulled at her sister's face making it—

The front door opened. Megan took a step back so she could see around Colleen. Before she could focus on the customer who had just entered the store, her breath caught in her throat. She didn't have to look. She knew.

She must have made some sound, for Colleen turned slowly.

"Ah, Sheriff Kincaid." Colleen said the words as if they left a bad taste in her mouth. "I believe you spoke with that dreadful woman yesterday and her bastard brat. I've given the situation some thought."

Justin stared at her. Morning light shone through the freshly washed windows, surrounding him with a golden glow. Megan knew she was being fanciful, but at that moment he looked as invincible as a warrior. He stood tall and strong, his feet spread slightly, his hands hanging loosely at his sides. His dark beaver-felt hat hid his eyes, but she knew they would be burning with an angry fire. She clutched the box of buttons close to her chest and smiled. Colleen had met her match.

"I don't want to listen to anything you have to say, madam," he said curtly.

"You will listen," Colleen told him, walking toward him. "The church is prepared to—"

There was a slight movement behind Justin. A small girl stepped out from behind the tall man. She was thin, with big eyes and beautiful dark hair. Her coat and dress were worn, her shoes in tatters. Even from halfway across the store, Megan could see the bruise on the little girl's face.

Her heart went out to the child. She looked about six or seven, with the most solemn expression, as if she'd never had a reason to smile. Megan had only been a few years older when she'd lost her own mother. She remembered how alone she'd felt, and she'd still had her sister and father. This girl had no one.

The child bit her lower lip and pointed. "That's the church lady. The one who said my mama was a postute."

Justin place his large hand on the girl's shoulder. "I know, honey. Don't worry. I won't let her hurt you." He looked at Colleen. "You've already done enough. I'll take care of the girl."

"You?" Colleen shuddered as if she'd just seen a mouse. "That's hardly appropriate."

"It's a damn sight more appropriate than anything you've got planned. I wouldn't trust you to take care of a stalk of corn, let alone a child."

Colleen puffed up, her chin thrusting forward defiantly, her hands clutching together in agitation. "Don't you dare swear in front of me."

"Colleen, you're making this more than it has to be," Megan said, stepping closer to her sister. "If Justin doesn't want your assistance, then don't give it to him."

"I don't need you to fight my battles." Colleen glared at the child. "I will do my Christian duty, despite your interference, Justin Kincaid. As I was saying, the church is willing to buy her a train ticket East, so she can go to an orphanage. We simply don't have the facilities in Landing to take care of a child like her."

The little girl had been following the conversation, turning her head from one adult to another. At Colleen's pronouncement, she froze in place. Her face went pale and her big eyes filled with tears. "Don't let her send me to an orphanage."

"I won't," he said, never taking his gaze from Colleen.

"I suppose *you* plan to keep her yourself?"

"If I have to."

Colleen laughed. The harsh, brittle sound echoed in the store like a sharp explosion of shattered glass. "In your hotel room? What will you do with her while you visit your—"

"Don't say it," he growled. "I won't be responsible for my actions if you do."

"Justin?" The girl tugged on his pant leg. "Promise me I don't have to go to the orphanage." Her voice shook so much, she barely got the word out.

He crouched down beside her. "I promise, Bonnie."

A single tear rolled down the child's cheek. He brushed it away with his thumb. Megan set her box of buttons on the glass counter and moved over to the girl.

The child looked up at her. The fear in the little girl's eyes hit her square in the midsection. She forced herself to smile. "If Justin says he's going to keep you safe, then you can believe him."

The girl sniffed. "I don't wanna go. Mrs. Jarvis said they beat children there." Another tear fell.

Justin smoothed his fingers over her cheek. The tender gesture should have been awkward and out of character, Megan thought, but he had always been good at doing the unexpected.

"A pretty story," Colleen said. "Very touching, I'm sure. However, the town doesn't have any room to keep her."

Justin stood up. "I said she's staying with me. I want to help Bonnie find her family."

"You really think she has any? If her father cared about her, he would have married her mother. But then, that's probably why the two of you get along," Colleen continued. "You're a bastard, too, aren't you, Justin? Like meets like."

"Colleen, leave Justin and the girl alone. You should be pleased not to have to pay for the train ticket. Let that be enough."

"Don't you tell me what to do," Colleen said coldly. She started toward the door. When she reached it, she paused and looked back. "You'd better take care, Megan. You're just an old maid and your good reputation is all you have. If people find out you're associating with this man and that brat, they'll take their business elsewhere rather than deal with someone of loose moral character.''

''I have the only store in this town. Where would they go?''

''This isn't the only town, though, is it?''

Megan stared at her sister. At her expensive clothes and fancy coiffure. She didn't know this woman at all.

''Oh, and Justin, don't bother trying to find someone else to take in the child. I'll make sure none of the decent women in town will have anything to do with her. If you get tired of playing nursemaid, my offer of a ticket to the orphanage still stands. If not, there's always the saloon. Perhaps you can find her relatives among the whores. After all, that's where you found her mother.'' Colleen laughed.

''Get out!'' Megan said loudly.

Colleen sobered. ''Don't push me, Megan. I can destroy you.'' With that, the door slammed shut behind her.

Chapter Six

Megan stared at the closed door and wondered when she would stop shaking. It wasn't anger as much as shock that made her tremble. Justin Kincaid had been back exactly three days and already her life had been completely disrupted.

She glanced around the store. Neither of the customers were paying any attention to her, but she doubted that they could have missed the argument. It could have been worse, she told herself. At least neither Cameron nor old Zeke were likely to spread rumors. Imagine what would have happened if Mrs. Dobson had been here to listen. By noon, the entire town would know Megan's business.

"Are you all right?"

She looked up at Justin. He'd moved next to her. His hand rested on her arm much as Cameron Forbes's had done moments before. The question was the same, as well. Only her reaction was different. Justin's words soothed her and his touch warmed her clear down to her toes, giving her much-needed strength.

"I'm fine," she said, then wondered if he'd heard the quaver in her voice.

"I'd like you to meet a friend of mine." He smiled down at the girl. "Megan Bartlett, this is Bonnie Smith."

Bonnie looked up at her. "You're as pretty as my mama."

Justin's fingers tightened on her arm. She knew he thought the comparison might make her angry. She shrugged him away impatiently, then crouched. "Hello, Bonnie." Megan reached forward and gently touched the child's unmarked cheek. "I didn't know your mama, but I thank you for the compliment. You're so pretty yourself, she must have been very beautiful."

"She's dead. Mrs. Jarvis says she went to hell."

Megan glanced up at Justin, then turned back to the girl. "Who is Mrs. Jarvis?"

"She's the lady who takes care of me. She doesn't like my mama."

Megan touched the very edge of the bruise on Bonnie's cheek. "Is she the one who hit you?"

Bonnie nodded. "It doesn't hurt anymore. I told Mama once what she did. She yelled at Mrs. Jarvis, but it didn't matter. When Mama left, Mrs. Jarvis hit me again." Her small dark eyebrows drew together. "Am I going to get a whippin' now?"

Megan's eyes burned from threatening tears. Still, she forced herself to smile. "No. Justin and I don't believe in hitting little girls." She pointed to the far counter. "Do you see that big jar there?"

"Uh-huh."

"There's some candy inside. If you're real careful, you can use the step stool and get yourself a piece. Would you like that?"

Bonnie nodded vigorously. "I had candy before, and it was good."

"All right. Be careful on the stool."

The little girl ran off, her dark hair swaying with her movements. Megan had never seen Laurie Smith, but the young woman must have been stunning. No wonder Justin had preferred her bed to the chaste kisses Megan had offered.

"You surprise me," Justin said, holding out his hand to assist her to her feet. "I didn't think you would ever stand up to your sister."

She shrugged off the compliment as she tried to ignore the feel of his strong fingers against hers. When he didn't release her instantly, she found herself wanting to stand there forever.

She stared at the swept wooden floor of the store, then at the front door and finally at the buttons of Justin's white shirt. His fingers tugged her closer. She took a single step, but didn't look any higher than the third button from his collar. She could see the rise and fall of his broad chest, and the open collar of his shirt. She could inhale the clean scent of him and almost feel his heat. She should be furious about Bonnie, about Laurie Smith and the time he'd spent with the woman. She should be terrified about what Colleen had threatened. She should throw Justin out of her store. But she found the only throwing she wanted to do was herself— into his arms.

"Colleen was wrong," she said at last. "Bonnie isn't responsible for who her parents are or what circumstances she finds herself in."

"Colleen is a—"

"Don't." Megan raised her eyebrows. "I know she can be difficult, but I'll thank you to remember she's still my sister."

"You're nothing alike, thank God."

She risked glancing at him and was rewarded by his most devastating smile. The one that made her forget things like her name and where she was. The flash of white teeth against his tanned face, the deeper lines beside his eyes, the flicker of appreciation as his gaze swept over her. This was the Justin she remembered. The young man she'd never been able to forget.

The front door opened. Two women came in. Megan instantly stepped back from him and walked toward the candy aisle. Bonnie had taken her treat and was now exploring the store. Megan stepped behind the counter and began rearranging glass bottles.

"I remember when Colleen was young," Megan said. "She was wild, always getting into trouble. Papa used to despair of ever getting her to understand about manners and acting like a lady."

"Something got through to her. She's turned into a—" Megan threw him a sharp glance at him. He took off his hat. "I won't say it, just for you."

"Thank you." Megan glanced at the girl gazing at a display of rings. "How did you end up with her?"

"After your gentle sister threw Bonnie off church property, Mrs. Jarvis brought her to me. She told me in no uncertain terms that if she wasn't going to continue to get paid, she wasn't going to take care of Bonnie."

His hands lay on the counter. As he spoke, he curled his fingers toward his palms until he'd made tight fists. She could feel the anger radiating from him. Without thinking, she reached forward and covered his hands with hers.

"I'm sorry, Justin."

He looked at her. Those stunning dark eyes, eyes that she'd dreamed about for the last seven years, seemed to see past her exterior self and down into her soul. She was afraid then, afraid of the old feelings, afraid of what he might make her feel. She couldn't be what he needed her to be. The failing had always been hers. She knew that in her most secret self. Frightened and ashamed, she withdrew her hands and turned away.

"Bonnie is very thin," she said, to change the subject.

"I don't think she was fed much. She's got bruises on her legs to match that one on her face. Her clothes are filthy. I had one of the maids at the hotel give her a bath and then do what she could with the child's clothes, but Bonnie doesn't even have a decent pair of shoes, let alone a spare anything else."

"I can fix that," she said and started toward the other side of the store. The two women shoppers smiled a greeting. They glanced from her to Justin, but Megan simply nodded as she walked past them to the shelf of ready-made garments.

"There should be several things here," she said, pulling down a pile from a high shelf. "She'll need a couple of dresses, a coat, underthings, a nightgown. What else?"

She sorted through the clothes, finding two items, putting the rest back. The smallest nightgowns were up on the top shelf. They didn't sell many of those. Most women simply made over already worn larger gowns for their children. She grabbed a step stool and brought it back to where she needed it, then climbed up. The pile was still almost out of reach. She stretched high.

"You could take her in, Megan. You have that big house all to yourself."

Justin's words shocked her. Take in Bonnie? Herself?

She got a hold of the nightgowns and drew them down. Still staring at the full shelves, she turned the idea over in her mind. Colleen's threats presented the first obstacle. She wasn't worried exactly, but her sister could be a problem. There was also the question of work. Bonnie would have to stay in the store all day since the town didn't have a school. Megan wasn't sure a little girl would enjoy that much. Of course, the general store had to be better for her than Mrs. Jarvis's house. Megan stepped off the stool and moved to the counter.

"Never mind." Justin's voice was low and angry.

Startled, she looked at him. "What do you mean?"

He grimaced. "I should have remembered that nothing is more important to you than your reputation. Colleen's threats really bothered you, didn't they? Don't worry, Bonnie and I don't need you."

"Justin, no. You're not being fair." She saw the two women across the store glance toward her. She spoke more softly. "I was thinking about all that's involved with taking in a child."

"You didn't have to think about taking in the kitten."

"They're hardly the same thing."

He placed his forearms on the counter and leaned toward her. "You know what I mean. No one cares about a damn cat, so that's safe. But when it gets a little dangerous, you back off. You're so frightened of not doing exactly what everyone expects. Fine, then. If that's all that matters to you, keep your reputation."

She set down the nightgowns and glared at him. "Don't be ridiculous. Are you planning to take her back to the hotel with you? She's just a little girl. She needs more than that."

"She's a damn sight better off with me than she was yesterday."

"I agree with that. But you can't keep her. You're a single man."

"You're not married, either."

"At least I'm a woman."

"I care about Bonnie, and you don't."

"Of course I care. You're being completely unreasonable, Justin. I'll take her home with me."

He stretched forward until their noses were less than six inches apart. "No."

She did her best to hang on to her temper, but he was trying her patience. If truth be told, there was a small amount of guilt fueling her argument. She *had* thought about what Colleen would think. She hated that. She didn't want to be tied down by others' opinions, but she couldn't seem to help herself. If only she didn't know the dangers of flouting convention.

"You didn't even give me a chance to think about it," she told him. "So if I don't instantly say yes, without considering the consequences that just might have more to do with Bonnie than with me, you assume the worst. I don't get a second chance."

"You haven't changed, Megan," he said, straightening.

That hurt more than almost anything he could have said. She glanced down at the counter so he wouldn't see the flash of pain in her eyes. "You're wrong."

"Am I? It doesn't matter. Bonnie will stay with me. She has her own room. She seems happy enough."

An excited squeal made her look up. Bonnie came running toward them from the back of the store. She clutched something in her hand.

"Look," she said, her mouth quivering with excitement. "Look what that man gave me. Look." She held out a small corn-husk doll. The facial features had been drawn with charcoal, the clothes made from scraps. But from the expression on Bonnie's face, the child had been given a gift more precious than gold.

"Isn't she beautiful?" she asked reverently, then smiled shyly. "He said she's for me."

Cameron strolled up behind the child. He cleared his throat, then shrugged uncomfortably. "Please put it on my account, Miss Bartlett," he said.

Justin was still staring at Bonnie.

"What's wrong?" Megan asked him.

He shook his head. "I've never seen her smile before." He glanced at the other man. "Thanks."

"Every little girl needs a doll." Cameron shuffled his feet. "I'm going to take two more hoes," he said to Megan. "They'll need to go on the bill, as well."

"I'll take care of it," she said.

Cameron's dark hair was in need of trimming and his shirt was a little ragged around the collar. It wasn't lack of money that had Cameron Forbes looking a little shabby. He was the most successful farmer in any of the nearby counties. He needed to get married. The women around town whispered that he'd lost his wife and daughter a few years before and had never recovered. Megan vaguely remembered a pretty blond woman who'd loved to dance and who'd made everyone around her smile.

"I'd best be going," Cameron said. He tipped his hat, then walked toward the front door.

Megan turned to Justin and saw him watching her with the most peculiar look on his face. There was an angry, knowing glint in his eyes.

She wanted to throw her hands up in frustration. She settled on taking the clothes Bonnie would need and stacking them into a pile. First Justin judged her because she didn't instantly beg him to let her take in Bonnie. Now he was obviously wondering if there was something between her and Cameron Forbes. Men. She would never understand them.

She shoved the pile of clothing at him. "This should solve Bonnie's immediate clothing problems," she said curtly. "I have some shoes in the storeroom. I'll go see if there's a pair that will fit her."

"You don't have to do this."

"I want to." She took two steps, then turned and grabbed the clothing. "On second thought, I'll keep these here."

"Why?"

"Because I'm going to keep Bonnie with me today."

He shoved his hat back on his head and drew his eyebrows together. "No, you're not."

"Oh?" She smiled sweetly. "What are you going to do with her while you're working?"

"I..."

She waited. He glanced at the little girl who was sitting on the floor whispering secrets to her new doll.

"I . . ." He muttered something under his breath. She thought he might be swearing. That thought perked up her spirits considerably. "All right, but just for today. I'll come get her at closing."

"Oh, thank you, Justin. How gracious you are."

He glared at her.

She laughed, then held out her hand to Bonnie. "Come on. Let's look for some new shoes. We'll see you later, Justin."

Bonnie waved her new doll and trotted along obediently. When Megan reached the curtain dividing the front of the store from the back, she wanted to turn around, but she didn't. It would spoil the effect. Besides, she knew Justin was fuming and that was enough for her.

Justin came through the bare trees just as the last curve of the sun dipped below the horizon. It had been another day of mild weather. Winter was almost over. He could see the small buds on some of the bushes, and the first leaves daring to make their appearance.

He paused in the clearing and stared at the lone three-story house perched at the top of the rise. Light twinkled from behind curtained windows, casting a welcoming glow onto the porch. How many times had he stood here and stared at that house, like a starving man hungering for food? How many nights had he listened to the sound of the family within, knowing they possessed a magic of belonging he could never understand?

He approached the front porch, but hesitated before climbing the three steps up to the door. Megan waited for him. She'd left word at the store that she'd taken Bonnie to the house to try on clothes and for him to come along when he was able. Andrew had spoken the message in a normal tone of voice, allowing whoever was within earshot to hear.

Justin told himself it didn't mean anything. Megan hadn't changed and she wasn't going to change. She would always worry about her reputation. He shouldn't allow himself to hope, to believe there could ever be anything between them.

The young man who had promised her forever didn't exist anymore. They were different people, strangers, really, and the past was simply a collection of what-should-have-beens.

He shook off the fanciful thoughts. They were the product of a too-long day after a night of little sleep. He would collect Bonnie and return to the hotel. Nothing more. He was here about the child, not about the woman.

That didn't stop the anticipation from coiling low in his belly as he raised his hand to knock on the door.

She opened it before he had a chance to rap a second time.

"Justin," she whispered and held a finger to her mouth. "Shh. Bonnie's sleeping." She stepped back and motioned for him to come in.

When he was inside, she closed the door quietly behind him, then reached for the hat he'd automatically removed. She held out her hand for his coat. He shrugged out of it, then wondered if he should tell her he wasn't staying. Before he could decide, she led him toward the parlor.

The room was still full of too much furniture. Chairs and tables crowded together. On the settee closest to the fireplace, he saw Bonnie curled up asleep. A light blanket covered her to her shoulders. The kitten he'd brought Megan slept by the girl's feet. One of Bonnie's hands was tucked under her cheek, the other held her precious corn-husk doll. On the table in front of her, clothes had been stacked into neat piles.

"Isn't she sweet?" Megan asked quietly.

He glanced at the woman standing beside him. A fire flickered behind the grate, providing warmth and the only light in the room. Since his return, he'd only seen her with her hair pinned back in a respectably plain style. Tonight she wore her hair in a loose braid, with gold-blond strands drifting across her cheek. Her green dress brought out the matching color in her hazel eyes. Something was different. He frowned. Softer, maybe.

It might be the edge of lace at the collar of her dress, or the fact that she didn't seem to be wearing as many petticoats. She looked relaxed, even content. He envied her that.

"Justin?"

Her voice caught on his name. Instantly, his gaze locked on her mouth. Her full lower lip quivered slightly. He remembered how she'd tasted when he'd kissed her. Was it just two days ago? He felt as if he'd been back a lifetime. What was it about Megan Bartlett that made him forget? Why did she have to be the one who turned his head? She was determined to live a respectable life. To her, he would only ever be that bastard Justin Kincaid. They had nothing together.

"Let's let her sleep," he whispered, then headed for the hallway.

Megan followed him. "I tried to keep her awake, but she just nodded off," she said as they paused by the front door. "We've had a busy day."

"It looks like it."

She held her hands together in front of her waist. "I've roasted a chicken. Will you stay to supper?"

One persistent strand of hair brushed against her temple. She reached up and tucked it behind her ear. He reached toward her and fingered the loose hair on her shoulders.

"You aren't so tidy tonight."

"I know." She glanced down. He thought he saw a faint blush on her cheeks. The color made her skin glow. "We were playing with her doll and Bonnie asked if she could brush my hair. She said she used to brush her mother's. It seemed like a small thing, really." Her gaze flickered over him. "She wanted to do my hair in a braid." She raised her hands to her braid and pulled it over her shoulder. After glancing at the uneven sections, she smiled. "I know I look a mess."

"No," he said, tucking another strand behind her ear. "Not at all. You look..." Perfect, he thought, but he couldn't tell her that. She stared at him so earnestly, as if his comment were the most important in the world. As if her life hung in the balance. As if she still cared. But she couldn't. He'd thought she had, once. He'd been wrong. "You look fine."

"Oh." Her head dipped toward her chest. "So you'll stay?"

He shouldn't. Eating with her would bring the ghosts to life. But he was too tired to resist her. He would be strong another time.

"Sure."

Her brilliant smile caught him like a sharp blow to the belly, but it didn't blind him to the truth. Megan was trouble for him. She always had been, she always would be.

She led the way into the kitchen. A large black stove dominated one wall. The smell of cooking chicken and potatoes made him swallow. He realized he hadn't stopped for dinner at noon. Breakfast had been biscuits and coffee while he'd watched Bonnie consume enough flapjacks to feed three farmhands.

"It'll just be a few minutes," she said, walking toward the counter. "I've already mixed up the biscuits. I just have to bake them." She picked up a thick towel and opened the oven door. After carefully pulling out a large baking dish filled with the chicken and potatoes, she set it to one side, then put the biscuits in their place.

She dropped the towel next to the dish and walked over to the kitchen table. Stacks of clothes covered the wooden surface. She scooped them up and dumped them on two chairs.

"I'll get you coffee," she said, pulling out an empty chair that faced the rest of the kitchen. "Sorry this is such a mess. Bonnie and I spent our afternoon in the attic, going through clothes. There were several things from when Colleen and I were little. Dresses, a couple of pairs of shoes. Even dolls, although she likes her corn-husk doll better than any of them."

Justin took the seat she offered. He stretched his feet out in front of him and rested his hands on the table. "I don't think Colleen is going to approve of Bonnie's wearing her old things."

"I know." Megan gave him a quick smile. "But I don't care. She wouldn't use them for her own daughter. When I offered, she said she'd rather buy all new. It's a waste, if you ask me. I'm glad Bonnie can use them."

As she spoke, she moved efficiently around the kitchen, getting a mug out of one of the cupboards, pouring the coffee, setting it in front of him, then walking to the buffet next to the table and pulling out a tablecloth. She flipped up the cream-colored fabric and let it fall neatly in place. Before he'd stirred sugar into his cup, she'd placed a napkin, knife and fork beside the mug. She did the same at her place setting, then returned to the counter and started carving the chicken.

"You act like you've spent time in this kitchen," he said.

"Of course. Did you think I had a cook?"

"Your father did."

She shrugged. He liked the way her quick movement drew the back of her dress up slightly, molding it around her behind. Her lower half wasn't as curvy as her upper half, but there was plenty there to squeeze, he thought, then grinned. Megan was all friendly and open. She'd shut up quick enough if she knew what he was thinking.

When she turned to glance at him over her shoulder, he looked down at his coffee.

"I pensioned her off when Papa died. It was silly to have live-in help for just me."

"And the maid?"

Megan chuckled. "She's gone, too, although I admit I have a lady in twice a week to clean and I send out the laundry. By the time I get finished with the store, I'm too tired to dust. Colleen is scandalized by the whole thing. She thinks I should hire a manager to take care of the store. The trouble is, I don't know what I would do with my day then. I like working."

"Colleen is a—"

"Justin."

"Yeah, I know. She's your sister."

She wiped her hands on a towel, then moved to the oven and opened the door. "About five minutes." She walked to the table and sat across from him. "You look tired. Did you have a difficult day?"

"You could say that," he answered, trying to ignore the domestic nature of their evening. He was sitting in her kitchen answering questions about his day. As if they'd done this a thousand times before. Or maybe it was familiar because he'd imagined his life with Megan being made up of moments like these. His fantasies about her hadn't all been hot images of her naked beneath him. Some had been quiet. Loving. They'd all been unrealistic, he reminded himself.

"You didn't find out anything about Bonnie's mother?"

"No. Everyone claims they never knew the woman. A few even admitted it's no great loss that she's gone. Mrs. Greeley wanted to know why I'm wasting my time with the investigation."

"I'm sorry."

She placed her hands flat on the tablecloth and leaned forward. Several strands of hair fell around her cheeks. She brushed them back impatiently. Her heart-shaped face was as beautiful as he remembered, her skin clear, her eyes large and expressive. He could read her sincerity in their depths. Suddenly, the need to talk to someone who would listen overwhelmed him. There was no one else he could trust.

"Colleen made good on her threat," he told her. "Before I could even ask, just about every woman I spoke to told me she wouldn't take Bonnie in. Some couple with a small farm on the edge of town said they had room if they got paid enough." He shook his head. "Doesn't anyone in this town give a damn?"

"I do. I'll take her, Justin. I would have this morning, but you wouldn't give me a chance."

"No."

"Why? You're being unfair. Do you think because I live alone I don't have the womanly skills to provide a home for Bonnie?"

"It's not that." He grabbed his mug and traced a circle on the cloth. He could smell the faint fragrance of rose water. Megan used it to rinse her hair. He studied her dress. The green calico complemented her coloring, but it wasn't an extravagance. Despite the warmth of the kitchen, she hadn't unbuttoned even one tiny button on her collar or turned up her cuffs. She wore less petticoats but would never consider not wearing them at all. The only thing out of place was her mussed hair. From the top of her head down to her sensible buttoned shoes, she was respectable.

He'd spoken to the citizens of this town. If they were so uncharitable about a child, imagine what they would do to

Megan if she flouted convention. He'd always mocked her fears of what others might think. For the first time, he began to see the power they wielded in Landing.

"It wouldn't look right," he said.

"What? It wouldn't look right?" She stood up and grabbed the towel, then pulled the biscuits out of the oven. They were perfectly browned. She served the rest of the meal. "Did someone hit you on the head? The Justin Kincaid *I* know wouldn't give a...a..."

He raised his eyebrows.

She plopped a full plate down in front of him and placed her hands on her hips. "A darn about how it looked."

"Maybe I'm learning."

"I don't mind," she said, serving herself. "I like Bonnie."

"I know, but I'll keep her."

"It looks less right for you to have her than for me."

"I don't care what they say about me, Megan. I've heard it all before. They can't hurt me."

"They can't hurt me, either."

He picked up his fork and smiled. "You never were much of a liar."

"So tell me what's different from what you remember," she said as she picked up his empty plate. He started to stand up to help her, but she waved him back down. "Sit. You're my guest. I don't get many of them anymore, so I'm having fun." She grinned. "Plus, we ate in the kitchen. That's scandalous enough without you cleaning up the dishes, too. So how has Landing changed?"

"It's bigger," he said, leaning back in his chair. The meal had been excellent. The company better. Megan still had the ability to make him laugh. "There are more people, more businesses. I heard there's going to be a newspaper soon."

Megan sighed as she scraped the plates. "I know. Colleen wants Gene to write a column on morality. His sermons are long enough to sit through, as it is. It would be awful to have to read them, as well. What else?"

"The livery stable. It's new."

She carried over the coffeepot and poured, then sat next to him and rested her elbows on the table. "The old one burned down a while ago."

"There's a new saloon."

Megan raised her eyebrows and blinked several times. "I'm sure I haven't noticed," she said, the haughty tone of her voice a close imitation of Colleen's.

He smiled. "The old one is still here, though." His smile faded.

She reached out her hand and covered his. "I'm sorry."

"About what?" She started to pull back. He grabbed her fingers. "I didn't mean that in a bad way. I'm curious what you're sorry about. It wasn't your fault my mother had to work in the saloon."

"I know, but I always felt, oh, not responsible, but guilty, maybe. Everyone was so cruel. I hated that."

He studied her hand. Her slender fingers were pale, the nails neatly trimmed. He turned it over. More smooth skin. "She served drinks," he said, without looking up. "Cleaned the place when it closed. Helped keep inventory. She never went upstairs with a man." He felt Megan stiffen, but he didn't release her hand. He swept his thumb across her palm, back and forth until she relaxed.

"They offered her money," he continued. "I heard them. No matter how little we had, my mother wasn't a whore."

Megan jerked her fingers free and quickly stood up. Her chair went skidding across the wooden floor. "I'm sure she wasn't. Would you like some cobbler? Bonnie and I made it this afternoon. I had to use dried apples, but I soaked them and I'm sure it's delicious." She hurried to the cupboard and pulled out the dessert. "There's fresh cream, too."

He rose from his chair and walked over to her. She blindly reached for a knife and continued to babble on about her cooking. Before she could plunge the blade into the dish, he grabbed her wrist and pulled the knife away from her. Then he placed his hands on her shoulders and turned her toward him.

"I didn't mean to embarrass you," he said.

"I wasn't embarrassed." She addressed the center of his chest.

"No? Then why are your cheeks red?"

"Because I'm flushed from the warmth of the stove."

"You're still a poor liar." He liked how she felt where he touched her. He liked her scent and the heat of her body. He liked how she was fidgeting, twisting her fingers together nervously, but not pushing him away.

"I'm a little embarrassed. But it's all right. We can talk about your mother if it helps you."

"It's not just her. I didn't know the memories would be so ugly."

She raised her gaze to his. "Are they? Why?"

"Nothing good ever happened to me in this town."

She bit her lower lip. It wasn't hard to figure out what she was thinking. She wanted to know if his opinion of the town included his time with her. Thank God she didn't have the courage to ask that question, because he didn't have an answer.

"What happened when you left? Was it better?"

"Yeah, a hell of a lot better than this place."

"Where did you go?"

"It doesn't matter."

She stepped to the side, away from him. "Why won't you tell me?"

"It's not important. I left here, swearing never to come back. I should have stuck with that decision instead of being a fool and changing my mind."

"Yes, you should have."

She picked up the knife and attacked the dessert. He'd hurt her feelings. He could see that. Justin leaned against the counter and folded his arms over his chest. He didn't have a choice. If he started talking about where he'd been, he would remember why he'd gone in the first place. Next thing he knew, he would be remembering how much he'd loved her. If he thought on that too long, all the feelings from the past might rise again and drown him. He had to keep them dammed and avoid the river of memories, no matter what it cost.

"I'm sure your year here will pass very quickly and then you won't have to come back again," she said. "Just take everything that belongs to you and—" She put the knife down and clamped her hand over her mouth.

"What is it?" he asked.

She stared at him, then slowly lowered her hand to her side. "I just remembered something. Excuse me."

Before he could ask what was wrong, she hurried out of the room. He heard her footsteps on the stairs.

He couldn't call out to her without waking Bonnie, so he went after her. At the top of the stairs he followed the sound of drawers being opened and closed, then the *thunk* of something heavy being moved.

The long narrow hallway had several doors, but only one of them was open. As he approached it, he told himself to go back to the kitchen and wait. Megan had gone to her bedroom. Obviously, the only emergency was in her mind.

He was about to turn around, when he heard a muffled "Darn it, anyway, where *did* I put that key?"

Curiosity got the better of him. He walked silently to the open door and looked inside.

From the corner of his eye, he saw Megan bent over an open drawer in a dresser. A large locked box sat on the floor, obviously the source of the loud thump he'd heard. But that wasn't what caught his attention. Instead, he stared at her bed.

He opened his mouth to speak, but couldn't think of anything to say. If someone had told him Megan Bartlett had secrets, he would have laughed out loud. If someone had told him Megan could shock him, he would have assumed the person was drunk. He would have been wrong on both counts.

He took one step into the bedroom, then another. At the foot of the bed he stopped. The coverlet was hidden under piles of women's undergarments. That wasn't the shocking part. Of course Megan wore them. But sensible, respectable Megan would wear cotton, or delicate lawn. Perhaps a pink ribbon on her camisole, a touch of lace on her petticoat. But the shimmering fabrics in front of him were satin. He fingered some exquisite lace. And silk.

A slow smile pulled at his mouth. One of the many advantages of growing up around women who entertained men for a living was that he knew the difference between silk and cotton. He knew about expensive, imported French lace and fancy corset covers. He knew what a store owner in Kansas was likely to wear under a conservative calico dress and it wasn't this.

He picked up a sheer nightgown worked with intricate beading. The pale pink garment slipped through his fingers like cool water.

"Got it," Megan said triumphantly. She held up a key, then dropped to her knees and opened the box. After digging around for several seconds, she pulled out something small, then started to stand up.

Their eyes met. If he'd thought she'd blushed before when he'd said his mother wasn't a whore, he'd been mistaken. The color that flooded her face, climbing from her collar to the roots of her hair in less than a heartbeat, was vivid tomato red. Her almond-shaped eyes widened.

"W-what are you doing here?" she asked. She sounded on the verge of choking.

"What are you doing with this?" He held up the nightgown.

"I—I...I—I..." She cleared her throat. "I don't have to explain that to you. This is my bedroom and I'll ask you to leave. Right now."

He didn't budge. "Megan, I admit I'm stunned. French lace and silk? No one knows, do they?"

She rose to her feet. "My undergarments are not your concern, Mr. Kincaid. Now, leave my room immediately."

His gaze dipped to her bodice, then lower. "You're wearing something like this right now, aren't you?" He smiled. "I'm impressed."

"Justin!" He slowly released the nightgown, letting it slide sensuously through his fingers. She stepped around the bed and grabbed his arm. "I can't believe you are this rude. How dare you come into my private room and fondle my personal things? Have you no manners? No decency?"

"No," he admitted happily. "None. Apparently, neither do you. I would take a guess that the ever-moral Colleen knows nothing about your wicked indulgence."

She hustled him out of the bedroom and closed the door. "It's not wicked. I bought a few things for the general store on my last trip to St. Louis. They didn't sell so I brought them home. I don't want them going to waste, not that it's any business of yours."

Most of her blush had faded, leaving only a red splotch on each cheek. She was shaking. He could feel it where her hand held his arm.

"Lying is useless," he said. "I've already told you, you're not good at it. Besides," he added, stepping closer and touching her chin. "I like knowing you're hiding silk and lace under that very respectable dress."

Her skin was silk, he thought as his fingers traced a line from her chin to the sensitive spot under her ear. She shivered delicately. And her mouth...

He swallowed. "Damn you, Megan. Were you always this much temptation?"

Her lips parted as her breathing increased. Her hazel eyes darkened to the deep gray of an approaching storm.

"I think so," she whispered.

He lowered his mouth to hers. "I think you're right."

Chapter Seven

Megan braced herself for his tender touch. A fleeting thought warned her she should push him away while she still had a scrap of common sense. She knew it was foolish to kiss Justin. It would get her into trouble somehow. It always had.

If she lived to be a hundred, she would never forget the sight of him as a young man. Or the memory of him standing in her bedroom holding her unmentionables. She was humiliated and ashamed and incredibly...

His lips pressed against her. It was as if a strong gust blew through her mind, scattering her thoughts to the four winds. Her fingers curled into her palms. In her left hand she felt the object she'd come upstairs to find. She slipped it into her skirt pocket, then reached up and wrapped her arms around his neck.

She was a lady. She should be retiring and coy, holding back in fear of a man's animal nature. She should play the reluctant virgin. But this was Justin and she'd never been able to do what she should around him.

As he pressed harder against her mouth, she raised herself on her toes, molding her body to his. She needed him to hold her this night. Perhaps it was her argument with Colleen that made her weak. Or the past. Or maybe it was because she was starting to think she might be more like Justin than she'd been willing to admit.

She slipped her hands down the length of his arms, then up again, savoring the heat of him and the smoothness of his woolen shirt. She squeezed his shoulders, then moved lower,

down his chest. She rubbed small circles across his broadness and wrapped her arms around his waist.

He groaned low in his throat. Contentment filled her. She
still affected him. Whatever had happened in the seven years
he'd been gone, she still had the power to move him to passion.

Her self-congratulations were lost to mindlessness when
he probed at her mouth. She parted her lips in anticipation.
But instead of plunging inside as she expected, he drew her
lower lip into his mouth and tenderly sucked on the sensitive skin. He nibbled the curve, then licked it thoroughly. He
swirled his tongue around her mouth, dampening her,
making her breathing more difficult. She clung to him as her
legs trembled.

He moved his hands from her face to her shoulders, then
down her back to her derriere. Through the layers of her
petticoat, she felt him cup her curves. When he pulled her
closer to him, she arched against him. Once, years before,
when they'd been kissing on the bank of the stream, her
hand had strayed between them. As his tongue had danced
in her mouth leaving her hot and breathless, he'd pressed her
palm against a hardness. She'd known only the most rudi-
mentary facts about men and women. The strangeness of it
all had both frightened and excited her. Before she could
explore him or ask questions, he'd drawn her fingers away
to the safety of his chest.

Now, as he moved his narrow hips against her, she cursed
the layers of clothing that prevented her from feeling that
mysterious part of him.

His hands slipped up to her waist. Her breathing increased. She liked the feel of his body so close, the touch of
his fingers. But she wanted more. He continued to tease her,
circling her mouth, nibbling at the corners, but not really
kissing her. Not the way she wanted him to.

She sensed he was holding back, but didn't know why.
Frustration made her bold. She drew away from his assault.

"Justin." Her voice was low and shaky, as if passion
robbed her of the ability to speak.

Dark brown eyes met her own. She saw the fire and understood the source of those flames. She felt them, as well. They flickered along her body igniting fires in her breasts and, embarrassingly enough, between her legs. They left her hot and hungry for something she didn't understand.

"Kiss me," she whispered.

"I am." He smiled slightly, exposing that surprising dimple in his left cheek.

"No, you're not. You're playing."

The smile faded and his face took on a knowing expression. "You've grown impatient in my absence."

She couldn't admit to that, but she could taunt him as he taunted her. Her arms were wrapped around his waist. She lowered them slightly until her hands rested above *his* derriere. Slowly, all the while telling herself she was wicked and would probably burn in hell, she slipped her hands down his dark trousers until her fingers encountered the first hint of his male curves.

Their eyes locked together. The fire in his gaze blazed hotter. His square jaw tightened.

Lower and lower until her palms embraced him and the tips of her fingers rested just above the backs of his legs. She felt a heated blush on her face. She told herself she didn't care, then realized Justin was right. She *was* a lousy liar. But she wasn't going to stop now. Not with him looking at her as if he was drawn so tightly together he was about to explode into a hundred pieces. Besides, it felt good to be touching him. She'd always liked how he felt next to her. She liked the contrasts between them, the way he smelled, and how he looked at her.

She squeezed gently. He drew in a sharp breath. The hands at her waist tightened. She squeezed again and this time tilted his hips toward hers. The bonfire between them erupted and sparks landed everywhere singeing her skin.

"Damn you." He said the words as if they were the most tender caress, then he bent over her and claimed her mouth.

There was nothing tentative, nothing teasing this time. His tongue plunged inside of her, seeking her secrets, demanding a response. He gripped her firmly, holding her in place.

Her heart pounded harder and harder. She met his intimate kisses, mirroring his sweeping actions, clinging to him as her world faded away, leaving nothing but the man and the sensations he created. Her trembling increased.

He drew back slightly and kissed her jaw, then her neck. She arched her head. The moist heat from his mouth made her tingle. She couldn't catch her breath.

The whisper of cool air on her chest surprised her. Then she felt his fingers on her bare skin and knew he'd unfastened her bodice. Shock froze her in place. She should protest this liberty, she told herself. His knuckle brushed the side of her breast. She jumped.

He straightened, forcing her to stand upright. She clutched at his shoulders as he continued to kiss her neck and nibble on her ears. It felt wonderful. Better than wonderful. It was more perfect than she remembered.

His hands moved between her breasts, unfastening more buttons. A vague feeling of panic threatened the moment. She didn't know what to do. She wanted Justin to show her more, but she was afraid. No one had touched her there before.

She stared at him, at the dark hair tumbling over his forehead, at the familiar shape of his face. The hardness there was new, as were the lines by his eyes. But he was still Justin.

As if he sensed her gaze, he looked at her. The fingers partway between her breasts and her waist paused. His mouth was damp. Damp from her. She raised her hand toward him and drew her thumb across his lower lip. He bit gently on the tip of her thumb, then touched her with his tongue. She shivered as a ripple of heat slipped down her spine.

"You're beautiful," he whispered, even as his hands moved higher. She could feel the pressure and warmth against her. She tried to draw in a deep breath but couldn't. "Don't be afraid."

"Justin, I—"

"Trust me."

He drew her bodice apart, then untied the ribbon closure of her corset cover. She held on to his upper arms, concentrating on his strength rather than on what he was doing. Then his mouth touched her chest. Hot and wet, his tongue circled against her sensitive skin. She gasped. His hands moved higher. Slowly, definitely, as if there was no plan to stop, as if he really meant to touch her breasts. As if she would allow him to. He moved up her ribs. At the top of her corset he paused. There was nothing between him and her bare skin except for a thin silk chemise. She held her breath, half hoping he would move away, half praying he would continue.

He moved his head up and kissed the side of her neck. Instinctively, she arched to give him more room and his hands swept over her breasts.

He held her without moving as she absorbed the feel of him against her. She was both hot and cold. She couldn't believe those two parts of her could feel so much at one time. Then he squeezed gently and she moaned. His fingers drifted across the silk, sending sensations shooting in all directions. Down her arms and legs, through her stomach and most especially to her female place. She felt funny there. Sort of achy and out of sorts. She squeezed her legs tightly together.

He brushed his thumb across her nipples. She gasped. She didn't know it could feel better, but it did. Back and forth he moved. Her nipples puckered. He raised his head and she glanced down, seeing his tanned hands against her pale chemise. Her breasts filled his hands. Over and over he stroked until she had to cling to him or fall. Until she couldn't catch her breath and the need inside, so wild and uncontrollable, made her want more.

Then he did the most amazing thing. He placed his mouth against her breasts. He drew the hard tip inside and suckled like a babe. Her eyes widened, then closed. She cupped his head, holding him in place.

"Justin, oh, Justin. How can you do that? How can you make me feel that?" He moved to her other breast and repeated the exquisite torture. When he would have pulled away, she slipped her fingers through his hair. "No, don't stop."

He laughed low in his throat. The soft sound made Megan aware of herself and what they were doing. Her hands moved from his silky hair to his shoulders and she pushed him away.

He straightened slowly and looked at her. Then his gaze dropped to her chest. She glanced down and saw the damp silk clinging to her. The material was transparent and left her breasts practically bare to his gaze. He touched the hardened tips.

"You're more beautiful than I imagined," he said softly. "Especially in silk."

He was teasing, but that didn't stop the feeling of guilt that flooded her. "Justin!" She swatted his hand away and pulled on the ribbon of her corset cover. When it was fastened, she tugged her bodice closed and began on the buttons.

"Megan, look at me."

She didn't want to. She was still blushing. She was afraid of what he'd made her feel and what she would see in his eyes. But she couldn't resist him forever. Slowly, she raised her gaze to his.

He smiled gently. The fire flaring between them had been banked, but she could see the lingering embers. It wouldn't take much to make it explode again. Despite the fact that he'd frightened and shocked her, she was pleased to know he wanted her again. She would hate to think the wanting was only hers.

"Your guilty secrets are safe with me," he said.

"Is that supposed to make me feel better?"

"Yes. Imagine what would happen if the good women of Landing knew what you wore under your dresses." He grinned and reached for her bodice, but she turned away. "Don't be shy now."

"I can't help it." She secured the last of her buttons. "I'm shocked at what we did."

His smile faded. "I'm glad you said 'we.'"

She raised her chin. "I won't deny I didn't object when you..." Her hand fluttered close to her chest. "But, no one can know."

He drew in a deep breath. "I've always kept your secrets, Megan. You can trust me with these."

The last glow of the passion between them flickered and died. She knew what he was talking about. Their "understanding" seven years ago. He'd never said anything about that. He'd never repeated those horrible things she'd said to him. Even now, she could hear her own words echoing loudly in the silence.

"I'm sorry," she murmured.

"Why? You meant what you said."

Her head jerked as if he'd slapped her. But she couldn't dispute the words. At the time, she would have said anything to convince him she didn't love him anymore.

"Besides, if you get lucky and the town accepts me, you can confess one of your secrets without anyone thinking less of you. With the possible exception of Colleen. I don't think she's ever going to see me other than—"

"Don't say it," Megan demanded, glaring at him. "Stop saying that about yourself. I won't listen to that word again."

Justin looked at her for several seconds, but she couldn't read his expression. She didn't want to know he still thought of himself as a bastard. He was too good for that. He'd always been too good, but seven years ago she'd been too young to see the truth.

"I'd better go," he said, and started down the stairs. "Bonnie should be in bed."

She trailed after him. "Leave her here with me. She's already asleep. I know you think I don't want her here, but I do. I'm sorry I hesitated when you asked me before, but you judged me unfairly. I care about her."

"I believe you." He reached the bottom of the stairs. "But I still have to take her with me. I understand Bonnie and she needs that right now."

Megan was one step above him, so she could stare directly into his eyes. "I understand her, too. I wasn't much older than her when I lost my mother. I know how she feels. I can help."

He shook his head. "It's not about that. You came from a respectable home. Bonnie's mother was a saloon girl. How are you going to explain it to her when she starts asking questions?''

She had no answer for that. What would she say to the child? Justin was right. Again. Before she walked past him, she reached into her skirt pocket and pulled out the object she'd raced upstairs to get.

''This is yours,'' she said, handing it to him. ''I meant to return it that last night, but I forgot.''

He stared at the pocketknife. The light in the hallway reflected off the polished surface, illuminating the initials carved there. She was surprised they could still be seen. How many times had she traced those letters with her fingers, as if rubbing them again and again would bring Justin back to her?

''Why did you keep it?'' he asked.

''I don't know,'' she answered honestly. ''I tried to throw it away, but I couldn't. I'll get Bonnie's things.''

She placed the girl's new clothes and shoes in a cloth bag, then put Bonnie's precious corn-husk doll on top. Justin picked up the sleeping child and held her against his chest. Megan handed him the bag.

When she opened the front door, he stepped onto the porch. ''Good night,'' she whispered.

He didn't answer for a long time. ''Was there anything between you and that farmer?'' he asked abruptly.

''Cameron? Of course not,'' she answered without thinking, then bit back a groan. She should have been coy.

''Good,'' Justin said. He started across the porch.

Megan watched until he disappeared into the night. Good? He thought it was good that she hadn't been involved with the handsome widower? Why?

She'd already closed the door and was dousing the lights downstairs when she got her answer. Justin had been jealous. There was no need for him to be. There had never been anyone but him. She was starting to wonder if there ever would be again.

''Will there be lace, too?'' Bonnie asked eagerly.

''Yes, here on the collar, and on the cuffs.'' Megan picked

up the dark blue dress and held it in front of the little girl. "See how pretty? It matches your eyes."

Bonnie grabbed a piece of lace and held it up to her face. "The white part, too!"

Megan laughed. "Yes, the white part, too." She leaned over and squeezed the child against her.

It had been over a week since Justin had first brought the thin, scared girl to her store. Since then, they'd spent most of their days together. Justin brought her to the store after breakfast and picked her up on his way home. There hadn't been a repeat of that first night, with Justin staying to supper, and then—she cleared her throat and searched frantically for her scissors on the table—what had happened later. She brought Bonnie back to the house, but she always returned her to the shop before sundown.

"This was your dress?" Bonnie asked, fingering the heavy cotton.

"Yes, when I was a little older than you. I'm going to cut it down. I think I only wore it one or two times, so it's almost new. It's going to look much prettier on you than it ever did on me. You have such beautiful dark hair."

Bonnie smiled shyly, as if compliments were as foreign to her as regular meals had been. But in the last few days, her bruises had faded and her face had lost its pinched, hungry look. She smiled often and even laughed on occasion.

"We're going to a social, huh?"

"Yes," Megan said, laying the dress flat on her dining room table. She began to carefully tear out the neat stitches. "After church on Sunday."

"I've never been to church."

Megan stared at her. Never been to church? But the child was six years old. She opened her mouth to say something, then clamped it shut. Of course Bonnie hadn't. Who would take her? Her mother wouldn't have been allowed inside Landing's most sacred building, and Mrs. Jarvis hadn't taken the trouble to feed and clothe the girl decently. Why would she have bothered with the state of the child's soul?

"It's very lovely," Megan said, and smiled at her. "There's singing and the minister reads from the Bible. He talks about God." She sighed. "Sometimes he talks a little too long, but he has a nice voice, so we don't mind."

"Is there singing at the social?"

"Sometimes. It's mostly a picnic to welcome Justin as the new sheriff."

Bonnie's big blue eyes got bigger. She laid her corn-husk doll on the table and leaned closer. "A picnic? I've heard about that. Is there going to be fried chicken?"

"Yes. And lemonade and cakes."

"Do I get some?"

"Of course."

"I'm glad Justin's the new sheriff," Bonnie said fervently.

Megan laughed. "I bet you are." She turned back to the dress and continued tearing out the stitches. Unfortunately, not all the townspeople shared Bonnie's enthusiasm. Justin continued to investigate Laurie Smith's murder and many citizens resented his spending so much time on something they considered worthless. She'd had an argument about it with Mrs. Greeley just yesterday. In a fit of temper, she'd told the older woman she should be grateful Justin cared that much. If anyone ever did in her husband for overcharging in his butcher shop, Justin would be sure to bring the man to justice.

Megan bit her lower lip. It had been a silly thing to say. She'd known that as soon as the words had slipped out. No doubt, news of the words she and the butcher's wife had exchanged were already spread all over town. Part of the reason she'd brought Bonnie back to the house had been to work on the dress, but the other had been to avoid her sister. It had rained yesterday, turning the path between town and the Bartlett house into a muddy trail. Colleen would never risk her shoes over a visit, so Megan and Bonnie were safe today.

At least Colleen and Mrs. Greeley seemed to be in the minority. There were enough new settlers to tip the scale in Justin's favor. He was also getting support from the most surprising places. Megan had been shocked when she'd found out Mrs. Dobson had been the one who'd suggested the social. The older woman had always talked about Justin's being as handsome as sin, and sin making its own kind of trouble. Maybe the widow didn't think trouble from sin that handsome was a bad thing. Megan smiled at the thought.

When the dress was in pieces, she picked up the heavy paper she was using as a pattern. She pinned it to the cloth, then carefully cut around the edges. Bonnie sat on the floor and played.

"Can we make a dress for my doll?" she asked.

"I think so."

"And Alice?" The kitten had awakened from her morning nap and had come to investigate their activities. She was still small enough to sit in a teacup, but she was growing. Her bright green eyes didn't miss anything, Megan thought as the kitten swatted at a falling bit of fabric.

"I think Alice likes her calico coat just fine."

The cat meowed her agreement, then hopped into Bonnie's lap.

"What are you going to wear?" the girl asked.

"Oh, I have lots of dresses."

"But you have to wear something special."

"I'll find the right dress."

Bonnie picked up Alice and cradled her in her arms. "Let's go pick one now."

Megan set down the blue fabric. She could finish the dress later, while Bonnie was taking a nap, or even that evening. It wouldn't take long. "All right." She took the little girl's hand and led her upstairs to her bedroom. There was a large armoire opposite the bed and another one beside the big window.

She opened the one opposite the bed. "I have a pretty pink dress," she said, pulling out a floral print calico that had to be at least four years old. It was wearing a little at the shoulder seams and the fabric had a decided droop to it.

Bonnie climbed onto the bed and shook her head. Alice flopped down beside her and started to purr. "It's not pretty, Megan."

"All right." She reached into the armoire again and brought out a light blue gown. It had pleats across the front and a big lace collar. The back pulled up into a cascade of flounces. The style was nice, but the color was a little off for her. Even before Bonnie wrinkled her nose, she was already hanging it back up.

They went through three more dresses. There was a second pink dress of silk that Bonnie admitted might be all right. Then the girl pointed at the other armoire. "What's in there?"

Megan hesitated. She shouldn't really show her. It wasn't as if she could wear the dress. It was completely scandalous. But no one had ever seen it, and suddenly she desperately wanted to know what the little girl would think.

"This is very special," Megan said as she approached the armoire. "But it's a secret. You can't tell anyone. Do you understand?"

Bonnie nodded so vigorously, the bed shook. Her eyes widened in anticipation.

Megan opened the armoire. One half was shelves where she kept most of the silk and lace lingerie that Justin had seen the other night. She flushed at the memory. She'd been rearranging her things while Bonnie slept that evening and he'd seen her room before she'd had a chance to put everything away. But she didn't reach for any of the fancy undergarments. Instead, she pulled out a cream-colored silk dress.

The neckline dipped scandalously low in front, and was edged in deep rose-colored rosettes. The tiny sleeves would just cover her shoulders and leave her arms completely bare. The tightly fitted bodice flared out at the hips before the luxurious fabric draped down to the underskirt. Rows and rows of gathered flounces had been edged in rose ribbon. The last foot of the skirt was pleated. She turned it slowly so Bonnie could see the back. A bustle of rosettes and ribbon cascaded to the ground.

It was a dress made for a princess. Bonnie stared openmouthed. "Oh, Megan, that's so pretty. It's the prettiest thing I've ever seen forever."

"I know. It's a Worth gown." She brushed a speck of lint from the shoulder seam. "Three years ago, I was in St. Louis buying for the store. This gown had been ordered for a lady who changed her mind about it. The gentleman I purchase my ready-made clothing from showed it to me, and I simply had to have it." It had been wicked of her, she knew, but she didn't care. The gown had been too beautiful to resist. The previous year had been her best yet, so she'd told herself she deserved a reward.

"Wear that," Bonnie said.

"No. I can't." Megan put the gown back. Just thinking about what the townspeople would say—what Colleen would say—was enough to make her shudder. Like the lingerie, this was a guilty secret. She had more than anyone suspected.

"The earth dress is pretty. You should wear it. My dress is going to be pretty and I'm wearing mine."

"It's a 'Worth,'" Megan said, closing the armoire and sitting next to the girl. "He's a famous dress designer in Paris."

"Worth," Bonnie repeated. "Doesn't he want you to wear your dress?"

He might, Megan thought, but probably not in Kansas. She smiled. "I'm sure he does. But not to the social."

Bonnie seemed to accept that. "You can wear your pink dress, then. We'll be pretty together."

"Yes, we will." Megan leaned over and hugged her close. Bonnie clung to her.

Deep in her chest she felt a sharp pain. She tried to ignore the cause, but she couldn't. She loved her job at the store. It made her happy and kept her from going slowly mad from being trapped in this big house. For the last few years she'd told herself the store was enough. That she was lucky to be able to work. Most women couldn't. Their children or society kept them at home. But as Bonnie snuggled closer, Megan realized she'd been fooling herself. Just as being home all the time wouldn't please her, the store by itself wasn't enough, either. She'd been lonely for a long time.

As she straightened, Megan wondered what she was supposed to do about that. She wanted the normal joys of womanhood. A family and husband. But how? And who? Since age sixteen, there had been only one man in her life. And in a year, that man would be leaving.

Chapter Eight

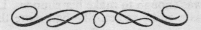

"**I** don't want to be here," Justin mumbled under his breath.

Bonnie, skipping along at his side, glanced up at him. "Megan says there's singing at church," she said, as if that made it all right.

"I know." The singing was the least of his problems but it sure didn't make it all right with him. He tugged on his collar and adjusted his string tie, then pulled at his black jacket. He didn't give a damn about how he looked. He wanted to be anywhere but fifty feet from the white clapboard church in front of him. The townspeople were starting to assemble. He'd hoped to get to church early and find a seat in the back so he and Bonnie wouldn't be noticed. However, more people were out than he'd thought. If having to go to church wasn't bad enough, afterward there was going to be a social.

The old-timers hadn't forgotten who he was and why he'd been run out of town. Most of them were offended by his investigation into Laurie Smith's death, despite the fact that he hadn't found out a damn thing. The new settlers didn't care who or what he was as long as he got the job done, but they would hear the talk today, if they hadn't already. He didn't care for himself, but Bonnie was another matter.

He glanced down at the girl. Alice, the maid, had come in early and done Bonnie's hair in ringlets. Her new blue dress with its big lace collar was the exact color of her eyes. She was beautiful, and almost a replica of her mother. If nothing else cast a pall over the social, the men who had visited Laurie were bound to be unnerved by Bonnie's likeness to her. It was going to be a long day.

As they approached the church, Justin noticed several clusters of people talking. One by one they grew silent and stared. Bonnie gripped his hand tighter. She clutched her doll to her chest and crowded him.

Mr. and Mrs. Greeley were closest to the path. Justin nodded.

"Morning, Sher—" Mr. Greeley stopped abruptly when his wife elbowed him in the ribs.

The sun was shining brightly in the morning sky. Birds swooped down from budding trees. The collection of fancy dresses and hats, men in suits and children giggling in their Sunday best should have made him feel welcome. It didn't. He wanted to turn on his heel and walk away. He couldn't. Because it was important to have Bonnie accepted by the town. Although he was starting to wonder if that was ever going to happen.

"Good morning, Sheriff."

He turned toward the familiar voice. Mrs. Dobson walked in his direction from the side of the church. Her large, feather-covered hat bobbed with each step.

"Mrs. Dobson." He tipped his hat.

The large-bosomed woman bent at the waist. "Bonnie, don't you look pretty."

The girl dimpled. "Megan made this dress for me 'cause it matches my eyes."

"It does indeed. You have very pretty eyes." She straightened. "Justin Kincaid, I'm very unhappy with you."

He stiffened, prepared to whisk Bonnie away if things got too ugly.

"You've been keeping this precious child all to yourself. You could have brought her to me. I would have taken her in."

He stared at her. "You?"

"Yes, me. Close your mouth and stop looking so surprised. I know what people have been saying. I'm very angry you would think that of me, however. After what happened before." She clamped her lips together and glanced significantly at the obviously listening people around them.

She was referring to her bedside vigil when his mother had been dying. He didn't know what to say. He'd never thought of taking Bonnie to Mrs. Dobson's house because the woman had always sided so firmly with the town. As a boy, she'd often scolded him for getting into trouble. He drew his eyebrows together. Maybe she wasn't as horrible as he'd thought then. Maybe she'd only been concerned about him.

"Justin?" Bonnie tugged on his coat sleeve. "Don't send me away."

He smiled at her. "You're going to stay with me, honey. Don't you worry. Mrs. Dobson was just offering her hospitality."

The widow nodded. "You're a sweet little girl and a bright spot to my day in the store." She turned to Justin. "I'm teaching her numbers and some ciphering. She's quite intelligent. Now, are you going to stand there like a clod, or are you going to escort me into church?"

He glanced back at the Greeleys openly listening to the conversation, then down at the small woman. "You amaze me, ma'am." He held out his arm. She slipped her gloved hand in the crook of his elbow. "Is that a new hat you're wearing? It's lovely."

She tapped his hand. "Don't you try your sweet talk on me, young man. I'm too old for your wickedness." She paused just inside the church, then pointed. "We'll sit there, next to Megan." She started walking. "No, I'll go in first." She slid into the pew and adjusted her voluminous dress. Bonnie went next and Justin sat on the aisle. He tried to see around Mrs. Dobson to greet Megan, but the widow's hat was too large. He settled for looking at the church.

Not that much had changed in the last seven years. The pews were still backless benches, the pulpit simple. He'd never spent much time in church, but occasionally his mother had made him go. He saw a mousy young woman sit down at an organ. She barely looked big enough to reach all the keys, but when her fingers began to move across the instrument, the music that swelled out through the church was stunningly beautiful.

"That's new," he said to Mrs. Dobson.

She glanced up. "Oh, yes. Megan donated it three years ago. We're fortunate to have our own organ and a minister in residence here in Landing. The other neighboring towns have to make do with occasional visits. We get him three Sundays a month."

"It's very fortunate," he mumbled. Mrs. Dobson shot him a look, but he ignored her. He would bet his salary Colleen had blackmailed the organ out of her sister. He would pay that amount again to find out how.

Mrs. Greeley and her husband started up the center aisle. As they passed, Justin put his arm around Bonnie.

"Good morning, Anabell and Winston," Mrs. Dobson said. "How are you?"

The couple paused. Justin saw the emotions flicker across Mrs. Greeley's middle-aged face. Finally, she turned toward their pew. "Good morning, yourself, Catherine. We're fine."

"Good." Mrs. Dobson smiled. "You've met Justin, of course, and this is Bonnie."

Anabell Greeley gripped her reticule so tightly, Justin thought she might tear it in two. She inhaled sharply and the color fled her pinched face. Finally, she nodded. "Megan, Sheriff." She gritted her teeth. "Bonnie." Then she turned away and marched up the center aisle, leaving her husband to tip his hat and trail after her.

The widow kept at the people arriving, until the entire congregation had been introduced to the child. Bonnie smiled winningly, showed a select few her precious doll and snuggled close to him for protection when the sharp stares got to be too much. By the time the service started, Justin was too exhausted to do more than listen.

Gene Estes's choice of sermons got his attention, though, when about ten minutes into his preaching the minister started going on about the wages of sin. Justin could feel the stares of the townspeople. Those words were meant for him and little Bonnie. But their impact was lessened by Mrs. Dobson's unmistakable acceptance of the child. She'd smoothed the way.

He leaned over toward her. "Thank you for making them accept her," he whispered, ducking to avoid being slapped by her ridiculous feather-covered hat. "I don't suppose you'd tell me why?"

She gave him a knowing smile and patted Bonnie's shoulder. "I always said you were handsome as sin, Justin Kincaid. I might be old enough to be your grandmother, but I'm not dead or blind. Besides, I like the child. Now, hush and pay attention to the preaching."

By the time the sermon ended, Justin's legs were cramped and his back ached from the uncomfortable pew. "No chance of falling asleep here, is there?"

Mrs. Dobson laughed. "No, Gene wouldn't like that one bit." She rose and tapped her foot impatiently. "Hurry up, Justin, we've got a social to get to. You're the guest of honor, you shouldn't be late."

He stood up and waited in the center aisle. People flowed around him, some giving him greetings, others simply smiling politely, but no one daring to ignore him or Bonnie. Not while they were under the protection of the formidable widow.

Mrs. Dobson moved past him to speak to one of her friends. He waited until Megan made her way to the center aisle.

"Good morning," he said.

Megan mumbled something he couldn't hear, then ducked her head. He saw the faint blush on her cheek. Only when he noticed her biting her lower lip did he realize the reason for her shyness.

Today she looked different than she had just a few nights before. Her blond hair was pulled up into an elaborate coiffure, with a small straw and ribbon hat perched on her crown. Her pink silk dress outlined her curves enough to help him remember what he'd seen, touched and tasted. As if he could forget. He didn't even have to close his eyes to recall exactly what had happened between them, and how much more he'd wanted. This morning she was every inch the respectable lady. He missed the mussed young woman more than he would have imagined. He missed her easy smile and teasing, he missed the sense that she was approachable. This Megan Bartlett was as remote as her sister.

He glanced down the center aisle to the entrance of the church. Gene Estes and his wife stood greeting parishioners. Colleen was in an overstarched green dress that looked stiff enough to hold up a building. Her tightly pursed lips and military posture made him shudder. Perhaps he'd been hasty in comparing Megan to her sister.

"What are you smiling about?" Megan asked.

"The fact that you don't look much like Colleen anymore. There was a time people had trouble telling you two apart."

"You always knew."

He stared into her almond-shaped hazel eyes. He could smell the scent of roses from her hair and feel the seductive warmth of her body. She swayed toward him. There was a time he'd thought he would marry Megan Bartlett. When he'd proposed and she'd accepted, he hadn't believed his luck or the fact that a woman like her would want a man like him. She'd promised to be his bride back when the most he'd been able to offer was the hope that one day he would be able to buy the old livery stable in town.

None of his dreams had come true. He'd been forced from town, and when he'd asked her to go with him, she'd refused, lashing out viciously so he wouldn't make the mistake of asking again. Now he was back in Landing, back where he never thought he would be, and Megan still had the ability to bring him to his knees.

"Bonnie and I made a cold dinner yesterday for the picnic. Would you like to sit with us?" she asked.

He raised his eyebrows. "You know what sitting with me at the social will mean?"

She nodded slowly.

"Colleen won't approve."

"I don't need her approval."

Brave words, if he didn't look too closely and see her lips quivering at the corners. "All right, Miss Bartlett, I would be honored to join you." He bent his arm and offered it to her. She took it with one hand and with the other pulled her skirt train out of the pew. With Bonnie walking in front of them, they made their way outside.

Families had already collected on blankets spread under the many trees around the freshly painted church. Megan led him to a basket she'd left in the shade. Before they could find a place to settle, Mrs. Dobson called to them from where she was already reclining. "Megan, Justin, I've saved room."

Megan looked at him and shrugged. "She means well."

"I don't mind."

"I'm surprised."

"Why? Mrs. Dobson thinks I'm handsome as sin."

Megan ducked her head as she chuckled.

By the time everyone had been seated and served, Justin was growing more comfortable with the crowd. He was aware of the stares sent their way, but no one had said anything bad to Bonnie. The little girl sat next to Mrs. Dobson and ate from her own plate, all the while prattling on about secrets her doll told her.

"If you're here having fun, Justin, who's on duty?" Megan asked, pouring him a tin cup of lemonade.

"Wyatt said he'd keep an eye on things, but everyone in town has come to the social so if there's going to be trouble, I'll be in the middle of it."

"You usually are." She made the statement casually, as if stating a fact. He had to agree she was right. He always had been in the middle of trouble.

She sat up against a tree, most of her weight resting on one hip, with her legs bent under her. The pink dress brought out the color in her face, and again and again he found his attention wandering to her mouth.

"What are you staring at?" she asked quietly enough so that neither Mrs. Dobson nor Bonnie could hear.

"You. You look lovely today." He cleared his throat. "Your dress is pretty," he said a little louder.

"She's got a prettier one," Bonnie said, raising herself on her knees. "It's white with flowers here." She motioned to the top of her chest. "And there's ribbons down the back with a big bow."

Mrs. Dobson picked up a chicken leg and waved it in the air. "It sounds wonderful, Megan. Why didn't you wear that one?"

"It's not appropriate," she answered, then turned to Bonnie. "You weren't supposed to say anything about that dress."

"Oh." Bonnie covered her mouth with her hand. "I forgot."

Justin stretched out on the blanket at Megan's feet and rested his head on his hand. "What *is* it appropriate for?"

Megan glared at him and took a bite of potato salad.

He watched her, knowing this must be another of her guilty secrets. His gaze flickered to her bodice and he wondered what she wore underneath. Satin and lace? Perhaps silk whispering against her creamy skin. Instantly, his blood heated and he pulled at the collar of his shirt. He forced his mind to consider less appealing questions. It wouldn't do for anyone to notice his physical reaction to Megan's closeness. There would be a scandal the likes of which this town had never seen.

"What's so special about this dress?" he asked.

She set her fork down. "Nothing. It's fancy, that's all. Not something I would wear to an outdoor social."

A small bird fluttered low and captured Bonnie's attention. The girl squealed and pointed. Mrs. Dobson stared at the tiny winged creature, then leaned closer to tell Bonnie what kind of bird it was. Justin took advantage of their momentary distraction. He raised his eyebrows.

"Another secret then?"

Megan surprised him by smiling. "One of many, I'm afraid."

"Don't apologize. Your secrets are intriguing."

"Are they?"

There was something odd about the light in her eyes. Something that made him want to pull her close and kiss her. Or hold her at arm's length and force her to tell him what she was thinking. In the seven years he'd been gone, Megan had changed. The shy young woman he'd given his heart to had grown up. She was still too easily swayed by the concerns of others, but she'd managed to rebel enough to wear French lace.

His good humor fled as he reminded himself French lace wasn't enough. He sat up slowly. Passionate kisses and soft female curves wouldn't be enough to allow him to forget the past.

"Justin, did you see the bird? Mrs. Dobson says I can take some bread to the woods and leave it for him to eat!" Bonnie bounced on her knees and clasped her hands together as if she'd been given the most wonderful gift. Her blue eyes glowed with happiness.

He reached out his hand and tweaked her nose. "I'm sure the bird will enjoy his meal."

Bonnie threw herself into his arms. "I like church, and I like socials more!"

Small hands held on to his coat. Her face burrowed into his chest. He could feel the two women watching him, but he didn't look up. He just held Bonnie close and stroked her hair.

Inside of him, in the place he'd ignored so long he'd been sure it had died, a flicker of feeling stirred his heart. He cared about this child. Almost as much as he'd once foolishly allowed himself to care about Megan.

"I can't believe this is the same little girl you brought to the store almost two weeks ago," Megan said. "She's blossomed under your care."

Her praise embarrassed him. And pleased him. "We understand each other," he said.

Bonnie tilted her head back and smiled at him. "We're going to be together forever."

"Yeah." He tapped her nose. He hadn't been faithful to all his promises, but this was one he was determined to keep. She was just a little girl, yet she'd been the one to show him how empty his life was and how hard it had become to spend it alone. The child wasn't enough to fill up the hole inside, or take away the bitterness from the past, but she blurred the edges enough that he could forget what had happened and ignore the taunting of what should have been.

* * *

"All right, children. Line up here for the egg race," Mr. Greeley called from across the clearing.

"Can I? Can I?" Bonnie asked eagerly. She looked from Megan to Justin and back.

Justin grinned. "Go on. But if you get covered with broken eggs, don't expect me to wash your dress."

Bonnie sprang to her feet. "I'll be extra, extra careful."

She raced toward the children milling around the butcher. Megan watched her go, waiting tensely to see what would happen when she arrived. Mr. Greeley glanced at the girl, then handed her a spoon. Several of the children stared curiously. Colleen's daughter sniffed imperiously, just like her mother, then one redheaded boy, about seven or eight, elbowed the girl in the ribs and grinned at Bonnie.

Megan relaxed against the tree. "I think she's going to be all right with the children."

"Good." Justin stretched out on the blanket at her feet. As the temperature had climbed, he'd taken off his jacket. His long-sleeved white shirt contrasted with his tanned face and hands. He closed his eyes as if preparing to doze. Mrs. Dobson had gone off to talk with some of her friends, so the two of them were alone on the blanket, surrounded by the rest of the town. It was the most public of privacies.

Megan stared at Justin, at his familiar features. His mouth relaxed into a faint smile. She could see the tail of the scar under his lower lip, and the lines beside his eyes. His jaw had always been square, but his face had grown leaner in his time away. His breathing slowed. She admired the length and breadth of his chest, remembering how it had felt when she'd touched him there. Her fingers tingled, as did her breasts and between her—

She swallowed hard, trying to ignore her lascivious thoughts. She still couldn't believe what they'd done, what she'd *allowed* him to do. It wasn't right. Not just because they weren't even courting, let alone engaged, but because Justin would be leaving Landing. What if she continued to allow him liberties? Wouldn't she then be risking more than her body and reputation? Wouldn't she be risking her heart? She couldn't. If it was broken again, it wouldn't mend.

But it was difficult to ignore the handsome man stretched out before her. She rose to her knees and began collecting plates and placing them in the basket she'd brought. Silverware clinked as she tossed it on top of the dishes. She left out their tin cups in case anyone wanted more lemonade. She picked up the chocolate cake she'd brought and was lowering it into the basket, when something grabbed her ankle. She almost dropped the platter.

Half turning, she saw Justin's arm sticking out from the hem of her dress. She could feel his warm fingers against her skin. His thumb moved slowly back and forth over her anklebone.

"What are you doing?" she asked softly, then darted a glance around to see who had noticed. The children were lining up for their race and everyone seemed to be watching them.

"You're making too much noise," Justin said without opening his eyes. His words were slow and lazy, his voice so low her mouth watered. "I couldn't sleep."

"You could have told me to be quiet instead of accosting me."

"Darlin', you don't know the first thing about being accosted."

His hand moved a little higher up her calf. Megan froze in place, awkwardly stretched out on her knees, one hand supporting herself, the other holding a half-eaten chocolate cake. Her arm cramped up, but she didn't move. A delicious lethargy swept over her. Justin Kincaid had his hand on her leg. In front of the entire town. And no one had noticed. Then his fingers moved again and she didn't care about the town or her muscles. She didn't care about anything but the stroking against her skin and the heat that spiraled up her thighs and higher to her female place. Her breathing increased.

Then his hand was gone. Despite the burning protest in her arm and bent leg, Megan stayed in her position, hoping his magic touch would return. When that didn't happen, she glanced at Justin. Both his hands lay on his chest. His expression hadn't changed at all.

She placed the cake in the basket, then humphed loudly and sat back against the tree. Irritation fed the passion inside of her until she was overheated. She wanted to scream at him, or kiss him. She contented herself with glaring at him.

"You would tempt a saint," he murmured.

She almost didn't catch the words. When she did, it took a moment for them to sink in. Her ill temper extinguished as quickly as it had flared. Justin was certainly no saint. He was the best kind of sinner.

"Thank you," she whispered.

In the center of the clearing, Mr. Greeley called, "Go!"

The straggly line of children began to move forward. Bonnie was on the end closest to them. Megan smiled as she watched her. Bonnie held the spoon out in front of her. The egg wobbled back and forth with each step, but didn't fall. Megan laughed.

"Good for you, Bonnie!" she called. The girl looked up and grinned.

"Is she winning?" Justin asked without opening his eyes. He bent his arms at the elbow and rested his head on his hands.

"No, but she's having fun. Go to sleep."

He mumbled something and sighed deeply.

Megan ignored the temptingly masculine picture he made and looked back at the racers. The first accident had already occurred with one of the children tripping and dropping his egg. Bits of shell and yolk scattered everywhere. A couple of the little girls shrieked and jumped out of the way. Bonnie glanced at the commotion, but kept going forward. Parents started standing up and cheering.

A girl of four or five dropped her egg, splattering her white dress. She promptly sat down and started to cry. Her older brother swerved over to talk to her. He got in the way of another child who tripped and, on the way down, bumped a little boy in short pants out of the race. The boy struggled to stay on his feet. His egg teetered precariously before slowly rolling off the edge of his spoon and dropping directly on top of Gene Estes's polished black shoes.

Megan clamped her hand over her mouth to hold in her chuckle of amusement. She glanced around at the crowd, but everyone's attention was focused on the crying little girl and the fallen boy next to her. Megan looked back at Gene.

Her eyes widened with disbelief. Her brother-in-law, the admired minster of the town of Landing, grabbed the boy by his arm and scolded him. She couldn't hear the words, but he pointed to his shoes and shook the child. There was something tight and ugly in the man's face. He turned his head as if trying to see who was watching, then backhanded the boy across the face. The child fell to the ground, too stunned to cry. Gene said something else, then walked away.

Megan stared at the child, then at her brother-in-law. He was standing beside Colleen and calmly wiping his shoes. As she watched, he even smiled. As if nothing had happened. As if he hadn't hit the child. No one else seemed to have noticed. She returned her attention to the boy. He'd started to cry and ran over to his mother. Megan didn't recognize her. She must be one of the new settlers, a farmer's wife. She had probably been in the general store, but Megan didn't know her name.

The boy rubbed the side of his face, then pointed to the minister. The mother frowned. She shook her head and grabbed the boy by the ear, pulling him away.

"She doesn't believe him," Megan said.

"Who doesn't believe whom?" Justin asked, his voice sounding sleepy.

She rose to her knees. "That woman. She doesn't believe what her son is telling her, but I saw him."

Justin yawned and raised himself on one elbow. "Saw what?"

"A boy dropped his egg on Gene's shoes. Gene scolded him, then hit him across the face with the back of his hand. He knocked the boy down, then calmly walked away as if nothing had happened. When the boy tried to tell his mother, she didn't believe him."

Justin frowned. "I understand his being upset about the raw egg, but that reaction seems a little harsh for our esteemed man of God."

"I agree." Megan stood up and looked around the crowd. She wanted to find that mother and tell her the boy wasn't lying. She started in the direction they'd gone.

"Megan, Justin, I got a ribbon!" Bonnie came running across the field holding a scrap of white ribbon in her hands.

"Good for you," Justin said, smiling as she approached. "Third place. That's wonderful. There were lots of kids bigger than you."

"I know." She quivered with pride. "I got a ribbon."

Megan bent down and gave her a hug. "I'm very proud of you, Bonnie. I saw how you concentrated on the race when other children were distracted by what was going on."

Bonnie grinned. "I'm gonna be in the sack race next. This time I'm going to win!" She pressed the ribbon into Megan's hand, then took off running, back to the center of the field.

"Is that them?" Justin asked, pointing.

Megan turned and saw a wagon driving away. She recognized the boy in the back and nodded. "Yes. The next time they come into town, I'm going to tell that woman what really happened." She glared at her brother-in-law. But he was across the crowded lawn and didn't even notice. "I can't believe he did that." She sat back down under the tree.

Justin flopped down next to her and picked up a piece of grass. "Believe it," he said, and started chewing on the short stalk. "People are basically bad."

"You can't mean that."

"No? Look at what just happened. Gene slapped a kid and no one will believe the boy."

"That's different. Gene is a minister. He's not supposed to behave that way."

"People always act worse than you think they're going to. That's what I've learned."

She shifted against the bark of the tree. The scent of springtime drifted to her. The grass and flowers, the lingering smell of fried chicken and stew, of biscuits and ale from some barrel down by the stream. The calls of the children, the buzz of flies and conversation. It was all so normal.

"I refuse to think the world is a bad place."

"It's not the world, it's everyone in it."

"You're a cynic."

"You're too innocent."

He lay next to her on the blanket, his long lean body stretched out, his booted feet crossed at the ankles. She was between him and the crowd on the lawn. She felt a faint tug on her sleeve. He pulled her hand down between them and covered it with his own.

She'd turned her wrist so they were palm to palm and their fingers laced. Only then did she think she probably should have pulled back rather than allow him the liberty. It wasn't safe. Then she leaned her head back and stared at the perfect Kansas sky. She was tired of doing the right thing. The right thing left her feeling alone.

"There's no news on Bonnie's family," Justin said, breaking into her thoughts.

"I didn't know you'd been checking."

"I promised her I would."

Justin's word meant everything, she thought sadly. When he made a promise, he kept it. Unlike herself. She'd given her word, then gone back on it.

"I've sent telegrams to several towns, but I'm beginning to wonder if Laurie Smith was her mother's real name."

"It would be easy to change it and start over," she said.

"Not as easy as you would think."

She glanced down at Justin, but his eyes were closed. If not for the thumb rubbing along the back of her hand, she might have thought he was asleep. "Did you try to start over?"

"Sure. And look where I ended up."

"Landing's not so bad."

"Maybe not for you. But for Bonnie and that boy Gene slapped, it's not perfect."

"I know it's not perfect, it's just..." She shook her head. Why was she defending this town? She had her own troubles, trying to find a balance between being respectable and living her life. As she grew older, she found she wanted more. Seven years ago, everything had been so clear. Now she wasn't sure.

She watched the children line up for the sack race. Bonnie looked over at her and grinned. Megan waved. Sunlight caught the child's long dark hair, making it shine. Bonnie grabbed the edge of the sack and pulled it up to her chest. Her chin thrust out in determination.

Bonnie was six. Megan bit her lower lip. She could have had a child that age. If she'd married Justin and gone away with him. What would have happened to them? Her father would have disowned her. Colleen, as well. At seventeen she hadn't been able to imagine a worse fate. Better to live out her days alone than risk her family's and the town's disapproval.

Now she wasn't so sure. She looked at the man lying next to her, at the slow rise and fall of his chest and the lean length of his body. She thought about his gentle smiles and the way he took care of Bonnie. She thought about the way he ignored the conventions of the day and did what *he* thought was best.

Falling in love with Justin all those years ago had been the most wonderfully terrifying experience of her life. Seven years later, she was grown up enough to admit that if she had it to do over again, she would go with him this time. But the Justin who had loved her enough to want to marry her no longer existed. The man who had taken his place might have feelings for her, but he would never forgive her the betrayal and pain she'd inflicted on him. He would never trust her enough to fall in love with her again, no matter how much she might want him to.

Chapter Nine

Justin braced the railing between his knees and pounded in the nails. The sound echoed in the crisp spring morning. After a few seconds, the front door of the house opened and Mrs. Dobson stepped out onto the porch. She clutched a shawl around her ample chest. The knitted wool was a pale shade of pink.

"What's that racket? Justin Kincaid, are you the one making all that noise? Do you know what time it is? How do you expect a body to sleep with you pounding away like the devil himself?"

"Morning, ma'am," Justin said, and grinned. He bent over and picked up the top railing. After balancing it in his arms, he heaved it up high and dropped it into place.

"You didn't answer my questions."

"I'm fixing your fence. A while back, you said it had fallen down in the winter."

She walked to the edge of the porch. "Why are you doing that?"

"Just being neighborly."

"I might be old, but I'm not foolish. You're the sheriff. You don't have time to be mending fences. Why aren't you off making our town safe for decent citizens?"

He wiped his hand across his forehead. "Landing seems plenty safe for decent citizens, ma'am. It's everyone else who has to worry."

"You're talking about that dance-hall girl, aren't you?" The older woman sighed. "It's a shame about her. But you still haven't told me why you're bothering with my fence."

He adjusted his hat, then picked up the next railing. "It needed doing. Besides, if it wasn't for you, Bonnie would have been turned away last Sunday. I'm grateful for what you did."

She tisked, but he could have sworn he saw a faint blush on her cheeks. "Just doing what I think's right. You eat yet?"

"No, ma'am."

"When you get done with that racket, you come inside here. I'll make some breakfast." She walked across the porch and opened the door, then turned back to him. "But don't you go around mentioning this to anyone. I've got a reputation to uphold. I don't want people gossiping that I'm entertaining a young man in my house."

He grinned. "I won't say a word."

It took him about a half hour to finish mending Mrs. Dobson's fence. He washed up at the pump in her yard, then straightened his shirt and climbed the stairs to her front door. After a quick knock, he stepped inside. The house was small, but surprisingly bright. Lace curtains hung at the windows. Little china figurines and picture frames sat on small tables. He edged around them, trying not to bump anything, and made his way to the kitchen.

The smell of bacon, ham and baking bread greeted him. There were two place settings on the small table, and a hot cup of coffee.

"That's yours," she said, motioning to the mug. "Drink it while it's still steaming. I'm glad you washed outside. I don't want some man's dirt in the same sink as my dishes."

He took a seat and eyed the widow. Something was different about her. Something that— He grinned. "Why, Mrs. Dobson, I admire your shawl. It's a pretty shade of pink," he said meaningfully.

The woman spun toward him. Her bright green eyes widened. She glanced from the offending shawl to him and back. Then she smiled. "It's been more than ten years since Mr. Dobson went to his reward. I thought it was time for a little color."

"I would say so."

"Some folks would be surprised if they knew I was thinking of ending my mourning."

He nodded slowly. "Not as surprised as they would be if they knew how you'd helped my mother."

She stared at him. "Imagine the talk if people realize you're keeping company with Megan."

He opened his mouth to protest.

"You were holding hands. Don't deny it. I was there Sunday, young man, and I have eyes."

"Sharp ones."

She checked the food, then turned back to him. Without one of her large hats, with her red hair not as tightly drawn up on her head, she looked softer, not quite as old. There was an intelligence and quickness in her expression that warned him Mrs. Dobson wasn't a fool. He leaned back in his chair and folded his arms over his chest. "So we both have secrets."

"I can keep my mouth shut if I think it's the right thing to do. What are your intentions toward Megan?"

"I don't know."

He'd answered without thinking, then realized he'd spoken the truth. He didn't know what to do about Megan because everything about her confused him. He hadn't expected her to still be in Landing, and he'd never thought she wouldn't have married. The fact that she was here and single had been enough of a shock, but in addition to that, there was the matter of the attraction between them. He could still feel the heat of their passion, the taste of her kisses. She dressed and acted like a perfectly proper spinster. But she wore French lace and kissed him with an abandon that left him wanting more.

"I suppose I trust that answer more than one you've had time to polish," Mrs. Dobson said. "What about Bonnie? Are you going to keep her?"

"Yes."

She raised her thin eyebrows. "As easy as that. You're a bachelor, Justin. She's just a little girl."

"She needs me."

"I suspect you need her, as well." She nodded as if she'd finally figured something out. "I know why you didn't bring the child to me. Of all the women in town, I was the only one you were afraid might say yes. You didn't want to give her up, did you?''

"You're as clever as a fox."

She preened, then turned back to the stove. "Don't try sweet-talking me, young man. It's true, isn't it?" She turned over the bacon and ham slices, then poured out flapjacks onto the griddle.

"Once I got used to the idea, I did want to keep her."

"What did Megan say about that?"

"She was concerned about her reputation."

"Don't despise her for that. You might think you know everything, but you don't."

He frowned. "What does that mean?"

"Oh, just that you shouldn't be so quick to judge her. After all, although you're keeping Bonnie because she needs you, there's a part of you that's enjoying the trouble you're making."

"That's not true. I care about her."

"Of course you do. But the trouble is an unexpected advantage. Don't bother telling me otherwise." She flipped over the flapjacks, and reached for a plate. By the time she'd served the bacon and ham, the pancakes were ready. She slid three onto his plate and set the food in front of him. "You never could resist trouble, Justin Kincaid."

"I'm not that boy anymore."

"I know. I hope the change is enough, because there's going to be more trouble than either of us can imagine. There's a feeling in my bones that says it's all going to get a lot worse."

"You're making a mistake," Megan said as she dried the silver coffeepot.

Colleen poured sugar into the server, then set it on the tray. "I know exactly what I'm doing. This should have been taken care of from the beginning. If I'd realized what that man meant to do." She sniffed. "It's scandalous."

"She's just a little girl. Why can't you leave it alone?"

Colleen straightened and glared at her. Her dark dress should have been flattering, but the rust-colored flowers seemed to pull all the color from her face. With her hair drawn tightly back into a bun and her mouth pinched together, Colleen looked unattractive and matronly.

"I hold you as much at fault as that man," Colleen said. "Because you're my sister, I won't mention your part in this debacle, but I'm very disappointed. I can't imagine what Father would have made of this."

Megan told herself to stay calm. Colleen was on a rampage. It didn't mean anything. She had these fits from time to time. Everyone around her had to listen to her rage on and on, then it died down. Megan should just smile sweetly and go along with her as she usually did. Except this time it was different. This time Colleen was raging against Bonnie. Megan wouldn't let anything happen to the little girl.

She checked the coffee. Sounds of conversation and laughter drifted in from the parlor. Most of the women in town and from the surrounding farms had been invited to Colleen's house for tea. Unfortunately, the mother of the boy Gene had hit wasn't among them. Megan had tried to talk to her sister about the incident, but her sister had dismissed it, saying the child obviously deserved slapping.

"Is the coffee done?" Colleen asked.

"Not yet." Megan began slicing the cake she'd brought. What would her self-righteous sister say if she knew Bonnie had helped with it the previous afternoon? Megan decided to wait until Colleen had eaten a slice before telling her.

"I think you're wrong about this," Megan said.

"Fortunately, your opinion doesn't matter to anyone."

Megan gritted her teeth. Getting angry wouldn't accomplish anything. "Justin is being very sweet to that child. When no one else would take her in, he did. He's seeing that she's fed and clothed. Why is that so terrible?"

"He's a bachelor living in a hotel, for heaven's sake. That child is the daughter of a whore, and a bastard to boot. She should be in an orphanage, with others like her. Not prancing around town, or corrupting our God-fearing children with her filthy language."

Megan set down the knife and wiped her hands on a towel. "The only one with a filthy mouth that I know is you, dear sister. You find pleasure in those words, don't you? Does it make you feel powerful or wicked to say them?"

Colleen drew herself up to her full height. Angry, righteous fire shot from her hazel eyes. "How dare you?"

"You're the one who dares. Bonnie is an innocent in all this. Why can't you see that?"

"I see you're being swayed by that man. I didn't know how far things had gone." Colleen's gaze narrowed. "What sins have you committed, Megan Bartlett?"

"I'm not the point. Bonnie is. You're being unfair."

"I forbid you to see her, or that vile man."

Megan was glad she'd put the knife down. She planted her hands on her hips. "You don't have the right to forbid me to do anything."

"Of course I do. I'm your sister, and married. I'm responsible for your reputation in town, and for what you've been doing. I know that you defended that man to Mrs. Greeley. Heaven only knows what other things you've done."

"Stop talking about me," Megan demanded. "We're discussing the little girl. She has no family, no home. She's only six years old. How can she be responsible for her parents' actions?"

"The sins of the father shall be visited upon the children." Colleen picked up the coffee and poured the steaming liquid into the silver serving pot. "Finish putting that second tray together."

Megan reached for the bottle of milk, then stopped. She stared at her sister. "I don't know you anymore, Colleen. We used to be close, but now you're a stranger to me."

"That's your own doing. I haven't changed at all. You have. You're the one associating with the sheriff and his—"

"Stop it," Megan said firmly. "Stop calling her names and saying those evil things. I won't listen."

Colleen slammed the empty pot onto the table. "Don't you tell me what to do."

"Colleen, don't be like this." Megan stared at her sister, wondering when they'd become enemies. This isn't what she'd wanted. Why wouldn't Colleen listen? Why was the truth so difficult for her to hear? "When we were younger and our mother left—"

"No. Mama didn't leave. She's dead. I've told you and told you, she's dead." Color flared on Colleen's pale face, staining her cheeks with an unhealthy-looking flush. "Mama died. There was a funeral."

"That's not what happened."

"No! I won't listen to this." Colleen adjusted the silver service on the tray, and picked up the plate of sliced cake. "You make up your lies to torment me. I know you do. You spend your entire life tormenting me. It's bad enough that you run that store. Do you know how that's shamed me? My own sister working like a common laborer? You're a spinster, as well. Sometimes I can barely lift my head for the shame."

Megan was used to this particular lecture. She'd heard it several times before. "Your shame comes and goes with amazing convenience," she snapped. "The matter of the child is still unresolved. I don't understand your reluctance to deal with her. That is, however, your choice. But why do you protest when someone else gets involved? What happened to Christian charity?"

"I save it for good Christians." Colleen picked up the full tray and motioned for Megan to follow her with the second one. "Mark my words, Sister. I will not tolerate your wickedness much longer. One whisper from me, from Gene, and no one will frequent your store."

"You're wrong about that."

"Am I?" Colleen smiled. "Shall we find out?"

"I'm your sister. Doesn't that mean anything?"

"Not if you persist in acting this way." She walked from the kitchen.

Megan sat in one of the chairs by the table and rested her chin in her hands. She could hear the faint laughter and conversation from the parlor. She felt out of place and unwelcome in her sister's home. That made her sad, but wasn't surprising. This had been coming for a long time. Perhaps it had all started that cold November day their father had told them their mother was dead. As far as she knew, it was the only time their father had ever lied.

The back door opened and Gene walked in. His bare scalp and temple glistened from the heat. He wore a white shirt and vest, and carried his black jacket in one hand. When he saw her, he stopped and smiled. There was something peculiar and a little frightening about his eyes.

"Megan. What are you doing here?"

"Colleen is having a meeting." She rose to her feet and approached the stove. "I was just waiting for the coffee." She opened the pot and glanced at the dark liquid. "Oh, look. It's ready." She poured it into the silver service.

Before she could pick up the tray, Gene moved close and placed his hand on her arm. "Colleen is very worried about you."

Despite his lack of hair and his chilling expression, Gene wasn't unattractive. He was tall and lean, with a studied but graceful carriage. When they'd first been introduced, she, along with her sister, had thought him handsome. Her opinion had quickly changed as she'd spent more time with him. She'd even tried to talk Colleen out of the engagement.

Now, with his fingers gently stroking her forearm, she had to fight the urge to put as much space between them as possible. "My sister is overly protective. I understand her concerns, even if I don't agree with them. Don't worry yourself, Gene. Everything is fine."

"I do worry about you. With your father gone, I consider you my responsibility." His brown eyes met hers. Something flared there. She didn't want to know what it was so she turned away and swept up the heavy tray.

Gene seemed to take the hint and moved to the hallway and held open the door. It was an unnecessary task; the door stayed open on its own. Still, she thanked him graciously.

Before she could escape completely, he spoke again. "The child will be sent away."

"You, too?" she asked, resigned. "What is it about this little girl that has everyone so afraid?"

"I'm not afraid. I'm just warning you. Bonnie's presence in this town is divisive. The Lord wants all of us to love one another and live in harmony."

She gripped the tray tightly. "Except for Bonnie or her mother."

"Exactly."

"She's just one little girl."

"It only takes one pair of hands to do the devil's work."

Megan started down the hallway toward the parlor. She didn't know who was worse—Colleen or her husband. They both made her shudder.

She entered the parlor and realized she'd gone from bad to worse. The discussion there was already heated.

"It's disgusting," Mrs. Greeley said, reaching forward and pouring herself another cup of coffee.

"I can't imagine what happens there," another woman said.

There were ten ladies in all sitting in Colleen's parlor. She'd inherited their father's penchant for overfilling a room. Settee and sofas, chairs and tables were crammed into every available inch of space. Lacquered boxes and figurines littered the surface of the tables. Megan had to hold the tray while Mrs. Dobson made room. She set it down, then settled next to the older woman, all the while wondering how long she had to stay before she could politely escape.

"She sleeps in his bed," Mrs. Greeley said knowledgeably. Several of the ladies gasped. They were all the best of Landing society, such as it was. The butcher's wife, the widowed sisters who owned the founding farm, Colleen, Mrs. Dobson, Megan and a few others Megan didn't know that well.

Mrs. Dobson straightened on the overstuffed settee. "Anabell, I'm ashamed of you for spreading lies like that. Bonnie has her own room."

"But it's *next* to his, isn't it?"

"She's six years old," Megan said heatedly. "She gets frightened at night. She's recently lost her mother."

"Good riddance," Colleen said, then sniffed.

Megan started to stand up, but Mrs. Dobson placed a restraining hand on her arm. "Hush, child," she said softly. "Getting angry won't solve anything."

"Why are you here?" Megan asked in a whisper. "I thought you liked Justin."

"I do. Finding out what your sister has planned seemed the most sensible route."

Mrs. Greeley was speaking again. "Whether or not the child has her own room isn't really the point, is it? That girl is a problem. A blemish on our town and a reminder of the kind of sin we're struggling to get rid of. If Sheriff Kincaid doesn't agree to the church's most generous offer—" she paused while Colleen smiled modestly "—then I say he should be fired."

"He has a contract," one of the widows reminded her.

"I'll have Winston check with our lawyer this week," Mrs. Greeley said.

"Sheriff Kincaid is a good man, and we're lucky to have him," Mrs. Dobson said.

Colleen arched her eyebrows. "What an interesting point of view. Are we to ignore the fact that seven years ago he was run out of town for beating a prostitute nearly to death?"

"He was cleared of that charge," Mrs. Dobson reminded her.

"Yes, she cleared him of it. If I remember correctly, I heard that she knew him intimately enough to be able to say it wasn't him in the dark. Curious, don't you think? That he's taken such an interest in that same woman's child."

Megan knew what she was implying. "Bonnie is only six. Justin's—" She swallowed hard as eight pair of eyes focused on her. She should have called him Sheriff Kincaid. Too late now. "Justin was gone over seven years ago," she continued. "Bonnie couldn't be his."

"Oh, but we only have the child's word on her age. It's likely her mother lied about it, to save her lover."

Several of the women nodded in agreement.

Megan shook off Mrs. Dobson's restraining hand. "You're all mad. Bonnie is just a little girl, like your own children. She's done nothing wrong. Justin has done what you were afraid to do." She pointed at her sister. "You don't know the meaning of Christian charity. You're heartless and cruel. I don't know you anymore."

"Watch yourself, Megan. Don't forget who I am."

"I know exactly who you are. Who all of you are. I'm ashamed I once thought of you as my friends." Megan made her way out of the maze of tables. She gathered her shawl and reticule from a table by the hallway. "I'm sorry, Mrs. Dobson. I know you're on Justin's side, but you're wrong if you think these women can be reasoned with."

Colleen stood up. "Megan, you're hysterical. Come back and sit down."

"I won't." She started toward the door.

Colleen came after her and followed her onto the porch. "You're acting a fool," her sister said, her voice low and angry. "Don't fight me on this, Megan, or I swear I will destroy you."

"I'm not afraid of you." She started down the stairs.

"You will be," Colleen called after her. "You will be."

Chapter Ten

Megan stormed into the sheriff's office, pushing open the door so hard it bounced off the wall. She shouldered past it and stomped toward Justin's desk. He looked up at her and raised his eyebrows. At the desk to his left, a young dark-haired man sat staring at her, his mouth partly open.

She barely spared him a glance. "I must speak with you, Sheriff Kincaid," she said through clenched teeth. Fury filled her.

"So I gathered." He jerked his head toward the door. "Take a walk, Thomas."

"Yes, sir." Thomas scrambled to his feet and crossed the room to the hooks by the door. He picked up his hat. "Ma'am," he said, then closed the door behind him.

Justin motioned to the empty chair in the center of the room. "Have a seat."

"Thank you." She sat down, then stood back up. "I can't sit. I'm too angry."

She pulled off her shawl and dropped it onto the seat, then slipped her reticule off her wrist and placed it on the shawl. Her heart was pounding in her chest, her breathing came in rapid pants. Her anger energized her and frightened her in equal measures.

Justin rose to his feet and came around the desk. He leaned one hip on the corner of it and folded his arms over his chest. "You look mad enough to spit."

"I never spit. But you're right. I could today." She drew in a deep breath and faced him. "I've been visiting Colleen."

"That's enough to put anyone in a bad mood." A faint smile pulled at his firm mouth. It tempted her to let go of her temper, but she couldn't. The problem was too serious, and far too dangerous.

"Don't try to tease me," she said quietly. "She wasn't alone. Several women were having a meeting."

"I don't care."

"You should."

"Because they want to fire me?" At her start of surprise, he shrugged. "I'm not stupid, Megan. Of course Colleen and her friends want to get rid of me. I'm making them uncomfortable. However, I haven't done anything illegal. They can't hurt me."

"You're wrong." She stepped closer to him. Dark hair tumbled down his forehead and in the back to the middle of his collar. He needed a haircut. "They're saying ugly things. Rumors, really, but they could be damaging. They're saying that Bonnie sleeps with you."

He clenched his jaw and narrowed his gaze. "Who said that?"

"That's not important. Mrs. Dobson said it wasn't true, and of course the hotel staff can confirm it. Colleen also hinted—" Megan stopped midsentence and swallowed. She didn't want to say it. She was afraid of the truth. No, she was jealous of the past, of what he'd done with Laurie Smith. She lowered her gaze to her hands and noticed that she was twisting her fingers together. She tried to stop, but couldn't.

"Megan?" Justin touched her upper arm. "What did Colleen say that upset you?"

"She said Bonnie was your child. That's the reason you're taking such an interest in her."

She kept her gaze centered on his chest, at the place where his black vest met his white shirt. She watched the slow rise and fall as he breathed in and out. She waited for him to say the words that would destroy her forever.

He swore.

Megan jerked her head up. Her eyes widened in shock. Justin glared at her. "I won't apologize for saying the word. Your sister is a conniving, lying... Damn her." He flushed under his tan. "I never thought much of Colleen, and now I think even less."

Megan turned away. Her heart continued to pound hard in her chest, but now it felt heavier. He hadn't denied it. He was angry that Colleen had guessed the truth. She blinked several times before realizing she was fighting tears.

"I understand."

"I don't think you do." She heard his footsteps on the wooden floor, then felt his hands on her shoulders. "You believe her, don't you?"

"I don't know what to think. Laurie said she could recognize you in the dark, and you said you'd...done that with her." She bit hard on her lower lip. She wouldn't cry. She *wouldn't*. She'd given up tears long ago.

"You think so little of me. No wonder you didn't come away with me when I asked."

She closed her eyes. She could feel him standing behind her, but she refused to turn around. She didn't want him to see the pain in her face; she didn't want him to know how much she still cared. Had she ever stopped caring? Her affections had changed over the years, mostly because she'd changed, but they'd never died. There had only ever been Justin in her life.

"Yes, I visited Laurie on occasion. Yes, I did 'those' things with her. But not after you agreed to marry me."

She spun around and her hands came to rest on his chest. She stared up at him, at his deep brown eyes. The stranger was gone. This was the Justin she remembered, the young man she'd been in love with.

"We were engaged for several months," she said.

He nodded. "If Laurie had been pregnant with my child, it would have been obvious at the time of the attack." He smiled. "Can you imagine how fast that sort of news would have traveled in this town?"

"Like a fall wildfire." She felt her mouth tugging up at the corners. "Thank you for telling me that. You didn't have to. It—" she ducked her head in embarrassment "—it means a lot to me."

He touched his finger to her chin and tilted her face toward him. "You believe me?"

"Of course."

His mouth straightened. "Every time I think I understand you, you surprise me."

He took her hands in his and pulled them away from his chest. When she would have protested, he glanced significantly to the freshly washed windows at the front of the office. She nodded her understanding. Anyone coming by could have seen them. A wave of embarrassment swept over her as she thought about how they'd been standing so closely together. Then she forced her head higher and squared her shoulders. She'd done nothing wrong, she had nothing to hide. Colleen's never-ending threats had done the reverse of what her sister had intended. Instead of being cowed by her harsh words, Megan felt stronger.

"I recognize that stubborn tilt to your head, Miss Bartlett," Justin said, holding out the chair for her. "What are you planning now?"

She picked up her reticule and shawl and set them on the corner of his desk, then took the seat he offered. He went around to his chair and sat down.

"I was thinking brave thoughts," she admitted. "You know, defying Colleen, that sort of thing."

"Good for you. Tell me what else happened at this meeting of hers?"

"They want you fired, and one of them is going to have her lawyer look at the contract."

He shrugged.

"Don't you care?" she asked. "I thought this job was important to you. You said you came back because you have something to prove. If you lose your position, they'll have won."

He leaned forward, resting his forearms on the desk. "They can't win, Megan. I've accomplished what I set out to do. I've made peace with some of the townspeople, I've faced my ghosts. Leaving wouldn't be the worst thing in the world."

It would be to me, she thought, and realized she didn't want him to go. A dangerous line of thinking, she told herself. Things were different between them. They couldn't go back to where they'd been before. But she still didn't want him to go. Not yet. He might have made his peace with some people in the town but not with her. She and Justin still had something between them. They needed time to settle it.

"Let me take Bonnie," she said impulsively. "If you don't have her with you, they won't have anything to complain about."

"No," he said sharply. "You've always cared too much about what other people think. Since Mrs. Dobson smoothed the way, I find your willingness to take Bonnie now a little too convenient."

"That's not fair," she said, springing to her feet. "I was willing to take her, but you didn't give me a chance to say so. I might be concerned about what others think, but you've always been very quick to judge me. I didn't instantly say yes. Is that so awful?" She curled her fingers into her palm. "I'm a businesswoman. I spend most of my day at the store. My concern was for the child, not myself. I see now that she enjoys being in the store and visiting with people. But I didn't know that before. Mrs. Dobson is teaching her her numbers. I've started her with her letters. I was worried about her. Of course, you won't believe that, will you?" she asked bitterly. She glared at him. "You still think I'm the girl you left seven years ago. You still think I'm a fool and afraid, but you're wrong."

He leaned back in his chair. "A very nice speech. If only it were true. You've always been ruled by what other people think."

Not five minutes ago she'd been thinking about how much she cared for him. Now she wanted to scream in frustration. "You're not listening to me. I want to take Bonnie. I don't care what Mrs. Greeley, my sister or the entire town has to say about it. She's just a little girl. She needs a home and food and caring. I can provide those things for her."

"She already has them."

His quiet words doused her temper. Megan moved next to the desk and stared down at him. She thought about Mrs. Greeley's ugly accusations and her own sister's uncharitable attitude. No one understood why Justin had taken in the child. Megan had thought it had something to do with his and Bonnie's both being fatherless and growing up in a town that didn't want them. Perhaps that's how it had started, but it wasn't that way anymore.

"You care about her," she said with surprise.

"What did you think?"

"I wasn't sure. I thought it was an obligation, or that you were doing it because it annoyed people."

"I'm flattered by your high opinion of me."

She waved her hand at him. "Don't be that way. You know what I meant. But it's more than that. You really love her."

He shifted on his chair, but didn't deny her statement. "Bonnie's easy to love," he said. "She doesn't care about who my parents are or aren't. When she does find out, it will just bring us closer. She doesn't care about the town, or what it thinks. She gives with her whole heart. There's no holding back. No lies."

Megan raised her hand to her cheek as if she could feel the physical imprint of his verbal slap. Bonnie was easy to love for all the reasons she, Megan, had left him. Bonnie was honest, Bonnie didn't care about the town, Bonnie didn't lie. Bonnie gave without question.

Megan walked to the window and stared out onto the street. She recognized most of the people walking by or riding in wagons. She knew the sounds of Landing, the seasons, the changes. Justin was right. She'd loved her position, her reputation and good name more than she'd ever loved him.

Loving him had been the most wonderful thing she'd ever done, and the hardest. No matter how much she'd cared, there'd been no sense of rightness or freedom. In the deepest part of her heart, she'd known it wasn't meant to be. She didn't have the courage to walk away from everything. She didn't trust him enough. The fear had been bigger and stronger than both of them.

Those idyllic months, that perfect summer, was a lifetime ago. The girl who'd promised, then broken her word was gone. Only the fear remained. She clutched at the windowsill, feeling the wood and the cool panes of glass. She swallowed against the tightness in her throat.

What would happen if she let go of the fear? What would happen if she gave in and did exactly what she wanted to do? She closed her eyes and thought about what had happened to her mother. She could hear her father's voice telling Colleen and herself that their mother was dead. She'd known it was a lie, but she'd been too afraid to say anything.

Afraid. There was that word again. Would she ever escape?

She thought about explaining why. Justin would listen, he might even understand. She opened her eyes and drew in a deep breath. The explanations didn't matter. Not anymore.

"I'm sorry," she said. "I know the words don't mean much, but I want you to know what happened that day has never left me. I was wrong to react that way. I was wrong to say those things."

I was wrong not to go with you.

But she didn't say that. It was too late for those regrets. Telling him that truth would only make *her* feel better.

"I know you're sorry," Justin said. He stared at Megan standing in front of the window, at the stiffness in her back and shoulders, at the way she clutched at the window frame, as if it were all that held her upright. "That doesn't change the past, or the fact that I left here alone."

He'd waited seven years to hear her apologize and mean it. He would have thought he would feel more when she said those words. There was a time he would have sold his soul to hear them from her. Now they left him empty. It was nice of her to apologize, but it didn't change what had happened. It didn't erase her betrayal.

"I know it doesn't change those facts," she said without turning around. "I wish ... I suppose my wishes aren't important." She sighed. "Where did you go when you left here? I always wondered what became of you. The next morning you were just gone. The sheriff talked about rounding up a posse, then Laurie woke up and said you weren't the man who had attacked her."

Megan wore a blue calico dress, similar in style and print to the green one she'd worn the night he'd stayed for supper at her house. The night they'd kissed and he'd touched her breasts. The night he'd discovered that no matter how

he hated her, the passion between them flared as bright and
hot as it ever had. That evening her hair had been down in
a loose braid. Today she wore it up. She looked respectable. No blond curls defied her tightly twisted bun. She
should have looked severe.

She was merely beautiful. The afternoon sun filtered
through the window and illuminated the side of her neck.
He'd touched that sweet skin, had tasted it and kissed it.
She'd arched against him in pleasure.

He could have walked away from that. He could have
bedded her or not, and let her go. It wasn't the passion that
kept him wound up like a too-tight watch spring. It was the
fact that she'd wondered about him after he'd gone. That
she'd thought of him, perhaps even mourned him. He was
supposed to be tough and unflappable. Around Megan he
was as stupid as a day-old calf.

"You don't have to tell me if you don't want to," she
murmured, still not looking at him.

"It doesn't matter," he said. "I left here determined to
prove the entire town right about me. If they thought I was
a criminal, then I was damn well going to be one."

That got her attention. She turned slowly until she faced
him. The sunlight danced around her, outlining her shape,
creating a pale halo from hair.

"You never broke the law."

"Folks around here didn't seem to notice that. If there
was trouble, I was usually in the middle of it." He tilted his
chair back and raised his feet until his heels rested on the
corner of the desk. He crossed his ankles and smiled in re-
membrance. "I was going to rob banks. I figured it was the
quickest way to make a name for myself."

"You wouldn't do that."

He shrugged. "I rode north for days while I made my
plans. I came to a small town. I wasn't even sure where I
was. Wyoming, maybe. Anyway, there was a bank there.
I decided that was the one. I went into the local saloon. I
needed a drink for courage."

The memories quickly came back to him. The sawdust on
the floor, the scarred old bar and the gray-haired man serving drinks. There had been something kind about the bar-

keep's eyes, something that had made him confess his secrets.

"After a couple of whiskeys I started shooting my mouth off, bragging about what I was going to do. I even showed the barkeep my gun. He was real impressed."

Megan moved closer, then sank onto the chair on the other side of his desk. As she tilted her head, the light brushed against her cheek, turning her pale skin to cream and darkening her eyes to the color of a moonlit sky. Hazel to gray, fear to curiosity, curiosity to caring. He didn't want to know she cared. It wasn't enough.

"Did he help you?" she asked.

"Yeah, but not the way you'd think. He kept asking me questions about how I was going to rob the bank, then pointing out problems I hadn't thought of. After a few minutes, I realized I wasn't prepared to pull off the job." He grinned. "I felt awful then. I wasn't even a good criminal. When I admitted that to the old man, he smiled at me and told me it was for the best. Then he pulled out his badge and tossed it on the table. In addition to owning the saloon, he was the town sheriff."

Instinctively, Justin reached up for the badge on his chest. It was a different shape, a circle surrounded the star, but the meaning was the same.

"You must have been shocked."

"That's putting it mildly. I just about sh—" He glanced up at her and cleared his throat. "I about embarrassed myself something awful. But Williams was a fair man. He said I hadn't committed a crime and someone's just thinking about committing one wasn't enough to get a body arrested. Then he did the damnedest thing. He asked me if I needed a job, then offered to hire me as a deputy."

It was as if that had happened yesterday. Justin could still feel the intense jolt of pleasure, followed by anger as he'd assumed the old man was taunting him. Bullying him the way the children at school had until he'd gotten big enough to make them stop. But Williams had been serious. His kindly eyes had squarely held Justin's gaze as he'd explained the duties involved with being a deputy in the tiny town. Last of all Williams had pointed out that Justin would have to stop his plans for a life of crime.

"He believed in you," Megan said slowly. She leaned forward in her seat. "He was the first one. No one here believed. Not even me."

He didn't think she would figure it out so quickly. "I owe him a lot. I paid back some of my debt to him when we had trouble a while back, but it's not enough. He's the reason I came back here. He told me I had to make peace with this town before I could go on with what I wanted to do."

He'd been staring at the toes of his worn boots, but from the corner of his eye he saw Megan stiffen. "You didn't know I was going to be here, did you?" she asked.

You didn't come back for me. She didn't have to say it. He heard the words echoing in the silence of the small office.

"I thought you were married and gone," he admitted.

"Of course. Why wouldn't I be?"

The tightness around her perfect mouth could have been hurt. Except hurting would mean she still cared. And she couldn't. Not about him. He was still the town bastard, and she was the respectable Megan Bartlett. They'd never had a chance.

"What happens when you've made your peace?" she asked.

"We're leaving."

"You and Bonnie?"

"If I can't find a relative of hers, I'm going to adopt her."

"Because of what Williams did for you?"

He nodded. "And because I don't want to lose her."

"I wish I had known more back then." Megan stared at her lap. "I wish I could go back and change what happened between us."

"Why?" He lowered his feet to the ground with a thump. "Nothing would be different. You still wouldn't have left with me."

"I might have," she said softly.

"I don't believe you."

"I know. You think it's all about what other people think, and that I should just dismiss their feelings. It's not that easy. I was raised differently than you. I never learned how not to care about the opinions of others, especially people who matter to me. My father would have disowned me. I was only seventeen, Justin. I was wrong, but I wish you could understand how hard it was for me. How hard it still is."

"No, I don't understand." He waved his hand toward the window. "What is so frightening about Landing? Who has this hold on you?"

"I can't explain it."

He watched her as she reached across the desk and picked up the pocketknife that had been resting there. It was the same one she'd returned to him the night he'd been at her house. He still didn't know why she'd kept it all these years.

She turned the knife over in her hands and traced the initials with her fingertips. There was something familiar about the gesture, as if she'd done it a thousand times before. As if the knife had meant something to her. A dangerous line of thought, he told himself. One best left alone.

"Colleen doesn't like me working in the store," she said. "She thinks it's shameful that a single woman, a spinster, really, is engaging in commerce." She smiled slightly. "I think she's been reading too many society pages. It's not as if we have a social standing."

"You do in Landing."

She shrugged. "That doesn't count. But she keeps telling me that my working is wrong. That I should hire a man to manage the store for me and spend my time doing..." Her voice trailed off. "I'm not sure what I'm supposed to be doing."

"Looking for a husband," he offered.

"Yes, that, of course. Charity work, but only for those people whom she has deemed worthy."

He made a noise low in his throat. Megan glanced up at him. The gray had faded from her eyes leaving them hazel again, and sad. "You think this is funny. It's not to me. Colleen is the only family I have left. After what happened today, I'm not sure we'll ever speak again."

He tried to find it in his heart to be sorry, but he couldn't. Not being around Colleen might be best for Megan, if she could get over the guilt. He thought about her store, about

how well she was doing. If the wide variety of items for sale
and the steady stream of customers were any indication, she
was doing better than her father had done. He couldn't
imagine Megan sitting home knitting socks for needy orphans. Nor could he imagine her married to someone else.

"There were no proposals after mine?" he asked.

She placed the knife back on his desk and folded her
hands on her lap, looking as prim as a schoolgirl. "I was
engaged for a short time, but when my father passed away,
my fiancé didn't agree with my desire to postpone the wedding until after the year of mourning. He broke off the engagement and married someone else."

"You must not have wanted to get married all that badly
if you were willing to wait a year."

She straightened in her chair and glared at him. "You
have no business—" She paused, then grinned. "You're
right. I didn't love him. I couldn't. Not after—" she cleared
her throat "—that is, not after everything that had happened to me."

Not after you. Is that what she'd been about to say? God,
he didn't want to know that. It would change too much.
He'd accepted the fact that Megan was still in Landing and
that there was still something very strong between them. But
he was going to do his damnedest to make sure nothing
came of it. He'd been weak once before and she'd almost
destroyed him. He wouldn't survive a second time. But even
if he could, he wouldn't risk Bonnie's heart. He'd already
explained to the child they would be leaving in a year. He
knew she didn't understand the reference to time, but she
was willing to be with him. She trusted him.

Yet, the past flickered through Megan's eyes and taunted
him. He wanted to reach across the desk and pull her close
to him. He wanted to kiss her and forget his good intentions. He wanted to touch her and take her right here on his
desk, the rest of the world be damned.

Instead, he pushed her from him the only way he knew
how. "Did Colleen and your father approve of your fiancé, or did you keep that engagement a secret, as well?"

Her gaze held his steadily. "No more, Justin. You win this
game. I can't play anymore. I can't go back and forth,

tender, then hurting." She stood up and smoothed her palms against her skirt. "I'm not good enough for my family, yet, in your mind, I'm too good for you. I don't seem to belong anywhere."

"Make your own damn place, woman. Don't depend on me or anyone else to do it for you."

"That's so easy to say. I admire your ability to do exactly as you please. I've always thought it was a strength. One I couldn't seem to summon. You must be pleased we never married. Think how I would have disappointed you."

She wouldn't have at all, he realized, then found the answer to a question that had puzzled him for years. As her pain swept over him, shaming him, he knew why he'd never found another woman, why he'd so easily walked away from that widow in Wyoming who'd offered her ranch and herself. He wasn't afraid of being tied down. He was afraid he couldn't be with anyone but Megan. Worse, he was terrified that she'd been right about him. That they'd all been right. Even now he lived with the fear that he was nothing but a bastard and a troublemaker.

He'd let her walk away from him seven years ago because he'd feared the truth in her words. Hating Megan was so much easier than watching her come to despise him.

He stood and moved around the desk. When he was in front of her, he reached for her hands and clasped them in his. Hazel eyes watched warily, as if she feared this act of kindness was to lull her before he attacked again.

"I'm sorry," he said. "For everything. It's not my place to judge you." He brought her hands to his face and pressed her warm palms to his skin. Her mouth parted, tempting him. He ignored the need that flickered through him. "You're right. The game has gone on too long. I'll stay out of your way. I'll be respectful and distant. Even Colleen won't be able to fault my behavior around you."

She jerked her hands free. "Is that what you think I want?" she demanded.

"It's best."

"For me, I suppose. Oh, you make me so angry." She planted her hands on her hips. "You're as bad as Colleen, you know. She tells me what to think, what to do. Now you're doing the same.''

"I thought this is what you wanted."

"No." She shook her head, then pointed her finger at his chest. "You *assumed*. You didn't ask. No one ever asks. They tell me what they think is best."

"Dammit, Megan, I'm trying to do the right thing, here. You're the one who has to live in this town. I thought I was making it easier on you. You should be grateful."

"Don't tell me what I should be and stop swearing." She glared up at him. Her mouth trembled with fury.

"You don't want me to stay out of your way?" he asked, still confused.

"Oh!" She stamped her foot on the floor. "I want—" She drew in a deep breath. "I want to decide. I want to be the one who controls my life."

"So control it." His temper flared. "When you make up your mind, let me know."

He started to turn away.

"No," she said forcefully. She reached up and grabbed the front of his shirt, pulling him down until their faces were inches apart.

He recognized the light of battle in her eyes, and something else. Something decidedly passionate. "Megan?"

"Oh, hush up!"

She placed her mouth on his.

If she'd pulled a gun on him, she might have gotten his attention quicker, but he wasn't sure. Her hold on his shirt-front loosened. He could have pulled away. She parted her mouth slightly and swept her tongue across his lips. Then he couldn't do anything but wrap his arms around her and draw her close.

She pressed herself against him. He could feel her breasts against his chest. Her tongue moved back and forth until he opened to admit her. She plunged inside, sweeping past his teeth to duel with him. When he would have angled his head over hers, she reached up her hands and held him still. Despite his greater height and strength, she was the aggressor.

Her fingers plunged into his hair and massaged the back of his neck. Her teeth nibbled his bottom lip. She murmured his name, then pushed at his chest. He moved backward until the desk stopped him.

"Sit down," she said, between quick breaths.

He settled on the wooden surface and spread his legs. She stepped between his thighs. The sway of her skirts brushed against his groin. The slight caress made his hips flex toward her. Heavy need there pulsed in time with his rapid heartbeat, urging him onward to a madness he'd been careful to avoid in the past. Those long nights by the stream, even more recently, in Megan's bedroom, he'd been carefully in control. He'd set the pace and had been able to back away when the time came.

This afternoon, Megan had something to prove. He wanted to resist her, but he couldn't. Not when she touched him so tenderly. Not when her soft, unintelligible whispers came from her honestly. Not when there was nothing between them but the need.

"I decide," she said, moving her mouth from his lips to his jaw. He bit back a groan as small, perfect teeth bit down on his chin. "It's my choice. Not yours, not Colleen's, not anyone's."

Her hands moved to his chest and he felt her unfastening the buttons of his shirt. He thought of the window behind her and the fact that anyone could see in. He thought of how Megan would hate him if anything happened. She was igniting a fire she couldn't control. She expected a slight heat; he was ready to explode.

"Megan, you have to—"

"No," she said, and pressed her mouth to his chest.

He grabbed her upper arms, prepared to push her away. Instead, he held her close as her tongue stroked his flesh. She'd only undone three buttons, but it was enough to threaten him with madness. Moist warmth sent his blood racing. His maleness surged against his trousers. When one of her hands slipped to his thigh, he had to grit his teeth against the urge to press her untutored palm along him. Just the thought of her sweet caress had him thrusting toward her, the layers of her dress and petticoat preventing any real contact or satisfaction.

"Damn you, Megan," he growled.

She raised her head. Passionate desire darkened her irises, even as her lips curved up in a smile. "I've decided this is very nice."

"Might I point out to you that we're in my office?"

"I don't care." She leaned against him and slowly wrapped her arms around his shoulders. "I don't care about anything anymore. Kiss me, Justin."

He gave up. He'd never been strong enough to deny her in the past. Why would now be any different?

He had just angled his mouth on hers, when he heard the door open. Even as he pulled back, a loud gasp filled the room. Megan jumped and spun toward the sound. He didn't need to look to know who had caught them in each other's arms.

"Megan Bartlett, I've never been so ashamed in my life," Colleen said, her voice shrill enough to threaten the windows. "I can't believe what I'm seeing."

Megan stepped away from him and pressed her hands to her chest. "Colleen! What are you doing here?"

Her sister glared at her. "I had heard an ugly rumor at my house this afternoon. Mrs. Greeley said she thought the two of you were keeping company. Like a fool I defended you." Her pinched mouth twisted down. "You slut."

Megan flinched. Justin rose to his feet and stepped in front of her. "Hold on, Colleen. There's no need to call anyone names. If someone's at fault, it's me."

"I have no doubt of that, Sheriff, but don't bother defending my sister. I know she came to you willingly."

"I don't need defending," Megan said, pushing him out of her way. She moved closer to her sister. "It was just a kiss. So what? I haven't done anything wrong."

"Forgive me if I can't share your sense of humor. I *saw* what happened here. How could you? With him, of all people."

The contempt in her tone made him curl his hands into fists, but he didn't move. No matter what he thought of Colleen, she was still a woman, and his mother had raised him to respect that. Even when he didn't want to.

Megan shook with fury. "Leave him out of this. It's not his fight. It's between you and me. Yes, we were kissing. Do

you know why, my pure and holy sister? I wanted to. *Me.*"
She pointed at her chest. "I decided to kiss him. And if I
want to do it again, I will. You can't stop me."

Colleen stared at her, then slowly shook her head. "I pity
you, Megan. I've long suspected your unmarried state
preyed on your mind, but I didn't know it had gone so far.
It must be difficult to live with the knowledge that you've
never been wanted by a man. You're not terribly unattractive. Perhaps it was your independence that turned men
away. I can understand you're tired of being an old maid,
but did you have to pick him? Surely the pain of being alone
is easier to bear than the stigma of being with someone like
him."

Justin stepped toward her. "Just one damn minute, Colleen."

"Justin, no." Megan motioned him to stay back. She ad-
vanced toward her sister. "I won't listen to your lies," she
said. "I don't believe you anymore. You'll say anything to
make me pay attention to you, but it's too late. As for my
choosing Justin . . . It's the smartest thing I've ever done. I
wish I'd done it years ago."

Colleen laughed. "You think you know everything, Megan, but you don't. He's making a fool of you. Everyone in
town knows. Everyone is laughing. Megan Bartlett, that
fussy old maid, is chasing after the handsome sheriff. He's
using you to help him with that bastard brat and you think
he really cares. The whole town is laughing at you. I pity
you. I've always pitied you."

Justin reached toward Megan, but she slipped from his
grasp and ran to the door. She pushed past Colleen and ran
down the boardwalk. A quick glance told him she was in
tears.

He started to go after her, but Colleen closed the door
from the inside and leaned against it. "She doesn't need
you," she said.

"Get out of my way." He stalked over to her and glared
down menacingly.

"You don't frighten me." She smiled a cold sickening
smile. It was as if she were that five-year-old girl again,

lisping along with the other children in the school yard, singing "Justin is a bastard" in that endless refrain.

"Get out of my way."

She stepped aside. "Don't bother going after her. It's too late. You see, she can't be with you now. She'll never believe they aren't laughing. Even you can't fight that."

"She doesn't trust your lies anymore."

Colleen smiled again. "We'll see. Megan has always been easily controlled. A little rebellious from time to time, but she'll get over it."

"You really hate her."

"Of course not. I love her. She's my sister. I'm doing this for her own good."

Chapter Eleven

Megan stumbled through the back door of her store and hurried to her small office. Once inside, she turned the key in the lock, then leaned against the smooth wood. Her heart continued to pound wildly in her chest, her throat hurt and her eyelids felt puffy.

Yet none of that compared to the ache in her chest or the heat of the shame that continued to flow through her.

"Everyone knows the fussy old maid is chasing after the handsome sheriff. The whole town is laughing." Colleen's voice filled the small space as the words repeated over and over in Megan's mind.

She closed her eyes, but that didn't shut out the vision of people laughing. It didn't stop her from wondering if Justin found her pitiful. What if he did? What if he was using her as a source of amusement while he was here? She raised her hands to her face and cupped her flushed cheeks. Please, Lord, it couldn't be true. Not Justin. Anything but that.

Then she remembered what had happened just before Colleen had walked in. How she'd pulled him close and kissed him. Like some wanton. She'd thrust herself at him. What if he hadn't really wanted to kiss her back? What if he'd acted out of pity?

The thought was too horrible to consider. Yet she couldn't let it go. A strangled gasp of pain escaped her lips and she sank down until she was huddled on the floor, her hands clutching at her knees. The tears returned and flowed down her cheeks. She ducked her head toward her chest and let them fall.

"You're not terribly unattractive."

Megan bit down on her lower lip, but that didn't stop the sob. Not terribly unattractive. What did that mean? That she was simply ugly rather than hideous?

"Surely the pain of being alone . . . alone . . . alone."

Would she always be alone? She hadn't meant to be. She'd thought she would marry. But she hadn't. Colleen was right about that. After Justin had left, she hadn't been interested in being courted by anyone else. Then, when she'd finally gotten engaged, her fiancé had broken off with her. She'd had to deal with the store and mourning for her father. She hadn't had time to miss the man. By the time she'd figured out she could successfully run the business, there had been no one left to marry. Before she'd known how much time had passed, she was an old maid with no prospects.

That wasn't so bad, she thought, wiping away her tears. She didn't mind being alone, as long as people weren't laughing at her. As long as Justin hadn't kissed her out of pity.

Megan wasn't sure how long she sat there in the dark office. When the tears dried and her legs started cramping, she rose to her feet and walked over to the mirror on the wall. She studied her face, searching for signs that she'd been crying, trying not to think about her sister's pronouncement that she wasn't "terribly unattractive." Her eyes were swollen, her nose a little red. She poured cool water into the basin and splashed her skin until it tingled. She used the towel hanging on the hook to wipe away the moisture, then smoothed her still-neat hair.

She had a store to run and customers to take care of. Perhaps in time she would have the courage to ask Justin the truth, perhaps not. It didn't matter. She had done what she'd done, and all the wishing in the world wouldn't change that. She placed her hand on the doorknob and turned it. If the truth be told, she wasn't sorry about kissing Justin or having him kiss her back. Being with him, in his arms, had always been wonderful. She refused to let Colleen steal those memories.

Drawing in a deep breath for courage, she opened her office door and walked into the hall, then past the curtain and into the store. A half-dozen customers circulated between the aisles or leaned over display cases. Bonnie was playing with another little girl her age under Andrew's watchful eye. Her assistant had turned out to be wonderful with the child, sneaking her penny candy and playing endless games with her when the store was quiet.

"Megan!" Bonnie looked up and grinned. "We're playing pioneer. Andrew made us a log cabin for our dolls."

"Good for you."

The girl turned back to her playmate.

Megan moved down the center of the store. Watch as she might, nothing seemed different. No one looked at her knowingly. There were no secret smiles, nor was there condescending laughter. Little by little she relaxed. By the time she reached the pattern books, she could breathe easily.

"There you are," Mrs. Dobson said loudly and squeezed out from behind her desk. "I've been waiting for you to come back. Colleen is looking for you. She was very angry that you left."

Megan began straightening the bolts of fabric and didn't answer.

"Are you all right?" Mrs. Dobson asked, stepping closer. The older woman peered at her. "You've been crying."

Megan touched her hand to her cheek, then glanced self-consciously around the store. No one was paying any attention to them. "Colleen found me," she admitted.

The widow leaned closer. "You weren't the only one who left," she whispered. "A couple of other women walked out after you, saying that they expected better from the wife of a minister and that it seemed to them Sheriff Kincaid was exactly the right kind of man to have in town. I thought Colleen was going to swear, she was so angry. I stayed until the end. I wanted to know what she had planned." She shook her head. "They're going to have a lawyer look at his contract, but that's all. Even Anabell Greeley admitted her husband didn't want her making trouble." Mrs. Dobson smiled and bobbed her head. "You mark my words. That boy is going to convince everyone."

"Except my sister," Megan said softly, fingering a bolt of red calico. "Did she say anything else? Anything..." She paused. She didn't want to give away everything if she didn't have to, but she needed to know how much of what Colleen had said was the truth. "Anything about me?"

"About you and Justin keeping company?"

She stared at the older woman. Bright green eyes met her own. "Everyone knows," Megan whispered in horror. "Colleen was right." She started to turn away.

"Just hold on a minute." Mrs. Dobson grabbed Megan's arm and kept her in place. "Colleen didn't say anything. Mrs. Greeley mentioned the two of you seemed friendly at the social last Sunday. Colleen denied it, saying you had more sense than to associate with someone like him." Mrs. Dobson sniffed. "That girl is about as silly as an Easter bonnet on a hog. Even someone my age can see Justin Kincaid is a good man. You can tell a lot about a man by how he treats his mama and little children. Seems to me he did himself proud on both accounts."

Megan listened to her prattle on about Justin's attributes. She wasn't sure if Mrs. Dobson was telling her she approved of him, or trying to tempt her into setting her cap for him. It didn't matter. If people were talking, they weren't doing it around Mrs. Dobson. Which meant they couldn't be talking at all. The widow knew everything.

On the heels of relief came anger. Colleen had been difficult in the past and had twisted the truth to manipulate everyone around her. But never before had she been deliberately cruel.

"I can't believe she said those things," Megan said. "She's my own sister."

"What does that have to do with anything?" Mrs. Dobson asked.

"What? Oh, I'm sorry. I was thinking about something else."

"I'm here telling you Justin is handsome enough to tempt an old woman like me and you're thinking... Oh, Lord, have mercy, look over there."

Mrs. Dobson straightened to her full height, which was about three inches shorter than Megan's, and cleared her throat. Twin spots of pink flared hotly on her wrinkled cheeks.

Megan turned to look at what the woman had seen, then suffered her own attack of embarrassment. Justin had entered the store without either of them noticing. He stood less than ten feet away, obviously listening. Her gaze skittered away from his and as she glanced down she saw he'd brought back her shawl and reticule.

"Mrs. Dobson," he said quietly.

"Good afternoon." The widow swept past him and returned to her desk by the front window. When she was seated, she picked up a stack of letters and stared at them as if she'd never seen any like them before.

He moved close to where Megan stood. "We need to talk."

She nodded, then started toward the back of the store. When she'd ducked behind the curtain, she moved into the storage area rather than risk being with him in the close confines of her office. She stared at the canned goods she kept back there, and started counting the row of green beans. Even when she heard his boots on the wooden floor, she didn't lose her place.

"Megan?"

"Yes." Sixty cans of green beans. How many corn? She began to count again.

"Dammit, look at me."

Before she could turn toward him, or duck away, he placed his hand on her arm. Involuntarily, she raised her gaze to his face. Dark brown eyes stared at her. She was terrified of pity or disgust, but once again the stranger had returned. The high cheekbones, the square jaw and full mouth, the shape of his eyes, the dark layered hair were all familiar. But the essence of the man, his soul, was concealed. For once, she was grateful.

"No one's laughing," he said.

She could feel the heat starting to climb from her collar to her face. "Yes, well, they don't seem to be here, do they? I'm sure Colleen exaggerated to prove her point."

"She lied," he said flatly. "About everything."

"Not exactly. I *am* an old maid." His gaze became more intense and she had to turn away. "As for the rest of it, I'm sure it's nothing."

"Are you?" He placed her shawl and reticule on a shelf, then grabbed her other arm. He drew her closer and shook her gently. "Are you sure? I don't believe that. Everything she said was a lie. Every damn word. No one is laughing. No one even knows."

"Mrs. Dobson knows and Mrs. Greeley suspects."

"And I know."

She felt as if he'd stripped her naked and mocked her frailties. She twisted to get away, but he didn't release her. The burning in her eyes warned her that tears were not far behind. She struggled to keep them at bay. She wouldn't let him know how he'd hurt her.

"Stop struggling," he said, holding on to her more tightly. "I do know the truth and you're going to listen to it whether you want to or not."

"No! Just go away, Justin. You've done enough." She pushed at his chest, but he was as immovable as the building in which they stood.

"I haven't begun to do anything yet. You've always been the most beautiful woman I've ever known."

She froze. Her hands dropped to her sides. "What?"

"When you were fifteen years old, you came to church in a white dress with a pink ribbon at the waist. Your hair was long, down to your waist, and when you walked into the building that morning, I thought you were an angel."

Her mouth opened but she couldn't speak.

"Colleen is nothing but a pinch-faced prune. She's married to Gene Estes and she wants everyone to be as miserable as she is. She uses self-righteousness to hide the fact that she knows everyone dislikes her. As for chasing after me, if you ever kiss me like that again, I'm going to take your clothes off layer by layer, down to and including your French silk chemise and I'm going to show you exactly what goes on between a man and a woman. I don't care if we're alone in your house, in the store or in the middle of the road." His dark eyes blazed with passion. "You are a beautiful, desirable woman. Apparently, the entire town of Landing is populated by fools.''

He released her, but she couldn't seem to find the strength to move away from him. He reached between them and took her hand, then drew it toward him and pressed it against his groin. She blushed when she felt the hard ridge of his maleness. Before she could move her fingers to discover more, he let go of her wrist and stepped away.

"Do you understand?" he asked.

"Yes," she whispered. "I think so."

He stared hard at her mouth. "I don't suppose you'd consider kissing me right now?"

His words about stripping her bare and showing her the secrets between men and women filled her mind with erotic images. She didn't know exactly what happened in the marriage bed, but she'd heard enough to picture herself in Justin's arms, with his bare chest pressed against her exposed breasts. She should have been appalled, but instead she found herself swaying toward him.

He closed his eyes briefly and swore. "Don't tempt me, Megan. This afternoon you pushed me past the point of control. I'm doing my best to get it back, but I need your help."

Boldly she allowed her gaze to slip past the fire blazing in his eyes, past his full mouth and broad chest to his trousers, to the hardness straining against the wool. She'd done that to him. They hadn't even been kissing or touching and he was obviously... She didn't know exactly what he was, but it looked painful and intense.

"Can you keep Bonnie tonight?" he asked.

The abrupt change of subject startled her. "Yes, of course. Why?"

He grimaced. "I feel the need to get stone-faced drunk, and I'd rather she not be around to see that."

Drunk? Why? "Justin—"

"I've got to go." He turned on his heel and walked out of the storeroom. She could hear his footsteps on the wooden floor of the store, then the front door opening and slamming shut.

She stared at the place he'd been standing as if she could find the answers to her questions. Then she smiled. It didn't matter. Nothing mattered. Not Colleen or the town or any of them. Even if it wasn't true, Justin had made her feel pretty and feminine. She'd obviously inspired him physically. She giggled, then touched her hand to her heated cheek. Such wicked thoughts in the middle of the day.

She picked up her shawl and reticule and took them into her office. When she sat at her desk to do paperwork, she couldn't concentrate. Images of Justin kept showing up on her ledger pages. He'd only been back a short time, but he'd managed to win over most of the town. Colleen would continue to wage her campaign against him, as would Mrs. Greeley and some of the others, but Megan was beginning to think Justin would triumph. If two women had had the courage to walk out of her sister's meeting, then others might not go along with Colleen, as well.

Megan gave up her ciphering and leaned back in her chair. There had been so much fear for so long. She'd allowed her sister to dominate her life, threatening her every time she tried something Colleen didn't approve of. It wasn't right. And Megan had no one to blame but herself. Was she ready to stand up to her sister? Was she ready to risk her place in the town, possibly jeopardize her store?

Did she have another choice? Since their father had died, Colleen had been the one to say what was right and acceptable.

"It's not as if I want to become a dance-hall girl," Megan muttered. She just wanted a little life of her own. It didn't seem too much to ask.

She knew her sister well enough to suspect she would be getting a visit from her in the next couple of days. Colleen would stop by to make sure she was doing well, and to explain that she said those ugly things "for your own good."

Megan didn't believe that anymore. She was beginning to think her sister had never cared about her.

A knock at her office door brought her to her feet. Had Justin returned? She quickly stepped to the threshold and pulled open the door.

Instead of Justin's handsome face, her brother-in-law stared down at her. His few wisps of hair swayed gently as he shook his head back and forth.

"I don't know what to say," he murmured as he moved into her small office. "Colleen told me what happened. While I don't agree with what she said, I certainly share her concerns."

"Thank you," she said, forcing herself to smile. "If that's why you stopped by—"

"It's not the only reason." Gene held his dark hat in one hand. With the other, he touched her shoulder. "I came by to see you."

She stared up at him, not quite sure what he meant. Despite his regular features and impressively broad frame, she couldn't believe she'd once thought him handsome. There was an edge to him, an air of coldness. He had a vicious temper. She remembered him slapping the child at the social and tried to back away. The wooden cabinets containing her records stopped her.

"I wish you'd spoken to me, Megan. I *am* your minister."

"Of course you are," she said brightly. "Spoken to you about what?"

"Your needs." He moved closer. "I should have realized a woman all alone would feel a certain . . . emptiness inside. I could have helped you with that."

She panicked. He couldn't be saying what she thought he was saying. It didn't make sense. He was married to her sister.

She darted her gaze around the room, searching for an escape. He was standing between her and the only door in the room.

"I think you might want to consider some spiritual counseling."

"Spiritual counseling?" She could have laughed with relief. Colleen had gotten to her more than she'd realized. She was seeing danger where it didn't even exist. "Oh, that. I see. I'm rather busy at the moment, but it's so kind of you to offer."

His hand moved from her shoulder to her neck. His thumb traced a line along her jaw and he licked his lips. "I have much to offer you, Megan. You're a very attractive woman. Colleen can be difficult at times, as I'm sure you can imagine." He moved closer until his bulk pressed against her. "You must be lonely. I can help with that."

"No!" She pushed hard against his chest. When he didn't budge, she ducked under his arm. She turned around to face him and backed up until the door was behind her. "You've misjudged me and the situation, Gene. You're my sister's husband." A shudder raced through her.

He glared at her. The warmth fled his eyes leaving only anger. She'd disliked her brother-in-law before, but she'd never feared him. A cold knot formed in her stomach. "I see."

"I don't think you do," she said quickly. "I understand how I might have led you to believe . . ." She paused. She'd never been a very good liar, but the last thing she needed was Gene for an enemy. "I appreciate your kindness to my sister and myself. Let's simply put this unfortunate incident behind us."

He began moving toward her. Megan gripped the door handle behind her, prepared to jerk it open and throw herself into the hallway. From there, people in the store would be able to hear her screams. Oh, but she didn't want to have to do that.

"Whore," Gene said.

"What?"

"Daughter of Satan. You've tempted me from the path of righteousness." He glared at her, his eyes wide, his mouth moist and disgusting. "I will call you out."

"What does that mean?"

"Sunday morning I'll denounce you as the sinner you are. I'll expose your seductive evilness before the townspeople, and they will all turn their backs on you."

"That doesn't make any sense. You're the one who started touching me."

"Your body is a temptation. Your hair." Before she could move away, he snaked out his arm and grasped her bun in his hand. He jerked hard, making her yelp in pain. Several strands fell free, over her chest. He moved closer and reached for them.

"No!" She twisted the door handle and dived into the hallway. Gene followed.

"Colleen was right. She told me she found you in the arms of that man. I didn't believe her, but you're the liar, not her. I will expose your secrets to the world, Megan Bartlett." He placed his hat on his head and started toward the back door.

"I haven't done anything," Megan called after him.

He turned toward her. "Your soul is black with sin."

"You don't know that. You don't know me at all. None of you do." She motioned with her arm. "This entire town thinks it knows me, but you're all wrong. You want to denounce my sin. Fine. But before Sunday, I swear I'm going to give you something worth denouncing. You'd better hurry home, Gene. If you thought Colleen was upset today, wait until she finds out what I'm going to do next."

He glared at her. "May God have mercy on your soul."

"And on yours," she called. She balled up her fists, wanting to do something physical, but not knowing what.

"Megan?"

She spun toward the sound and saw Mrs. Dobson standing in the store, holding the curtain to one side.

"I couldn't help overhearing part of your conversation with Mr. Estes. Is there a problem?"

"No," Megan said automatically. "Yes," she amended. "There's a big problem. Gene thinks I'm a daughter of Satan." She stared after her brother-in-law. "The worst of it is, I've never done one really bad thing in my whole life. I've been slightly wicked from time to time, but that's all."

Mrs. Dobson stepped into the hallway and let the curtain fall behind her. "What happened? What did he do to you? Your hair is all loose."

Megan laughed. There was a slightly hysterical edge to the sound. She closed her lips tightly and covered them with her fingertips.

"Oh, Megan." The older woman moved closer and held out her arms. "Hush, child. You'll be fine."

Megan let herself be folded into Mrs. Dobson's embrace and pulled against the widow's ample bosom. She started shaking and knew the tears weren't far behind.

"I think he wanted to kiss me," she said, her voice shaking. "He said he understood that a woman like me has needs. It was awful."

"I've never liked that man."

"Me, neither. But he and Colleen are the only family I have. I don't think either of them is ever going to speak to me again."

Mrs. Dobson patted her back. "That isn't such an awful thing."

"I know. Except Gene is going to tell the entire town I tempted him. I'll be ruined." She drew back and looked at the other woman. "I wouldn't mind so much if I'd done something bad. At least then there would be a reason."

"You've always been a good girl." Mrs. Dobson smoothed Megan's hair off her face.

Megan squeezed her tight, then stepped back. "Why do I care so much what other people think?"

"Because that's a sensible attitude."

But was it? Megan wasn't so sure anymore. She was about to get into trouble and Gene was the one who had made advances at her. At his own wife's sister. It was appalling. She could try telling the truth, but who would believe her? Mrs. Dobson did already. Justin would. But what other citizen would take her word over the preacher's? Sunday morning he would call her a sinner before the entire congregation and there was nothing she could do to stop him.

"I'm ruined."

"Hardly that. You'll put this behind you. In time—"

"No. I don't want to wait. It's not fair. It's never been fair. I'm tired of being judged by other people's standards and rules. I'm tired of being the one who always has to bend."

"Be careful, Megan. Don't do something you're going to regret. Don't forget that you're the person who has done the most judging. You judge yourself the hardest."

"You're right. And for what? What insignificant sin have I committed?"

She paced toward the back door, then turned and started the return trip. She stopped suddenly. The plan came to her fully formed. It was impetuous, foolhardy, even. She knew if she didn't do it, she would never forgive herself. She'd promised to shock the town before Sunday. This was the best way she knew how. "Will you keep Bonnie tonight?"

"Of course. Why?" Green eyes narrowed. "What are you planning?"

"To sully my reputation."

Mrs. Dobson put a restraining hand on Megan's forearm. "Once your good name is lost, you can never get it back."

"After Sunday I won't have one, anyway. What does it matter?"

The older woman studied her. "I hope you know what you're doing."

"No, I don't. Probably for the first time in my life." Megan ducked into her office and came out holding her shawl and reticule. She paused. "I appreciate everything. Don't worry, I'll be fine. I promise."

Mrs. Dobson nodded. "I'll be home tonight if you need somewhere to go."

Megan bent down and kissed the old woman's papery cheek. "Thank you for understanding."

"I was young and impetuous, once." She smiled, then her mouth straightened. "Be sure, Megan. Very sure."

"I am. I have to do this. I'm not sure why, or what I'm going to prove, but at least I can say that I've done one impetuous thing in my life without considering the consequences." She draped her shawl over her shoulders and stepped into the store.

One of the Greeleys' boys was staring longingly at the candy display. His mother kept him on a meager allowance. Megan marched over to him and pulled out a handful of sweets from the closest jar. "Winston, all this candy can be yours if you'll take a message to the sheriff's office for me. Can you do that?"

The boy's eyes widened as he stared at the bounty in her hands. "Yes, ma'am. Right away."

"Good." She placed the candy in a paper and twisted it into a cone. Then she quickly wrote a note and folded it twice. "The candy will be here when you get back. Just ask Andrew."

Winston grabbed the note from her and raced out the door. "I'll be right back."

"I'm sure you will be." She smiled, then told Andrew to give him the candy when the boy returned. She asked her assistant to close the store at the regular time, and left quickly, before her courage deserted her.

Forty minutes later, she stared at herself in the glass over her dresser. The Worth gown fit as well as it had when she'd bought it in St. Louis three years before. Unfortunately, the bodice was as low-cut as she remembered. She tugged at it, but it didn't budge. It clung to her breasts, exposing far more than it covered. She tried to convince herself the rosettes cast a shadow that concealed her curves. She turned a little in front of the mirror and knew she exaggerated the truth.

Aside from the shameful bodice, she was pleased with the dress. The creamy silk made her skin glow, and the flounced skirt reduced her waist to nothing. Ribbons and rosettes cascaded down the bustled back, and the pleated under-skirt swished as she walked.

There was no time to curl her hair. She pulled out the remaining pins and brushed it smooth. She drew the top half up into a loose bun and pinned it in place. On either side of her ear, she made a braid about an inch thick, then weaved the two braids around the remaining loose hair, drawing it up off her neck into a coiled rope. She twisted the rope, then pinned it under the first bun. Several rosettes had been sewn onto a ribbon. She pinned these around her crown and secured loose ones to various points on her braid.

She stepped back to study the effect. She almost didn't recognize herself. Perhaps it was for the best, she thought, smiling nervously. If she did recognize herself, she might lose courage, and she didn't want that to happen now.

Her finishing touches included a pair of gloves made of the same silk as the dress and embroidered with rose-colored flowers, and a small silk bag. She glanced once more in the mirror, then reached up and pulled at the tiny sleeves that barely rested on her shoulders. At least it was warm outside. If it had been cold, or raining, her entire plan would have been ruined. For once, the weather cooperated.

She made her way down the stairs, then outside toward the path to town. Fear knotted her stomach but she ignored the sensation. She was tired of doing what everyone expected. Of being the fussy old maid. She was determined, for once, to give the good citizens of Landing something to talk about over their evening meal.

Chapter Twelve

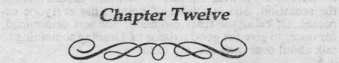

Justin stared out the hotel's front windows, then glanced back at the note in his hand. Megan had asked him to meet her here. He looked up at the clock above the great stone fireplace. She'd said to be here in an hour. She was ten minutes late.

Something was wrong. He could feel it in his gut. It was the same feeling that had caused him to push Sheriff Williams down suddenly when they'd walked into the bank during a holdup. His fast actions had saved the older man's life. He'd almost taken the bullet instead, but his aim had been better than the robbers. He would gladly do it a hundred times over for his friend. Williams had been the first and so far only person to believe in him.

He reminded himself Megan had believed, but he knew it was only while it had been easy to do so. If things got hard again, she would disappear as quickly as she had before.

So why did she want to meet with him? And why at his hotel? He returned his attention to the window and watched the people along the boardwalk. Her reasons had something to do with what had happened that afternoon. He shook his head, wishing his mother hadn't taught him to respect women. Or that Colleen could spend five minutes in male form. Then he could show her exactly what he thought of her and leave her as broken and bleeding on the outside as she'd left her sister on the inside.

He glanced back at the letter, as if the few scrawled words would give him answers to his questions. Had he said the right things to her at her store? Had he convinced Megan that Colleen was lying about all of it? He wished he was one of those educated men with a couple of ten-dollar words to help her see the truth. He wished a lot of things.

The feeling in his gut got stronger. He looked up through the sparkling clean hotel window. Across the street a woman paused to check for wagons before stepping daintily out onto the road. She had to pick up her skirt to keep it from trailing in the dirt. The train was long, so she was exposing her entire foot and a bit of ankle. Another time he might have enjoyed the unexpected view. Today, he didn't even notice it. He was too busy staring at the woman's face and dress.

"Megan?"

Not only had growing up above the saloon with whores in the neighboring rooms given him an appreciation of fine lingerie, he recognized an expensive gown when he saw one. She would have looked at home at a fancy dress ball somewhere back East. Or maybe even in a French drawing room. But in Landing, Kansas, dressed as she was, she was as foreign as Napoleon brandy.

He wasn't the only one who noticed. Several people stopped and stared as she stepped onto the boardwalk, then paused in front of the hotel. He walked around to the open front door and watched as she nodded graciously.

"Good afternoon, Mrs. Jones. Lovely day we're having."

The other woman spoke, but he couldn't hear what she was saying. Megan's voice, however, rang out clear and strong. "My gown? It's beautiful, don't you think? Yes, all the way from Paris, France. It's a Worth gown. I bought it in St. Louis. If you'll excuse me, I have an appointment to see Sheriff Kincaid. In the hotel . . . What? Yes, we're meeting in the hotel. Just Sheriff Kincaid and I. Good day."

She came through the open door, smiling as if she'd just learned a wonderful secret.

"Justin, how good of you to be waiting for me down here. It wasn't necessary, though. I'm sure I could have found my way to your room."

"I don't know what kind of a game you're playing, but I won't be a part of it. We're not going to my hotel room and that's final."

"Oh, how disappointing." She pursed her lips into a pretty pout.

"Megan, what the hell is going on?"

"You haven't said anything about my dress. What do you think?"

She walked in a small circle in front of him, giving him a clear view from all angles. Megan had always been beautiful. Earlier that day he'd been telling the truth when he'd said she was the most beautiful woman he'd ever seen. With her heart-shaped face and large hazel eyes, she could capture any man's attention. Her womanly shape had been tempting him since she'd first started filling out. She was the kind of woman a man dreamed of being with. It didn't matter whether she was dressed in simple, worn calico or stunning silk. At least, that's what he told himself at first.

As Megan continued to turn in front of him, he found his heartbeat increasing and his palms growing damp. He'd never imagined she could be more lovely, but he'd been wrong.

The elegant gown clung to her breasts, leaving most of her cleavage exposed. He swallowed hard. Rose-colored flowers perched in the deep vee, the soft petals providing the only hint of decency. From the top of her intricately done hair, to her silk-covered shoes, she was a female designed to reduce a man to incoherence. He was far from immune.

"I'm trying to decide if your silence is a good one or a bad one."

He cleared his throat. "You look perfect."

She arched her delicate eyebrows. "Perfection. That's exactly what I'm trying to leave behind. Still, it will have to do. Perhaps we can work on something else, privately."

She winked slowly. Suggestively. His blood boiled, coursing through his body, raging through his chest and exploding into his groin. He was hard and hungry in less than a heartbeat.

Who was this woman?

She tossed him a quick smile, then turned toward the front desk. Newt stood there, his mouth hanging open. When her gaze lingered on him, he blushed.

"Hello, Newt," she said in a sultry whisper.

"Ma'am." His voice cracked.

"What room is Sheriff Kincaid staying in?"

"Two-twelve. Miss Bonnie's next door in two-eleven."

"Thank you." She moved toward the wide curved staircase that circled down to the ground floor.

"Ma'am, Miss Bartlett, you can't go up there."

She paused and looked at the clerk. "Why not?"

He got redder. "It ain't, ah, isn't right."

"Oh, is that all?"

"Megan?" Justin said, still not sure what she was after.

She looked at him. "Come now, Justin. We have things to talk about."

His gaze narrowed. He took in the fancy gown, the faintly suggestive tone in her voice, the unexpected cleavage. It was hard to think straight when every time she looked at him all he could stare at were her pale white breasts.

Two men entered the hotel. Their conversation came to an abrupt halt when they spotted her. Justin didn't bother turning around. He didn't care who they were. All that mattered was Megan. His gaze drifted down her bare arm to her hand holding onto the banister railing. She was gripping the wood as if she was terrified of falling. Or just plain terrified.

The fog in his brain lifted and he could think again. He looked at her other hand. She was holding on to her bag just as tightly. He could detect a faint tremor in her body. She was out to prove something. But what? Why this way?

"Are you sure?" he asked quietly.

Their eyes met. The hazel irises had faded to gray, but he didn't know what emotion had caused the change. Fear? Anticipation? Determination? He could read all of them there.

She nodded. "For the first time in a long time, I'm very sure."

She started up the stairs. With three long strides, he was beside her. He offered her his arm. When she took it, he could feel her shaking. At the curve of the staircase, he paused, bringing her to a halt. "There's still time," he said, motioning to the men openly watching them from the lobby. "You've flaunted yourself, but you haven't come to my room yet. You could go back."

"I'm never going back." She straightened her shoulders, and walked calmly to his hotel-room door.

He fumbled with the key. Her closeness was making him as nervous as he'd been his first time. Not that anything was going to happen between them. He didn't know what her game was, but it didn't matter. He wasn't going to play.

"Nothing's going to happen between us," he said as the key finally slipped into the slot and he opened the door.

She glanced up at him and smiled. Her hazel-gray eyes met his, then skittered away. "I'm sure I don't know what you're talking about."

"Yeah, I'm sure, too." He followed her into the room.

He thought about not closing the door behind them. That would give them the illusion of convention, if nothing else. He shook his head. Who was he kidding? Megan Bartlett had just walked into his hotel room. Half the town already knew about it and the other half would know within the hour.

He shut the door behind him, then stood beside it with his arms folded over his chest. She circled the large bedroom, glancing at the armoire, at the wing-back chairs by the fireplace, then moving over to the bay window and leaning over the window seat to look out.

"You can see the entire town from up here," she said. She gave him a quick smile over her shoulder, then turned back to the view. "People are stopping and staring at the hotel. Do you think they've already heard that I'm here?"

"I'm sure of it."

"How fascinating. I suppose I've created a scandal."

He moved to the foot of the four-poster bed and grasped the column of dark wood. It wasn't just that damned dress, although it was making him hot and hard. Being this close to Megan, seeing her, knowing they were alone and remembering the kisses they'd shared not three hours before was enough to make him want to pull her onto the wide bed in front of him and have his way with her.

He wasn't going to do that. No matter how she tempted him. At least he was going to do his damnedest not to do that, he thought grimly as she placed one knee on the window seat and bent forward to get a better view. Her action raised her bustle, allowing the yards of silk to drape over the length of her legs. The position was provocative. He turned away.

"Why are you here?" he asked.

"I thought we could talk."

"What?" He glanced at her. She'd turned back toward the room and was perched on the edge of the window seat. Her hands were folded modestly in her lap, her gaze firmly locked on the floor. She was the picture of innocence, except for the expanse of pale bosom that rose and fell with each breath. If she took a really deep breath, he wondered if she would pop out, then got disgusted when he realized he was holding his own breath in anticipation. "What do you want to talk about? No. First tell me why you wanted to talk in my room. And why the hell you're wearing that dress."

She stood up quickly and smiled. "My Worth gown? Isn't is wonderful? I've had it for three years." She held the skirt out at the sides and glanced down at the fabric. "It was the most beautiful thing I'd ever seen. I knew I shouldn't buy it. After all, where was I going to wear it in Landing?" Her smiled faded. "But I bought it, anyway. What was it you said? Another of my guilty secrets."

She released her skirt and walked across the floor until she stood directly in front of him. He could smell the rose water she'd used in her hair.

"I don't expect you to understand," she said quietly. "You think I'm playing a game, but I assure you, I'm quite serious. I've realized that I'll be judged no matter what happens, so I want to do something wicked. Just once. All my life I've done the right thing. The expected thing. I know you can't understand that, either. You've always flouted convention."

"I do understand," he said, risking contact by taking one of her gloved hands in his. At least he couldn't feel her soft skin, even if the heat of her was enough to drive him mad. "More than you might think. But are you sure this is what you want? Have you given enough thought to what you're doing?"

"No." Her soft laughter made him smile in return. Megan's almond-shaped eyes glowed with humor as she wrinkled her nose. "I haven't thought about it at all. That's the perfect part. I'll stay an hour. Long enough to ruin myself. Then I'll go home. I hope you don't mind."

"That you're using me as the method for your social demise?" Oddly enough, he did mind. He tried to keep the edge from his voice, but he knew she'd heard it. She withdrew her hand from his.

"You're angry."

"No, disappointed. You didn't give me a choice. Did it ever occur to you that one of the things I liked best about you was your innocence and pure reputation?"

She backed up slowly. "I wasn't sure you liked me at all, anymore. As for my reputation, why would you care about that? You've always scolded me for caring about what other people think. You've mocked my concerns for respectability." When she reached the window seat, she sat down in a cloud of silk and flowers. She glared at him. "Make up your mind. Either you like my position and standing in this town, or you want to help me dispose of it. You can't have both."

She was right, he thought, chagrined. Her willingness to let her life be governed by what other people would think made him furious, and frustrated. If not for what her family would have said and done, she would have left with him seven years ago. He studied her, the fire in her eyes, the faint color on her cheeks. Or would she? Perhaps she had simply used her family as a convenient excuse. Maybe she'd never planned on marrying him at all. Maybe...

He rubbed the bridge of his nose. He could go crazy thinking about this. The past was long over. He would never know what could have been. It didn't matter anymore. Nothing mattered except the fact that coming back to Landing had been a mistake. Williams had been dead wrong on this one.

"You want a drink?" he asked suddenly, crossing the room to the tray Alice kept set up beside the fireplace.

He poured two fingers' worth of brandy into an expensive crystal glass, then turned and raised his eyebrows expectantly.

Megan blinked. "I've never had spirits before." She blushed. "Except for that sip from your flask. It wasn't very good."

He thought of the cheap liquor he'd barely been able to afford. "This is better," he promised.

She looked doubtful, then nodded.

He carried the drink to her, then returned and poured himself a slightly more generous serving. After capping the decanter, he raised the glass. "To your soiled reputation."

She smiled tightly and took a tentative sip. She didn't gag, but her grimace had him fighting back a smile.

"Yes, it's much better," she lied, and quickly leaned forward to place the drink on the nightstand.

She didn't fall out of her bodice. He was torn between being grateful and disappointed. It was going to be a long hour. He glanced around the room, searching for the safest place to sit. Probably outside, he thought humorlessly. He settled on one of the velvet wing chairs by the fireplace.

"What are we going to talk about?" he asked as he rested one booted ankle on the opposite knee.

She looked at the ceiling as if searching for a topic. Her fingers tapped together. "Bonnie!" she said at last. "She's learning to read. Just yesterday..."

But he didn't listen to what Bonnie had done just yesterday. He took another sip of the brandy and watched Megan speak, without hearing the words. Her mouth moved, and she smiled often. Her arms raised as she used her hands to describe something. Her bare skin gleamed like the silk dress she wore. A shudder raced through him as he thought of how she would feel if he was to touch her, stroke her, love her into mindlessness.

With her hair done up so intricately and her dress billowing around her, he thought how he'd like to take her in his arms and dance with her. Around and around the room until they were too exhausted to do anything but hold each other.

His direct gaze unnerved her. He could tell by the way she darted quick glances at him, then looked away. Her presence here would start a scandal the likes of which Landing hadn't seen in years. Probably not since he'd left. He shouldn't have let her come in his room. She'd caught him so off guard, he hadn't been thinking. It was too late now, he told himself. The cards had been dealt and she would have to play the hand. As he had seven years ago.

"You're not listening to me," she said.

"Sorry. What were you saying?"

"It doesn't matter. Is there any news on the investigation into Laurie's murder?"

He shook his head. He didn't like thinking about that, but it was better than wondering if Megan was wearing her French silk and lace undergarments. "Nobody here knows anything, either about Laurie's murder, or the murder of the saloon girl four years ago. I've been thinking of going to neighboring towns and seeing if anyone there had heard of similar crimes in their area."

"Why would they?"

"I know it's not likely," he admitted. "However, if other towns have had the same sort of murders, we might be able to find a pattern."

She shivered. "It's so awful. Why would anyone do something so horrible?"

"People do strange things."

"This investigation is very important to you, isn't it? Is it because you don't want to let your friend, the sheriff, down?"

"Partly." He took a sip of the brandy. He hadn't poured enough to affect him, but he wished he had. He'd planned on coming back to his room tonight and getting drunk. He didn't know how else he was going to forget what had happened this afternoon in his office. Even now he could feel Megan's eager body pressing up against him, and her tongue penetrating his mouth. He bit back a groan.

Forget it, he ordered himself. Think of something else. Think of the murders.

"Part of it is Williams. He would expect me to do my best. Part of it is that someone died."

"But it's about you, too, isn't it? You want to prove yourself."

He raised his eyebrows. "You see too much."

"I know you." She shifted on the window seat, settling into a corner.

Justin set the drink down, then leaned forward, resting his elbows on his knees and clasping his hands together. His boots needed polishing, he thought absently. "Being here isn't what I thought it would be. Landing is different. Or maybe it's me. Sometimes I wonder if any of this makes a damn bit of difference. Williams was so sure I had to make peace with the past."

"Have you?"

"Maybe. I'm beginning to understand that I contributed to my own reputation. Like the time somebody burned down those three outhouses. Everybody said I'd done it, so I didn't bother telling them otherwise. I figured no one would have believed me." He shook his head. "A dumb idea. I should have stood up for myself."

"You were just a child."

He almost asked her what her excuse was for not believing him, but he didn't. He liked the quiet conversation and the slightly charged air in the room. He didn't want to change anything between them; he didn't want Megan angry. Not tonight. Not at him. Later they would have to discuss the past and place blame, but not right now.

"I've figured out that there's always going to be folks who don't like me. That's fine. I probably don't want them to like me."

"I wish I could be more like that," Megan said softly. She studied her fingernails. "Are you still planning on leaving in a year?"

"Unless they fire me first. As you know, some of the ladies in town are intent on doing just that."

"A lot of them are also changing their minds. Mrs. Dobson told me a couple of women left Colleen's meeting after I did. They said you were the right kind of sheriff for our town."

"It's not enough to keep me here."

"Oh."

It was the way she said the single word that caused him to look up at her. She was staring at him intently, as if she'd never seen him before. He straightened slowly.

He wanted to demand to know what she was thinking. At the same time, he reminded himself he couldn't do this again. It was too dangerous. The citizens of Landing changing their minds about him wasn't enough to keep him in town. Unfortunately, a word from Megan was.

He'd been running from the truth since the day he'd arrived. There was no point anymore. The truth was sitting in the window seat not ten feet from him. She'd always been the one to get to him. She would never believe that, no matter how many times he told her. She would never know the extent of her power, or his love. In a way he was glad. If she didn't suspect the truth about that, she would never know how much of him she'd destroyed when she'd sent him away.

He wanted to hate her for making him weak. He couldn't. He'd spent his whole life caring about Megan Bartlett. He knew now he always would.

The truth hit him square in the eye, like an unseen first blow in a fight. He jerked his head back, reeling from the impact. Damn it all to hell. He couldn't escape her.

"Why are you looking at me like that?" she asked.

"Like what?"

"As if you'd like to strangle me . . . and kiss me, all at once."

He straightened and gulped down the rest of his brandy. "I would like to do both."

Her big eyes widened. "I wouldn't mind the kissing part, but I'd prefer not to be strangled."

He swallowed. Hard. "That's the brandy talking. I warned you what would happen the next time we kissed. Have you forgotten so quickly?"

She flushed the color of the rosettes sewn on the bodice of her gown, then wiped her hands on her dress and slowly rose to her feet. "I—I haven't forgotten. I'd still like you to kiss me."

"You'd sound a lot more sincere if you'd stop shaking with fear, little girl." He told himself the growl in his voice was from anger and not sexual anticipation. Megan didn't know what she was asking. He had to be strong for both of them. It would have been easier if she would quit looking at him as if he was the most wonderful man in the world—they both knew that wasn't true—and as if she wanted him as much as he wanted her.

"I'm a little nervous," she admitted, taking a step toward him. "But it's not the brandy talking, it's me. I only took one sip. You were wrong. It doesn't taste better."

"That's the only thing I've been wrong about today," he muttered. "It's time for you to go, Megan. You've stayed in my room, you've shown everyone in town. Try as you might to change my mind, I'm determined to send you home as innocent as you were when you arrived."

"Is that a challenge?"

He nearly groaned aloud. He didn't need her untutored seduction. He wasn't strong enough to resist her. He'd never been strong enough.

"Why the sudden change?" she asked, stepping closer. "Seven years ago, you were furious at me for wanting to keep our relationship and engagement a secret. Now you're the one who wants to hide everything."

"I'm older and wiser, and you should be grateful one of us is still talking sense." He wanted to stand up, but he knew if he did, she would move closer. He didn't think he would have the strength to let her go once he'd touched her, or worse, once she'd touched him. He wasn't sure he could make it to the door before they came in contact with each other. His only hope was to force her away with words, to hurt her enough that she would leave on her own.

"I'm talking the best kind of sense," she said and took the last step between them. When she was directly in front of him, she leaned forward and placed her gloved hands on the arms of his chair.

An audible groan escaped his lips. Her cleavage was directly at eye level. It would take a better man than himself not to look, and everyone knew he was just the town bastard. He feasted visually on her generous white breasts, remembering how they'd filled his hands, recalling the tightness of her nipples, the sweetness of her through the thin layer of her silk chemise. His fingers curled into his palms as his hardness throbbed heavily against the placket of his trousers. *Dear God, give me strength.*

"Kiss me, Justin. I want to know. I need to know, just once. After today, I won't have another chance. I'm going to be ruined, anyway."

She closed in on him. Her mouth was inches away. He could feel her warm breath on his face. Her silk skirt rustled against his legs.

He'd wanted her since the first day he'd seen her, nearly a lifetime ago. He'd loved her just as long. For years he'd denied himself the one thing he wanted most, coveted most, needed most.

He stood up, forcing her to take a step back. Her eyes held his. Their hazel depths asked questions, but there was no fear in them. Only the purest of desire mingling with excited expectation.

She trusted him. The weight of that trust nearly brought him to his knees. He knew it was wrong. He knew there would be regrets. He could handle his own. He would regret the briefness of this moment, the realization that none of this had anything to do with him and everything to do with what she'd decided she had to prove.

Her regrets would destroy him. She would regret what they'd done. She would hate him.

"You'll be sorry," he said softly.

"Never." She placed a gloved hand on his chest.

Did she know she lied?

"Leave now, because if you don't, I'm going to take you to my bed." And never let you go. Only, he couldn't say that part.

"I'm not going anywhere."

He stared into her eyes, then at her trembling mouth. He should be stronger, but she'd always been his greatest weakness. He'd never been able to resist her. That hadn't changed in the seven years he'd been gone. Neither had the fact that he'd always loved her, that he still loved her.

He lowered his mouth to hers.

Chapter Thirteen

Megan thought she'd prepared herself for Justin's kiss. They'd kissed many times in the past. Heavens, they'd kissed just a few hours ago in his office. She hadn't expected this time would be any different. She hadn't expected to be plunged into a sensual whirlpool, to be swept away by heat and taste and feeling. She hadn't thought he would reduce her to mindlessness.

His mouth touched hers, molding itself to her, taking her without pausing for question or permission. Before, he'd teased her into delighted acquiescence; this time, he plunged forward, daring her to keep pace. His tongue slipped between her parted lips and swept toward hers. He brushed against her waiting moistness, circling, thrilling her beyond reason.

She clung to his shoulders because there was nothing else solid in her world. She held on because she would fall if she didn't. Not just to her knees, although her legs trembled violently, but into another place, another realm of living where there was only sensation and desire and she felt as lost and confused as a newborn babe.

His hands touched her back, her sides, then pulled her closer and tilted her hips against his. He was all male need, frightening and very exciting. Through the layers of her dress, she felt little except for the vague outline of his form. Was he engorged as he had been in her shop? She wanted to look, or even touch, but she didn't dare. She was still in shock from her own bold behavior. She couldn't believe

she'd actually invited him to teach her about those secrets
that had always intrigued her.

"Megan." He whispered her name like a prayer. As if his
desire for her was greater than both of them combined.

He moved his mouth from hers and trailed kisses along
her jaw to her neck, then lower, lower still, until firm, warm
lips traced the curves of her bosom. Until her fingers curled
into his white shirt.

Instinctively, she arched her head back. It was difficult to
breathe, so very difficult. Everywhere he touched was like
fire on her skin—searing heat that made her blood run
faster, and her heart flutter in her chest.

He dipped his tongue into the shadowed valley between
her breasts. She nearly swooned from the sensation. Again
and again he licked her skin, sipping deeply, slowly, taunting her with silent promises.

When she thought she would perish from pleasure, when
she knew that this magic touch was the most wonderful she
had ever encountered, he moved from her breasts and nibbled along her chest up her neck, until he reached her ear.
In the back of her mind she wondered if she should protest
his liberties, then almost laughed aloud. She wanted this.
She had deliberately come to his room, knowing what might
happen. At first, she'd just thought to stay for an hour or
so, just long enough for the scandal to begin. But after she'd
watched him watching her, after she'd seen the passion flare
in his eyes and felt the flickering answer deep in her soul,
she'd known she couldn't leave. Not until she knew. Not
until she'd been with him.

It wasn't just about learning the mysteries that had been
denied her, or the fact that once she was ruined, no one
would ever want her. It was that Justin had said he was
leaving. Still. In a few months he would be gone, taking
Bonnie with him. Megan knew he would never trust her
enough to ask her to go with him. She would never be able
to make up for what had happened between them all those
years ago. No matter how she protested youth, or fear, he
wouldn't forgive her. There might never be another time for
them. Colleen might very well force her from town. She
didn't know, and as he took her earlobe in his mouth and

sucked, she found she didn't care. This was wrong, by the world's rules. It was probably the worst thing she'd ever done. Yet nothing else had felt so right.

He returned his lips to hers. He kissed her slowly, thoroughly, until she was sure every inch of her mouth had been attended to. Until she was tingling down to her toes curling in her shoes. Her breasts ached, as if they were calling him back to them. Her nipples pressed against her chemise. Even the cool silk was too much of a barrier. She remembered how he'd placed his mouth on her nipples once before. She wanted him to do that again.

She arched against him, turning her head slightly so he could deepen the kiss between them. She moved her hands from his shoulders to his head. His hair slipped through her fingers as she held him still. She rubbed her chest against his, trying to get closer, to be with him, a part of him. His hands cupped her waist, then moved up her back to the long row of hooks. She'd about dislocated her shoulder getting them all fastened. Justin unhooked them easily, one by one.

Fear nibbled at the edge of her consciousness. She pushed it away, but the insidious creature returned. She didn't want to be afraid. She wanted to be with Justin. She needed this.

Squeezing her eyes tightly closed, she thought about how much she cared for him, about the contrast between his silky hair and the stubbly line of his jaw. She stroked his throat and neck, finding the line where the stubble ended and his smoother skin began.

His mouth slid away from hers. "Did you do this with him?" he asked.

"Who?"

"That man you were engaged to. Did you do this with him?" He bent low and placed his lips against her neck. She felt the intensity of his sucking, followed by the nibble of teeth. She inhaled her pleasure.

"No, never. He kissed me a few times, but not like you do."

"So he never unhooked your dress?"

His question once again focused her attention on his fingers along her back. They'd passed her waist and were reaching for the last few hooks over her derriere.

"No," she whispered.

"He never did this, then," he said, stepping back and tugging her dress down her arms until it pooled at her waist.

She resisted the urge to cover herself. Justin stared at her as if she was the most perfect thing he'd ever seen. Dark hair tumbled onto his forehead. His brown eyes glowed from an inner, raging fire. That same heat reached out to warm her, sending sparks along her arms and belly, settling in her breasts and her female place.

Justin moved behind her and untied her petticoats. He pushed them and her dress off her hips, until everything was bunched around her knees. Then he bent over and slipped one arm behind her legs and the other behind her back. After picking her up, he held her against his chest.

She clung to him, her right arm around his neck, her left hand pressed against him. She could feel the strength of his arms through the thin layer of her pantaloons.

Brown eyes held hers. "Tell me you want this," he commanded.

She'd never felt so safe, she realized. Held like this in Justin's arms. The vague unease at being undressed in front of him didn't matter. Nothing mattered but the moment and the man. Nothing mattered but how he made her feel and the knowledge that in the seven years he'd been gone, he hadn't forgotten her.

Her free hand reached up to touch his face. She traced his mouth, then touched the scar across his chin. She remembered the knife fight he'd gotten into so many years ago. Three boys had jumped him from behind. One had pulled a knife. Megan had been walking home from her father's store and had seen everything. Even now she could remember the taste of fear and how she'd prayed he would survive.

Before she'd gathered herself enough to go for help, he'd subdued two of the boys and had turned on the third, the one with the knife. They'd fought silently. The boy had lashed out, cutting Justin's face, but that had been his last act. Faster than her eyes had been able to follow, Justin had punched the boy, knocking him to the ground. The other two had carried away their defeated friend. Without stopping to think about what would happen if they were seen talking together, Megan had pulled out a handkerchief and taken it to Justin. She'd been fifteen at the time. A girl. He'd been nearly eighteen, and very much a man.

"What are you thinking?" he asked.

"About how you got this." She touched the scar.

He grimaced. "I should have been paying attention. I knew they were following me, but you distracted me."

"Did I? Really?" She didn't bother pretending not to be pleased.

"Oh, Megan, if you only knew the truth." Sadness doused some of the fire in his eyes.

"Justin, don't. Don't think about it. Don't think about anything right now. Please." She didn't know what else to do, so she bent her head toward him and kissed him.

At the first touch of her lips, he squeezed her tighter against him. As she parted her mouth and eased her tongue inside of him, he shifted her slightly so that she was flat against him and her legs slipped down along his. He supported her with his arms wrapped tightly around her waist.

He answered her kiss and the past faded away, leaving nothing but the feelings between them. When he flexed his hips, she felt the hard ridge she'd thought about. It pressed into her belly, sending an odd aching up her thighs. Nothing seemed to help and squirming against him only made it worse.

He groaned low in his throat. She felt him moving, then he lowered himself to the bed. Her knees bent and she found herself straddling his lap. The moist, aching part of her came in contact with his maleness and she jumped.

He grinned. "Scared?"

"Of course not."

His smile faded. "You never were a good liar." He reached up for the ribbon of her corset cover and pulled the edge of the bow. "The first time is painful," he said quietly, staring into her eyes.

She swallowed. "All right."

"I've heard it can be a slight pressure or a lot of pain. I can't tell you which."

"You can't make it not hurt?"

He shook his head. "I wish I could, Megan. I'd do anything for you."

"I know." She bit her lower lip. "I'll be brave."

"You don't have to look like that. It's not as if I'm asking you to take medicine. It'll be worth it, I promise."

She was doubtful. Colleen had never mentioned pain. But then, Colleen had never mentioned much of anything. Her entire discourse on the subject had been a smug reminder that it was something Megan was unlikely to ever know.

Justin pulled off her corset cover. She turned to let him tug the fabric down her arms. He started on the hooks down the front of her corset.

Wait until Colleen finds out about this, Megan thought with glee. Her sister was going to be so surprised, she would probably—

Then Megan felt her corset fall away. She stared down at herself in amazement, then blushed. She could feel the heat flaring on her chest and face. She'd been so caught up in thinking about her sister's reaction, she hadn't paid attention to what Justin was doing.

"My clothes," she said, protesting their loss after the fact.

"You're not going to need them."

She opened her mouth to speak, then couldn't think of anything to say.

"Don't be afraid," Justin said softly, and drew her onto the bed. In the process, she lost her shoes. As she stretched out on the coverlet, she tried not to think about the fact that she was wearing her chemise, pantaloons, stockings and nothing else. She also tried to ignore her shaking.

"Don't be afraid," he repeated.

"I'm not."

"Yes, you are. Would you feel better if you kept on the rest of your clothing?"

She smiled with relief. "Could I? That would be wonderful. I wouldn't feel so vulnerable."

"It's not a problem."

"Good. It's very sweet of you to be so thoug—"

His mouth came down on her nipple. She forgot what she'd been saying and closed her eyes. The warm heat was exactly as she remembered it from when he'd touched her there before. Only this time, he drew more of her breast inside. This time, she didn't have to worry about falling down in the hall. This time, she could cling to him, then fling her arms out in abandon as he suckled her and flicked his tongue back and forth against the hardened tip of her nipple.

He was at her side, barely touching her at all. She raised her knees and rotated her hips as the sensation shot through her. His hand reached for her other breast. She held her breath in anticipation. He was warm through the thin layer of her chemise. The calluses on his palm caught at the delicate fabric. She loved the faint rasping sound as he moved against her, circling her breasts, then slipping closer over the full curve, touching the underside, the top. He teased her nipple with his thumb, brushing it back and forth slowly. Then he took her hard point in between his thumb and forefinger and squeezed gently.

"Justin?" she breathed.

He squeezed again and tugged. Her hips arched upward, her toes curled, as did her fingers. He raised his head and blew softly on the dampened fabric. She shivered as the cool air tingled against her flesh.

He raised himself on one elbow and stared at her. "You're very beautiful," he said. "More perfect than I'd ever imagined you to be."

His words soothed her, even as the fingers still on her breast made her feel warm inside, as if she'd been sleeping under a too-heavy quilt.

"How does it feel?" he asked.

"Wonderful," she admitted shyly. "I feel tingly inside."

"You're flushed."

"It's a little warm in here."

He raised one eyebrow. "It's all the clothes you're wearing."

"Oh." She glanced down at herself. Dry, her chemise was sheer. The damp portion over her breast was transparent. "Do you think it would help?"

He nodded solemnly.

"All right." She reached for the ribbon between her breasts.

"Allow me."

He tugged on one end, then helped her into a sitting position so he could pull the garment over her head. As it fluttered away, she started to bring her hands up to cover herself. Before she could, he lowered his head to her other breast.

His touch was as delicious as it had been before. She vaguely noticed he lowered her back to the bed. She felt him moving over her, his chest pressing against her side as his hand came up to tease her other nipple. The heat was overwhelming. Removing her chemise hadn't helped at all. If anything, taking it off made the situation worse.

He drew his mouth down from her breast to her belly. His lips tickled her skin. When he came to the waistband of her pantaloons, she had the thought that she should push him away. Touching her in other places was one thing, but touching her *there* had to be wrong. Everyone knew that.

Yet when he stroked her thighs, she was surprised to find it felt almost as nice as when he touched her breasts. And when his fingertips whispered across the fabric covering her blond curls, she was struck with shivering, not disgust. It didn't seem so odd then to part her knees a little.

He ran his hands down the tops of her legs, then up the outside. His thumbs swept dangerously close to her most secret place. She jumped in anticipation or perhaps even in shock when he paused and deliberately touched her there. Just one finger, just for a moment.

Delight ripped through her. She thought about opening her eyes, but she didn't want to look at him. Not just after he'd done that. She shifted against him, feeling the hard strength of his legs beside hers.

He returned his attention to her chest, touching her with his mouth, making her forget everything. She felt his hand moving once more over her belly. She didn't mind. He could stroke her legs if he wanted to. It didn't matter if he—

Her eyes flew open. He put his hand there. Right there! Over her. She glanced down. Justin wasn't looking at her. He was poised over her throbbing nipple, his eyes closed, his mouth parted. She told herself to look away, but she couldn't. It was too amazing. He lowered his head slowly, achingly slowly, then stuck out the tip of his tongue. As she held her breath in anticipation, he touched the tip to her nipple. The combination of watching and feeling what he was doing almost made her faint. He did it again and again, until she was forced to close her eyes in ecstasy. She arched her hips, then felt the weight of his hand.

She'd been able to forget it for a while, but now she felt each individual finger through her pantaloons. The middle one started to move. Up and down, moving lower and lower with each stroke. Pushing the loose fabric against her until he suddenly touched something that made her gasp. A tiny jolt of heat singed her, like an ember from the stove. Only better. She froze. Would he do it again? Should she let him?

He did. He touched that place again. It was wrong, she told herself. It had to be. Nothing right could feel that good. She should tell him to stop. But his finger circled the magic place and she didn't want to tell him to stop.

Just a few more minutes, she promised herself. She would count to a hundred, then make him stop.

"One," she whispered. "Two, three—"

Justin raised his head from her breast. "What are you doing?"

"Counting. When I get to a hundred, you have to stop."

"Why?"

"It feels— Ah!" He brushed over her again and her thighs parted completely. Again and again, and the bottoms of her feet started burning.

"Go ahead and count," he said. "I'll stop when you get to a hundred. Don't forget to tell me."

She could have sworn he was laughing, but she didn't have the energy to open her eyes and look. It didn't matter, anyway. She would remind him. Now, what number was she on?

She thought it might be ten, then decided it couldn't be more than five. He moved his finger slowly against her. Around and around, building a sensation she didn't understand. It was as if every muscle in her body was straining toward a common goal. She tensed and relaxed. She tossed her head from side to side. Nothing helped. It was definitely warmer in the room.

"Justin, it's hot."

"Maybe it would help if you took off your pantaloons."

She opened one eye. "You think so?"

He nodded solemnly. "What number are we on? I don't want you to lose track."

Number? Oh. "Ah, twenty-five."

"Is that all?" he murmured as he untied her pantaloons. He slipped them off her legs, leaving her only in stockings and garters. Somehow, she knew taking them off wouldn't help at all. "Twenty-five? You're sure?"

"Yes, yes, hurry, we have to get to a hundred."

The first time he stroked the dampness between her legs without the barrier of clothing between them, she forgot to count. The second time he did it, she didn't care if he continued to touch her forever. Nothing mattered except the magic he created. She hadn't known there could be such sensation or feeling. Every inch of her quivered. She couldn't focus, couldn't breathe, could only feel those gentle fingers moving back and forth, around and around.

And then she couldn't feel them anymore, either. There was nothing but tension and heat, the deepest of aches as she arched herself upward, her hands clinging to the coverlet.

She spoke his name, at least she tried to. She wasn't sure what sounds escaped her parted lips. She inhaled deeply, needing to breathe, to find the surface of this sensual pool into which she'd fallen. Justin was close by. She could feel his sweet breath on her face, hear his whispers of encouragement. His fingers moved faster now, faster and lighter, brushing over her until she couldn't think, could only wait for something, anything, to rescue her.

Then his hands froze in place and she cried out her need. He moved swiftly, carrying her deeper into the pool, farther down than she'd known she could go. Her muscles clenched one last time, tighter, then tighter still until there was nothing left to do but explode back to the surface of the pool.

She cried out as her body flew upward, as the waves swept over and around her, as his fingers continued to touch her, still moving quickly and lightly, still urging her on even as she broke the surface and could gasp for breath. Even as sanity returned and she could speak his name. Even as the tears fell softly, rolling down her temples into her hair. Only then did he stop touching her so he could hold her against him.

Their hearts thundered in unison. He brushed her tears, then kissed her mouth. She stared up at him.

"What happened?"

He smiled gently. "We almost made it to seventy-five."

"But there was something different, something—"

"Wonderful?" he offered, settling next to her and pulling her against his side.

"Oh, yes, wonderful. Even more than wonderful." She snuggled close, absorbing his warmth and curious about the lethargy that seemed to be stealing over her.

He stroked her hair, gently tugging at the pins and loosening the braids until the long strands fanned out over her shoulders and back. With his other hand he unbuttoned his vest and shirt and drew her palm close to his exposed chest. "Touch me, Megan."

Her first thought was that she was suddenly far too shy to agree. But when he kissed the top of her head, she reminded herself this was Justin and that they'd just shared the most incredible experience of her life. Besides, she'd been wanting to touch his chest, really touch it, for years.

She slipped her fingers under his shirt. His skin was hot and smooth, the hair there cool and crinkly. He felt different, harder than she'd imagined. She closed her eyes and absorbed the sensations. The clean scent of his body, the sound of his steady breathing, the heat their bodies generated and the achiness that slowly slipped between her thighs.

Over and over she stroked him, finally raising herself onto one elbow to tug his shirt free of his trousers and part it. She stared down at the broad expanse of him, then at his face. His eyes were closed. The trust in that gesture made her swallow thickly. She leaned toward him and kissed his cheek.

Her hair fell around her like a silk drape, shielding them from the outside world. She moved to his mouth and paused, knowing he would part his lips for her. When he did, she dipped inside delicately, tasting him, teasing him, taunting him as he had done her just a few moments before.

She felt his arms move for a second, then he pulled her closer. This time, as her hand moved lower on his chest, there was no barrier of trousers to stop her. She lifted her head and stared at him. His eyes opened. Fire burned there. Hot, passionate fire. She wondered if the flames would consume her.

"I want you," he whispered.

A ripple of pleasure swept through her. She hadn't known he felt like that. She'd hoped, but hearing the words, seeing the proof in his eyes, erased the last of her fears. Boldly, she moved her hand lower until she encountered his maleness.

She froze, feeling suddenly awkward. She could have copied the motions he'd used on her earlier, but judging by the shape of him—that ridge she'd felt before now rested on the back of her hand—it wasn't going to work. She didn't know what to do.

"It's all right," he murmured and rolled her over until she was on her back. He pushed off the rest of his clothing, then knelt next to her. His hands rested casually on his thighs, his crotch almost at eye level.

She thought she should look away. Then she reminded herself she might never see one again, so she should look while she had the chance. Then she wondered what on earth he was going to do with it.

"It's very large," she said at last, because it was the only thing she could think of to say.

He grinned. "Thank you."

She hadn't meant it as a compliment, she was simply stating a fact, but she was glad he was pleased. "Should I touch it?"

"Yes."

She stared at it, then looked up into his face. He was smiling, but the fire still raged inside. She could feel the heat and it empowered her.

"Let me show you," he said, and took her hand in his. He placed her palm against him and wrapped her fingers around, then showed her how to move her hand back and forth over him.

The sensation was quite pleasant. He felt dry, which was odd. Her woman's place was distinctly moist. The hardness below the soft skin felt taut, almost painful. She wanted to ask if it hurt, but he closed his eyes and arched into her embrace. She remembered how his touch had made her feel. Was it the same for him?

She experimented with rhythms, moving quickly, then slower, finally shifting so that she could touch him with one hand and also press her mouth to his chest. He tasted slightly salty. As her lips brushed against his skin, he threaded his fingers through her hair and raised her face to him.

The lines of his face were harsh, his eyes almost glazed. "You're pushing me over the edge," he murmured.

"Good." She smiled but he didn't return it.

"I want more, Megan. I want to be inside of you. But I don't have to be. You can keep doing what you're doing. It's enough. You'll still be a virgin."

But then she wouldn't really know. When Justin was gone, she would wonder what it would have been like to know all of it with him.

She shook her head. "No, I want you to be inside of me, too." She knew she was blushing and prayed he didn't notice.

"You're sure?"

She nodded. "What should I do?"

He eased her back on the bed, then moved between her thighs. She'd spread her legs for him before, but with him between them now, she felt awkward and exposed. Before she could tell him, however, he bent over and pressed his mouth to her breasts. Within minutes, her blood was hot and moving quickly, and her hips arched toward him.

She felt him probing her female place, pushing forward. She shifted slightly, not sure if she should move toward him, or away. He answered her unasked question by straightening and holding her hips still. Slowly, he filled her. She felt her insides stretching to accommodate him. It was unlike anything she'd imagined. He was actually going to be a part of her.

She stared up at his body, enjoying the size of him, the differences in their forms. She watched the lines of his face tighten and his eyes drift closed. She didn't mind this at all. It was actually kind of fun, in an embarrassing sort of way.

Then he stopped suddenly. She felt a mild pressure. Before she could react, he thrust in deeply. She bit back a cry. It was more surprise than pain, although she'd felt an unpleasant twinge.

Justin opened his eyes. "Megan?"

"I'm fine." She smiled. "I promise."

He muttered something she couldn't hear, then bent down and wrapped his arms around her. Kissing her deeply, he started to move in and out of her body. They touched everywhere. His chest to her breasts, their legs tangling, their tongues dancing with each other.

Her hands clutched at his back. As he thrust in again and again, his muscles tightened. His breathing became more rapid. She wondered if he was experiencing what she'd felt before. One of his hands cupped her breast and played with her nipple. The twinge between her thighs became something else, something like what had happened before, as her blood had heated and she'd felt herself pulled under. It wasn't going to happen again, was it? Could it? So quickly?

He kissed her neck, then her shoulder. She caught her breath. He raised himself and touched both her breasts. The pleasure increased, as did the rhythm of his thrusts. She arched against him, needing more. Needing to feel that same intensity.

Without thinking, she drew her legs back toward her chest.

"Oh, Megan," he breathed.

She opened her eyes and stared at him. He was looking at the place where they joined. By her innocent actions, she had exposed herself completely. He raised his head and their gazes locked. The intensity there seared her down to her soul. She forgot to be embarrassed. She forget everything except the feelings that passed between them.

He lowered his right hand and pressed his fingers to her most secret place. Rubbing slowly, he brought her deeply into the sensual pool. He drew her under, down and down until she knew she would drown with him. She needed to look away. She needed to close her eyes, but she couldn't. She had to bare herself to him. All of her. It made no sense, but she didn't question the need. She drew her legs back more, bending them at the knee so he could see all of her. She forced her eyes to stay open, even as her muscles contracted and she felt herself thrust up to the surface. Even as he stilled suddenly and groaned her name. Even as his face tightened into a grimace and his thighs turned to rock beneath her hands.

Only when they stretched out together under the coverlet, did she sigh softly and let her lids sink closed.

Justin held her close to him. She could hear his heart beating as she rested her head on his chest. She'd never known such a feeling of contentment and intimacy. It was as if they were the only two people in the world.

"Does everyone do this?" she asked softly.

He chuckled. She heard the sound and felt the vibration against her cheek. She liked it.

"Everyone doesn't do it all the time," he answered. "Most married couples do."

"Even Colleen and Gene?"

He laughed again. "Let's not think about that."

She didn't want to, either, but she couldn't forget what had happened in her store when her brother-in-law had talked about her "needs." She shuddered at the thought of him wanting to touch her the way Justin had. As for her sister, she couldn't imagine her taking her clothes off completely, let alone being quiet enough for she and her husband to... Justin was right. Better not to think about it.

She shifted until she was facing him with her palm on his chest and her chin resting on her hand. "Is this what you did with Laurie?"

His dark eyes met hers. He stroked her temple, brushing aside a loose strand of hair. "Why do you ask?"

"It makes more sense, now," she admitted, then grimaced. "I never understood why men would want to visit, you know, those kind of women. But for something this wonderful, who wouldn't pay a dollar?"

"Megan!"

She gazed up at him, then touched his face. "Did you want to do this before? With me, I mean."

"Oh, yes." He lowered his head and touched his lips to hers. "All the time," he said between kisses.

"All the time? How often do people do it?"

"As often as they want."

"Really?" That was an intriguing thought. "So we could do it again? Right now?"

He grinned. "You'll be the death of me."

"Why?"

He shook his head. "Hush. I thought you wanted to do it again."

She had another question, but he reached his hand up to cup her breast and suddenly she couldn't remember anything at all.

Chapter Fourteen

He woke with a feeling of foreboding. Without stirring, Justin knew Megan had left his bed. He didn't want to open his eyes to see where she'd gone to. He didn't want to know if she was dressed or still delightfully naked. He didn't want to admit that it was dawn and that yesterday was gone forever.

He lay still, breathing deeply, as if by pretending to be asleep, he could hold on to what they'd had together. Those few hours had changed everything. She was too innocent to know, of course. She assumed everyone felt the same kind of passion that had flared between them. It wasn't true. He'd been with women before. He'd felt excitement and a release. But nothing like the pleasure he'd found with Megan. Perhaps it was the anticipation. He'd wanted her for as long as he could remember. Perhaps it was a foolish trick of fate, to bind him to the one woman he could never have.

A small sound caught his attention. A slight sigh. Steeling himself against the inevitable pain that was sure to strike his soul, he sat up and opened his eyes.

Megan stood in front of the window seat, looking out. She'd drawn the coverlet around her. Long blond hair cascaded down her back. He looked at the piles of clothing scattered on the floor. She hadn't dressed yet. She was naked under the coverlet. Yet the most male part of him didn't stir. There would be no fire between them this morning; only pain.

He stood up and walked over to her. Without stopping to consider the fact she might hate him, he wrapped his arms around her and inhaled the familiar sweet scent of her body. She relaxed against him.

"The sun's barely up," she said, still looking out the window. "But people are already stirring."

He glanced toward the eastern horizon. The first sliver of sunlight could be seen stretching across the sleepy town. Megan was right. Mr. Greeley was making his way toward his butcher shop.

"They'll know." Her voice was troubled.

Regret. That which he'd feared most. He'd known she would regret their night together and the tenderness and love their bodies had shared. He'd warned himself about this, but he still felt the icy fingers clutching at his heart.

He stepped back. "If you hurry, you can get home without anyone seeing you."

"No. It's too late."

She shook her head. Long strands of hair shimmered around her. He wanted to touch her hair, touch her, anything to make it all right. But he couldn't. She was right. It was too late. For both of them.

He stood behind her in the cool morning air, clenching his hands at his sides. He didn't want to know about her regrets. A flare of anger surprised him. "You should have thought of that before you came here," he said. "You're the one who insisted on coming up to my hotel room. You wanted to plan your own scandal. Now that it's happened, why are you surprised? Of course there's going to be a price to pay. There always is."

"At least we're even."

He stared at the back of her head, then placed his hands on her shoulders and turned her until she faced him. He'd half expected to see tears, but there weren't any. Her large hazel-gray eyes met his unflinchingly.

"What do you mean?" he asked.

"I'll have my comeuppance this morning. You should be pleased. At last I'll pay for those things I said to you seven years ago."

He stared at her. "Is that what you think last night was about? That I bedded you to punish you for what you said?"

"No, of course not. Punishment wouldn't be that sweet." She stared at the center of his chest. "But can you tell me it never crossed your mind? As we climbed those stairs, wasn't a small part of you secretly pleased at what I would have to face today?"

"Never."

She swallowed. "I wish I could believe you." She tossed her hair over her shoulder and raised her gaze to his. "Do you forgive me, Justin Kincaid? Genuinely? Can you forget the past between us?"

She'd always been beautiful, but this morning, with the fragrance of their night together clinging to her skin, with a faint flush of color staining her cheeks, with her full mouth trembling, he knew beautiful didn't begin to describe her. She was the only woman he'd ever loved. She'd broken his heart and shattered his soul. She'd known his greatest weakness and she'd profited from it. Loving her had always been easy, but forgiving her?

She nodded faintly. "I suspected as much. You can't forgive me. No matter. I can't forgive myself, either." She moved away from him and sat in the window seat. The coverlet she clutched around her made her look young and vulnerable.

"I loved you," she said, then smiled. "I know you don't believe me, but I swear, I did. More than anything. That morning." She shuddered. "It was awful. I'd heard about the beating. Colleen could talk of nothing else. My father knew you'd been accused. He was disgusted, saying the most awful things. He frightened me. Gene came calling. He told me more details of the beating. He was the one who told me they'd accused you."

There was a velvet chair by the fireplace. Justin walked over and sat on it. The faint chill in the room made him glance toward his clothing, but he didn't bother to pull on his trousers.

"I believed you to be innocent," she went on. Her gaze was firmly fixed on the floor, her fingers twisted the edge of the coverlet. "Then Gene took my father aside and told him you'd admitted to being with Laurie. That you'd paid her to do those things." She paused and swallowed, as if fighting for control. "We were supposed to be engaged, Justin. You said you loved me, but you'd admitted to being with a wh-whore." Her voice cracked.

"I explained that," he said.

"I know. But I needed the truth seven years ago. Not last month."

"You should have trusted me."

"Perhaps." She looked up at him. Tears glistened in her almond-shaped eyes, but they didn't fall. "I was destroyed at the thought of you being with another woman. I didn't understand about needs and longings. I didn't know how wonderful it was and why you'd want to do that with her."

"Dammit, Megan, you're the one I wanted. You're the one I loved." He wanted to go to her and hold her, but he couldn't. Not yet. She had more to tell him. He wondered if her words would continue to rip his heart, or if eventually it would eventually become numb to the pain.

"I wanted to believe you," she continued. "When we met by the stream, I really wanted to hear that you were innocent. I kept waiting for you to explain about being with Laurie. But you never said a word."

"I didn't think you knew. It's not something I'm proud of."

"I felt that if you were lying about that, you might be lying about everything." He started to interrupt, but she held up her hand to stop him. "I see now that I was afraid to believe in you. If I really thought you were innocent, I would have to be at your side defending you. I couldn't do that. I was too afraid. Afraid of what my father would say. Afraid of what Laurie had been able to give you that I couldn't. I was afraid of everything."

"You could have just said that," he told her, then leaned back in the chair and closed his eyes. The demons returned and he didn't know if he had any strength left to fight them. It had been seven years since that afternoon. Why did it still matter what she said?

"I know. But I knew if I admitted that to you, you would convince me. You were always very good at convincing me of things."

"Not good enough."

She shifted on the seat. He didn't bother to look at her. He could hear the rustle of the coverlet. "I didn't mean to say those things. They just came out."

Then the demons won. He was swept out of the hotel room toward the bank by the stream. He could see the green leaves on the trees, feel the heat of the summer afternoon. Megan stood before him, a frightened young girl, not yet sure of her way. Her face had been pale, her eyes wide with apprehension.

"I won't go with you," she'd said, her body stiff with what he'd thought was disgust but now understood was fear. "I won't. Leave me be, Justin. It's over. If you're going, then go, but I don't want any part of you."

"I thought you cared about me. We're engaged." His body was numb. He'd had to force the words out slowly.

"Not anymore." She'd raised her hand to her neck and taken off the delicate chain that he'd given her as a symbol of their pledge. The chain had been the only thing of his mother's that he'd kept. Megan had tossed it at him. He hadn't bothered to put out his hand, and it had fallen to the ground.

"Just like that," he'd said sadly, wondering how much this was going to destroy him. Each breath hurt more than the last. Every part of him screamed with pain, with emptiness. Not Megan. He couldn't lose her. She was the only decent thing in his sorry life. "I love you."

"I don't love you," she'd said spitefully. "You're a fool if you thought I ever did. Who do you think you are, anyway? I'm Megan Bartlett. I know who my father is. You're just that bastard Justin Kincaid. You'll only ever be a bastard. Go away. Go away!"

Her shriek had rebounded through the forest, vibrating against the trees and the ground, forcing him to run. He'd turned from her and fled into the cool silence, away from the words that would forever echo in his mind.

He'd left the next day. Had left Landing determined to become that which the town believed him to be. A criminal and a troublemaker. He'd been determined to forget Megan, as well. He had done neither. In the end, he'd found himself facing what he'd fled from. Here he was, seven years later, listening to Megan say she'd been wrong.

But it was still too late.

"I'm sorry," she whispered.

He opened his eyes and stared at her. "Why do you care about them?" he asked, fighting his anger. "Why the hell does it matter what other people think? What is the hold everyone has on you? Damn you, tell me why."

Her mouth opened twice before she could force out the words. "I can't."

"Is it me?" he asked, clenching the arms of the chair to keep himself from rushing to her side to grab her and shake her until she confessed. "Is it your sister? Is it Gene?"

She shook her head. "No. None of them. It's me. It's always been me." She bent her head toward the floor. Her long hair fell forward, concealing her features. He didn't want to know that she cried. Despite the pain, despite everything, her tears would tear him apart.

"Megan—"

"No!" She raised her head and glared at him. Tears trembled on her lower lashes but didn't fall. "Do you want to know why?" She paused as if waiting for him to answer. When he didn't, she shook her head. "Don't change your mind now, Justin. I'll tell you everything."

She drew in a deep breath. "When I was almost nine I came home early from school because I didn't feel well. I walked into the kitchen, as I always did, and I heard voices coming from the parlor." She pulled her knees up to her chest and gazed past him, as if seeing that long-ago afternoon. "It was my father and another man. I went down the hall and saw my mother was there, as well. They all started yelling. It was so loud, I couldn't understand what they were saying at first. Then I knew. My mother was going away with this man. She wanted to take Colleen and me with her, but my father wouldn't let her. He called her awful names."

Megan started rocking back and forth. He wanted to go to her and comfort her. More than that, he wanted to stop her words, for they obviously caused her pain. But he couldn't. Selfishly, he had to know why she'd acted as she did. He had to know why she'd been so willing to destroy them both.

"I couldn't bear it anymore, so I ran out and hid until it was the regular time to come home from school. I made Colleen swear not to tell them I'd left early." She tilted her head back and stared at the ceiling. A single tear rolled down her temple and into her hair.

"He said she'd died."

Justin straightened in the chair and stared at her. "Your mother?"

She nodded. "He said it had been very sudden. She'd fallen down the stairs. At first, I thought he'd killed her. When they brought in the coffin, I was sure of it. That night, I crept downstairs and looked inside. It was empty. She'd gone away. Two days later, he buried that empty coffin and from then on spoke of my mother as if she were really dead."

"You never saw her again?"

"No. I tried to tell Colleen what had happened, but she wouldn't listen." She turned to look at him. Sunlight caught the side of her face, illuminating her skin until she looked otherworldly. "You asked me once when my sister changed from being a wild hooligan to a proper lady. It was the day we buried that coffin. I think we both knew if we ever did anything wrong, we would be dead to our father. Dead and buried, or sent away. We were so young. We never forgot the lesson. Colleen won't speak of it, but I know she remembers."

He went to her then. He didn't remember standing up and walking across the room, but suddenly she was in his arms and he was holding her close. Her sobs sounded loud and harsh in the morning stillness, her body shook as he wrapped his arms around her.

"Hush, Megan. No one is ever going to hurt you again," he whispered, then knew he would do anything in his power to keep that promise.

She raised her damp face to him. "Don't you see?" she said intently. "I finally understand. My mother took a lover. Papa was so difficult and exacting. I never knew why he was so concerned about our actions and reputations, but as I grew up, I finally understood. Yet in the end, all his effort went to waste."

He knew what she was about to say, but he couldn't stop her. He tried pressing his fingers over her mouth, but she jerked her head away impatiently.

"I'm just like her." Her eyes held his. "I've taken a lover, too. I know Papa was difficult at times, but taking a lover is wrong, don't you think? I'm ruined, just like she was. Only I can't be dead to the world. I have to face them. Everyone. Mrs. Dobson warned me. She said I would never be able to get my reputation back, and she's right."

Her mouth trembled so hard, she couldn't speak anymore. The mute pain in her eyes was his undoing. He cursed her father, the town and most of all, himself.

"You're not like her," he said, tucking her head under his chin. "I promise. I promise." He stroked her long hair and her back, trying to comfort her. The sobs had grown silent, but he could feel the tears as they continued to drip off her cheeks onto his bare arm. Their legs tangled together, reminding him they were both still naked. She was warm in his arms. A stirring of interest flared between his thighs, but he ignored the feeling. This wasn't about him; it was about Megan and what he'd done to her.

He'd known the first minute she'd walked into the hotel that she'd been hell-bent on destroying her reputation. If he'd walked out of the lobby and gone back to his office, she would have been left without a plan. Given a few hours to think things over, she would have come to her senses. But he hadn't given her the time to reconsider. He'd been so damn pleased to see her, so caught up in the thought that he might be able to kiss her again and hold her that he'd only thought of himself and what he wanted. This was his fault and he had to make it up to her. Not just because her reputation had been destroyed but because he'd only ever loved Megan. Seven years hadn't changed that fact. A hundred lifetimes wouldn't made a difference.

He cupped her face in his hands. Using his thumbs to wipe away the tears, he smiled at her. "I can make it right," he said.

Her eyes got wider. "How?"

"Just get dressed."

His statement reminded her of her nudity. He saw it in the sudden blush that swept up her cheeks. "Justin, what are you going to do?"

"It's what you're going to do."

"Which is what?"

"Marry me."

The church was unfamiliar, as was the minister. Megan stood in front of the altar in her Worth gown trying to keep her legs from shaking.

She was getting married. Even as the familiar words of the ceremony washed over her, she felt as if she were caught up in some madness and in a few minutes she would find out none of this was real.

Except Justin's hand felt real as he held hers. Behind her, Mrs. Dobson sat with Bonnie. She could hear the child's excited questions, then her whispered conversation with her precious doll. Everything had moved so quickly. One minute he'd announced they were getting married and the next they were dressed and walking toward the livery stable where Justin had spent five dollars to rent a buggy for the day. She'd protested the expense, saying a wagon was good enough, but he hadn't listened. From the livery stable, they'd driven to Mrs. Dobson's house where they'd picked up the widow and Bonnie. By mutual agreement, they'd left Landing. Neither of them wanted to be married by Gene.

"Do you take this man to be your lawfully wedded husband?" the minister asked.

Megan looked up at Justin. He wore his black coat over a clean white shirt with a string tie. Dark eyes met hers unflinchingly. "Only if you're sure," he said quietly, ignoring the minster's raised eyebrows at the interruption.

Only if she was sure. He still wondered, she realized, watching the emotions flicker across his face. He still wondered if she was ashamed of him.

The pain in her chest was so sharp, she almost cried out. It wasn't fair that this proud man would be so afraid of what she might think of him. She wanted to blurt out that she cared for him, but was caring enough? She'd done wicked things to Justin and he hadn't forgiven her yet. He might never forgive her. But he'd been willing to marry her, to save her good name. He'd protected her from her own foolishness. He'd offered her his name. And still he wondered if it was enough.

"I'm proud to marry you," she said, then glanced at the minister. "I do."

Justin repeated the vows. His voice was low and strong as if saying the words didn't trouble him at all. With a bolt of self-realization, she knew she didn't deserve him now, and she certainly hadn't seven years before. She'd been a fool and a weakling. Closing her eyes briefly, she prayed for the strength to make it right.

The minister closed his prayer book. "I now pronounce you husband and wife. You may kiss the bride."

She raised her head slightly and prepared herself for the impact of his touch. His lips brushed briefly across hers, making her yearn for more, then he pulled back and looked at her oddly.

"We're married," he said.

"I know." Her smile felt shaky. When he held out his arm, she tucked her hand into the crook of his elbow and allowed him to lead her down the two stairs to the first pew, where Mrs. Dobson sat sniffing into a handkerchief.

"That was so beautiful," the older woman said and wiped her nose. "I've always loved weddings. Megan, that dress might not be a traditional gown, but I doubt any bride has looked more lovely."

Megan glanced at the Worth gown and shrugged. "At least it's special. I'll remember this day if I ever wear the gown again."

Bonnie bounced to her feet. "What's married mean?"

"It's a holy institution sanctified by God," Mrs. Dobson said importantly, the perky feather on her black hat quivering with agreement. "A man and a woman live together for His glory."

"Does that mean you go live with God?" the girl asked.

Megan smiled. "No, honey. We still live in Landing."

"Good," Bonnie said, and grinned. "I like it there."

"I'm glad," Mrs. Dobson said. "Now, you go wait by the buggy, while I talk with Megan and Justin. And don't get too close to the horses, you hear me?"

"Yes'm," Bonnie said obediently as she raced out of the church. Her shoes clattered loudly on the stone floor, then were silenced as she skipped outside onto the new spring grass.

Mrs. Dobson cleared her throat. "If you choose not to take me up on my offer, I'll understand, but I thought I would make it all the same."

She paused. Megan didn't have any idea what the other woman was talking about. She glanced at Justin. He shrugged.

"It would be a simple thing to explain to people that the two of you left Landing last night, rather than this morning." Mrs. Dobson looked at Megan and nodded significantly. "If you get my meaning."

At first Megan didn't. Then she understood. The widow was offering to tell everyone that Megan and Justin had been married *before* she'd spent the night in his hotel room. The lie would go a long way to salvaging her reputation. She looked at Justin. "What do you think?"

"It's up to you."

She studied the handsome lines of his face. The scar on his chin, the full mouth, the dark eyes. Familiar yet unfamiliar. He was her husband now. He was also a stranger. They were finally married—seven years too late. Or was it? He hadn't forgiven her for what had happened between them. Was this wedding the finest form of revenge? Did he plan to exact a price for the rest of her life? Or was their marriage a second chance? Would it give them the time to learn about each other and perhaps even fall in love again? Did marrying him to protect her reputation mean she was destined to an unhappy life? Did she want the marriage to be successful?

She waited, hoping he would give her a hint as to what he was thinking, but he didn't. It was her decision. To save herself and begin with a lie, or to begin with honesty. To begin as she meant to go on.

She turned to Mrs. Dobson. "No lies," she said. "Let them think what they want. I'm not afraid."

"I'm not afraid." Easy words for Megan to say while they were still two hours away from Landing, Justin thought. More difficult to believe now, as they drove into town.

He could feel her apprehension. She huddled close to him on the seat. Behind them, Mrs. Dobson and Bonnie had grown silent. It was late afternoon. Before starting the long journey back, they'd stopped and eaten. At the time, Justin had wondered if Megan was putting off the inevitable. Did she already regret the wedding?

He told himself he didn't know that for sure, but he couldn't let go of the thought. Why wouldn't she regret it? He was still just that bastard, Justin Kincaid.

His hands tightened on the reins and the black gelding tossed his head. Justin loosened his grip and took a deep breath. He had to consider the facts. First of all, he *wasn't* just that bastard kid anymore. He was the sheriff. Seven years had passed. He was older and, hopefully, wiser. He and Megan were married. That couldn't be undone. Even if she wanted it to be.

The horse trotted down the main street, past the hotel, past the new saloon. The animal's pace increased as he apparently realized he was close to home. Justin reined him in. They had to take Mrs. Dobson to her house first. He felt Megan inhale sharply. He glanced at her. She'd put on a bonnet to protect her skin from the bright spring sun. Gloves covered her pale hands and she'd pulled a thin shawl over her bare shoulders and bosom. She looked every inch a lady.

But she was still wearing her Worth gown. She'd still spent the night in his hotel room, then disappeared with him out of town that morning. People were talking. And stopping to stare. And pointing. He was used to being the center of attention, but she wasn't. He could feel her shrinking against him.

"Take me to the store," Mrs. Dobson ordered from the seat behind theirs.

"Don't you want to go home?"

"No. If I'm at the store, tending to my duties, it'll be easier for folks to come ask me questions. The quicker everyone knows you're married, the quicker things will settle down."

So she'd noticed the crowds, too. "You all right?" he asked Megan.

"Fine." The single tight word conveyed several emotions. So much for not being afraid.

Justin slowed the gelding and moved him to the side of the road until the animal stopped in front of the general store. Andrew rushed outside and helped the older woman down. The teenager stared up at Megan.

"I opened the store like you said, Miss Bartlett. It's been real busy. You gonna come close up?"

"I don't think so, Andrew. Can you take care of it for me?"

"Sure thing, Miss Bartlett."

Megan stared at the boy for a second, then laughed. If her humor had a slightly strangled sound, Justin wasn't going to say anything.

"It's not Miss Bartlett anymore, Andrew. I'm married. I'm Mrs. Kincaid, now."

Andrew looked at her. "You married the sheriff?"

She nodded.

"Well, I'll be. That's just fine." He came around the horse and held out his hand to Justin. "Congratulations to you both." Justin shook his hand. "Sheriff, Miss Bartlett, ah, Mrs. Kincaid, is a fine lady. Married. Don't that beat all."

He kept them for several more minutes while he explained how pleased he was, then he escorted Mrs. Dobson into the store. Justin picked up the reins, but didn't urge the horse forward.

"Where are we going?" he asked.

"What do you mean? I thought we were going home."

"That's what I'm asking, Megan. Where's home? Bonnie and I live in the hotel."

Her hazel eyes darkened to gray. "Do you want me to come live with you there?"

"I wasn't sure we were going to be living together."

"But we're married. What else would we do?"

It wasn't a conventional marriage, so he didn't know. He'd been half expecting her to assume they would continue living separate lives. He hated the relief that filled him with the knowledge that she expected them to share a roof. Which only left the questions of which roof, and, more importantly, would they be sharing a bed?

"Where will we live? At your house or the hotel?"

She bit her lower lip and twisted her hands together. "Would you mind terribly if we lived in my house? The hotel is so public."

He didn't mind at all. "That's fine. I'll drop you and Bonnie off, then go back to the hotel and collect our things."

Megan placed her hand on his arm. "Couldn't I come with you? It would be faster that way. I can pack for Bonnie while you take care of yourself."

He could feel her trembling. Dark shadows stained the delicate skin under her eyes. She looked ready to cry. This had been hard on her. Considering all she'd been through, she was holding up very well.

He glanced over her shoulder to see what Bonnie was making of this conversation. The small girl was curled up in a corner of the seat, her arm tucked under her head, her free hand clutching her doll. It would be better for Bonnie to have a real home, he thought. Megan was great with her, teaching her to read and sew. He faced front and saw the crowds collecting on the sidewalk. He couldn't hear what they were saying, but it was obvious the gossip was spreading.

He flicked the reins and the gelding started walking in a wide half circle toward the hotel. When they reached the three-story building, he jumped down, and held out his arms for Megan. She placed her hands on his shoulders while he helped her down. Her body felt warm and familiar next to his. He wished she would look up and smile at him, but she didn't. Several people paused to watch them.

Someone came rushing out of the hotel. "Sheriff Kincaid, I need to talk to you."

"Not now, Newt."

The young man moved closer. "I must insist. I've spoken with the owner about what happened yesterday. He was understandably upset. I'm afraid I can't allow you to take this lady up to—"

"Newt," Justin said, interrupting him, "have I introduced you to my wife?"

An audible gasp went up from the bystanders. Megan raised her head, so he could see her face. Her expression sent a chill through his body like a long ribbon of ice. It coiled in his belly and knotted, twisting tighter and tighter. Fear and regret. Of course. What else would she be feeling?

He tried to control his anger. He shouldn't be surprised. He'd known this was what was going to happen.

Newt was still babbling. "I'll be checking out," Justin said, cutting him off. "Send one of the bellboys up to carry my things. Prepare the bill and have someone watch the buggy. Bonnie's sleeping inside." Then he took Megan's cold hand and led her into the building.

It was nearly dark by the time they arrived at the large house on the edge of town. Justin stared at the structure. Old man Bartlett's house. He was going to live here now. But it wouldn't be his home. He knew that. Megan had barely spoken to him the entire time they'd been in the hotel. They'd worked quickly, in separate rooms. The maid, Alice, had come up to offer her assistance. At least having a third person there had taken some of the edge off the tension.

Who would do that tonight? Where would he spend the night? In Megan's bed? Or alone?

"Are we there yet?" Bonnie asked as she stirred on the seat behind them. She bounced to her feet, making the buggy rock slightly. "Oh, we are. Are we going to stay here forever and ever?"

Justin didn't know how to answer that. Were they? His plan had always been to leave in a year. But he was a married man, now. Could he still think of leaving? Did he want to?

"Can I have my own room?" Bonnie asked, holding on to the back of their seat.

"Of course. I'll even let you pick it out," Megan said as she turned and smiled at the girl.

Justin waited, but she never answered Bonnie's original question. She didn't say if they were going to live in the house forever or not.

"And are we a real family? My mama always promised me a real family."

Megan smiled at the child. "We'll do our best, Bonnie."

He wondered if their best would be good enough. After climbing down from the rented buggy, he walked around to the other side and held out his arms to Megan. She placed her hands on his shoulders as he lowered her to the ground.

Just for a moment, before he released her and she stepped back, their eyes met. He searched for some hint as to what she was feeling. He could see that apprehension was foremost, mingling with fear. He turned away. He didn't want to know what else swirled through the hazel-gray depths. Not yet. He wasn't strong enough to face her censure. Not when he could still taste her passion on his lips.

Bonnie jumped down and ran up the steps to the porch. Megan moved after her and opened the front door. Justin unloaded the luggage and started carrying it inside.

Half expecting to see old man Bartlett jumping out to bar him entrance, he crossed the threshold. The house was cool and dark inside. It smelled faintly musty, as if daily cleaning wasn't enough to disguise the fact that only one person lived in the three-story mansion.

While Megan removed her hat and shawl, Bonnie danced impatiently at the foot of the stairs.

"Go on," Megan said, and laughed softly. "Go pick out your room."

"I know exactly which one I want," the girl answered as she tore up the stairs. Her footsteps thudded loudly on the wooden floor, then muffled as she reached the landing and ran across the carpet.

He set down the small trunk Megan had packed Bonnie's things in, then lowered his valise next to it. "Do you know which one she'll choose?" he asked.

"I think so. There's an oddly shaped room in the corner. It's tucked under the eaves with a view of the forest. She seemed to like it the best."

"Is it close to your room?"

She suddenly seemed to find the ribbons of her bonnet fascinating. She looped them around her fingers. "No, it's on the opposite side of the house. I have a small bedroom up on this side."

A small bedroom. With a virgin's narrow bed. He looked at the expensive wallpaper brought out from St. Louis, or maybe even New York. The floors under his feet gleamed with polish and care, the furniture was large and substantial. Hard to believe he was less than half a mile from the room above the saloon where he'd grown up.

This wasn't his home; it never would be. It was Megan's. For the hundredth time since morning, he wondered why she'd married him, and what he was going to do when his year was up.

"There's a large guest suite just off the stairs," she said softly.

He glanced at her. She was staring intently at her hands as if the task of removing her gloves required her full attention. There was little light in the hallway, no flicker of a candle to catch the gold-blond color of her hair. He could see her profile, the straight line of her nose, her full lips. He knew that mouth in exquisitely intimate detail, yet he ached to know it, to know her, again.

A large guest suite, with an equally large bed. If they shared that bed, he would touch her and claim her long into the night; he would never grow tired of being with her.

His throat tightened against the pressure of emotion. If he shared that bed with her, in time her belly would swell with his child. And when his year was up, he would be forced to stay. He could never abandon a child.

He glanced at her bare shoulders, at the tendril of hair brushing against her spine. He remembered the feel of her skin against his fingers and the warmth of her body pressed against his as she slept. If he stayed, she would destroy him. Living with her and knowing she wouldn't love him would slowly eat away at his soul. He'd only ever wanted to love and be loved by Megan Bartlett. Like most men, he yearned for the one thing he would never have. He could claim her body, but as he held her, he would know she neither trusted him nor thought him good enough. That she had married him to save herself from the scandal.

He picked up his valise. "I'll take the room next to Bonnie's" he said, ignoring Megan's start of surprise. He didn't meet her eyes as he walked past her toward the stairs. "It's better if I'm close. Sometimes she has nightmares."

Chapter Fifteen

Megan told herself she wasn't going to cry. She blinked several times, then sniffed and stamped her foot. Crying didn't accomplish anything. Besides, it would make her nose red and her eyes puffy. Not that Justin would care one way or the other; he didn't even want to share her bed.

The burning behind her eyes increased, but she ignored it. What had happened? How had she angered him, or upset him so much? Last night had been so...so—she clutched her hands together in front of her waist and exhaled slowly—wonderful. She leaned against the wooden cabinet and sighed. She hadn't known such sensations existed. That her body could feel that kind of tingling magic. She hadn't known it was possible to want and ache and need with an intensity that had left her breathless. She was quite annoyed that no one had ever explained about the exquisite pleasure.

But she must have done something wrong. Had she offended Justin, or had her untutored enthusiasm embarrassed him? There had to be a reason he didn't want to share her bed. She wouldn't know what it was without asking him and she would rather be publicly flogged than expose herself to that kind of torment.

She stared moodily at the large hamper that had been delivered a few minutes before. One of the boys from town had run over, practically dragging the straw container behind him. Inside she'd found a cold supper, a bottle of French champagne and a note from Mrs. Dobson wishing she and Justin happiness as they started their married life together.

"Married, but not together," Megan said softly, running her finger down the side of the bottle. It was still cold and drops of water coated the outside. She'd never had champagne. Her father hadn't approved of drinking spirits. She wondered if it tasted better than the brandy Justin had given her the night before.

"Don't think about it," she ordered herself, then shook her head. How was she not to? She and Justin were married, sharing the same roof. Her body still ached pleasurably from his attentions last evening. She didn't even have to close her eyes to see him looming over her, his face taut with passion, his bare, broad chest so close, so warm, so—

A pounding on the back door brought her out of her reverie. Before she could cross the few steps to answer it, the door was flung open and Gene stepped inside.

He was properly dressed in a shirt, vest and jacket, but the jacket hung open and his hat was askew. Dark red stained his cheeks and his eyes burned as if lit with the fires of hell. Instinctively, she took a step backward, bumping her hip against the hamper.

"Gene, this is a surprise."

"For us, as well, Megan." His voice was low and controlled. She could hear the effort it took him to keep it so. That frightened her more.

"What are you doing here?"

"I came to see for myself," he said, advancing farther into the room. His censorious gaze raked over her, making her realize she still wore the Worth gown. She wanted to tug the bodice higher and wished she still had her shawl for protection.

"You look like a whore," he said, removing his hat.

She caught her breath. "How dare you?"

"How dare I? Madam, you have disgraced this family more than once. I have often considered you a specific test from our Lord and have borne your wildness gladly. But this time—" he motioned toward her chest "—you have gone too far."

Megan opened her mouth to answer him, but she couldn't think of any words. He dared to accuse her of going too far when just yesterday he'd been in her store talking about ministering to her *needs?* "I've done nothing wrong," she said at last.

"Oh, Megan, don't add lying to your list of sins." He shook his head slowly. "Are you denying you spent the night with that man? In his hotel room?"

Megan reached behind her and grabbed the edge of the counter. She could feel the flush spreading up her face. No, she couldn't deny that. "I'm a married woman."

Gene's gaze narrowed. "You married Kincaid? That no-account bastard?"

"Don't you say that about my husband. Like it or not, Gene, he's your new brother-in-law. I suggest you get used to the fact."

"Never." Gene moved closer. Before she could back away, he grabbed her arm. "You're a stranger to me, Megan. To your sister, as well. Her shame is so great, she couldn't rise from her bed this morning."

If I had to be intimate with Gene every night, I wouldn't want to face a new day, either, Megan thought spitefully. She tried to pull herself free of him, but his grip was surprisingly strong. She glared at him. "I don't care about Colleen and her shame. She's threatened me for the last time. I won't be cowed anymore, Gene. Not by her, or by you. I have my own life, and it now includes a husband and a child."

"Child?" His eyes bulged with the word. "A child? You plan to house that spawn of Satan under this roof? I won't allow it."

Megan jerked her arm free, then rubbed the red marks he'd left. Tomorrow she would carry a bruise. "May I remind you, sir, this is not your house? It's mine."

He drew himself up to his full height and glared down at her. "May I remind *you,* madam, that I am a man of God. The Lord is on my side."

"I don't think so, Gene. Not this time."

She was starting to shake, but it was from anger, not fear. The words came easily to her and she was pleased to realize that she meant them. She wasn't afraid of him anymore. She wondered why she had ever been.

"Justin is my husband," she said, meeting his gaze unflinchingly. "Bonnie is as much my child as if I had borne her myself. I expect them both to be treated with respect and courtesy. If you won't accept that, then you are no family to me."

He reached his hand up toward her. She stood her ground, sure he wouldn't hit her. He didn't. He placed his hand over her throat. Not pressing hard, just holding his fingers against her skin. She shuddered, but didn't move back. There was something odd about his expression. Something feral. But she couldn't believe he would really hurt her.

"Don't you dare defy me. I'll destroy you," he threatened.

She swallowed, ignoring the first tendril of fear that coiled through her belly. "Now you sound like Colleen."

The fingers around her throat tightened. Without thinking, she grabbed his wrist with both hands and pulled hard. His fingers jerked free.

"Don't ever do that again," she said, the rage giving her strength and courage.

"I will do as I please, Megan," Gene said. He glanced at the deep vee of her bodice and smiled lasciviously. "Who will tell me otherwise? I will order the members of my congregation to boycott your store. I will brand you as a whore, as a lover of a whore's bastard."

His voice didn't change from its low monotone. A shiver rippled down her spine. Raising her chin slightly, she stared at him. "Do what you must. I'm not afraid. I have the only general store in Landing. Some will stay away because of you, but most won't. I've always been honest in my dealings with the people of this town, and I'm fair with my prices. You can rant at me all you want, but that doesn't change the truth."

"The truth?" Gene leaned closer. "The truth is you bedded that bastard."

"After you offered to take care of my needs yourself, you hypocrite," she retorted hotly. "You're married to my sister. Don't speak to me of sinning in the eyes of God."

"Never!" His eyes widened and all color fled his face. "Never. Liar. Whore. You must be stopped! You must be punished!"

Megan stared at him. She'd never seen Gene like this. Her heart thundered in her chest and she started inching sideways along the counter. He was crazy.

Before she could duck away, he grabbed her arm. "It is the will of God. You must be punished." He raised his hand high. She twisted, but he didn't release her. She steeled herself for the blow.

It never came. Suddenly, Gene was wrenched away from her. He flew across the kitchen and hit the back door before sliding into a heap on the floor.

"If you *ever* touch my wife again, I'll kill you," Justin said through clenched teeth. He towered over the fallen man. "Get up, you worthless piece of—"

"Justin?"

He turned toward her. Fire burned in his dark eyes. Not the fire of passion, but something darker and more deadly. She didn't recognize this man at all. Even so, she trusted him. She ran to his side.

"Hush, Megan. It's all right."

Gene rose slowly to his feet. "This isn't finished," he said.

Justin stiffened but didn't move. "I've warned you. Your being a man of God doesn't make a damn bit of difference to me."

The minister glared at him, then stumbled out the back door. When he was gone, Megan gave in to the trembling and clung to Justin. He held her tightly against him. His hands felt warm and sure as they moved up and down her back.

"Dammit it all to hell, Megan, why didn't you call me?"

"I didn't think of it."

"Why the hell not?"

"Stop swearing at me." She shifted her face against his chest and inhaled the scent of him. He'd come to her rescue. Despite the mistakes she might have made last night, he cared enough to defend her. The thought left her giddy with relief.

"Did he hurt you?"

She shook her head.

"Megan." He took a step back and glanced down at her. "Are you sure?"

One of his hands closed over her upper arm. Before she could fight back the sound, she whimpered. Justin turned her so she was facing the lamp on the kitchen table and studied the darkening red marks. They were large and the exact shape of a man's fingers, standing out garishly on her pale skin.

He cursed low and long, using words she hadn't heard before. "I should have killed him," he muttered.

"It's nothing. Besides, you're the sheriff. You can't go around killing people just because you want to."

"A lot of good being sheriff does me, if I can't even protect my wife."

Gene had scared her with his physical violence, and worried her with his threats of turning the town against her. But none of that mattered. She glanced up at Justin's familiar face, noting the intensity in his stare and the straight set of his mouth. His large body vibrated with the need for revenge. The burning behind her eyes returned, but this time it wasn't from sadness or confusion. It was from happiness.

He looked down at her. "Why are you looking at me like that?"

"Like what?" She sniffed.

"Like I'm responsible for the sun coming up in the morning."

She smiled and could feel her mouth trembling. "You defended me."

"You're my wife, Megan. What would you have me do?"

"No one's ever defended me before."

His stare intensified and she had to look down as she realized how close they were standing and how silent it was in the kitchen. She could hear the ticking of the clock in the hallway and the echoing beating of her own heart.

A few minutes ago, she'd run to Justin without thinking about what she was doing. Now, with less than a foot separating them, she wanted to hold him again. She wanted to feel his body pressed against hers, to inhale his scent and steal his heat. He'd defended her because she was his wife. If only he knew how willing she was to take on every part of that role. Or did he already know and not care?

She stood there in front of him, her head bowed, her heart praying. But he didn't touch her. The moments ticked along. At last, he moved to one side and glanced into the hamper.

"What's this?" he asked.

"Mrs. Dobson sent a cold supper."

"It looks good. I'll go get Bonnie."

She watched him leave the room and listened for the sound of his footsteps on the stairs. Tonight she would be alone in her narrow bed with only her memories to keep her warm. A single tear slipped down her cheek.

It wasn't only that Justin didn't want her to share his nights, it was the fact that this marriage was a farce from beginning to end. For now, they shared a roof, but what would happen when his year was up? Would he still be leaving? What would they do about Bonnie? Would they separate? Get a divorce? It was unthinkable. Megan turned back to the hamper and started unpacking food. She wasn't worried about the scandal his leaving would create. Instead, she wondered how she would survive losing Justin for the second time in her life.

"You let me know if you want my special recipe." Mrs. Brown winked, then tapped the side of her nose. "It sure keeps men coming back. Not that a pretty thing like you will have any trouble keeping your husband happy."

Megan smiled. "Thank you. You're too kind."

The farmer's wife picked up her basket of supplies and left the general store. Megan stared after her, then glanced around at the crowded aisles. It had been three weeks since she'd married Justin, three weeks since that night they'd spent together at the hotel and three weeks since Gene had threatened her.

Megan picked up a bolt of fabric from the others that were scattered on the counter. Mrs. Brown had been choosing cloth to make her eldest daughter a dress. The weather had been fine this year, and crops were growing well. If the grasshoppers didn't come back, if the prairie fires kept west and north of them, if it didn't hail in July, then this would be the best harvest in almost ten years. Everyone seemed happy and optimistic. Even friendly. Gene had threatened her with ruin, but so far nothing had happened.

She climbed up her short ladder so that she could push the bolt of fabric in place. Since her first day back at the store, people had been stopping by to congratulate her on her marriage. She'd been afraid of censure, especially from Colleen's most loyal supporters. Mrs. Greeley had sniffed a rude comment, one or two others had stopped frequenting her store, but the rest of the town had seemed pleased. Megan smiled to herself. Everything was working out.

"Megan, Megan, come quick!" Bonnie dashed into the store and across the swept floor. Her new shoes skidded on the smooth surface. "They're here, they're here!"

She climbed down the ladder and turned to the child. Bonnie's big eyes glowed with excitement. Her braids flapped with each turn of her head. "Who's here?" Megan asked, teasing her by pretending ignorance.

"The supply stage." The little girl practically quivered with anticipation. "You think they brung my readers?"

Along with her regular order, Megan had sent for some primers for the girl. Bonnie had been waiting impatiently ever since she'd finally mastered her letters and had started reading simple words. She was anxious to "read a whole story by myself."

Megan crossed over to her and bent down to smooth the child's lace collar. That morning, Bonnie had left the house all clean and tidy. Now there was a smudge of dirt on her cheek, her shoes were scuffed and there was a new tear in the elbow of her blue calico dress. "I'm sure they *brought* your readers. But let's go find out for sure." She took Bonnie's hand and led her to the door.

Outside, a crowd was already collecting around the stagecoach. There was only one passenger climbing down. He was dusting himself off as if he'd had to share his seat with dirty cargo. Megan grinned. He probably had. Every inch of the vehicle had been filled with boxes, barrels and sacks.

"Where are they?" Bonnie asked, dancing and ducking, trying to look around the people in front of her. "I don't see 'em."

"They'll be in a box for the store," Megan said. "Don't worry. I'm sure they're here."

Mrs. Dobson came out onto the boardwalk and marched over to the stage driver. "Don't forget to give me the mail, young man."

The driver, closer to fifty than forty, looked down at the darkly-clad woman and grinned, exposing white teeth. "Now, Miz Dobson, did I ever forget your mail?"

"Just because you haven't yet, doesn't mean you won't."

"All right, ma'am, I'll be gittin' it fer you right quick." He leaned close and winked. "I don't suppose you'd have time to share a cuppa coffee with me?"

Mrs. Dobson glanced from his shiny, leather boots to his black Stetson. Megan watched the exchange, all the while wondering when the widow was going to light into the man. She'd taken hides off of much bigger men than this one, and for much less of an offense. It was a pity, though, she thought sadly. The driver was handsome, in a gruff sort of way, and he was a lot cleaner and better mannered than many men in town.

Mrs. Dobson drew herself to her full, if unimpressive, height. "Young man, I am a respectable widow and you have a schedule to keep."

The driver winked again. "I ain't so young, Miz Dobson, and you ain't so old. As for me being on a schedule and you being a widow, I don't see what one has to do with the other. But I'll tell you what. Next time I come through here, I'll make sure my overnight stop is right here in Landing. That way, we'll have plenty of time for coffee."

Megan glanced around. Everyone was eagerly watching the boxes and barrels being unloaded and didn't notice what was happening between the widow and the driver. She held her breath, wondering how loud the explosion would be. However, Mrs. Dobson didn't puff up her large bosom in indignation or begin a long, shrieking speech about her dignity. Instead, she raised a hand to her head as if making sure her hair was in place. Then she smiled slightly.

"I think that might be agreeable." With that, she turned and walked back into the store.

"Close your mouth."

Megan glanced up and found Justin standing beside her. "What?"

"Your mouth is hanging open. What are you staring at?"

It was warm out today. Spring had arrived and was already hinting at summer. Justin wore a black vest over his blue-striped shirt, but no jacket. The sheriff's badge gleamed on his chest. He was handsome and tall, proud and formidable, and her husband. Her chest swelled with pleasure.

"Megan?" He raised his eyebrows expectantly.

"Oh! Sorry. I was just—" she tried to think of something to say "—watching the crowd. What are you doing here?"

"I'm always around when the stage comes in."

Funny, she didn't remember him being here for it before. Bonnie tugged on his shirtsleeve. "I'm gettin' a reader."

"Good for you." He touched the girl's head, then pulled gently on her braid. Bonnie grinned in response.

Megan liked watching them together. They seemed to fit. The large man and the happy little girl. They understood each other. Their past formed a bond that she could never understand, yet they never made her feel left out of their circle.

"Will you look at that?"

The loud call made Megan glance back at the stage. Three tall plants were being unloaded from the passenger compartment. The roots had been wrapped in wet burlap and set into big metal pots. More burlap had been wrapped around the plants themselves. She couldn't see anything at all except for one perfect pink rose peeking over the top.

"I wonder who ordered that," she said, knowing it hadn't been her. Most people made their special requests through her store, but a few people telegraphed directly to St. Louis.

"I did." Justin stepped through the crowd over to the plants. He glanced at the tags and spoke to the man there, then started unwrapping them.

The roses were almost as tall as he was, with long graceful branches that swept toward the ground as he unwound the burlap. One of the farmers' wives sighed audibly, then said, "Climbing roses. My mother had some just like 'em back when I was a little girl. They were her pride and joy. I always thought they were the prettiest things I ever saw. Just look at the color of those blooms."

Megan moved closer to the plants. "What are they for?"

Justin looked at her. The brim of his hat shaded his eyes, hiding his expression. His lips pulled into a straight line. "The house. I thought you'd like to plant them by the front porch. It's a little late in the year, but these are strong enough that they should survive. I thought they'd look nice wound around the railings." His mouth turned down at one corner. "I know I should have asked first, but I thought I'd surprise you. They're a wedding present."

She stared at the perfect blooms fluttering in the slight breeze, then at the handsome man waiting for her to pass judgment on his gift.

"They're beautiful," she said quietly.

He pushed his hat back, so she could see his eyes. The wariness there made her want to weep. No, it made her want to go to him and press her lips against his until he forgot everything but the wondrous feelings they always seemed to create between them. But the crowd of people around them reminded her they weren't alone. She would have to save her impulse until later.

It was only after he'd peeled away the rest of the burlap, then loaded the roses into the back of a wagon that she remembered that even when they were together at the house, she wouldn't be offering him her kisses. Despite their sharing a common roof, they spent their nights in separate beds.

"Where are my readers?" Bonnie demanded as Justin tied down the plants.

"They're probably inside the store with the other supplies," he said. "You'll get them later."

"I want them now."

He jumped off the wagon and bent down to gather the child up in his arms. She squealed as he tickled her. "When did you get to be so bossy?" he asked, his voice muffled as he buried it in the curve of her neck. She shrieked with excited laughter, claiming his whiskers were itchy.

"Itchy?" He held her high in the air. "I'll show you itchy. I'll bury you in an ant farm, little girl."

Bonnie wrinkled her nose. "I'll bury you in a bear farm. The big old bears will eat you for breakfast. Every day."

He tossed her high, then caught her. She threw back her head and laughed. "Again!"

"Again?" He grinned. "If I've been eaten by bears, who are you going to order around?"

"I won't let them eat all of you," she said.

"Just part?"

She nodded. "Again!"

He threw her up. Her shrieks of excitement made Megan smile. While the two played, she went inside the store and started sorting through the boxes. Andrew had already opened most of them and was checking the contents against what she'd ordered. The young man worked quickly and efficiently. He was good at his job.

Megan tried to concentrate, but again and again her gaze was drawn back to the play outside her window. The stage had moved on and most of the people were gone. The few that stayed also watched their sheriff and the child he'd taken in. They all nodded and smiled as Bonnie laughed. People on the other side of the street called out greetings. The scene was so different from the first few days Justin had been in town. It was hard to believe so much had changed.

He'd found a home in Landing. Why now? she wondered. Why had it taken seven years for everyone to see the truth about him? Had the passage of time made the difference in him or in everyone else?

"Here are Bonnie's readers," Andrew said, handing her several slim books.

"Thanks. She's going to be very excited to start them."

Andrew nodded, then continued emptying the last of the boxes and cataloging supplies. He'd worked for her since her father had died. Mrs. Dobson had told her he was courting a farmer's daughter. Soon, Andrew would be marrying and starting a family. She looked out the window at Justin and Bonnie. The child needed more attention than Megan could give her, working in the store as much as she did. She'd already inquired into hiring someone to help at the house. Perhaps she should think about giving Andrew more responsibility and cutting back her time in the store.

Justin flung Bonnie high in the air and caught her. She laughed again and grabbed his hat from his head. Sunlight highlighted his dark hair. His good looks made her catch her breath.

She studied the lines of his face and body. How well did she know this man she'd married? She was his wife, yet not his wife. For the first time since the rushed wedding ceremony three weeks before, she acknowledged she wanted more. Having Justin and Bonnie in the big house with her made the old mansion feel like a home. But it wasn't enough. She wanted them to be the family Bonnie had requested; she wanted to be the wife Justin deserved.

Was that possible? Could they both let go of the past and begin again? She wasn't sure. Seven years ago, she thought she'd loved him, but she'd been wrong. She'd been afraid of what people would think, of what would happen to her if they knew about her and Justin. The fear had been bigger than the love. She'd hurt Justin horribly, said things that weren't true, things that would always be between them. He hadn't been able to forgive her yet. Would he ever?

Justin set Bonnie on the ground. The little girl clung to his leg and stared up at him, love and trust shining in her eyes. His hand swept over her head, brushing her bangs out of her eyes. She smiled.

Megan felt her heart squeeze tightly in her chest. She wanted Justin to look at her with that kind of affection. She wanted to convince him it was safe to care for her again. She wanted ... Everything.

"Megan, dear, I'm more than happy to keep Bonnie with me tonight."

Megan glanced up and saw Mrs. Dobson scooting out from behind her desk. She frowned. "I don't understand."

"The meeting is tonight. Have you forgotten?"

Apparently, she had. Megan rose to her feet and wiped her hands on her calico skirt. "Meeting?"

Mrs. Dobson shook her head and sighed. Her large bosom rose and fell with exaggerated movement. "There is a town meeting to discuss what to do about hiring a teacher. All parents are expected to attend."

"But I'm not—" She clamped her mouth shut. She'd been about to say she wasn't a parent. Her gaze returned to the small girl standing on the boardwalk. She and Justin were responsible for Bonnie. That made them parents, in her eyes at least.

"You're right," she said. "Thanks for the offer. We'll pick her up on the way back."

The older woman waved her hand in the air. "Don't hurry on my account. I enjoy having the child."

"I do, too," Megan said. She did enjoy Bonnie's presence in her life. She'd tried to ignore the needs inside of her for so long that she'd finally forgotten about wanting a husband and children. But Justin and Bonnie reminded her of all of that. They made her remember her dreams from long ago.

Megan resumed sorting through the supplies, but her mind was far away, wondering what it would be like to hold a baby in her arms. Her baby, the one she'd made with Justin. She touched her hand to her flat belly. There'd been no child from their one night together. But if they were still sharing their nights, who knew what might happen.

Was that the reason he avoided her? Was he afraid of having a child? Or was he afraid of having a child with her?

Megan closed her eyes and fought against the longing. She wanted a baby, and she wanted her husband to be more than a stranger in their home. She wanted... She sighed. For some reason, she'd been given a second chance with Justin and this time she just had to get it right.

Chapter Sixteen

Justin kicked a small rock out of their path and watched it roll away.

"You look as unhappy as an eight-year-old boy who would rather be fishing than going to church," Megan teased.

He grinned at her. "I sure don't want to go to this meeting. Do you?"

"No, but we have to. Getting a teacher in Landing is important for everyone with children. We have to think about Bonnie."

"I think you and Widow Dobson are doing just fine teaching her."

"What about the children who don't have anyone to teach them?"

He grimaced. That argument worked. Who would have taught him if there hadn't been a teacher? When he and Megan had been young, there'd been a small single-room schoolhouse on the edge of town. A series of young women had come, spending a year, sometimes two, on the lonesome prairie. A fire had destroyed the building eight years ago. Between the hard winters and grasshoppers, there hadn't been any spare time or money to think about rebuilding. The children in town had had to make do without formal instruction.

"Something tells me the other parents of Landing aren't going to appreciate our presence at their meeting," he grumbled.

"I know."

Nothing in her tone gave away her feelings, but he could feel her tension in the way the hand holding on to his arm tightened slightly, and the way her body stiffened.

"If you'd rather not go," he began.

"No. I want—" She drew in a steadying breath. "We need to be there, Justin."

He sure as hell didn't know why, but right now he wasn't inclined to argue. Not with Megan walking beside him in the cool evening. She wore a green calico dress that brought out the color in her face and eyes. After her day at the store, she'd freshened up, smoothing her hair back in place so that no strands escaped the elegant upswept twist. It should have looked severe. Instead her coiffure emphasized the heart shape of her face, her stubborn pointed chin and the fullness of her lower lip.

They walked easily together, her skirts swaying against his legs like a forbidden caress. Around them, other couples strolled in the direction of the church, where the meeting would take place. He didn't want to think about having to face Gene again without having the pleasure of smashing the man's face in, so he stared up at the darkening night. Stars were slowly making their appearance. Landing was so flat, it felt as if he could see the whole sky at once.

"Thank you for my roses," Megan said softly. "It was very sweet and thoughtful. How did you think to order them?"

"Wyatt mentioned his mother's roses to me once, and when I was walking back to the house, I saw the porch looked sort of bare. They're just roses, Megan." They didn't really mean anything. Except he was glad she was pleased with her gift.

He glared at the white building up ahead. Why did the meeting tonight have to be held in the church? He hated walking into Gene Estes's territory. It made the hair on the back of his neck stand up.

"It's a beautiful night," Megan said, stopping and staring at the sky.

"Beautiful," he echoed, watching the play of shadows on her features. She'd always been the loveliest woman he'd ever seen. He knew there were many who wouldn't agree with him, but he didn't care about anyone else's opinion. She had always been his ideal. It was going to be hell to leave her. Even for a few days.

"With the weather fine like it is, I've been thinking of traveling around to some nearby towns," he told her.

Her gaze met his. "You're still concerned about Laurie's murder." It wasn't a question.

"I want to see if they've had any murders, or even beatings. Maybe I can figure out a pattern. That would help me find the killer."

"You still believe it wasn't a drifter?"

"Yes. One thing I learned while I was away is that life isn't that tidy. Bad people don't just come into a town, murder someone and leave. Most people are killed for a reason, and usually by someone they know."

"I'm glad you won't let this go," she said.

He drew his eyebrows together. "Why?"

She tucked her hand more firmly against the crook of his elbow and leaned her cheek against his arm. "It reminds me of the kind of man you are. I'm very proud of you, Justin."

He didn't know what to say to that, so he didn't say anything at all. They moved toward the church, joining other couples who had come to decide about hiring a teacher. As they approached the few steps leading up to the church, Megan came to a stop.

"You're worried about Gene and Colleen," he said.

She nodded. "They have two children, and this is his church. I know they're going to be there. It's just that I haven't seen Colleen since—"

Since the day before the wedding. Since Megan's evil sister had come into his office and tossed her lies around like rocks thrown with deadly accuracy.

"We don't have to go," he said softly.

"Yes, we do. I refuse to let her frighten me. Besides, I have to face them sometime."

He'd been doing his damnedest not to touch her. It hurt too much to be close to what he would never have. But she needed his touch tonight, and he'd never been able to deny Megan anything. He raised his hand and brushed a knuckles down her cheek. "I'll go beat up Gene for you, if you'd like."

His offer was rewarded with a trembling smile. "Somehow I think you might enjoy that a little too much."

"You're right."

She stared up at the building and straightened her shoulders. "Thank you, but no, I'll face them on my own. If they give me too much grief, I'll simply take back that organ I donated."

He grinned. "I'll help."

They entered the church and found most of the townspeople already in place. Justin was grateful that the only seats still available were at the back. Gene was going to be running the meeting, because he controlled the church. Justin knew if he had to sit up front and stare at the man, he would be forced to violence. He didn't think the good citizens of Landing would take kindly to their sheriff and minister brawling by the pulpit.

They slid into one of the pews. Justin tried to get comfortable, but the benches didn't have backs. He shifted a couple of times, then resigned himself to a long, boring evening and a stiff back, come morning.

Gene walked to the front of the church and cleared his throat. "I appreciate all of you attending tonight. As you know, we're here to decide what we're going to do about educating our children." As he droned on, his snakelike gaze slipped over the assembled group. When his eyes met Justin's, he faltered for a moment, before going on.

Justin smiled. It was an insignificant victory over a man he would easily best in any competition. He shouldn't care that his presence upset Gene Estes, but he was damn pleased, anyway.

The minister outlined several proposed plans. When he was done, one of the farmers stood up. He was dressed in worn clothing, with several patches on his sleeves and trousers. The man removed his hat. "We can't pay no teacher's salary, and we ain't got no room to have her come stay with us for a month. I don't think no teacher will take kindly to sleepin' in the barn with the milk cow and that's all the room we got."

Gene thanked the man. "I understand your concerns, but this year's crop is going to be good for everyone."

The farmer shook his head. "You don't know about next year, do ya? Not unless the good Lord himself has been a' whisperin' in your ear."

Megan bit down on her lower lip, but Justin heard a small giggle escape. He leaned over and nudged her. "Shh. He's stating his opinion, not being disrespectful."

She looked up at him, her hazel eyes alight with amusement. "I know, but I don't think Gene or Colleen see it that way," she whispered.

Justin glanced over at Megan's sister and saw Colleen stiffening in her seat. If she sat any straighter, she was going to pull her hips clean off her legs.

The farmer twisted the hat in his hands. "I'm willin' to pay my share. I want my young'uns to learn to read some and do cipherin'. I'm just pointin' out that we don't know what's gonna happen next year. I can't make no promises about salaries 'til I know."

"Good point," another farmer called. "We ain't all rich like you, Reverend."

Gene cleared his throat. "My wife has a small inheritance. That hardly classifies us as rich."

"Richer than us," someone in the middle of the church mumbled.

Justin was surprised when Megan rose to her feet. She was the first woman to speak. At the sight of her, Colleen blanched and drew her mouth into a straight line. Gene tugged at his collar.

"Perhaps we should consider a different plan of payment," Megan said. "What if, instead of everyone paying the same amount, which could be a hardship for many, we have people pay according to what they earn? If there's a bad year for crops, those of us whose income doesn't depend on the favors of weather and pestilence could pick up the extra. In years with good crops, farmers could pay more."

Several people mumbled their agreement. Justin looked at his wife. Her idea made sense.

"I've never heard anything so stupid." Mrs. Greeley bounced to her feet. "Megan Bartlett, you sit down and be quiet. You don't even have a child."

Justin started to stand up. Megan placed a warning hand on his shoulder. The room grew quiet.

"My name is Megan Kincaid, and I'm responsible for the welfare of a child. My concerns are as great as yours."

"Sit down!" Mr. Greeley tugged his wife's arm until she plopped down next to him. Megan stood for several more seconds, as if to show people she wasn't afraid, then she took her seat.

Gene cleared his throat. "Perhaps it would be best if the women left the decisions to the menfolk and—"

He was cut off by the sound of twenty women calling out protests. Justin grinned. Megan's brother-in-law was braiding the rope for his own hanging.

"Ladies, please. Ladies!" His voice rose as he tried to get order.

Justin leaned over to Megan. "Your idea was interesting. I liked it."

"Thank you. It'll get voted down, but I wanted to say my piece." She pointed across the room. "I don't suppose I've endeared myself to my sister."

Colleen was fanning herself and appeared to be breathing heavily. The flush of color on her cheeks added to her appearance of agitation. "I wouldn't let it bother you," he said, wondering how the same family could have produced such different women.

"But Justin, you should be more concerned." Megan's voice was teasing. He glanced down at her and raised his eyebrows. She leaned closer so that their arms were pressed together and their shoulders brushed. "After all, my sweet sister is now your sister-in-law."

He groaned softly. "You're a wicked woman to remind me of that."

Her smile was impish. He could hear the discussion continue to flow around them, but he didn't pay any attention to what was being said. Instead, he studied Megan and wished they were alone. He wanted to kiss her. It was a foolish desire that would only lead to trouble, but he couldn't not want her. Even knowing how she felt about him, even knowing she'd been forced into marrying him. He tried to summon male pride to combat the weakness, but it was useless. Around her, he had no pride, nothing but need and desire. She could leave him broken and bleeding, and he would still come crawling back to her.

"I promise we'll only have to spend holidays with them," she said, smiling softly.

"That's not much of a consolation."

"Maybe you'll get lucky and Colleen won't ever speak to me again."

"That would be nice," he admitted, then thought he wouldn't want that for her. Despite Colleen's priggish ways, Megan cared for her sister. He would suffer her presence if it made Megan happy.

We'll only have to spend holidays with them. He stiffened as he grasped the meaning of her words and the implication that they would still be together year after year. Would they? Would this mockery of a marriage endure? He thought not. He would perish from need if he had to continue living with her and not be able to claim her as his.

He shifted on the hard seat and wished the meeting would end. Conversations sprang up around them as small groups discussed the merits of each plan presented. Megan listened intently but didn't interrupt. Justin didn't care what they decided. He wanted to believe he would stay, that he and Megan would have a marriage in more than name, but it wasn't likely. She had been right when she'd accused him of being unable to forgive her for the past. He knew he was right about her being unable to love him for what he was.

Time ticked by slowly and the temperature in the small church increased. If the damn pew had a back, he could have relaxed and dozed off. He shifted again.

"Sit still," Megan whispered, tapping his forearm. "This is important."

He folded his arms over his chest and exhaled. "It's boring. I'm of a mind to just give them enough money to build the schoolhouse and hire the teacher."

"I'm surprised you'd offer so much of your salary for this."

She didn't know, he thought, feeling alert for the first time in an hour. Why would she? No one knew. He grinned. "I wouldn't have to use my salary," he said, realizing he was about to surprise her. Megan wouldn't care about money; she'd never worried about going hungry. But he knew what that felt like. When he'd been no more than twelve, he'd promised himself he would never be poor or hungry again. It had taken almost the entire seven years he'd been gone, but he'd kept the promise to himself.

"How would you pay for it?" she asked, her delicate eyebrows drawing together.

He leaned close and whispered in her ear. Not because he didn't want anyone to hear what he was saying but because he liked being close to her and smelling the rosewater rinse she used in her hair. "I'm rich."

"What?"

She turned and stared at him. Their faces were inches apart. If they hadn't been in the middle of a crowd, he would have kissed her. "I've invested heavily in the railroad. About a year ago, I sold all my shares at a great profit." He allowed himself a moment of pride. "I've got more money than you, your sister and everyone in this damn town combined."

"Then why did you bother coming back?"

Because I couldn't go on without seeing you again.

The thought sprang to his mind fully formed. He fought against it, but saw the truth. He'd gone on about making the past right, about proving the town wrong about him, but the real truth was he'd come back for Megan.

"I had some unfinished business."

Before she could ask another question, someone in the last pew stood up and started walking toward the front. Justin recognized the handsome widower, Cameron Forbes.

As Cameron walked the length of the church, all conversation ceased. Megan straightened and faced front. When he reached Gene, Cameron pulled a small bag out of his trouser pocket and placed it on the table at the head of the aisle. The bag clunked as it settled on the wood. Justin stared at the man. He'd just set down a lot of money.

"There's enough there to build the school and pay the teacher for the first year. Between now and the time that year is over, you can figure out how to keep her paid." Cameron's eyes swept over the assembly. Something dark and painful flickered in his gaze. "I'll build a three-room house on my property, by the main road. The teacher can stay there at no charge. The way I see it, if the teacher doesn't have to board from family to family, it'll be easier to hire someone good. I'll leave the rest of it up to you folks."

With that, he jammed his hat on his head and stomped out of the church. There was a moment of silence after his departure, then the room exploded into conversation.

"What the hell was that about?" Justin asked.

"I'm not sure." Megan turned and stared after the man. "He lost his wife and daughter a few years back. I don't think he's ever gotten over the loss. Maybe it has something to do with that."

Justin understood about a woman being hard to get over.

Gene pounded on the desk at the front of the church, but no one paid him any mind. As far as the townspeople were concerned, the issue of how to pay for a schoolroom and a teacher had just been solved.

Megan stood up and rubbed the small of her back. Justin watched as the movement thrust out her breasts, making him remember how her tender flesh had felt against his hands, and tasted in his mouth. He swallowed hard, knowing he was a fool to continually dwell on that which he could not have. He tore his gaze away, only to see Colleen sweeping down on them from across the room.

He bumped Megan's arm and jerked his head in Colleen's direction. "If we hurry, we can beat her out the door."

Megan hesitated, then shook her head. "I have to face her sometime." She waited until her sister was directly in front of her, then nodded. "Colleen, you're looking well."

"I wish I could say the same." Colleen gave an insincere smile, then glared at Justin. Slowly, he pushed up until he was standing. "I see marriage has not improved your manners," she said.

He grinned. "I'm sure you're right, however it's brought me into the warm bosom of your family. I know how much that must please you."

Colleen's thin lips pinched together as if she'd tasted something bitter. She huffed and turned her back on him. "I don't know how you stand him, Megan, however I didn't come to fight with you."

"Oh?" Megan met her sister's gaze squarely. Justin placed a supporting hand on her shoulder. He was grateful when she didn't shrug him off. "Why *did* you come over?"

"We're sisters. I know in my heart what you did was wrong. You're a sinner in the eyes of the Lord and in the eyes of this town."

"This is your idea of not fighting?" Justin blurted out. "Should Megan be grateful for your criticisms?" He'd never hit a woman before, but there was something about Colleen that tried his self-control. He gritted his teeth. "I warn you, Colleen, I won't stand here and listen to you speak this way to my wife."

Megan glanced up at him. The brief look spoke of her gratitude and her request that he let her handle the situation.

He growled an assent, all the while ready to protect her, by force if necessary.

Colleen ignored him. "However, you are my sister and I must ignore my distaste of what you've done. It wouldn't be seemly of me to turn my back on you."

"Go ahead and do it," Megan said softly.

Justin stared down at her. He couldn't have heard her correctly. But he must have. Colleen stared at her with an incredulous look on her narrow face.

"Pardon me?" she said.

"Go ahead," Megan repeated. "Turn your back on me, Colleen. I don't care anymore." Under his hand he felt Megan's muscles relaxing as she spoke. He squeezed her shoulder. She reached up and put her hand on top of his. "I've married Justin Kincaid and we've taken Bonnie in as our own child. Nothing you can say or do is going to change that. I'm not afraid of you or your threats. If you wish us to be a family, I'm very willing to accommodate that. You and I only have each other. But if you won't accept my husband and my child, I won't have anything to do with you. And I do mean *accept*. No snide remarks, or subtle references to lack of manners, breeding or whatever else you wish to spend your time finding fault with. Accept them as your equals, or lose me forever."

Colleen opened her mouth but no sound came. She tried again, her hands balling up into fists. "You dare to dictate to me?" she asked, her voice incredulous. Her gaze swept over Megan, then settled on him. Justin remained in place, his weight balanced on the balls of his feet. If he had to, he was prepared to move quickly. He wasn't afraid of Colleen for himself, but for Megan. Despite her brave words, she could still be badly hurt by her sister.

"I dare that and more," Megan answered. She turned toward Justin and nodded to the door. "Let's go home."

He stepped back to allow her to precede him. They'd almost made it to the front steps, when Colleen recovered. "It's him, isn't it, Megan?" she called.

Justin wanted to keep walking but his wife had other plans. She paused and glanced over her shoulder.

"This is all because of that bastard, isn't it?" Colleen pointed an accusing finger at him. There were only a few people left in the church. Her words hung inside the building and everyone turned to stare. "He's the reason you never married, even when you had your chance. You've been waiting for him to return. You're a fool, Megan Bartlett. He'll never care about you. He'll leave you stranded with more bastard brats to feed."

Justin thought about retracing his steps and shutting Colleen up. He watched her face turn red and her eyes disappear into slits as she spewed out her filth. Then he shook his head. She wasn't worth the trouble.

Megan turned away from her sister. "Let's go home," she repeated. She took his arm and they started down the stairs. Before they could even reach the path that led toward town and the Bartlett house, a man darted out of the shadows.

Mr. Greeley smiled nervously, then pulled off his hat. "I'm sorry about my wife, ma'am," he said, then glanced at Justin. "Mrs. Greeley isn't always a happy woman."

Justin didn't answer. He stared at the man for a moment, then nodded.

"I'm going to have a talk with her tonight. You've done a fine job, Sheriff. And Miss Bartlett, ah, Mrs. Kincaid, you're real fair to us folks. Your sister and her husband are trying hard to turn the town against you. I just wanted to let you know that we all stand behind you on this."

Justin stared at the smaller man. He pictured the butcher's tall dragon of a wife and felt a twinge of pity for him. He held out his hand. "Much obliged."

Mr. Greeley grinned and they shook hands. "You want anything special from my shop, you come tell me. It's never any trouble."

"We appreciate that," Justin said and watched the man walk away. He didn't envy him his conversation with Mrs. Greeley that night.

"You must be very happy," Megan said, taking his arm as they started toward town. "You're proving them all wrong."

"I suppose." He shoved his free hand into his trouser pocket. He'd waited seven years for the victory but it didn't taste as sweet as he'd thought it would. He would give it all back in a minute if it meant Megan would continue to hold on to him as they walked and trust him to keep her safe.

"I noticed at the meeting how many people greeted you. Quite a difference from your first day in Landing," she said.

A cold feeling slipped over him. He tried to ignore the sensation and its source, but it drew all the warmth from him until he had to clench his muscles tight to keep from shivering. A knot formed in his stomach. As Megan chattered on, the knot tightened.

"I'm not sure if Colleen is going to come around, but I have to say, I don't really care. She thinks she controls the town, but she's wrong. If she forces things between us, I believe she'll be the one cast aside by everyone." Megan cuddled close to him. "They respect you, Justin. I'm so proud of you."

He'd been ignoring the truth for days, but he couldn't any longer. The knot in his gut grew until the pain threatened to drop him to his knees.

Megan wasn't warm and friendly because she'd come to care about him. It didn't matter that he'd never stopped loving her, that he still loved her. What mattered to her was what other people thought. Now that the town had accepted him, she could accept him, too. It was safe for her to be seen with him now. He was respectable, so her reputation was safe.

He shouldn't have been surprised. Megan had always cared about what other people thought more than anything. He even understood why. But that didn't change anything. It didn't change the fact that she would never love him for himself. It didn't change the fact that her reputation mattered more to her than he did.

"What's wrong?" she asked. He kept walking, even when she tugged on his arm. "Justin?"

"I thought it was different," he said at last. "But it isn't, is it?"

"I—I don't understand. Why are you suddenly angry?"

He stopped and turned to face her. Moonlight illuminated her feminine features, the line of her cheek, her full mouth. God, he didn't want to still care about her. He didn't want to be trapped by a love that would never be returned.

"You must be happy," he said, trying to keep the bitterness from his voice. "How convenient that your husband has at last become respectable. Now it's safe to be married to me."

"What are you saying?"

"The truth, Megan. It's all right to tell it to me. We're old friends. I guess I know you better than anyone. I know how much your reputation matters."

She flinched. "Is that what you think of me?" Her eyes filled with tears. "That I've been waiting for the town to pass judgment before I sanction this marriage?"

"Don't worry. I won't walk out on you." He couldn't, damn it all to hell. Even if he wanted to.

"Oh, Justin, I suppose I know why you think that, but you're wrong. I care about you very much."

The pain was worse than he'd remembered, he thought, wondering how he managed to stay upright. She placed her hand on his chest. It burned, not with the heat of passion but with the fire of betrayal. He couldn't stand it anymore. Couldn't stand to be with her and know what would never be.

"Caring isn't enough," he said, stepping away from her. "Damn you, woman, how dare you tell me you care? As if I'm some maiden aunt you're going to tend in her dotage. I love you, Megan. I've always loved you."

She caught her breath. "Justin?" Her hand reached out toward him.

"No!" He moved back farther. "No more lies. No more pretense. No more betrayal."

"Justin, don't go."

The words were a whisper, but they came too late. He turned from her and disappeared into the night.

"But why isn't Justin here?" Bonnie asked, her voice plaintive.

"I told you, sweetie, he had to go back to his office. He'll be here in the morning, when you wake up." At least she prayed Justin would return.

"Promise?"

Megan bent forward and kissed the girl's cheek. "Yes. Now go to sleep. It's very late."

Bonnie snuggled under the quilt, her small world having been made right by a promise she believed. The trusting innocence jabbed at Megan's heart like a pinprick. As she rose to her feet and carried the lantern out of the room, she hoped she wasn't going to disappoint the child, come morning. Justin had to come back. For both of them.

At the top of the stairs, she hesitated, wondering if she should go down to the parlor and wait for him. She stared into the shadows below, then turned toward her bedroom. She trusted him to come home to his family. He wouldn't leave Landing without telling her.

She entered her room and closed the door behind her. Instead of starting to get undressed, she sat on the edge of her bed and stared toward the open window. She could hear the sounds of the night and inhale the fresh fragrance of spring. Soon the first shoots from her vegetable garden would be making their appearance. She set the lantern on the nightstand beside her bed, then lowered the wick until the room was plunged in darkness.

He loved her. Her eyes closed and she held the feeling of gladness close to her heart. He loved her. He said he'd always loved her. For the seven years he been gone and even before that, Justin had loved her. He loved her still.

Megan felt the tears on her cheeks. She didn't brush them away. She didn't want to. These were happy tears, joyful tears. Until he'd spoken the words, she hadn't known how long she'd been waiting to hear them, not wanting to admit her need, fearing she could never have that which she most desired. Until he'd said the words, she hadn't realized how much *she* still loved him.

She smiled, then laughed aloud and fell back on the bed.

"He loves me," she whispered. "Me! Justin Kincaid loves me."

She felt positively giddy at the realization. They could make it work now, she knew. Justin was the most honest, decent man she knew. He wouldn't lie about something that important. She could trust his feelings and him. His proposal of marriage had been the act of an honorable man, as was the way he always stood by her. Of course, there were problems to work out. The whole issue of their past. But if he loved her, he must forgive her. She laughed again, overwhelmed by joy and relief. At last they were together. In her heart, she knew she'd been waiting for him to come back to her.

She sat up suddenly and stared at the dark room. Was that why Justin had chosen separate rooms? Because he cared and thought she didn't? It made sense. She fumbled for the lantern and lit the wick. She would have to tell him the truth. As soon as she saw him. Then they could be together always.

A thought intruded on her happiness as she suddenly wondered if he planned to stay in Landing permanently. He hadn't said anything about it. If he was the rich man he claimed to be, not that she cared about the money, she had enough for them both, what would he do here? If he was planning to leave, would he expect her to go with him? Could she leave everything she'd known behind?

"It doesn't matter," she said aloud and picked up the lantern. "We love each other. Everything else will work out fine. I know it will." She walked into the hall. It had to work out. She refused to lose Justin again.

Chapter Seventeen

Justin didn't bother with a lamp when he unlocked the door and stepped into the sheriff's office. The faint glow of the moon outlined the three desks and he moved until he was sitting behind the one in the middle.

After opening the bottom right drawer, he pulled out an unopened bottle of whiskey. He set the bottle on his lap, then raised his feet until his heels rested on the corner of the desk and he could stretch out in his chair.

It was quiet tonight. No drunks slept it off in the lone cell in back. He hadn't had to arrest more than a half-dozen troublemakers since he'd taken over as sheriff. The job wasn't hard or even time-consuming. He could be doing something else if he wanted. Maybe start up that horse ranch he'd been dreaming about ever since he'd had that job at the livery stable when he was a teenager.

He picked up the bottle, then set it down on the desk and closed his eyes. Had it really been that long ago when he'd quit school so he could make money to help out his mother? It felt as if it were just a couple of months ago. He'd still been on the scrawny side, getting beat up regularly by bigger boys who had nothing better to do than taunt the town bastard. His mother had cried over his cuts and bruises. She'd wept silent tears for his pain, and by the time she'd finished tending him, he'd been the one offering comfort.

Had she known the truth? he wondered. Had she figured out that the reason he'd stopped coming back beat up was that he was sending other boys home that way? Or had she assumed he was getting along better? What would she say about his marriage to Megan Bartlett?

He didn't want to think about that, but he couldn't help it. Megan was as much a part of him as his soul. Ripping her out would cost as much. He suspected his mother would be pleased with the union and would only see what she wanted to see. That was how she'd survived her grim life living above the saloon, spending her days on her knees scrubbing and cleaning.

But it had all been for nothing. His job at the livery stable hadn't saved her. She'd died, despite his earnings. He'd come back to make the past right and had found himself caught up in it, instead. He was married to a woman who could never love him. The fragile peace with the town was meaningless in the face of his dilemma. How could he walk away from Megan? Knowing the truth, how could he bear to stay?

He leaned over and pulled open the top left drawer. In the back, tucked under a couple of wanted posters and some bullets, was a small cloth bag. He drew it out and held it in his hand. Seven years ago, he'd gone back to the forest and spent the better part of a night looking for this. He opened the bag and tilted it so the slender gold chain spilled out onto his hand. He'd given it to Megan the afternoon he'd asked her to marry him. She'd tossed it back at him the afternoon she'd sent him away.

Justin held up the chain, turning his hand so that it caught the moonlight.

"I don't love you. You're a fool if you thought I ever did."

Her words screamed in the silence. The fact that he'd heard them more than seven years ago didn't lessen their impact.

"I know who my father is. You're just that bastard Justin Kincaid. You'll only ever be a bastard. Go away. Go away!"

He closed his fist over the chain, squeezing as hard as he could. The gold work was too fine to bite into his skin. He knew he could never create a physical pain to match the bleeding in his soul.

And now she cared about him. Seven years too late he found favor. Not because she loved him or needed him, but because he was accepted by the town. Because it was easy and the right thing to do.

He knew now why the opinions of others mattered so much to her. What her father had done was inexcusable. But it wasn't enough. Justin knew he needed more. He needed to know she loved him for him and not because doing so was simple and correct. If only she'd come away with him when he'd asked her. They could have been together all this time. They could have had a child of their own, maybe a daughter like Bonnie. A six-year-old who—

Justin sat up suddenly. His boots hit the floor and the sound echoed loudly in the still office. Something nibbled at the back of his mind. Something that almost made sense, but not quite. Bonnie was six. Her mother had been murdered. Seven years ago, her mother had been beaten and left for dead. Had someone tried to kill Laurie because she'd found out she was pregnant?

He stood up and started pacing the office. It made sense. But why wait all that time to kill her? Why didn't the killer do it when he found out she was pregnant? Unless Laurie had known her killer and had been convinced the first attack was the result of temper, never to be repeated. Justin grimaced. A lot of men beat up women, and prostitutes were more susceptible to injury than most. From what he remembered about Laurie, if she'd known and cared about the man, she would have given him another chance.

He continued to pace. "Mama said we'd be a real family," Bonnie had told him.

He stopped suddenly. Had Laurie been pressuring her lover? If so, that meant he was married. Justin frowned. Almost all the men in Landing were married, and with the possible exception of Colleen's minister husband, most of them visited the saloon girls regularly. It could be anyone.

But it was a start. In the morning, he would leave for the neighboring towns and talk to the sheriffs there to find out if they'd had similar problems. If he could figure out a pattern, his gut told him he would have his answer.

He walked toward the door and stepped outside. After turning the lock behind him, he started down the boardwalk. As he moved through the quiet town, he wondered if he could consider staying here permanently. He would for Megan. Which made him an even bigger fool, he supposed.

He still held the delicate chain in his hand. He dropped it into his vest pocket and tried to think about something else. By the time he walked up the front steps to the Bartlett house, he'd managed to plan his routes to the nearby towns and come up with a list of questions to discuss once he got there.

The hallway was dark, but a lantern had been left by the stairs. He picked it up and carried it with him. At the second-story landing, he paused in front of Megan's closed door. How many times had he wanted to go inside and watch her as she slept on her virgin's bed? How many nights had he imagined opening the door and finding her waiting for him, her body clad only in her wicked French lingerie? He placed his hand against the wood as if he could feel her warmth through it. He swallowed hard against the need welling up inside of him and turned away. He only had to be strong for tonight. In the morning, he would be gone and when he returned, well, he would get through that night when it happened.

After checking on Bonnie and making sure she was covered and sleeping soundly, he started down the hall to his own room. The door was partially open. He pushed it and stepped inside. If he hadn't tightened his grip instinctively, he would have dropped the lantern on the floor and started a fire.

Megan lay curled up on top of his bed. Her long blond hair was loose on his pillow, her body covered only with the sheerest silk and lace. One bare foot peeked out from the hem of her robe. Her hands were tucked under her cheek.

Desire hit him like a thunderbolt. His legs almost buckled as his blood heated to boiling. Hot need swept through his groin, hardening him instantly. On the heels of the compelling urge to go to her and claim her was the thought that he should turn and run in the opposite direction. Bedding her would expose him even more. He was already too close to being destroyed by his feelings for her.

Then she stirred slightly and he was lost. It wasn't that he could see more of her perfect body, or inhale the sweet scent of her skin. It was that she trusted him enough to risk his rejection, and that she dared enough to come to him virtually naked.

"Megan," he said softly and put the lantern on the dresser by the door.

She opened her eyes and stared at him. He wondered if she would remember where she was, but she didn't look surprised or ashamed. Instead, she smiled and stretched. "I didn't mean to fall asleep. I was trying to wait up for you."

"Why? What do you want with me?"

She sat up and pushed her hair out of her face. Her expression was fearless. "I'm your wife, Justin. I want—" She ducked her head but not before he saw the first hint of a blush on her cheeks.

It took every morsel of his self-control to stay where he was. He wanted to go to her and take her in his arms, greedily supping on all she offered. But he couldn't. Not after what had happened between them. Not after he'd told her he'd never stopped loving her. He wouldn't bed her because she felt sorry for him.

She stood up slowly. The thin, delicate fabric and lace hid nothing. He could see the shape of her breasts, the elegant curve of her waist and hips, the shadowed place that hid her secrets. Her eyes met his. In the lamplight, the hazel faded to a pale gray. He'd always thought the color cold, but now he saw fire could burn there hotly. Desire straightened her mouth and won against her modesty. She untied her robe and drew it off her shoulders. It fell to her feet, leaving her dressed only in the sheerest of gowns.

Thin straps held embroidered lace against her breasts. The rest of the fabric flowed uninterrupted to the floor.

"I'm here because I—"

But he didn't let her finish what she'd been going to say. He'd thought of being strong and turning away from her. He'd thought he should protect the last whole part of his being so she couldn't leave him completely shattered. He'd been a fool. He couldn't resist her; he'd never been able to. And why should he? Wasn't a single night in her bed worth a lifetime in hell?

He crossed the room in two long strides, not caring that he crumpled her delicate robe beneath his boots. With one quick pull, he drew her gown over her head and tossed it behind him. Then he picked her up in his arms simply because he wanted to feel her naked body next to his. A fire ignited inside of him and it burned away his slender hold on convention and manners. He prayed Megan would not protest his possession, because he had to take her or die.

She wrapped her arms around his neck and pressed her head to his shoulder. He bent over and lowered her onto his wide mattress, then moved close to stretch out beside her. She was silk and satin, fresh cream and roses. He couldn't think of all the words he would need to describe her beauty, her softness. As she lay on her back staring up at him with wide eyes, he ran his hands over her. From her shoulders, down her pale arms to her long fingers. Across her waist, down her hips to her thighs. Below, to her slender calves and ankles, and finally to the arch of her foot. Everywhere he touched, she was smooth and soft. Sleek skin, sensuous curves, the supple willingness of a woman who trusts a man. She moved with him, her muscles rippling where he stroked her, her body shifting in subtle appreciation of his attention.

He knelt at her feet. Her nakedness pleased him. He smiled faintly. Pleased. What a foolish word to describe his feeling of awe. It was as if he gazed into the face of God this moment and saw a miracle. Her blond hair lay against the pillow like golden water spilling on lace. Every inch of her body, every line, every curve, brought him pleasure. He would touch them all this night, taste them, make her writhe and scream, make her cry. Only then would he claim her, and only then would *he* weep. Deep inside. Hard ugly tears for what would never be, and the permanence he would never know at her side. But the pain was for later. For this next hour, there was only this woman and her perfection.

He started to unbutton his vest. His finger bumped against his pocket and he felt the slight bulge there. The chain. He hesitated, then pulled it out.

"Justin. You found it."

He held it up so it caught the light of the lantern, then took her hand and pulled her until she was sitting up in front of him. Without saying anything, she moved her hair over her shoulder, leaving the back of her neck exposed. He unfastened the chain and slipped it under her hair. His fingers brushed against her bare skin, making her shudder and him clench his teeth with longing.

The tiny catch resisted at first, then he secured it and straightened. She drew her hair away from her chest. The gold chain rested on her bare skin, less than two inches below her throat. It clung to her as if it too had spent the last seven years wishing to return to her. She reached up and traced its curves with her fingertip.

"Thank you," she whispered. Her lips trembled.

He finished unbuttoning his vest and ripped it off. He pulled his shirt from his trousers and tugged at the buttons. When they were free, the shirt joined the vest on the floor. Then he bent over her and grasped her shoulders. She arched her head back, raising her chin toward him. Her mouth parted as if she needed no seduction to be ready.

He gave her none. He pressed his lips hard against hers and instantly thrust his tongue inside her mouth. She moaned deeply. Her fingers touched his chest and sides, moving up and down quickly, fluttering against his heated skin. He wanted to grab her hands and force them down so that she held his throbbing hardness, but he knew if she touched him there, he would explode. Not yet, he reminded himself. Not until he'd branded her with his passion. Not until she was mindless with exhaustion and could do nothing but feel.

He cupped her face, then slipped his fingers through her long hair. He drew back slightly and swept his tongue across her mouth, moistening her, then sucking her lower lip until her breathing increased. He kissed her cheeks, her nose, then nibbled the edge of her chin. Lower and lower he kissed along her neck, until he reached the curve of the chain.

There he bit down, making her jump, tasting her sensitized skin. He could feel a shiver as it raced through her. The hands on his body stilled as her attention focused on what he was doing.

After tracing patterns on her back, he lowered her to the bed and slipped between her knees. Her thighs parted willingly. He moved closer, until his crotch rested against her blond curls. He could feel the heat there. It burned him through the layer of his clothing. She rotated slightly, but he ignored the invitation. Not yet.

He bent over her and touched her breasts. Veins showed through, a faint blue line against pale skin. He traced the path with his tongue, then circled her already erect nipple. The small rose-colored point strained toward him. Her eyes fluttered closed and her head arched back in anticipation. He blew softly on the tip, but didn't touch it. He repeated the procedure with her other trembling breast, tracing the faint line, circling the sweet curves, savoring the taste and the anticipation.

He sat up and stroked between her breasts to her midsection, across her hips and close, temptingly close to her woman's place. Her hands curled into the coverlet. He reached for her wrists and brought her fingers to his chest. Eagerly she brushed against him, rubbing the hair, searching for his male nipples. When she found one, he sucked in his breath as sensation shot through him.

Her hips flexed against him. Up and down, she pressed herself along his hard length. He wondered if she was aware of what she was doing. He captured one of her hands and drew her first two fingers into his mouth. She tasted faintly salty. He licked the tips of her fingers, then bit down gently. When her skin was wet, he moved her hand back to his chest. Those damp fingers now toyed with his nipple, pulling it gently and teasing it into a tighter need.

He glanced down at her face. Her eyes were open and she watched the play of her hands along his body. There was nothing shy in her expression. Curiosity diluted by passion, perhaps, but no fear.

"Does that feel nice?" she asked and raised her other hand toward his mouth. He sucked on her fingers, then released her. She touched her damp skin to his nipple and squeezed gently.

"Yes," he said hoarsely, fighting the need to unbutton his trousers and bury himself in her waiting moistness. He leaned forward, pressing into her attentions. Her hips kept up their rhythmic assault on his self-control. The heat between them grew as he felt his clothing dampen from her body.

He sucked in a curse, then bent over her and drew her left nipple into his mouth. The tight bud tasted sweet. He touched his tongue to the sensitive point, then circled around. She moaned his name. Her hands kneaded his shoulders and his back, until mindlessly they slipped onto the bed. Her head twisted back and forth.

Again and again he drew her into his mouth. He toyed with her until her body was coated with perspiration and her legs trembled. Until rubbing her woman's place against him had left him as wet as her. Only then did he dip his head lower so he could kiss her belly. Her skin quivered. Her hands clung to the coverlet. Lower still, until he could feel the soft curls, then lower and lower until he touched his mouth to her most sensitive place.

She jumped. When she started to raise herself and say his name, he pushed her legs back and apart, exposing her fully to him. He began at the place that would shortly give him respite and slowly drew his tongue up to the tiny spot of her pleasure.

Her questions got lost in her gasp. He focused on that spot, circling it, loving it, gently, teasingly, drawing her tighter and tighter still. He listened for the sound of her breathing, for the ragged gasps and half-formed moans. He felt her body quiver and shake as pleasure rippled through her. He felt the sudden tensing as she neared her completion and he tasted her sweetness. He released her legs, but they stayed splayed apart. She dug her heels into the mattress and pressed her hips higher, her woman's place harder against him. He tasted her sweet saltiness and knew he could spend the rest of his life loving her this way.

Her hips thrust up again, then locked. He loved her quicker now, light, fast movements that sent her body into spasms. She called out his name, the word broken by a single sob.

He held her as she cried, feeling the tears on his bare chest. He kissed them from her face, then was still as she kissed him back and tasted her own sweetness. He allowed her to unbutton his trousers and caress him as he sprang free. When the tentative stroking brought him too close to the edge of madness, he tossed away his clothing and swept her onto her back.

There, buried in the wet tightness that massaged every inch of him, the pain at last eased. In those few moments of pure pleasure, he forgot. As her body matched rhythm with his, he told himself it would be like this always, and for once he didn't mock his own lie. As the ecstasy exploded and she held him close, he waited for the inevitable return of the ache.

When they were both still, he spoke at last. "Why did you come to me?"

Megan stretched against him, looking as contented as a cat in front of a fire. Her naked legs tangled with his, her hand rested on his chest. "We're married, Justin. A husband and wife should sleep together."

"I suppose."

"You don't mind?"

She raised her head as if she wanted to stare at him. He placed his hand on her hair and pressed her back into place so that her cheek rested on his shoulder. "I don't mind."

How could he mind? It was all he'd dreamed of. It would kill him later, but without her, what did that matter?

"I'm glad. I thought about a lot of things while you were gone." With each word, her breath puffed out along his chest. It tickled. He didn't want her to ever leave him.

"I'm sure you did."

"You said you loved me."

"I know." His telling her had been a mistake, a moment of weakness. But he didn't call back the words.

"Do you really?"

He closed his eyes against the light of the lantern. "Yes."

"But you can't forgive me?"

"No."

"I understand."

He doubted that she did, but it didn't matter. His fingers glided over her back and down to her rounded derriere. He squeezed. She hugged him closer.

"Justin, I—"

He knew what she was going to say even before she spoke the words. He didn't want to hear them. Not now. Not like this. Not when he had no way to protect himself. He wouldn't listen. But he had to.

"I love you, too," she said.

He'd expected the pain, so it shouldn't have surprised him. Still, as the agony ripped through him, he couldn't help stiffening against the hurt. His breath caught in his throat and his heart pounded painfully against his ribs.

"Justin, what's wrong?"

He sat up slowly and turned until his feet slid off the bed to the carpeted floor.

"Justin?" She touched his back. "What is it? You're frightening me."

"It's nothing."

"But—"

He shook his head. "Leave it alone, Megan. It doesn't matter."

"Of course it matters. I just told you I love you and you act like I stabbed you or something. Tell me. Are you afraid of what that means? Am I being difficult? Didn't you want me to love you?"

He jerked his body around until he was facing her. She'd sat up and her long hair tumbled over her bare breasts. How was he supposed to walk away from her? "Stop saying that," he ordered.

"Why? What's so terrible about me saying that I love you?"

"I don't believe you."

Megan stared at the man who had just touched her so intimately. The face, the body, even the voice was familiar. But she didn't know him. She couldn't. Her Justin would believe her, while this dangerous stranger simply stared at her with empty eyes.

"You can't mean that," she whispered, too numb to feel anything but shock and surprise. This wasn't true. It couldn't be happening. Not after what they'd just shared.

"Dammit, Megan, don't look so stunned. Did you think I was blind?"

"I—" She didn't know what to say.

He shook his head in disgust. "When I first came back here, you were terrified to be seen with me. You were worried about your precious reputation more than anything."

She winced. "That's not fair. I explained about my father and what he did."

"Yes, you did." He leaned close to her and brushed his finger against her cheek. "I'm sorry about what happened with your mother. I understand how it must have hurt and frightened you. But that was a long time ago. You're not that little girl anymore. I think you're using what happened then to excuse your fear now. You wouldn't risk anyone's knowing we had once been engaged, because you were afraid of what people would think. Now that I'm acceptable, it's all right to be seen with me, even to be married to me."

"I came to your hotel room, Justin. I purposely destroyed my reputation. Don't you dare tell me I care anymore what other people think."

He dropped his gaze to the rumpled bed. For the first time, she became aware of their nakedness. She wanted to pull the sheet over her, but was afraid of what he would say to that. She shook her head slightly so that her hair covered her breasts and tried not to think about the rest of her body being exposed.

"You reacted out of anger and frustration," he said quietly. "Your unconventional behavior had nothing to do with how you cared about me. If anything, you used my feelings against me. You knew I couldn't resist you."

Now it was her turn to look away. Shame crawled over her, leaving her skin hot and tight. He was right. She'd never thought that Justin would turn her away if she went to him. She hadn't planned on staying long enough for them to become intimate, but she had expected him to go along with her plan. Even when they'd spent the night together and she'd been frightened about what she'd done, she trusted Justin to protect her. And he had. He'd married her.

"You must hate me," she whispered, fingering the edge of the sheet and pleating the white linen between her fingers.

"No, never that. But I do know you. At the first sign of trouble, you'll turn away again."

"I won't." She looked up at him. "I swear, I won't. I've changed. I've grown up. I'm not that frightened young woman you knew seven years ago. I've had time to think about things."

"It's not different. Seven years ago, you claimed to love me and look what happened."

"Don't compare me now to who I was then. I've already admitted I was very young and afraid of what people would say. This is different."

"No, it's not."

He rose to his feet and towered over her. He seemed not to notice his nakedness, but she was aware of his body that had so recently joined with hers. How could they have shared such intimate passion and now be arguing? How could he do those things to her, make her feel so exquisite and then not trust her?

"I don't believe you," he said. "Just this evening, you said how pleased you were that the town had accepted me."

"I was happy for *you*," she said, staring up at him. "Not for myself. I want you to be happy here, with Landing and with me. You're deliberately twisting what I said. Why would I lie about loving you? Why would I pretend?"

"Because it amuses you to control me. You've always enjoyed the power you've had over me."

The unfairness of his accusations left her speechless. She stared at him and knew there was no way to reach him this night. Perhaps not ever.

She studied his face, his expressionless eyes and the dark hair that drifted to his eyebrows. She looked at his broad shoulders and the chest she'd caressed just a few minutes before. How could he have done that with her, all the while thinking of her as so shallow and cruel? She swallowed and tasted bitterness and defeat.

"You used me," she said, and shuddered. Suddenly, her nakedness was too much for her. She scrambled off the side of the bed and reached for her robe. The thin silk offered no protection against his gaze, but she pulled it on and knotted the belt tightly around her waist. Pushing her hair out of her face, she turned toward him. "How could you?"

His arms hung loosely at his sides. A cruel smile pulled at his straight mouth. She braced herself for the blow.

"Now you know how I've felt these past years," he said. "You used me, Megan. Back when you said you'd marry me, then a few weeks ago, when you came to my hotel. Even tonight. You came to my room knowing I wouldn't turn you away. Don't talk to me about taking advantage of someone. It's what you do best."

You said you loved me, that's why I came to you tonight. She opened her mouth to speak the words aloud, then shook her head. There was no point. She moved around him toward the door. How had this happened? How had their wonderful night become something ugly and mean? She reached for the door and pulled it open.

"I'll be gone in the morning," he said.

Her eyes burned, but no tears fell. Gone? He was leaving her? She'd only just figured out how much she needed him and now he was leaving? Oh, please, God, it wasn't fair.

"Wh-what about Bonnie?" Her voice cracked.

"Can't you take care of her? I'll be back in less than a week. With any luck, I'll have found the murderer."

Her knees trembled with relief. He wasn't leaving her. He was going to nearby towns to investigate Laurie's death. Of course. How could she have forgotten?

"Bonnie will miss you," she said, fighting against the tightness in her throat. She felt cold, although the night temperature was pleasant. Her skin was clammy, as if a fever raged, but the cause wasn't illness, it was the pain of her broken heart.

"I—" She stopped for a moment, then shook her head again. There was nothing left to say. "Good luck, Justin." She pulled the door shut behind her.

The hallway was completely dark, but she was able to find her way to her room. Once there, she huddled in a chair by the window and stared into the night.

Words and images from their evening together flashed through her mind. She turned them around and around, wondering what she could have done differently, said instead to have made it better between them. She fought against the instinct to lash out in pain and forced herself to be calm. She had to know if Justin was right.

But it was hard to think that way, when all she wanted to do was curl up in a small ball and disappear. She wanted to leave town and never look back; she wanted to run so far she would forget about Justin and what he'd said. That she didn't love him, that she'd used him her entire life, that she enjoyed the power she had over him.

"Never," she whispered into the darkness. "I'm not like that." But was she?

Megan searched her mind for the first moment she'd noticed Justin Kincaid as more than another boy around town. She'd been fifteen, caught between the worlds of children and young women, not sure what to do with herself. It had been at a dance, she remembered. He was popular with the young women. They liked his quick smile and easy good looks. She'd watched him circle the room, holding them in his arms, dancing and laughing. Justin had laughed so much back then. She'd been envious of those young women. She'd escaped outside and it was there that he'd found her.

Megan swayed in her chair, remembering the music and the faint sounds of conversation from the old barn the harvest dance had been held in. She could smell the food and the men's cigars, the faint fragrance of cider on Justin's breath.

"You're Megan," he'd said as he'd appeared beside her in back of the barn.

She'd been too nervous to speak. She'd simply nodded and stared at her shoes.

"Old man Bartlett doesn't like me much," he continued. "I don't suppose he'd take kindly to me asking his prettiest daughter to dance."

Megan could feel the flush of pleasure on her cheeks, as she had that night so long ago. Justin had taken her in his arms then and danced with her on the edge of the forest. They hadn't spoken, they hadn't had to. From that night on, he'd been there, waiting. When she'd managed to get free from her duties in the store, he'd been around to go for a walk. In the summer, they'd met down by the stream. Some nights, she couldn't get away and she'd thought about him waiting, but he'd always understood. They'd never discussed her father, or the town. They were never seen together by anyone. He knew her father would forbid them seeing each other, so Justin had made it easy for her. And she'd let him.

Megan drew her knees up to her chest and hugged her legs close. She'd let him. Because she hadn't wanted to fight with her father or stand up to him. She'd known she didn't have the courage to face him. For two years, she and Justin had crept around, seeing each other when they could and never telling anyone the truth. She'd been so sure she loved him, but when the moment came to prove her feelings, she'd thrown his affections in his face and turned away.

He was right about the past; was he right about the present? Did she profess to love him now because it was easy?

She thought about her sister and her threats. She thought about Gene and Mrs. Greeley and the other people in town who would never understand and never accept. She could survive without their approval. She thought about her store. It tied her to Landing. When his contract was up, Justin wouldn't want to stay here. Why should he? Could she leave everything behind and go with him? Could she love and trust him that much?

She squeezed her eyes tightly closed. She liked the store. She liked keeping the books and inventory in order, and dealing with the customers, and being responsible for her own well-being. But she loved Justin more. If forced to choose, she would go with him, because without him, she had nothing.

But would he even give her the chance to choose or would he simply leave her behind, turning away, as she had turned away in the past?

She reached up and touched the slender gold chain that encircled her throat. Whatever happened, she wasn't going to lose him again. If he tried to leave without her, she would follow him. If he rejected her again, she would keep coming back. She loved him. She believed that as surely as she believed the sun would rise in the morning. But her faith wasn't at question. How was she going to convince Justin? She could follow him for a lifetime and he might never trust her. What then? How exactly was she supposed to convince her husband that this time it was real?

Chapter Eighteen

At the loud crash, almost everyone in the store turned. Megan calmly finished counting the pattern books before drawing in a deep breath and looking behind her toward the most recent disaster.

A large glass jar of buttons had tipped over. The jar was intact, but several pounds of buttons had scattered over the counter and onto the floor. Bonnie stood in the center of the mess, biting her lower lip. However, the real culprit was halfway across the room, sitting on the jewelry display case and frantically licking her fur as if to reassure herself everything was fine.

Bonnie looked at her. "Alice got caught."

"I can see that." It was amazing what sort of damage a six-pound kitten could do in a general store, Megan thought.

"That cat is a menace," Mrs. Dobson said, coming up behind her and staring at the mess.

"I know. However, Bonnie has really missed Justin since he's been gone. Alice makes her feel better. I can't tell her she mustn't bring the cat with us. Can you?" She stared down at the widow.

Mrs. Dobson sighed. "The child does dote on Justin. We'll survive this, I suppose. But please keep that cat out of my stamps." She shuddered. "I can just see her getting them stuck all over her fur."

Megan laughed.

"It's not funny."

Megan stifled her humor. "I suppose not." She walked over to Alice and picked her up. Wide green eyes gazed back innocently. "Stop getting into everything."

Alice snuggled into Megan's arms and started to purr. Megan shook her head. To be honest, she liked having the mischievous cat underfoot. It helped pass the long hours. Like Bonnie, she, too, missed Justin. He'd only been gone four days, but it felt like a month. Probably because they hadn't spoken before he'd left that morning.

"I'm sorry, Megan." Bonnie puffed out her lower lip. "I'll clean it all up myself."

"That's a big job. It's probably going to take all afternoon."

Bonnie nodded, dejected. "Am I gonna get a whippin'?"

Megan's chest tightened. The girl always asked the same question when she got into trouble. Megan wished she could go out to Mrs. Jarvis's farm and give the woman a good whipping of her own. How dare she treat this little girl so badly? And Bonnie's mother, Laurie, should have known what was happening to her own child.

Megan set Alice on the counter by the spilled buttons, then touched Bonnie's face. It wasn't fair to judge Laurie. Megan didn't know much about the young woman, but from all Bonnie had said, Laurie had loved her daughter. Perhaps she'd done the best she could.

"No whipping," Megan told her. "Remember, I promised you that a long time ago. I'll never hit you, Bonnie. You're going to be punished if you do something bad, but you don't have to worry about being hurt or scared again."

Tears filled Bonnie's big eyes and spilled onto her cheeks. She flung herself at Megan and wrapped her thin arms around Megan's thighs. "We're sorry, aren't we, Alice? We didn't mean to make a mess."

"I know, honey." Megan knelt down and gathered the girl to her. "It's all right. I understand you and Alice were just playing."

Sobs shook the girl's body. "You're not gonna leave, too, are you? If I promise never to be bad, will you please stay with me?"

Was that what this was about? Megan pulled Bonnie's arms from around her neck and set the girl away from her. Bonnie's nose and eyes were red and her mouth puffy from crying. "Is that what you think? That Justin has left you?"

Bonnie nodded. "You said he'd come back, but he didn't."

"Oh, Bonnie, I'm so sorry. Justin came back that night, but then he left before you got up. He hasn't left you forever. Just for a few days. He'll be back. I promise."

Bonnie sniffed. Megan could see the child wanted to believe, but was afraid to.

"What's all this nonsense about Justin leaving you behind?" Mrs. Dobson asked, coming over to stand next to them. "Bonnie, you're a smart girl. You just think about Justin and how he's taken care of you. Would he go to all that trouble if he was just going to leave you behind?"

"N-no."

"Well, then. He's a fine father and you should be grateful to have him. Imagine how hurt he would be to find out you didn't believe in him."

Mrs. Dobson was speaking to the girl, but Megan wondered if the older woman could see into *her* soul. Imagine how hurt Justin had been when she, Megan, hadn't believed in him. She closed her eyes briefly.

"He's really coming back?" Bonnie asked softly.

Mrs. Dobson smiled. "Justin will never leave you, child. He loves you."

How simple, Megan thought, wishing the same logic applied to her situation. She knew Justin loved her, but he didn't trust her. Still, she'd made up her mind to prove her feelings to him, somehow. Hopefully, a plan would occur to her before he came back. If not, then she'd think of something before his year was up. She had that long.

"I made a cake last night," Mrs. Dobson was saying. She held out her hand. "Why don't you come with me to my desk and we'll share some. Then we can get started picking up these buttons." She glanced at Megan. "Is that all right?"

"Fine." Megan stood up and brushed off the front of her dress. "Are you feeling better?" she asked Bonnie.

The little girl smiled and nodded, then took the older woman's hand and skipped over to the front of the store.

Megan stared at the scattered buttons. She went into the back room and collected several tins. This was as good a time as any to get the buttons all sorted. At least it would keep Bonnie busy. Alice would have fun, as well, chasing shadows and generally making a pest of herself.

When she walked back into the store, Bonnie was already laughing with Mrs. Dobson. Megan smiled. The older woman had grown to care about the girl. So far, Justin hadn't been able to find out anything about Bonnie's family. He'd mentioned that if nothing turned up, he would speak with the circuit judge on his next visit and discuss adopting Bonnie. Megan set the tins on the counter. Perhaps by then they would be the real family that the little girl wanted and they could adopt her together. She touched her stomach. Perhaps by then she would already be carrying Justin's child. She hadn't figured out exactly how she was going to prove herself to him, but one thing was for sure, she was going to do her best to stay in his bed.

Oh, but it was difficult to keep hoping for the best when she didn't have any idea how to convince him she cared. She'd spent the last four days coming up with plans, only to abandon them. Everything she'd considered had sounded foolish or impossible.

The front door opened and Colleen strolled in. She was dressed in a blue gown with lace insets in the sleeves and over the collar. It was beautiful, and expensive, ordered all the way from New York. Clothing from St. Louis wasn't good enough for Colleen. The fact that the dress was completely inappropriate for Landing would never occur to her sister, but Megan figured she wasn't the one to point it out. After all, she had a Worth gown sitting in the armoire in her bedroom.

Megan smiled. Colleen could be difficult at times, but there was no denying they had some things in common. A love of expensive, inappropriate clothes was one of them.

Colleen saw her and walked down the center of the store to meet her. Other conversations in the store stopped as people turned to stare at them. Megan grimaced. No doubt, everyone had heard about their argument after the meeting last week. She held her ground and waited.

Colleen stopped in front of her. She glanced at the spilled buttons. "Was there an accident?"

"No, I was taking inventory."

Colleen's thin eyebrows drew together as if she wasn't sure if she was being mocked or not. "Gene and I have realized we must trust our faith to keep us safe from the devil."

Megan blinked several times, not sure what that meant. "I'm so pleased for you," she said at last.

"Yes, well, with that in mind, we would like to have you and your, um, family, over for supper." Colleen pulled a lace-edged handkerchief out of her reticule and sniffed it delicately.

"I'm overwhelmed by your gracious invitation," Megan muttered.

"You told me I must accept your husband and that..." She paused. "I must accept Justin and Bonnie if you and I are to continue to be sisters. Despite what you think of me, I do have your best welfare at heart. I don't agree with what you've done. However, I am willing to make the first step."

It was a big gesture for Colleen, Megan reminded herself. After all, her sister wasn't known for her generosity. She thought about refusing and severing the relationship completely, but she didn't want to. The momentary satisfaction would quickly give way to regret. Whatever Colleen had said or done, they were the only family each had left.

"I was thinking of tomorrow night," Colleen said. "About five-thirty. Is that convenient?"

"We can't. Justin's away for a few days. He's gone to neighboring towns to see if the same kinds of murders have happened there."

"A waste of time, if you ask me."

Megan drew in a deep breath and reminded herself Colleen had made the first move toward a reconciliation. She had to be willing to take that same step herself. "It's not a waste of time. You should be pleased he takes his duties so seriously."

"I think he takes this seriously because his mother was as much a prostitute as that dead girl. Good riddance. Have you thought of what he'll be doing while he's gone? Perhaps he'll need to question some of those *women* as part of his investigation." She said the word as if it were dirty. "Don't forget, Justin admitted he knew that whore seven years ago. Knew her intimately. I would be quite concerned if I were you." Colleen shook her head. "You're already having second thoughts, aren't you? You should have listened to me. I could have told you—"

"Stop it," Megan ordered, her voice low and angry. "Stop it right now! I should have known better. But no, you've tricked me again." She glared at Colleen. "Why am I so willing to believe the best of you when you forever show me how wrong I am?"

"I don't know what you're talking about. I'm simply pointing out the obvious. Your husband—"

"Is none of your concern," Megan interrupted. She placed her hands flat on the counter between them and leaned forward. "I'm only going to say this one time. So listen to me very carefully. If I hear of you saying one bad thing about Justin or Bonnie, anything, even the fact that you don't like the dress she has on or how he combs his hair, I'll never speak to you again as long as I live. I'm tired of watching you bully people in this town, and I'm especially tired of watching you bully me."

Colleen flinched, but Megan wasn't finished yet. "You constantly talk about your pious ways and your husband's position as minister, but you make a mockery of true Christian spirit and godliness."

"Don't you dare speak to me that way."

Megan leaned closer, until less than a foot separated them. "Don't *you* dare threaten me. I won't listen anymore. I'm not afraid of you or anyone. I don't care what you think. The only person whose opinion matters to me is Justin's."

"You're at least one step up from a whore, Megan. I'm sure he thinks you're perfect."

Megan narrowed her gaze. "You're pushing me too far, Colleen," she said quietly. "I don't need your business here. You and Gene never pay your bill, anyway. But you'll have a lot of time to think about that when you have to go all the way to the next town for supplies. As for my being perfect..." She drew in a deep breath and let it out with a laugh. "If only you knew the truth. You're right. One of us isn't worthy of the other, but I'm the one at fault. I'm the one whose reach exceeds her grasp with Justin. He deserves so much more, but he's stuck with me, because I love him and I'm not going to let him go."

Colleen blanched the color of her handkerchief. For a second, Megan thought her sister was going to faint, but she managed to clutch the counter in time and catch her breath. "Don't say that."

"Why not? It's true. I loved him before he left seven years ago, and I still love him. My only regret is that we've lost all those years together. We could have already had a family together."

"You're mad."

"Probably," Megan agreed, surprised at how relieved she felt to tell someone her real feelings.

"I don't know what to say." Colleen turned away and started for the door. When she opened it, she looked back. "I'll speak to Gene. We'll pray for you."

"Do that," Megan called as her sister left. When the door closed, she looked around the store and saw everyone was staring at her. She met each of their gazes, keeping her head high and her shoulders back. She had nothing to be ashamed of.

Bonnie put down her cake and ran across the store. When she reached Megan, she looked up and grinned. "I'm glad you love Justin. Now we can be a real family together."

Megan picked up the girl and held her close. "I'm going to do my best to make that happen, honey. I'm going to do my best."

Megan wasn't sure what she'd heard when she first woke up. She had the vague memory of a thud, as if something had hit the side of the house. Or as if someone had closed a door.

She sat up in bed. Had Justin returned? He'd said a few days. She didn't know exactly how long that was, but yesterday had been day four.

She swung her feet over the side of the bed and grabbed for her robe. It wasn't the silky sheer confection she'd worn to his room, although this robe wasn't something her dear sister would approve of, either. It was soft blue satin and edged in black lace. She drew it over her shoulders and fumbled for the matching slippers. By the time she crossed the room, she'd already fastened the tie around her waist.

She pulled open the door and peered down the stairs. "Justin? Is that you?" She kept her voice low, not wanting to awaken Bonnie. No sense in disappointing the girl if what Megan had heard was just the wind.

Silence answered her call. She waited, then spoke again. "Justin?"

Nothing. Megan took a single step down, then stopped and listened. There was a slight scratching sound. No, that wasn't exactly what it was. She tilted her head to try to figure out where the noise was coming from. From behind her, maybe? From one of the other bedrooms.

She turned slowly and looked down the hallway. All the doors were closed. For the first time since awakening, she felt a shiver of apprehension. Was a stranger in the house? The hairs on the back of her neck stood up.

Before she could decide whether to investigate or just grab Bonnie and run outside with her, she heard a loud thump followed by a scream.

"Megan!"

She raced down the long hallway and flung open Bonnie's door. Her gaze raked across the room to the empty bed. "Bonnie!"

The child screamed unintelligibly. Megan spun toward the sound and saw a tall dark shape carrying the girl toward the already open window.

"Stop!" she yelled. "Let her go."

Without thinking, she ran toward the man, stopping long enough to grab the poker from beside the small fireplace in the room. She could see his arm around Bonnie's waist as he hauled her along. He already had one leg out the window.

Megan raised the poker and brought it down hard on the man's shoulder. He grunted in pain. His head turned toward her. Instinctively, she shrank back. Dark eyes glared at her above the cloth he'd tied over his lower face. A hat had been pulled low on his forehead. She stared, mesmerized by his gaze. There was something familiar about his eyes, something horribly familiar.

Then it didn't matter who he was. She raised the poker again. He ducked away, in the process releasing the child. Megan grabbed Bonnie and thrust the girl behind her.

"Get out!" she screamed at the man. "Go away!" She hit him again and again until he stumbled out the window and made his way down a ladder. She kept screaming, even after he'd run into the forest.

Only then did the fear swamp her, leaving her shaken. Her teeth chattered and her legs refused to support her. She had to hold on to the window frame for balance. After catching her breath, she pushed the ladder hard so it slowly moved away from the house and crashed to the ground. She closed the window and then turned toward Bonnie.

The little girl huddled in a corner of the room, sobbing wildly. Megan dropped the poker and hurried to her.

"Hush, honey," she said, pulling her close and holding on tight. Bonnie trembled in her embrace. "I know you're scared, but it's all right now. You're safe."

"H-he s-said he was gonna h-hurt me," Bonnie whimpered, clinging to her.

"It's over. You're fine, honey. You're with me, now." Megan stroked Bonnie's back and arms, then smoothed the child's hair away from her face. "Come on, we're going to go to my room and stay in my bed. We'll be together. He won't come back."

Bonnie continued to hold on to her, so Megan picked her up and carried her down the hall to her bedroom. She closed the door and locked it, then set Bonnie on the bed. After settling her under the covers, Megan sat next to her with her back against the headboard. She leaned over and opened the nightstand drawer. Her father had left her capable of taking care of more than the store. He'd left her able to protect herself. She pulled out a derringer.

The small pistol was cold and deadly looking in her hand, but she was prepared to use it. Megan put her arm around the girl and fixed her gaze on her locked door. No one was going to hurt Bonnie. Not while she had any say in the matter.

A thousand questions filled her mind. Who would try to take Bonnie, and why? It didn't make sense. She wasn't a danger to anyone. She had no family, she didn't know anyone except for a few people in town. There had to be a mistake. But the man must have known he was kidnapping a child.

She caught her breath. Kidnapping! Was that it? Had someone tried to take Bonnie and hold her hostage? Was the man really interested in money?

"Megan?"

"Yes, dear?"

"Are you really gonna shoot him if he comes back for me?"

She thought about lying, but knew she couldn't. "Yes, Bonnie, I am."

"I'm glad." The girl sniffed. "The bad man scared me."

"I know, but I promise to keep you safe. Always."

Bonnie was quiet for a moment, then she spoke again. "Are you my mama now, Megan?"

"I suppose I am." She gave her a quick smile, then returned her attention to the door.

"I'm glad," Bonnie said softly and snuggled close.

"Me, too," she whispered back. "Try to sleep, honey. I'll be right here."

Bonnie took a deep breath and relaxed. Megan fought against the emotions roiling inside of her. The little girl trusted her with her life. It was a big responsibility, but she wouldn't give it away for anything. Reactions from what had just happened kept rippling through her as her body trembled and her mouth grew dry. She wanted to run and hide with Bonnie, but it was the middle of the night and they had nowhere to go. Town meant walking through the woods and that was the direction the man had gone. Better for them to stay in the house until daylight, then make their way to safety.

An hour before the sun crept over the horizon to begin the day, Bonnie fell asleep. But Megan didn't dare close her eyes. Still staring at her door, she prayed Justin would return to them quickly. She needed him to help keep their child safe.

Justin rode into Landing shortly before noon. He stared at the familiar buildings, nodded as people waved and called out greetings and wondered why he was fool enough to think he was going to miss this place when they ran him out of town.

He squinted up at the bright sun and figured he'd be gone before nightfall. He would be lucky to get away without a lynching. But he'd done what he'd set out to do. He'd found the killer.

Even now he couldn't believe it. The answer was so obvious, once he knew who it was. He'd been right. Laurie had been killed by someone she knew; the same man who'd tried to kill her when she'd told him she was pregnant.

He reined in his horse in front of the sheriff's office. After dismounting, he secured the animal, then made his way inside. Wyatt was pacing the floor. At the sound of the door opening, he spun around.

"Sheriff! You're back. Am I glad to see you."

Justin fought against the uneasy feeling that swept over him. "What's wrong?"

"You've got to go see Megan, ah, Mrs. Kincaid right away."

His heart beat faster. "Is she hurt?"

"No." Wyatt stared at him. "It's the damnedest thing. She was in here this morning demanding I tell her when you'd be back. I told her I didn't know exactly. She said that last night someone climbed in an upstairs window and tried to kidnap Bonnie."

Justin stared at his deputy, then swore loudly. He took off running. He tore out of the building and down the boardwalk. Wyatt followed on his heels. If anything happened to either of them— Dear God, he couldn't bear to think about it.

"Thomas is out questioning people," Wyatt said between breaths as he caught up. "I asked her if she wanted me to stay in the store with her, but she said she'd be safe with Mrs. Dobson and Andrew there with her. If you hadn't shown up by noon, I was going to start wiring the towns and find out where you were."

They ran across the dusty street, dodging a wagon and a man on horseback. Justin saw the gleaming front glass of the store up ahead. He raced to the door, then flung it open.

"Megan!" he roared as he entered the building. There were half a dozen shoppers who all turned and stared at him. Several of the women backed up a step or two. He looked around the building and saw Bonnie sitting beside Mrs. Dobson.

The little girl squealed with excitement and came running toward him. "Justin, you're back!"

She flung herself at him. He opened his arms wide and drew her up against his chest. She wrapped her legs around his waist and her arms around his neck.

"How's my girl?" he asked. He felt as if he'd been gone a year. He knew it was silly, but he thought she might have grown in his absence.

"I missed you."

"I missed you, too, Bonnie," he said quietly. He wanted to ask if she was all right, but he didn't want to upset her. Then he heard soft, familiar footsteps and turned toward the sound.

Megan walked down the left aisle of the store. Her blue calico dress was neatly pressed, her hair pulled back and tidy. But her appearance didn't deceive him. He saw the shadows under her eyes and her hands twisting together in front of her waist. After the way they'd parted, he'd been determined to maintain his distance, but he couldn't. Not after what he'd just been told.

He shifted Bonnie so he could support her with one arm, then held out his other. Megan ran those last few feet and threw herself against him. He drew her close.

"I'm sorry," he murmured. "I should have been here."

She raised her face to his. He saw tears glistening in her eyes, but she didn't let them fall. Even her smile was brave. When had Megan gotten so strong?

"It's not your fault. You couldn't know what was going to happen. Bonnie and I are fine, aren't we, honey?"

The little girl nodded. "Megan's got a gun."

Justin raised his eyebrows.

"It's just a little one. A derringer. My father bought it for me years ago, when I started staying late at the store."

"Your father had more sense than I did," Justin said, realizing he should have thought of that himself. But this was Landing and it had never occurred to him Megan or Bonnie could be in any sort of danger.

He looked down at the little girl and gave her a smile. "I need to talk to Megan for a couple of minutes. Can you stay with Mrs. Dobson?"

Bonnie nodded. "We're reading. I read a whole book by myself!"

"Good for you. Maybe tonight you'll read it to me." If he was still here.

"Really?" Bonnie's eyes widened. "All the story?"

"Sure." He set her down.

She grinned. "I'll go practice." She skipped across the wooden floor and excitedly told the widow her plan.

Justin looked around the store. The shoppers weren't even pretending interest in anything other than the drama unfolding around them. "Wyatt, stay here for a few minutes. I'm going to need your help. Megan, let's go in the back and you can tell me exactly what happened."

"Of course," she said, and started to lead the way.

They'd almost reached the curtain that separated the private part of the store, when he realized she was hanging on to his hand as if she would never let go. He studied her and saw the faint tremors in her shoulders and the way she held her head so stiffly. She must have been terrified last night.

His chest tightened at the thought of what could have happened to her. The other sheriffs had had more detailed reports about their towns' murdered prostitutes. The killings had been brutal; all the young women had been beaten to death. He sent up a prayer of thanks that Megan had survived. He didn't care if they did run him out of town, he was going to make sure that criminal never hurt anyone again.

Megan walked into her office, then released his hand. She leaned against her desk. "I woke up sometime after midnight," she began calmly. She stared at a point over his left shoulder. "There was a noise. At first I thought you had—"

Suddenly, he grabbed her shoulders and hauled her hard against him. Before she could protest or even speak, he lowered his mouth to hers. It was wrong to kiss her. Hell, it was a disaster. But he didn't care. She was safe and alive and that was all he cared about.

He brushed his lips against hers, slowly, gently, not wanting to frighten her more. Megan stretched her arms up so that she could slip her fingers through his hair. Before he could think about deepening the kiss, she had parted her mouth. He swept his tongue inside and tasted her sweetness. She was as hot and willing as he remembered, meeting him more than halfway, pressing her hips against his, murmuring words of encouragement.

He cupped her face and kissed her cheeks, her nose, her eyelids. She was the most precious part of his life. "I love you," he murmured, not caring that she would use the words against him.

"Oh, Justin." Megan rested her head on his shoulder and pressed her lips to his neck. "Believe me when I say I love you, too. For always. Later, we'll figure out the whys and hows. Later, I'll come up with a plan to convince you of the truth. But for now, for just this one minute, please, please, believe me."

He wanted to, more than he wanted to draw in his next breath. He would have given anything to trust her. But he couldn't.

He stroked her hair. "I'm glad you're safe."

"Damn you, Justin Kincaid, you're the most stubborn man in the world."

"Possibly," he admitted.

"Why won't you believe me?"

When she would have raised her head, he held her in place. He didn't want to look into her face and read her emotions. He didn't want her reading his. "Tell me what happened last night."

She wrapped her arms around his waist and leaned against him. In a few, brief sentences, she explained about hearing the noise then finding the man trying to escape with Bonnie.

"Did you see his face?"

"No. He had something tied over the bottom part, and a hat pulled low. I saw his eyes. Not that well, it was dark and I didn't have a lamp with me. They were..." She paused.

"What?" he prompted. "Anything you can tell me will help."

He felt her draw in a deep breath. "They were familiar, but don't ask me how... I don't know. There was something evil about him." She shuddered.

"It's all right, I'm here."

"I was so frightened. What if he'd gotten Bonnie? He might have hurt her."

The man probably would have killed her, but Megan didn't need to know that. "He didn't. You were very brave."

"I didn't feel brave. I just wanted her back. I knew he wouldn't let go of her, so I grabbed the poker and started hitting him."

Justin stared over her head toward the wall above her small desk. "How many times?"

"I'm not sure. Five, maybe six. Why does it matter?"

"Did you hit him hard?"

"As hard as I could, on his arm and shoulder."

"Good. He'll have bruises there. We'll be able to prove it was him last night."

She straightened and pushed at his chest until she could stare at him. "You came back. Does that mean you've figured out who the killer is?"

He nodded slowly.

"And?" She waited expectantly.

He touched her hair, then brushed the back of his hand along her cheek. Soft, sleek skin, so warm and supple. He prayed losing her again would kill him because he didn't want to spend the rest of his life missing her.

"I'm sorry, Megan," he said, releasing her and stepping back. "I want you to stay here until everything is taken care of. You'll be safer here."

"Safe from what? Who's the killer? Is it the same man who tried to take Bonnie?"

"Yes. The man responsible for all of that is your brother-in-law, Gene."

Chapter Nineteen

Megan looked up at him. She couldn't catch her breath, so she couldn't ask him to repeat what he'd just said. Gene? A killer? It wasn't possible. Her brother-in-law was a self-righteous prig who would rather be flogged than actually help a needy person, but a killer?

Justin grimaced. "I didn't expect you to believe me. That's why it's better if you stay here. There's going to be enough trouble with the town. I suspect the good citizens of Landing won't take kindly to me arresting their minister. If you want to salvage what's going to be left of your reputation, you'd better stay clear of the church. Later, you can divorce me and I'm sure they'll take you back to their collective bosom."

He spun on his heel and walked out of the office.

Megan stared after him. She blinked several times, then drew in a deep breath. He couldn't have meant what he'd just said. "Justin?"

But he was already gone. She ran to the curtain and thrust it aside. Justin was talking with his deputy, then both men started toward the front door.

"Justin, wait!"

He didn't bother turning around. He kept on walking, Wyatt at his side.

Mrs. Dobson squeezed out of her small post office. "What is it, Megan? What's happening?"

"Justin's gone to arrest Gene," she said woodenly, wondering what to believe.

"Arrest the minister?" Mrs. Dobson's disbelief was echoed by customers all around the store. "For what?"

"For Laurie Smith's murder and for—" she glanced at Bonnie who was staring at her wide-eyed "—other things." She looked back and saw Andrew stocking the canned goods. "Andrew, do you know where I keep my rifle?"

The teenager looked up, obviously startled. "Y-yes, ma'am."

"Do you know how to use it?"

He gulped, then nodded.

"Fine. Everyone, I'm sorry but the store is closing temporarily," she told the customers. "Just leave your purchases here. You can come collect them later."

She hustled everyone out of the store, then crouched in front of Bonnie. "I have to go check something. Justin thinks he's found the bad man who hurt you. I want to make sure he's going to arrest the right one. Can you stay here with Andrew? He'll keep you safe."

Bonnie nodded. "Don't let that bad man hurt Justin."

"I won't," Megan said, then prayed she could keep her promise. She waited while Andrew fetched the rifle she kept in the back. "I'm trusting you with my daughter," she told the young man.

"Yes, ma'am. I'll protect her like she was one of my own."

Megan blinked back the tears. When all this was through, she was going to have to give him a raise. "Lock the door behind me. Don't let anyone in but me or Sheriff Kincaid. Do you understand?"

He nodded and followed her to the front door. She waited until he'd secured the lock, then she grabbed her skirts and hurried toward the church.

The people she'd thrown out of the store were milling around on the street. Several tried to talk to her, but she just kept moving. Mrs. Dobson fell into step beside her.

"Are you sure about this?" the widow asked. "He's really gone to arrest Gene?"

Megan nodded and kept moving. Nothing made sense. Justin had to be wrong. Yet, she didn't care if he was. He'd made his feelings plain. He was her husband and she was going to support him.

"What proof does he have?" Mrs. Dobson asked as they hurried toward the edge of town.

"I don't know."

"He must have made a mistake. Why would Gene want to kill a prostitute? I would be surprised if he even knew what they were for."

"If Justin said he did it, then I believe him."

Megan saw the church up ahead. Justin and Wyatt were outside talking. Her husband looked up and saw her. He frowned.

"Dammit, Megan, get the hell out of here," he called, glaring at her.

She shook her head and kept walking toward him. Justin turned away and started up the steps. She rushed after him, leaving the widow panting behind her.

When Megan reached the steps, she could hear Justin inside calling for Gene. She raced up the stairs and stepped into the building.

It was dark and cool inside, a marked contrast to the bright, warm day outside. She paused by the door, letting her eyes adjust. Justin and Wyatt stood by the pulpit. Gene moved out of the shadows toward them.

"Good afternoon, Sheriff. What can I do for you?"

"Did I miss anything?" Mrs. Dobson asked between breaths as she entered the church.

"Hush." Megan started down the aisle. She wanted to be able to hear everything. The widow kept pace with her. Behind them, Megan could make out more sounds, as if the entire town was coming to join them.

Justin stepped toward the minister. Her husband was a few inches taller, but Gene was broader and heavier. Megan stared at her brother-in-law's face, trying to imagine him climbing a ladder to the second-story bedroom so he could kidnap Bonnie. Her imagination wasn't up to the task. What would Gene want with the girl? She clutched her hands together in front of her waist. Justin had made a horrible mistake. She squared her shoulders. It didn't matter. He was her husband and she would stand beside him.

"I'm arresting you for the murders of Laurie Smith, Ellen Morgan and Sharon Tyler. In addition to that, last night you tried to kidnap a little girl from her bed, with intent of murdering her, as well."

Megan hadn't realized how many people had entered the church until she heard their collective gasp. Justin didn't even turn around. He waited.

Gene stared at him, then stared to laugh. "Murder? You're accusing me of murder? Come now, Sheriff, I know we've had our differences, but even you wouldn't arrest an innocent man on such ridiculous charges."

Someone pushed Megan aside. She stumbled and had to clutch a pew to maintain her balance. Colleen marched up the center aisle toward her husband. She shoved Justin, but he didn't budge.

"What are you doing?" she shrieked, waving her hands in the air. "How dare you come into the church and try to arrest a man of God!"

"He might be a man of God, but he's got a taste for sin. Wyatt, give me the handcuffs."

"No!" Colleen threw herself at Justin and started beating his chest. He grabbed her arms and thrust her away from him. She kicked out with her feet.

Megan quickly walked toward her sister. When she reached Justin's side, she placed her hands on her hips. "Colleen Suzanne Estes, you stop that right now."

"Stay out of this, Megan," Justin ordered.

"I won't." She glanced at her husband. His dark eyes were cold and unfriendly. He didn't want her here; he didn't trust her. Well, she didn't give a damn about what he wanted.

Colleen glared at her. "Don't you see what he's trying to do? How he's trying to destroy everything you care about. He's evil, Megan. A wicked man. He's betrayed you and everything you've ever cared about. Save yourself while you can. Save yourself!"

Justin pushed her away from him. Colleen started to fall, but Wyatt caught her. "Ma'am, if you'll just calm down."

"Unhand me, sir," Colleen said, and wiggled free of Wyatt's grasp. She straightened, and tugged on her bodice. "You'll be sorry, Sheriff. I'll see you hang, if it's the last thing I do."

"Probably," Justin said. "But first I aim to arrest your husband." He took the handcuffs from his deputy and approached Gene.

Her brother-in-law stared at Justin, then slowly shook his head and held out his hands. "I pity you, Kincaid. And I pray for God's mercy on your soul."

"Thanks, I'm going to need it."

Megan watched as her husband slipped the handcuffs into place. The click was audible in the church. Behind them, several people spoke up.

"What's he doin' arrestin' the minister? That ain't right."

"Who does he think he is?"

"I told you, but you wouldn't listen. Justin Kincaid's always been trouble in this town."

Justin ignored them. "You're wanted for two murders in two towns and are the main suspect in three more. All the women, local prostitutes, were killed while you were preaching there."

Gene's good humor didn't falter. "Preaching is hardly the same as murder."

"That's right," Colleen said, glaring at Justin. "You'll be sorry you ever thought of doing this."

"Shut up," Megan said, stepping forward. She could feel everyone staring at her, judging her for defending her husband. A flicker of fear licked up her spine, but she ignored it. She trusted him. She'd always trusted him. She was finally ready to prove it to the world. "Justin knows what he's doing. I believe him. He's good and decent and honorable. He cares about this town more than anyone has in a long time."

Justin turned to face her. He raised one eyebrow. Before she could respond, Colleen moved between them.

"He's cast a spell on you, Megan. Don't listen to him." Her sister's pale eyes widened. "If you care for your immortal soul, you must turn your back on him."

Megan stared at the woman she'd grown up with. They'd been strangers for so long it was hard to remember when they'd ever been friends. She shook her head. "No. I love him and I believe him. Now, get out of my way."

She waited, but Colleen didn't move. Slowly, so no one could mistake her purpose, she stepped around her sister and moved to her husband's side. Justin stared down at her, then back over his shoulder.

"If I'm wrong about this," he told her, "you're in a hell of a lot of trouble."

She smiled briefly. "It doesn't matter, as long as we're together."

"Very touching," Gene said, "but hardly relevant to the arrest. I'm warning you, Sheriff, the crowd in the back of my church is about to become difficult."

Justin ignored him. "You know what you're risking?" he asked her.

She nodded. "Absolutely nothing. You're the only one who matters to me. I love you."

He grimaced and she thought she'd lost him forever, but then a fire flared in his dark eyes and his hand brushed against hers. "Hell of a way to convince me."

He believed her! She smiled up at him. "It was the best I could come up with, under the circumstances."

"You think on your feet."

"Thank you."

Justin turned back to Gene. "Ellen Morgan's sister also works for a saloon. She saw you two together several times."

Some of the minister's bravado slipped. "She's obviously lying. Who would believe her word over mine?"

"Seven years ago, you tried to kill Laurie Smith, but failed. Earlier this year, she came to you wanting you to make good on your promises of running away with her. You couldn't, of course. What would people think? So you beat her up again and this time you killed her."

A low moan filled the church. Megan glanced at her sister. Colleen was clutching her midsection. "No," she cried. "No!"

"Last night, you tried to kidnap Bonnie because you'd found out I'd left Landing for a few days. You had to get rid of her because she was your only link to Laurie."

"That's preposterous," Gene said, then swallowed hard. "Why would I care about some whore's castoff?"

"Because you're her father."

Colleen gasped and fell to the ground. Megan stared at her. Wyatt moved toward her. "Don't bother," Megan said. "She didn't really faint."

The deputy hesitated. Behind them, the crowd murmured in confusion. Colleen sat up.

"How dare you. How dare you!" she screamed.

Megan was prepared to defend her husband against her sister's rage, but then she saw her sister was pointing at Gene.

"A whore? You bedded a whore?"

Gene stared at her. "Shut up, woman. They're all lies. Lies, do you hear me?"

But he'd started sweating. Beads of perspiration rolled down his face. He trembled and his smile wasn't quite as broad.

"You have no proof," he said, his voice shaking. "None at all."

"What about this?" Justin asked, and stepped forward. He gripped Gene's shirt at the collar and jerked it down. Everyone gasped. Several welts had been raised on his pale skin. Megan felt sick to her stomach. She'd beaten a man last night with a poker and today her brother-in-law was bruised.

Gene raised his head and glared at her. His eyes. Those same eyes had met hers last night. They'd been as filled with hatred as they were now. It was him. Oh, how was that possible?

"They were all whores!" Gene screamed. "They were evil and they had to be punished. When I could resist them and preach to them, then I let them live, but if they tempted me, I sent them to hell where they deserved to spend all eternity. I'm right! I have done nothing wrong!"

Colleen sobbed loudly, burying her face in her hands. No one moved to assist her. Justin jerked his head and Wyatt took Gene's arm to lead him away. Only then did Megan glance back at all the people standing by the rear of the church. They parted to let Wyatt and Gene pass through, then they stared at Colleen.

Megan told herself she should go to her sister, but she didn't have the strength. When Justin placed his arm around her, she leaned against him.

"Take me home," she whispered.

A soft rain fell over the garden, muting the colors of the spring flowers. Justin released the curtain and stepped back into the parlor. Megan looked up from the coffee she was serving and smiled.

"I can't believe how quiet it is," she said.

"Or that we're finally alone."

At his comment, she held out the cup toward him and blushed slightly. He moved toward her. There was enough room on the settee for him, as well, so he settled next to her and took the cup.

"Did Colleen get off this morning?" he asked.

She nodded. "The stage was right on time. She'll take the train to St. Louis. I'm not sure what she'll do after that. With the money she inherited from our father, she's got enough to manage without Gene."

"Just as well. She'll never see him again."

Megan busied herself with her own coffee, then didn't pick up the cup. "Will you have to go to Topeka for the trial?"

"Probably, but I won't be gone long." He shifted on the settee so that he was facing her. His knee pressed against her thigh and his arm lay across the back. He reached up and placed his hand on her nape. "I'm sorry, Megan."

She glanced at him, her hazel eyes wide, her mouth trembling. "You have nothing to be sorry about. You should be very proud. You solved the crime and brought the criminal to justice."

"That's not why I'm apologizing."

A lamp hissed in the far corner of the parlor. The circle of light stopped short of Megan, so soft shadows blurred the edges of her perfect features. She sat with her back straight, her hands folded together in her lap. Only the slight tremor where his fingers stroked hers betrayed her nervousness.

"It's been five days," he said. "We can't avoid this conversation forever." He set his cup on the low table in front of them.

"I know." She drew in a deep breath. "I want to tell you that I love you, but I'm afraid you still won't believe me. I know you did, for a minute there in the church, but you've had time to think things over and, oh, it's silly, but...what if you've changed your mind?" She finished her sentence in a rush.

His fingers dipped under the collar of her dress until he felt the delicate gold chain there. It was warm from her skin. "I haven't changed my mind."

She looked at him. Her mouth parted slightly. "You're sure?"

He nodded.

"Oh, Justin." She flung herself at him.

He pulled her close to his chest, shifting so that their legs tangled and her arms slipped around his shoulders.

"I love you, Megan. For always." She pressed her cheek to his and he felt her tears. "Don't cry," he murmured.

"They're happy tears, my love. Very happy tears."

He touched her hair, smoothing his hand over her head, then lower, down her back. "I'm happy, too." He was. The unanswered questions could wait.

But as she had so many times in the past, Megan read his mind. "Now what happens?" she asked, raising her head to meet his gaze.

He brushed the back of his hand against her cheek. "I still have several months on my contract."

"And after that?"

He saw the worry in her eyes, the fear. "I don't know," he said honestly. "Your business is here, and I know that's important to you. However, I'm not sure I want to stay."

"The town adores you," she said. For once, the observation didn't upset him.

He smiled faintly. "That'll wear off quick enough."

"I'll go anywhere just to be with you. It doesn't matter about the store. I can sell it."

He pressed his mouth to hers. "Hush," he whispered against her sweet skin. "We don't have to decide all of this today."

"But I—"

He nipped at her chin. "You're wasting time. Mrs. Dobson is only keeping Bonnie until morning."

"Morning?" Her eyes widened. "I thought she was just keeping her for the afternoon."

"I had a little talk with her after you left."

"Oh." Megan looked away as color climbed her cheeks.

He felt a moment of panic. "Megan, I thought—" Damn. It was never easy with her. "I had hoped that after what happened in the church, after what you said..." He cursed silently. He was making a mess of this.

He shifted her off his lap and stood up. She watched him with wide eyes. Trusting him. He could have let it go and not said anything. Yet they both deserved better than that. He cleared his throat.

"I can't stay with you any longer unless this is a real marriage," he began. "It's too difficult to pretend I don't mind your sleeping in another bed. I want to be your husband, Megan. I want to touch you and hold you each night, and wake up next to you in the morning. I'm finished settling for less. You are either my bride in every sense of the word or we have nothing between us."

She stood up and brushed her hands against her sides. The deep rose-colored gown made her skin look as if it glowed from within. Her beauty made him ache with longing, but he remained silent. He'd meant everything he said. He wouldn't accept half a marriage from her. He would rather cut her out cleanly than suffer and die slowly.

"Have you forgiven me?" she asked.

He closed his eyes against her piercing gaze. Had he forgiven her? Could he let go of the past? It was a fair question, he thought, and realized he should have expected her to ask it. If he needed Megan to fully give herself, should she require less of him? But was he willing to ignore the pain, to turn his back on his constant companion? Sometimes it was all that had kept him going.

Could he forgive her? He opened his eyes and looked at her. How could he not?

"Yes," he whispered. "A thousand times, yes."

She moved toward him slowly, then placed her hands on his chest. "I'll be your bride, Justin. I'll share your bed, your troubles and your life, for as long as you'll have me." She smiled. "I had hoped we might reconcile this afternoon, so I took the liberty of preparing the master suite. I even moved our things in."

"What if I hadn't said anything?"

"I would have found a way to convince you." She raised herself on tiptoe and kissed his cheek. "We have a second chance. It's taken me seven years to find you again. I wasn't about to let you go."

He bent down and picked her up in his arms. She giggled, clinging to him fearlessly. "You're a wicked woman," he said.

"You taught me that, so don't you dare complain."

He walked out of the parlor and started up the stairs. "It wasn't a complaint."

When they reached the bedroom, he set her down gently and took her face in his hands. He'd waited a lifetime to claim Megan as his own. "I'll love you forever," he promised softly. "I'll worship your body and give you children. I'll be at your side and provide for you always. I've spent my life living for you. I don't know how to do anything else. I—"

"Stop talking so much." She grabbed his shirtfront and pulled him close. Their lips brushed once, twice, then she opened her mouth and taunted him with her sweet taste. He moaned low in his throat. Nothing had ever felt so right. Megan was his other half, his purpose for being. He breathed a prayer of thanks that he'd found her at last. He'd come back to Landing to make peace with his past. Instead, he'd found a future with the only woman he'd ever loved.

*   *   *   *   *

MILLION DOLLAR SWEEPSTAKES (III)

No purchase necessary. To enter, follow the directions published. Method of entry may vary. For eligibility, entries must be received no later than March 31, 1996. No liability is assumed for printing errors, lost, late or misdirected entries. Odds of winning are determined by the number of eligible entries distributed and received. Prizewinners will be determined no later than June 30, 1996.

Sweepstakes open to residents of the U.S. (except Puerto Rico), Canada, Europe and Taiwan who are 18 years of age or older. All applicable laws and regulations apply. Sweepstakes offer void wherever prohibited by law. Values of all prizes are in U.S. currency. This sweepstakes is presented by Torstar Corp., its subsidiaries and affiliates, in conjunction with book, merchandise and/or product offerings. For a copy of the Official Rules send a self-addressed, stamped envelope (WA residents need not affix return postage) to: MILLION DOLLAR SWEEPSTAKES (III) Rules, P.O. Box 4573, Blair, NE 68009, USA.

EXTRA BONUS PRIZE DRAWING

No purchase necessary. The Extra Bonus Prize will be awarded in a random drawing to be conducted no later than 5/30/96 from among all entries received. To qualify, entries must be received by 3/31/96 and comply with published directions. Drawing open to residents of the U.S. (except Puerto Rico), Canada, Europe and Taiwan who are 18 years of age or older. All applicable laws and regulations apply; offer void wherever prohibited by law. Odds of winning are dependent upon number of eligibile entries received. Prize is valued in U.S. currency. The offer is presented by Torstar Corp., its subsidiaries and affiliates in conjunction with book, merchandise and/or product offering. For a copy of the Official Rules governing this sweepstakes, send a self-addressed, stamped envelope (WA residents need not affix return postage) to: Extra Bonus Prize Drawing Rules, P.O. Box 4590, Blair, NE 68009, USA.

SWP-H595

Harlequin® Historical

WOMEN OF THE WEST

Exciting stories of the old West and the women whose dreams
and passions shaped a new land!

Join Harlequin Historicals every month as we bring you
these unforgettable tales.

May 1995 #270—**JUSTIN'S BRIDE**
Susan Macias w/a Susan Mallery

June 1995 #273—**SADDLE THE WIND**
Pat Tracy

July 1995 #277—**ADDIE'S LAMENT**
DeLoras Scott

August 1995 #279—**TRUSTING SARAH**
Cassandra Austin

September 1995 #286—**CECILIA AND THE STRANGER**
Liz Ireland

October 1995 #288—**SAINT OR SINNER**
Cheryl St.John

November 1995 #294—**LYDIA**
Elizabeth Lane

Don't miss any of our Women of the West!

Announcing
the New **Pages & Privileges**™ Program
from Harlequin® and Silhouette®

Get All This FREE
With Just One Proof-of-Purchase!

- **FREE Travel Service** with the guaranteed lowest available airfares plus 5% cash back on every ticket

- **FREE Hotel Discounts** of up to 60% off at leading hotels in the U.S., Canada and Europe

- **FREE Petite Parfumerie** collection (a $50 Retail value)

- **FREE $25 Travel Voucher** to use on any ticket on any airline booked through our Travel Service

- **FREE Insider Tips Letter** full of fascinating information and hot sneak previews of upcoming books

- **FREE Mystery Gift** (if you enroll before May 31/95)

And there are more great gifts and benefits to come!
Enroll today and become Privileged!

(see insert for details)
